I0685767

DIANA OF ORCHARD SLOPE

A GREEN GABLES VARIATION

LIBBIE HAWKER

RUNNING RABBIT EDITIONS

ALSO BY LIBBIE HAWKER

Tidewater

Mercer Girls

White Lotus

The Sekhmet Bed

The Crook and Flail

Sovereign of Stars

The Bull of Min

House of Rejoicing

Storm in the Sky

Eater of Hearts

Baptism for the Dead

Daughter of Sand and Stone

A VISIT FROM MISS CUTHBERT

Bowers of white blossoms arced above the Avenue, raining down late-season petals in a gentle shower as the Barrys' buggy rolled through. The wheels grumbled softly in the reddish ruts of the road, and all along the verge of the lane, ferns nodded and swayed in the summery breeze. The buggy's lacquered black sides reflected the Avenue's proliferation of apple blossoms like stars against a night sky.

Mr. Barry looked just as fine as his carriage did, sitting straight and proud in the driver's seat with his back to his young daughter, who gazed out dreamily at the landscape as the pair of them drove on.

When they left the flowery seclusion of the Avenue behind and the farmland around the village of Avonlea was revealed to them, Diana Barry sat up straighter, pulling her shoulders level and square, just like her mother had taught her... just in case anyone should see her. The day was lovely, without a single cloud to mar the smooth blueness of the sky, which was the same perfect azure tint as Aunt Josephine's prized Wedgwood vase. But Diana couldn't quite make herself enjoy the pleasures of the afternoon. Over the jolly rolling of the carriage's wheels and the rhythm of the horse's steady trot, the girl could hear her mother's voice chiding her from inside her own head. "Sit up straight, Diana. A lady's back is always straight. Don't run in the house, Diana. In fact, don't run anywhere. Ladies do not run. Diana, put your napkin on your lap. A lady doesn't go about with stains on her skirt."

She did want to be a lady... someday, when she was thoroughly grown up. But Diana was only eleven years old. She felt as if she still had miles and miles of growing up to do, and that the ladylike Diana whom Mrs. Barry worked so hard to cultivate was still like a sprout curled inside its seed. There was plenty of time yet for a proper lady to emerge... wasn't there? Now, with the Avenue in full flower and the red roads of Avonlea positively thick with the delicious, blossom-and-fern perfume of summertime, Diana felt sure that being a little girl was a much more pressing business.

"If only Mother saw things my way," she muttered as the cart rumbled over the bridge's split timbers.

The bridge spanned the narrow middle of the big pond—Barry's Pond, Avonlea folks called it, for Diana's family had lived beside that sparkling expanse of jewel-bright water since the first farmers on Prince Edward Island settled dear old Avonlea. Barry's Pond widened and spread to either side of the bridge; around its edges were fringes of dark-green reeds where blackbirds swayed and sang all summer long and where, in the spring and autumn, choirs of frogs filled the purple dusk with music.

Orchard Slope crowned the hill beyond, looking down on the pond like a gracefully aging monarch gazing with quiet beneficence upon her queendom. The grand old farmhouse was tall and white, with a wide porch along one side where cool breezes played in the summertime, carrying the scent of sun-warmed hay up from the fields beyond the pond. The windows below peaked gables caught the afternoon light, glinting with the sheen of gold. One of those windows was Diana's, her own little sanctuary of quiet hours and evening stillness, of thought and memory, which even at her tender age she was already learning to cherish.

The grand old trees that gave Orchard Slope its name spread like a softly colored quilt below the house's feet, stretching down the lazy hill to the reeds and willows of the shoreline. June had been mild and sweet thus far, and so most of the gnarled, age-bent boughs still bore their crowns of blossom. Apple and pear, plum and cherry, they shared their glories with bowers of white and pale green, and rose-pinks that ranged from the most delicate blush of dawn to a deep, passionate hue that could almost be called crimson.

Diana loved that ancient orchard. If her room under the gable was her sanctuary, then the orchard was her cathedral, the one place in all the world where she could walk alone, dreamy-slow and wandering through all her most precious and personal thoughts, without any fear of the judgment of family or peers intruding. To see Orchard Slope again after two long weeks in Carmody made her heart throb with delight—a delight that was almost equal to her worry.

The horses trotted on up the hill, and Father pulled them in smartly, so that the cart stopped in just the right place for Diana to jump off onto the old white house's porch. She smiled gratefully at her father as she swung over the side of the cart. His dark brown eyes twinkled in response, and his bristly mustache shifted with a conspiratorial grin. Jumping from the cart to the porch was a game they had played since Diana was a tiny girl.

And she should have known, as her father drove the horses on toward the barn, that her mother would see, and would disapprove. Mrs. Barry had never appreciated the sport, and had worked hard to quell Diana's taste for "wild acrobatics." Diana heard her mother's reproachful sniff, even before the hollow thud of her own boots against the porch wood had died away.

She turned quickly to face her mother, clasping her hands at her waist and looking up contritely, hoping her dress wasn't irredeemably wrinkled from the train ride from Carmody.

Mrs. Barry raked Diana with her eyes, from head to heels and back again. Diana's mother was a remarkably pretty woman, although she did tend somewhat toward stoutness, with smooth skin and neat black hair that had only a few strands of silver at the temples. She always kept her hair swept up in a bun that was neither ostentatious nor particularly stylish, but managed to look flawlessly elegant all the same... even when she was baking bread or sweeping the floor. She had dark, shining eyes that never missed a single detail of whatever she surveyed: kitchen, orchard, dining table or daughter. Her well-shaped lips were as pink as the pinkest blossoms in the orchard, but Diana had often thought she would like them better if they weren't so often pursed in disapproval.

"I'm sorry," Diana said quickly. She had learned that it was better to apologize for unladylike behavior before her mother had a chance to scold her for it.

Mother raised one black brow. "How was your visit with Aunt Josephine?"

Diana smothered a sigh. Aunt Josephine was her father's aunt, which made her Diana's great-aunt, though the whole family referred to her simply as Aunt. Doubtless to call her "great-aunt" would have incited that lady's considerable wrath. She was technically a spinster, having never married, but she lived like no other spinster did, enjoying a life of wealth and high style that fairly took Diana's breath away. Diana had been sent on plenty of visits to Charlottetown so that she might visit with Aunt Josephine. She was required to spend at least a few days with the chilly old maid on every school vacation. The visits were always dull and oppressive affairs, with Diana doing her best to exhibit perfect behavior, and failing more often than she dared admit. Meanwhile Aunt Josephine behaved in the stiffest and stuffiest manner at all times, in all circumstances, as if she thought little girls were made of spun sugar and Diana might shatter into a million pieces if she, the old dame, so much as looked at her in the wrong way.

Mother's plan, Diana knew, was to so impress Aunt Josephine with Diana's charm and ladylike grace that the spinster would divert a stream of her considerable fortune toward Orchard Slope, for the sweeping beauty of the farm was nearly all the riches this branch of the Barry family tree possessed. In recent years, Mother had grown fond of reminding both Diana and Mr. Barry that they scarcely had two pennies saved toward Diana's marriage and trousseau. For Diana's part, she didn't see why any quantity of pennies, even down to a paltry two, were necessary for a marriage. And anyhow, it was woefully premature to consider Diana's future now. Mother was locally famous for declaring that she would never allow her daughter to marry until the age of twenty-one. The Barrys had ten whole years to plan and save for their eldest daughter's wedding; twenty-one was a whole lifetime away.

She couldn't imagine what had inspired Mother's great urgency on the subject. During her private strolls through the twilit orchard, she often supposed (ungraciously, she admitted) that Mother simply wanted some of Aunt Josephine's fortune for herself, and thought Diana the likeliest way to get it.

But of course, she would never give voice to that thought, not for all the money in Canada. Diana squared her shoulders unconsciously, as she always did when facing her mother, and answered in a carefully cultured tone, "My visit with Aunt Josephine was very well, thank you, Mother."

Mrs. Barry's manner relaxed some... *some*. "Did you give her the cake I baked?"

"Yes. She said it looked good enough to eat, but I never saw her eat any of it."

Mother's lips pursed again. "That woman has always been as

skinny as a broomstick. I wonder if anyone has seen her eat anything, ever."

Diana knew Mother's pride was agitated, if not wounded. Her cakes were great favorites at the fair and at Avonlea society gatherings. Only Aunt Josephine, who was the very picture of austerity, could deny herself of Rebecca Barry's baking.

"And did you play the piano for your aunt?" Mother asked, after a pause.

Diana blushed despite her best efforts to remain unflustered. "Yes... ." She had played piano, after a fashion. "Aunt Josephine has offered to pay so that I might take music lessons."

At that happy news, Mother's smile seemed genuine rather than cool. The truth was, though, that Aunt Josephine had little choice but to contribute toward Diana's musical cultivation. Diana was all but certain that, if the Premier were to hear her play, he would outlaw her piano recitals, declaring them a form of unusual torture. She was simply dismal at the piano. It was Mrs. Barry's idea that Diana should learn to play, since she accounted musical accomplishment an essential feature of all true ladies. Diana enjoyed singing very much, and thought perhaps that she could have a very good voice, if it were trained by a proper instructor. But although Mrs. Barry's convictions were firm where music was concerned, she thought singing too ostentatious a pursuit for a proper young woman. *Ladies* did not warble in satin gowns and diamonds, before the eyes of crowds at concerts and recitals. They did not flaunt themselves before audiences, like peacocks strutting in a yard. *Ladies* sat sedately upon piano benches and tickled out gentle airs with their delicate, white fingers.

"Your dress is wrinkled," Mother said, bracing one fist against her rounded hip. "I have told you so many times, Diana, that you must be careful of your appearance."

"It's only wrinkled from the train ride," Diana protested.

"How am I to sit on a train bench for more than an hour without getting a few wrinkles?"

Mother's eyes flashed a warning. Diana knew she was tiptoeing dangerously around the edge of pertness. She lowered her face contritely. "I'm very tired, Mother. I'd like to change my clothes now and rest before supper, if I may."

Wordlessly, Mrs. Barry stepped aside to allow her daughter into the house. But her icy silence stifled any welcome Diana might have hoped to find upon her homecoming. "I'm a hopeless disappointment," she thought as she climbed the stairs to her room, "to Mother and to Aunt Josephine, and... oh, to everyone in the whole world, except maybe Father." She knew it was true, but try as she might, she couldn't make herself feel exactly terrible about it. She *liked* being Diana—Diana just as she was, with her tumbling black curls and her wrinkled skirt and her utter lack of talent for the piano. *She* was fine as she was. But somehow the rest of the world didn't seem to agree with her. More and more, she had begun to feel like a cast-off, like a dandelion seed blowing about on the wind and never finding any place to land, any place where she belonged. It was a terribly lonesome sensation.

When she had hung up her old dress and buttoned a new one, she peeked into the little cupboard beside her bed and found her trove of treasures: the beautiful, bright books she had been made to leave behind for her trip to Carmody. She had borrowed the books from some of her friends on the last day of school, trading old favorites for these new treasures, which she planned to thoroughly enjoy over the long, warm weeks of summer.

Diana lifted the books reverently, feeling the cool smoothness of their covers one by one, then holding them in a bundle to admire the rainbow their spines made, stacked one atop the other. She longed to delve into each and every one, and didn't know which to choose first. Every one seemed equally appealing, with gold-embossed titles that promised romance and adventure. *The Rose of Whitfield. Patricia's Pride. Envy and Eleanora.* It was a decision too great for any girl to bear. She spread the books across her chenille-covered bed, then closed her eyes and reached out, letting fate guide her hand.

She chose *Sunset Song,* the newest from Charlotte E. Morgan, whom all the older girls at school were simply wild about. Mrs. Morgan's stories were always deliciously tragic, with sad-eyed heroes and slender, pale heroines and shocking twists of the plot that often left Diana sleepless with excitement long after she'd blown out her candle at night. Rumor held that Charlotte E. Morgan lived not terribly far away from Avonlea, somewhere in the Maritimes. Diana secretly hoped there was no truth to that story. Mrs. Morgan was a heroine in Diana's eyes, a figure of impossible grandness. The cosmopolitan landscape was surely Mrs. Morgan's natural habitat. Diana felt that her image of the authoress would be somehow tainted, even ruined altogether, if she must truly picture *the* Charlotte E. Morgan living out her days in a prosaic, pokey old place of Avonlea's breed.

Sunset Song was small enough to fit in the pocket of Diana's skirt. Its weight against her hip felt friendly and encouraging. She slipped downstairs on quiet feet. Mother was working in the kitchen, so Diana was free to enjoy the stillness of the parlor alone. She settled on the sofa—a chummy old blue one that was much too faded and informal for Mrs. Barry's liking, but was as soft and comfortable as a cloud. It was Diana's favorite place for reading and dreaming. She paused for a moment, savoring the buttery yellow light that spilled into the parlor and cast its cheerful presence all around. The light itself seemed to carry the essence of the orchard trees in past the window—their warm stillness, their sense of wisdom and quiet dignity. When she had filled herself up with the peace and beauty of the afternoon, Diana opened her book and began to read.

Alas, she was only two pages into the story, reveling in Charlotte E. Morgan's lush description of a grand stone house that stood amid a garden of sweet peonies, when Father came in from the barn. She heard his low, happy voice as he greeted Mother in the kitchen, and then they began to talk, and Diana's concentration was ruined.

Diana Barry was a bright little girl, make no mistake… but she had always found it difficult to concentrate on her reading when there were noises about. Perhaps that was why she loved the orchard so much, and the territories beyond—the pond's green shoreline, the fringes of the dark wood where jaunty little ferns sprouted and the only sound was the soothing rustle of leaves overhead. As her mother and father talked, she read and re-read the lines of her book, but she could not return to the story's enchantment. She was caught up in the conversation from the kitchen.

"And where is my little Diana?" Father asked.

"Probably off reading a book somewhere," Mother said with a sigh.

"Then I won't disturb her."

"I wish you would, George. You encourage Diana too much in her reading."

"Come now, Rebecca. You know I believe girls ought to be just as literate as boys."

"I don't disagree with you," Mrs. Barry said, "*necessarily*. But there is a limit, George. There must be a limit. Time spent absorbed in novels is time Diana could spend learning useful skills."

"She is only eleven years old, darling!"

"Years fly by," was Mrs. Barry's prediction of doom. "If the time comes for courting and all Diana knows is how to read a novel, she'll have no prospects at all."

"Why, what talk! She'll have plenty of prospects. She's the prettiest little girl on the island."

Diana glowed with pride at that—pride, and affection for her father, whom she often suspected was the only person in all the world who truly understood her.

"I admit that she is very good-looking," Mrs. Barry murmured.

All of Avonlea said Diana was the very image of her mother, though she smiled a good deal more than Mrs. Barry ever did. For Mother to admit approval of Diana's looks was tantamount to approving of her *own* looks. It was so uncharacteristic of Mrs. Barry that Diana nearly giggled with surprise. She controlled herself at the last moment, for she was dreadfully compelled to hear what else her parents might say about her. Spying was a sin... or if not a sin exactly, then something awfully close to it... but what else was Diana to do, now that she couldn't enjoy her reading?

Mrs. Barry drove home her point forcefully: "But looks aren't enough to make a good match. We must start thinking now about how to provide for..."

Mother trailed off, then blurted in agitation, "Would you look at that, George! I declare! It's Marilla Cuthbert coming over the foot-bridge... coming from Green Gables."

"So it is," Father said, in a voice that was considerably less agitated than Mother's.

"She's got that *child* with her."

"Child?"

"Didn't you know? The Cuthberts have adopted an *orphan*." Mrs. Barry made that word drip with impossible scandal.

Diana dropped her book on the sofa and scrambled to the parlor window. Down at the foot of the long orchard slope, she could see the familiar figure of Marilla Cuthbert moving sedately up the path with her usual air of placid constraint. Marilla was tall for a woman, and could be called stately if not for her thinness and angularity. She was gray from top to bottom—gray of hair, which was pulled back severely in an unstylish bun, and gray of garb, in a dress like a storm cloud, devoid of the smallest ruffle, the least of modest pintucks.

The old maid Marilla was not a shocking sight. She and her aging bachelor brother, with whom she ran a small farm called Green Gables, were the Barrys' nearest neighbors. Despite her forbidding appearance and stolid personality, Marilla sometimes revealed to the world fleeting glimpses of humor, even warmth— both of which she seemed to work very hard at hiding. Diana quite liked the old lady, even if she was old-fashioned.

But the person who accompanied Marilla Cuthbert was certainly a cause for curiosity. A little girl walked at Marilla's side... though it would be more accurate to say that the little girl skipped, bobbed, and twirled, turning this way and that to take in the beauty of the flowering trees and the fairytale twists of their gnarled branches. The girl seemed to be about Diana's own age. She wore a dress of a horrid yellowish-brown color that didn't seem to fit her quite right, and below her straw hat, two long braids of copper-red hair hung down, one over each ear. The girl's mouth was moving, as if she chattered as she walked, though Marilla Cuthbert looked straight ahead and seemed not to respond to the cascade of words.

"Land's sake," Mrs. Barry said, "what *can* Marilla want?"

"You've never objected to a visit from Miss Cuthbert before," Father said, amused.

"But she never lost her head and took in an orphan girl before."

"Lost her head? It seems like an act of charity to me, Rebecca."

"It's no charity for a pair of old geese like the Cuthbert siblings to take in a little girl. They know nothing about raising children, George—nothing! Neither of them has ever been married, let alone dealt with the needs of children."

"Marilla and Matthew Cuthbert have both survived well into their fifties," Father said drily. "I guess that's testament enough to their good sense. What more is required to raise a child, other than good sense?"

Diana could hear mother's sharp sniff, even from the parlor. "A man *would* hold such an opinion. Fathers aren't the same as mothers, George, mark my words. Your permissiveness with Diana proves that much."

"In any case," Father said, "Miss Cuthbert probably wants to borrow something from you. Isn't that usually what brings her here?"

Mrs. Barry's silence gave Diana the impression that she was searching for something—an argument against her husband's own good sense, Diana supposed. Finally, Mother conceded, "Usually."

"You don't sound pleased about it."

"It's only that I've... I've *heard things* about the orphan child." Mrs. Barry deplored gossip—or claimed to, at least—so this confession was dragged from her as if by savage hooks.

Father laughed heartily. "Was Mrs. Rachel Lynde the source of these *things* you've heard, by any chance?"

"What difference does it make?"

"None in the world, I suppose," Father said, and Diana could still hear the humor in his words.

"Mrs. Lynde told me all about this orphan girl... how she flew into a rage and shouted and said the most awful things to poor Mrs. Lynde!"

"Yes, poor Mrs. Lynde."

"I tell you, that girl is trouble, and the Cuthberts will find out soon enough."

"Well, Miss Cuthbert has nearly reached the kitchen door with her troublesome orphan, so you had best put on a welcoming smile," Father advised. Then Diana heard his boots on the back staircase. Evidently he had no desire to remain in the kitchen and watch the orphan's sparks fly, if indeed any were to fly at all.

Diana hurried back to the sofa and propped her book in her lap. As her mother poked her head into the parlor, Diana casually turned the page, giving every impression of having been absorbed in her reading all along.

"What is it, Mother?" Diana asked.

"Miss Cuthbert calling, from Green Gables. She has a girl with her. Remember to be on your best behavior for company."

Diana couldn't keep the glimmer of interest from her eyes. She didn't need a mirror to know how the intrigue and curiosity shone out from her face.

"Don't go looking so hopeful, Diana Barry. It remains to be seen whether this girl of the Cuthberts' is fit company for you. I have my doubts... yes, very grave doubts indeed."

Diana nodded obediently, but when her mother turned away to answer Marilla's knock at the kitchen door, she smiled and felt her cheeks color with a secretive longing.

THE IMPORTED ORPHAN

THE KITCHEN DOOR SQUEAKED OPEN ON ITS ANCIENT HINGES.

"How do you do, Marilla?" Mrs. Barry said in her most even and unflappable tone. "Come in. And this is the little girl you have adopted, I suppose?"

"Yes, this is Anne Shirley." Marilla's voice was familiar to Diana, cracked and low-pitched with age.

A third person spoke up, directly on Marilla's heels. "Spelled with an E." The red-haired girl's words had a quiver to them, as if she were on the point of bursting wide open, thanks to some barely-contained, utterly momentous emotion.

A tingle rushed all through Diana, from her toes to her black-curled crown, for what the other girl had said might be accounted pertness, and no one Diana knew—girl or grown-up —ever dared to risk pertness with Mrs. Barry. It was terribly exciting. She longed to be in the kitchen so she could get her own measure of this orphan.

There was a brief pause, and then: "How are you?" Mrs. Barry inquired with measured politeness.

Anne-Shirley-with-an-E answered back promptly, like an

actress who had been waiting for a cue. "I am well in body, although considerable rumpled up in spirit, thank you, ma'am."

Diana's mouth fell open. What splendid talk! Why, the orphan girl spoke just like a figure from one of Charlotte E. Morgan's novels! Or from any other delightfully grand story-book. Awe surged in Diana like a cresting wave. It must be so romantic to be an orphan. Tragic, yes... but if novels had taught Diana anything, it was that one could never expect the grandness of romance without at least a little tragedy. The two went hand in hand.

The sound of three pairs of feet, crossing the wide fir planks of the kitchen floor, came to Diana through the parlor door. She gasped in surprise, suddenly all a-fluster at the prospect of meeting the other girl face-to-face. How could she, Diana, ever hope to make a favorable impression on one who had already lived a lifetime of grand adventures? She held her book up in front of her face to disguise her overwhelmed flush... and promptly dropped that same book on the sofa the moment the visitors stepped into the parlor.

"This is my little girl Diana," Mother said.

Diana stared wide-eyed at the adopted girl. Anne Shirley was about as tall as Diana was herself, but skinny as a half-starved pup. Despite her thin limbs and the sharpness of her features... and despite the threadbare, unattractive wincey dress Anne wore... Diana could sense an innate, unconscious grace in the girl. One day, when she was a girl no longer, Anne would be slender instead of skinny, and willowy in manner and move-ment... just like the heroine of a book. She would be everything Diana herself dreamed of becoming.

Anne's skin was very fair. A scattering of freckles lay like flecks of gold dust across her cheeks and the bridge of her nose, which was pointed in a remarkably pretty way. Her lashes were thick and dark for a red-head; they framed her gray eyes boldly, emphasizing the starry, awe-struck daze that had fallen over

Anne when she caught sight of Diana on the sofa. The two girls gazed at each other silently, both with an air of having stumbled upon an impossible, unlooked-for treasure.

"Diana, you might take Anne out into the garden and show her your flowers. It will be better for you than straining your eyes over that book."

Diana rose swiftly from the sofa, hoping she didn't leap up with too much eagerness (her mother would surely remonstrate with her later, if she had). She smiled, tremulous with excitement, as she approached the freckled little girl. Without a word, Anne turned and followed Diana back through the kitchen.

Mrs. Barry was complaining genteelly to Marilla of Diana's reading habit; Diana glanced back at her mother, and did not fail to note the swift, sharp warning in Mrs. Barry's eye. Diana could all but hear her mother's unspoken words: "Don't you dare get attached to this waif. You must be polite to guests, but you mustn't think that an orphan girl is fit company for you, Diana Barry."

Diana turned hastily away from her mother and impulsively hooked her arm through Anne's, leading her through the kitchen door and out into the garden. Anne gazed at her in disbelieving wonder, then looked down at Diana's hand resting on her elbow, then back to Diana's face again.

"Here are my tiger lilies," Diana said, gesturing to the showy, shoulder-high blooms of sunset orange. "I planted them here myself. I guess they grew pretty well this year. Last year I couldn't get tiger lilies to take at all."

The lilies smelled deliciously sweet in the warm, early-evening air. A few last, lazy bees hummed around the flowers.

"Oh, aren't they lovely," Anne said breathlessly. But she hardly glanced at the lilies at all. A ruddy flush tinted her pale cheeks, and Diana thought it had nothing to do with the reddish glow of sunset, which had begun to creep past the western wall of firs to lay in still, calm pools all around the garden. Anne seemed to be blushing with the effort of holding in some hectic, boiling emotion.

"I love flowers," Diana confided. "I think perhaps I'd like to have a floristry shop someday, and make big bouquets for ladies who live in spectacular mansions. Of course, I would have to do it in Carmody or all the way out in Charlottetown, for there are no ladies with mansions in Avonlea. But Mother says shop-keeping isn't a fit occupation for a lady, anyhow... at least, not past the age of twenty-five, or marriage, whichever comes first."

Anne stared at Diana over the tiger lilies. Her slightly cracked, rosy-pink lips were half open, as if she felt herself on the verge of saying something but couldn't quite make up her mind what she ought to say. And those eyes! Their gray depths were as stormy as a winter sea. For a moment Diana recalled that Mrs. Rachel Lynde had condemned this girl's temper and behavior, and she wondered, rather dizzily, if Anne Shirley were about to burst out with some shocking reaction. But the girl only shook her head slowly, side to side, as if unable to credit what she saw before her.

But all she could possibly see was Diana herself... Diana and her lilies.

"I know you've only just come to Avonlea," Diana said, "but do you think you might get to have a garden of your own someday, over at Green Gables?"

At last the orphan girl found her tongue. "I have always *longed* for a garden of my own." She sounded quite out of breath with rapture. "It has been my lifelong ambition. Gardens are so romantic; they just pierce my soul through with their beauty. I used to imagine, whenever I had a chance to think about it, how grand it must feel to be a lady with her own mansion. I would have a red brick one, with a mansard roof and a widow's walk that looked out to the sapphire expanse of the sea. Oh, but I couldn't come to own my mansion simply by purchasing it. That's not romantic enough, even for a lady who could afford extravagances. I would inherit it through a great tragedy... a heart-rending twist of cruel fate, which would hang sorrows all about the place like black draperies, so that I almost couldn't enjoy the splendidness of living in a mansion at all... almost, but not quite. I think... let me see... yes, this is suitably heart-rending: I would be married for one day only to a dashing, heroic man, Lord Bartholomew Fitzgerald. But before we could leave on our honeymoon, he would be summoned to sea by duty. He would bid me a regretful farewell with a kiss on my smooth white hand, and would promise to make it up to me with the grandest honey-moon tour of Europe, and we would part with trembling and tears and oaths that we would hold each other again. But then his ship would be sunk in a storm and he'd never return. Isn't that grand? And I would pace the widow's walk every night as the storm winds rose, gazing forever out to sea... but doomed never to see my beloved's face again in this world."

Diana sighed and pressed a hand to her fluttering heart.

"Of course," Anne went on quickly, "I couldn't do all this as plain old Anne Shirley. Glorious, tragic romances never happen to girls named Anne. I could only be the Lady Cordelia Fitzger-ald. And whenever I wasn't up weeping on my widow's walk, I would be down in my garden, clad in subdued silks... for, you know, I would still be in mourning... but even in my anguish, I would glide swan-like through the rows of lilies and peonies and roses. And with time, new suitors would come to try to win my heart—and my mansion—but I would never pay them the least mind. My flowers would be my only comfort... until I met my grave, and found my beloved husband again.

"So, yes, I have often imagined what it would be like to have a garden on my own. I think I should like it very much."

"My," Diana said. "You talk just like a story-book."

"Oh, I know I shouldn't." Anne's pale face flushed quite red. "I know I talk too much, and I'm awfully afraid that Marilla and Matthew will grow tired of it, or think I'm too silly to be put up with, and will send me back to the asylum. Well... Matthew never would, but Marilla might. She does seem like a very good woman, and charitable, to take me in... but one can never be too sure of one's place when one is an orphan. Anyway, I ought to talk less and listen more. Marilla and Mrs. Rachel Lynde have both told me so, and I know they're right. But it seems impossible sometimes. I have so many beautiful thoughts and fancies inside me, and if I don't let them out, Diana, then I'm afraid I might actually burst from them!"

"I like the way you talk," Diana said honestly. "And I think your story about Lady Cordelia Fitzgerald is perfectly tragic."

Anne's eyes glittered yet more. For one startled moment, Diana thought the red-haired girl was about to weep, but it was only the glow of passion that shone out from her... not tears. "Do you really? Oh, Diana, you have given me an immeasurable gift."

Diana laughed, uncertain whether Anne was being serious or not. The skinny, freckled imp darted around the bed of tiger lilies, her red braids flying, and hooked her arm through Diana's. Together they walked the paths of the garden, chattering as they surveyed the rows and arcs of flowers, all neatly corralled by the white "cow-hock" clam shells that were so popular in countryside gardens. Or, it is more accurate to say, Anne chattered while Diana listened in contented, fascinated silence. The sunset spilled its warm hues into the garden, setting all the petals and leaves to glowing. Bees, and the first moths of evening, moved in slow motion around nodding blooms; their tiny bodies and delicate wings were bright as candle flames, illuminated by the lowering sun.

"I always pictured Lady Cordelia Fitzgerald with hair just like yours," Anne said as the girls stopped to admire the spray of Scotch roses, which trailed in great, fragrant cascades over the paling fence.

"Did you, really?"

"Oh, yes... black as the raven's wing. Nothing could be prettier."

Diana's cheeks heated with pleasure. She did like her hair, though she had sense enough not to be vain about it.

"And your complexion is so rosy, Diana. Oh, what I wouldn't give to look just like you!"

"I think red hair is awfully pretty."

"No it's not." Anne toyed with the end of one braid, her narrow face falling despondently. "It's far too rustic to be pretty. With red hair, I can never aspire to any greater fate than... than a goose-girl or a milk-maid."

Diana laughed. "But that's not true, Anne! Once I read a book about a girl who had two lovers, and they warred with each other fearfully in order to win her heart, and accidentally killed each other in the fight, at exactly the same time, so that neither one of them got to marry her. And her hair was 'as red as garnets' and 'glittered like copper.'"

"But my hair isn't red like garnets. It's red like a Jersey cow. Or like a carrot. There is nothing romantic about cows or carrots, and copper is vastly inferior to gold, or even to silver. Yes, I'd much rather have silver hair like an old lady than pain old *red*."

"Anyway," Diana said resolutely, "I'm sure two lovers wouldn't kill each other at exactly the same time over a girl who wasn't worth the bother. So they must have liked red hair, at least. And now I suppose you'll say it was just a story," she added, laughing merrily, "but the author thought it up and wrote it all down, so she must have supposed the people who read the story would find it believable."

Anne tapped her pointed chin with one finger. She gazed off across the garden, distant in thought. Finally, she said, "Maybe you're right after all, Diana, and if so, you have fortified me with hope. But I still would like to have hair black as a raven's wing."

Suddenly Anne turned to Diana with hands clasped, a radiant burst of emotion shining from her trembling form. "Oh, Diana," she whispered, "do you think you can like me a little— enough to be my bosom friend?"

Diana laughed again. She found herself laughing often, in the company of this fervent little creature. "Why, I guess so. I'm awfully glad you've come to live at Green Gables."

Anne took a step closer. Her tempestuous gray eyes held Diana with an intensity that fairly took her breath away. "Will you swear to be my friend forever and ever?"

Now it was Diana who trembled. She had the sudden, queasy sensation that her mother was distressingly nearby, and was listening in on every word... but of course that was impossible. If Mrs. Barry and Marilla had come out from the kitchen, Diana would have heard the screened door slam. She resisted the urge to glance over her shoulder toward the house, half fearful that after all she would find her mother standing just there, tense and disapproving on the garden path, waiting with her judgment.

"It's dreadfully wicked to swear," Diana said.

"Oh, no." Anne shook her head. "Not my kind of swearing."

"I never heard of but one kind."

"Oh, it isn't wicked at all," Anne insisted with a touch of desperation. "This sort of swearing only means vowing and promising solemnly."

Diana gave a tiny sigh of relief. "Well, I don't mind doing that. But how do you do it?"

Anne looked around the garden for a moment, her freckled brow furrowed. "We ought to have running water if it's to be a *proper* oath. But here... we can imagine the garden path is a stream."

The girls each stepped into a garden bed, their toes against the cow-hocks, and faced one another.

"Now we must join hands," Anne said.

She extended her thin hands over the path. Diana took them, surprised at how warm they were. Anne was such a wispy, star-eyed thing that Diana had almost expected her to feel insubstantial and cool, like a spirit of the air.

Anne said, "I'll repeat the oath first, and then you must say it."

"All right," Diana said. Her stomach felt faintly sick with excitement, or maybe with guilt, for the proceedings had a heathenish air about them, and she knew her mother would never approve. But she made no move to withdraw her hands or to call the business off.

"I solemnly swear," Anne said, "to be faithful to my bosom friend, Diana Barry, as long as the sun and moon shall endure." She placed a weight of emphasis on every word. "Now you say it, but put my name in."

Diana swallowed hard, staring wide-eyed at the other girl, wondering whether she really ought to do it. But at last she shook off her doubts and gave a light-hearted laugh. "I solemnly swear to be faithful to my bosom friend, Anne Shirley, for as long as the sun and moon shall endure."

The oath did sound terribly inspiring, like something one might find in a grand old book of prose, from an age long past. Anne certainly had a knack for words.

When the oath was concluded, Anne broke into a wide grin. Diana couldn't help but smile back at her. Anne's volubility, to say nothing of her flights of fancy, were a world away from the proper, ladylike perfection Mrs. Barry strove to cultivate in Diana.

"You're a queer girl, Anne." Diana still held her new friend's hands. "I heard before that you were queer. But I believe I'm going to like you real well."

"And I believe Mother won't like it one bit," Diana added silently, to herself.

All too soon, Marilla's business at Orchard Slope was concluded, and it was time for Anne to depart. Dusk was settling in, a luscious, velvety-blue twilight that spread thick, fir-scented shadows between the domes of the ancient apple trees. Diana accompanied the visitors down the long, gentle hill, walking with her arm comfortably around Anne's shoulders. Anne clung to her, too, with a strength that said the orphan girl had found a treasure of immeasurable worth... something long sought, but never truly expected.

The girls parted ways at the log bridge. The brook murmured sleepily between its banks of ferns, and from the nearby pond the frogs had started up their nightly chorus.

"I must go back home now," Diana said. "If I'm not at the supper table soon, Mother will be cross with me."

"Oh," Anne sighed, "I feel as if I can't possibly bear to part with you, but I could never forgive myself if I endangered your happiness, dear Diana."

Marilla Cuthbert tapped the toe of her boot impatiently against the log bridge.

"Let's play together tomorrow," Diana suggested.

"Nothing could make me gladder. Good night, my bosom friend."

Diana stood at the bridge, watching Anne fade into the dusk. "She certainly is an interesting girl," Diana thought. Anne Shirley fairly brimmed over with adventuresome spirit. She was just like a heroine in a novel, if you disregarded her freckles and her wincey dress. "She's exactly the kind of girl I want to be."

Wanted to be... but couldn't.

Mrs. Barry's voice rose above the chanting of the frogs. "Diana! Diana, come in now!"

Diana gazed after Anne for a moment longer, then, with a long sigh of surrender to the inevitable, she turned and ran up the hill toward home.

IDYLLS AT IDLEWILD

"I'VE THOUGHT OF A NAME AT LAST," ANNE SAID. A RHAPSODIC note was in her voice, a musical quiver of delights anticipated—the sound Diana had grown to recognize over several days of friendship with Anne Shirley.

Anne and Diana walked arm-in-arm through the knee-high grass, pushing through early clusters of milk-white Queen Anne's Lace. The noon air was full of a bright, greeny smell: new oats growing in Mr. Harmon Andrews's field, just on the other side of Barry's Pond. (Or, as Anne had dubbed it, the Lake of Shining Waters.) They made their way along a narrow strip of land that ran beside the brook's southern bank, exactly between Orchard Slope and Green Gables. The land in question belonged to Mr. William Bell, but Mr. Bell had put it to no particular use and was always welcoming to children, so the girls thought it no great crime to colonize the enchanting stand of birch trees that grew there.

Anne led Diana into the ring of trees, which formed the walls of their secret playhouse. Then the red-haired girl threw her arms wide, taking in the circle of their small, shared world.

"Idlewild," Anne declared.

Diana gasped. "Oh! It's perfect, Anne... really perfect!"

The name did fit the place exactly. Diana surveyed their playhouse with a new appreciation of its glories. When they had first explored the birch ring, the girls had been delighted to find a few flat-topped stones already waiting for them, each with a carpet of soft green moss on top. Those served nicely for seats. They had brought down some old boards from the Orchard Slope barn and nailed them up between the birches, then filled those shelves with an array of treasures to delight a magpie. Pieces of broken pottery and cracked plates decorated with gay-colored flowers served as their china—it was the easiest thing in the world to imagine the pieces were whole, and exceedingly elegant—and, of course, the bit of broken crystal Diana had found out behind the hen house had pride of place. Its diamond facets sparkled in the sun with a hundred rainbows. Anne swore it was a glass the fairies had lost after a twilight fairy-ball. Diana knew it was only a bit of an old lamp, but she supposed there was no harm in making believe it was truly a cast-off from Fairyland.

To any outsider, the playhouse would be accounted the roughest, most rustic of camps. But to the girls, it was a realm of elegance and grown-up beauty. Sheltered by the magic circle of the slender white birches, they could be anything, say anything... and share any secret or ambition that hid down in the depths of their earnest little hearts.

"Idlewild," Diana repeated. "It's the perfect name for our house, all right. Anne, you do beat all! I've never met anyone who's better at naming places than you."

Anne sank down on one of the moss-covered rocks. She gazed up at the tangle of birch branches overhead, listening to the small, pointed leaves rustle and whisper together.

"I tried on one name after another for two days running, Diana, but none of them fit... not a one! It was just like trying on dress after dress, only to realize that each one was more poorly suited than the last.

"Or at least, I imagine it was like trying on dresses. I've never done it, myself. I've only taken whatever dresses kindly people gave to me, like this one Marilla made for me, and I've had to do it without complaint, because orphans generally can't complain about charity. No one should complain about charity, I suppose. It was awfully good of Marilla to make dresses for me, but I do wish she had more stylish tendencies. Still, I have often imagined what it must be like to be a beautiful princess in a castle that's generations old, and to face the impossible task of choosing a suitor for marriage, who will inherit the castle and the kingdom… and to try to dress for the occasion. I think it would be necessary to try on a dozen gowns at least, and discard every one of them, for it would be such a momentous occasion, and momentous occasions call for just the right kind of clothing.

"Anyway, I kept testing out names but none of them fit our playhouse. I was beginning to despair over it, and thought I'd never find a name to suit us… but then last night, as I was lying in bed and fighting against sleep so I could continue to ponder over the dilemma, 'Idlewild' just came to me. And I knew straight off that it was the right name, and that you'd love it, too. After that I fell asleep straight away, and slept so deeply the whole night through, for my heart was at last relieved of its burden."

"I'm having a new dress made this week," Diana confided. "Mother said it's time for a new one, since I'm growing so big. Only I'm growing *out*, not up. Oh, Anne, I wish I weren't so fat!"

Diana settled on the stone beside her friend, and Anne promptly threw her arm around Diana's shoulders.

"But Diana, you aren't *fat*. That word applies only to pigs and dumplings. You are *plump*, just like the girls in Charlotte Morgan's novels, and plumpness is ever so much more romantic than skinniness."

"Charlotte Morgan's heroines are all tall and willowy, Anne, like you."

"They are not, indeed! Not all of them. I've read at least two of her books that had heroines who were 'round and rosy and beaming.' Or they weren't in Charlotte Morgan's stories, they were in other books, equally as good. That's how I think of you, Diana: rosy and beaming. You're just like a rose, in fact, with your pink cheeks and your gay smiles. Oh, if only I could be as pretty as you! But with red hair, I never shall be, even if I were to succeed in getting plump. It's a sorrow I must resign myself to, for there's no way to change my fate."

Anne jumped up and took a cracked teacup down from the shelf. She presented it to Diana with a grand flourish; Diana sipped her imaginary tea with exaggerated good manners.

"But tell me about your new dress," Anne said. "I want to hear every last glorious detail."

Diana laughed as Anne took her seat again, sipping from a broken teacup of her own. "I don't know that there's much to tell you as yet. It hasn't been made yet. But the seamstress is coming over tomorrow morning to take my measurements."

"You must have lace at the throat and sleeves," Anne said, wide-eyed. "And seed pearls all along the bodice."

"Mother would never permit anything so fancy. But it is to be a *nice* dress... one I can wear to church and to parties."

"What color will it be? Oh, you must choose pink! I can never wear pink because it doesn't suit my hair, but how I have *longed* to, Diana! Let me live my dream through you. Please tell the seamstress to make it out of pink silk."

"I don't think Mother will pay for silk, either," Diana said doubtfully. "But perhaps some sateen, or maybe a very good cotton. Anyway, I know it's to have elbow sleeves. Mother was very firm on that point. They're so fashionable just now, and she wants me to look my best."

"You're lucky," Anne sighed. "What I wouldn't give to look fashionable. Marilla thinks fashion is the height of foolishness. She has strictly forbidden me to wear puffed sleeves!"

Diana set her china cup aside and all but wailed in despair.

"No, I'm not lucky, Anne! Oh, how can I make you understand? Mother is impossible... simply impossible! I don't know what I ought to do!"

Anne transferred herself again to Diana's side. "Dear Diana! Whatever do you mean?"

"Mother has everything all planned out... my whole life. But I'm still a girl, Anne! And that's all I want to be, for now. Oh, I like to imagine with you that we're grand ladies living in a beautiful mansion, but I don't want to *be* a lady... not yet."

For once, Anne had nothing to say. She looked steadily at Diana, waiting, her gray eyes widened by sympathy, her cheeks flushed pink with feeling.

"All Mother can think about is my marriage," Diana went on, her chin quivering with misery. "My marriage, my prospects, my reputation. It's all she ever talks about! And I know it's because she's so resentful, secretly. She would never tell a soul that she regrets becoming a farmer's wife, but I know... I know."

"Your father is the dearest, kindest man," Anne said. "Except for Matthew. And Mr. Barry is *almost* as nice Matthew, so really I don't see much to choose between them."

Diana sniffed and wiped a tear from the corner of her eye. "Father is a dear, sweet thing. I don't think Mother resents *him*... I think she loves him just as much as I do. But you know, Anne, Mother is awfully proud. She came from Charlottetown, and all her family lives there, and in Carmody. She even has cousins in Halifax, and they are highly regarded in the city... or so she has told me. I think Mother always felt she was destined for a better life, but here she is, in an old farmhouse in Avonlea. She's determined to see that I don't meet the same fate. She has never told me so, but I know I'm right."

Anne, sensing that their game was over, picked up the china teacups and returned them to the birch-tree shelves. "What fate do you want, Diana? What is your lifelong dream?"

Diana sat in silence for a moment, scuffing the heels of her boots against the mossy stone. At length, she said, "I don't know. I don't think I have a lifelong dream."

"Of course you do!" Anne insisted. "Everyone has at least one dream. Maybe a dozen! Haven't you ever closed your eyes and imagined out just exactly how your life should go?"

"No," Diana said honestly. "I suppose I've always been too busy trying to please Mother to spend much time imagining. But she's impossible to please, Anne! No matter what I do or how perfectly I behave, she always finds some fault with me. She's so determined that I shall be a perfect lady someday, and make the most successful match for a husband, I feel I can never catch my breath around her. There's no time for dreaming."

Anne took Diana's hands in her own, just as she had done when they swore their oath of friendship. "There's always time for dreaming. Why, sometimes there's too much time for it. I was forever getting into trouble with Mrs. Hammond for imagining too often, and letting it interfere with my work. Mrs. Hammond was one of the ladies I lived with, you know, just before I went to the asylum at Hopeton. I suppose I do let dreams and imaginings intrude on my duties, and I want to be good—really I do, especially for Marilla, who has been so kind to me—but sometimes the temptation is more than any mortal soul can resist."

Diana smiled tremulously, despite her tears. "I wish I had an imagination half as grand as yours, Anne. It might make life a little jollier, if I could imagine Mother was... was..."

"An elegant countess," Anne suggested with a half-wicked gleam in her eye, "sinking inevitably into old age, and you are her step-daughter, left alone to her care after your father, a gallant knight, died tragically. Not that I would hope for your *real* father to meet such a fate," she amended hastily. "But the countess... oh! She seethes with envy over your delicate, youthful beauty."

Diana laughed aloud at that; it seemed so absurd, to imagine a country girl like herself as a 'delicate' and beautiful aristocrat.

"And she plots to wed you to a horrible old scoundrel, who's balding and has warts on his nose. But you would rather marry…"

"A real hero, like the ones in my favorite books," Diana broke in. Her heart pounded with surprise when she realized that her imagination had sprouted wings. It seemed to respond to Anne's infectious presence, flourishing under her magic touch, as flowers bloom brighter near fairy-rings. "He'll be tall and serious —but not so serious that he can never laugh—with dark, curling hair and eyes like… like…"

"The tempest winds," Anne whispered.

A chill raced up Diana's spine. Anne did have such a knack for words. "Yes, exactly like that. And he'll seem cool and unapproachable, as if he has a secret he must guard, or as if he has some dark thought that follows him around all the time, which he can never be rid of. But he'll always be sweet to *me*."

"Oh," Anne sighed. She sank down beside Diana, drooping with the weight of awe. "That does sound so romantic. You see, Diana? You do have dreams after all."

"I suppose so," Diana said. Her cheeks felt very hot. "But my dreams will never matter to Mother. She'll have her way, whether I like it or not. And I must always be the perfect lady, like some society girl of Charlottetown. Always, even when I feel like being just a farm girl… just Diana of Orchard Slope."

All at once, Anne wrapped both her thin little arms around Diana, hugging her tightly. "I solemnly vow to you, dearest Diana, that you can always be Diana with me. And I will always adore you, exactly as you are."

"Will you really, Anne?"

"That's what it means to be bosom friends. I took our oath seriously, you see. I am yours forever."

The girls broke from their embrace and gazed shyly at each other. Both felt as if they had found something rare in the world, and neither quite knew what to do or say next. What does one say when one has found a treasure of immeasurable worth? But at last Anne scrambled up from the mossy stone.

"I do have to return to Green Gables now. Marilla is expecting me. I'm to do patchwork this afternoon. I *hate* sewing, but I guess it's an unavoidable task." She sighed deeply, pressing a hand to her heart. "There are so many unpleasant duties in this world, but I learned in Sunday school that all duties can be borne, no matter how unpleasant, if we but pray for patience. I will pray for it the whole time I'm doing my patchwork, I'm sure."

Diana sprang up, too, her tears drying in the warmth of her new excitement. "Oh, Sunday school! That reminds me: You are going to the picnic, aren't you?"

Anne stared at her blankly.

"There's to be a picnic next Wednesday! Just across the pond, in Mr. Harmon Andrews's big back field. He's mowing it down on Monday for the occasion. I expect nearly everyone in the whole church will be there."

"A picnic!" Anne clasped her hands before her, gazing far beyond the ring of birch trees to a glorious vista only she could see. "Oh, Diana, you don't know how often I've dreamed of attending a picnic. It has been one of my lifelong ambitions. I've never thought I'd be fortunate enough to actually go to one!"

"It's going to be ever so much fun," Diana said. "Some of the ladies are making ice cream, and—"

"*Ice cream!*" After that single, half-choked utterance, Anne fell silent with awe.

"And there will be games and prizes and the Avonlea brass band will play, too. I suppose that's one good thing about Mother insisting I have a new, more grown-up-looking dress: I'll be able to show it off to the Pye girls and make them positively sick with jealousy. I know I shouldn't flaunt any good fortune—it's terribly wicked—but sometimes I can't help myself where the Pye girls are concerned. I'll bet neither of them has elbow sleeves yet!"

Anne gave a little shiver, as if waking from a trance. "Thou hast given me a beautiful dream to guide me through the darkest night."

Diana nearly giggled at Anne's affected speech. She managed to stop herself by biting her lip as hard as she dared.

"I'll just run home now and tell Marilla," Anne said, reverting to a more prosaic mode. "Oh, what a thrill, just to *think* of a picnic! Nothing will keep me from it, Diana. Nothing!"

"Let's play again tomorrow."

"Tomorrow and every day, for the rest of our lives," Anne promised. "Well... except for Sundays. I suppose that wouldn't be reverent. And remember, dear Diana, you are always Diana to me, no matter what your mother may think or say or do."

DIANA FINDS HER VINEGAR

The seamstress rose gracefully from her knees, winding a long linen measuring tape around her hand.

"You may put your arms down now, Diana," Mrs. Barry said.

Diana did accordingly. Her shoulders had begun to tingle with weariness after holding her arms straight out to her sides for whole minutes at a time, while the seamstress recorded every conceivable measurement of her body. Diana was dressed only in her chemise and her knee-length pantalets, which really can't be said to be "dressed" at all. She was eager to get back into her frock of pretty, flowered calico, which lay neatly folded on the parlor sofa behind her.

"My, Diana," the seamstress said, "you have grown up like a weed since the last time I made a dress for you."

Her name was Miss Adams. She had clever, quick, small hands and a beaming smile that Diana liked very much. Her hair, a toasty, ash-like blonde, was beginning to show a few threads of gray, and some lines had formed around her twinkling, hazel eyes since the last time Diana had seen her. Diana thought her very pretty and regal, but she knew her mother didn't entirely approve of the woman, for Miss Adams had never married. That would have been acceptable to Mrs. Barry if Miss Adams had simply been unlucky in love, but word in Avonlea society held that Miss Adams had turned down a whole pack of suitors in favor of living and working on her own. "It's unnatural, bordering on sinful," Diana had once heard her mother murmur to another Avonlea lady. But Miss Adams was the very best seamstress for miles around... maybe the best on the whole island. Mrs. Barry was not about to spend her money on second-rate clothing for her little girl—not when the very best was close at hand.

"May I put on my dress now?" Diana asked.

"Yes, indeed," Miss Adams said, jotting a few last-minute notations on the small pad of paper. The pad hung by a ribbon that was pinned to her waist sash. Diana found the tools of the seamstressing trade endlessly fascinating. She remembered Anne's hatred for sewing and wondered at it. Perhaps Anne would like sewing better if she could see how jaunty Miss Adams looked, with her notebook dangling from her sash as if it were a beaded purse. And wouldn't Anne just love to jot down all her rainbow fancies as they came to her!

"Go on," Mrs. Barry prompted. "Don't stand about; get dressed if you're going to."

Blushing, Diana hurried to her calico dress and pulled it on while her mother opened the curtains, which had blocked the parlor windows while Diana's measurements were taken. There had been little sense in blocking them in the first place, as far as Diana could tell, for Father had gone into town on business, and the only other people at Orchard Slope were Minnie May, Diana's three-year-old sister, and the French girl who sometimes helped look after her.

Mrs. Barry extinguished the oil lamps that had kept the parlor lit, then settled on the sofa to look over the samples of fabric Miss Adams had brought. "Come here, Diana. We must choose the fabric for your new dress."

Diana sat close beside her mother and looked at each sample

with wonder and delight. It was perfectly delicious, to imagine herself dressed in such glorious textures and gay colors. There were cranberry cottons and linens in blue-and-white stripes, a satin-like weave of lustrous mauve and a leaf-green velvet with a silvery nap. Diana felt each sample with a near-reverent awe, and bubbled inside with secret mischief when she pictured the open envy of Gertie and Josie Pye.

"I think this blue will do very nicely," Mrs. Barry said.

Diana looked at the sample with fading enthusiasm. There was nothing *wrong* with the fabric. But it wasn't glamorous at all. It had no hint of sheen or luxury; it was as simple as could be. And worse, the color was a misty, powdery blue, better suited to a very small girl like Minnie May than to Diana, whose eleven years had surely earned her some claim to a little finery.

"I've thought so often that I only want to be a girl while I still can," Diana thought, resisting the urge to chew on her lower lip, "but this is entirely *too* girlish! Oh, couldn't Mother insist on growing me up a little *now*? She's so quick to do it at other times."

Diana, recalling Anne's request, pulled a vivid, rosy pink from the stack of samples. "This is such a pretty color. And it's so becoming on me... look!" She held it up beside her cheek so Mrs. Barry could appreciate how it harmonized with her complexion.

Her mother scowled. "Don't be ridiculous, Diana. Pink is far too showy a color. It's immodest! I won't have it."

"But..." Diana began.

Mrs. Barry collected the samples together and handed them back to the seamstress. "The pale blue will do very nicely, Miss Adams. I thank you."

"It's a very good weave," Miss Adams said, "and it wears so softly, Diana... it's just like silk after you wash it a time or two. I'm sure you'll adore it."

Diana lowered her eyes to the parlor rug, but she remembered to smile. "I'm sure I will, thank you, Miss Adams."

The seamstress gathered her supplies into her attaché case

and took Mrs. Barry's hand, a professional farewell. "I'll have the new dress finished in two days."

"Diana and I are both looking forward to it. Farewell, now."

When Miss Adams had gone, Mrs. Barry gave a loud sniff. Diana didn't know whether her mother's disapproval was for the unmarried seamstress or for Diana herself, but it hardly mattered. Mrs. Barry was in a mood, and would remain so for the duration of the afternoon. Diana steeled herself within.

"It's time to prepare supper," Mrs. Barry announced. "Come along, Diana."

Diana stifled a groan. She didn't mind cooking. In fact, she often enjoyed it. But the kitchen would be a terribly confined space with Mother simmering as she was. But like the good girl she always tried to be, Diana followed her mother into the kitchen without a word of complaint.

Mrs. Barry set her to work straight away, washing potatoes and carrots for roasting. When the last round little potato was spotlessly clean, Diana carried her bucket of wash-water outside to pour it in the garden. She dumped it onto the roots of the tiger lilies and paused, smelling their sweet fragrance and recalling the thrilling hour when she had first met Anne Shirley.

"How my life has changed, in less than a week!" Diana said to herself.

Anne had brought a new, indefinable feature to life, something Diana hadn't even known she was lacking until at last it was found. With her heartbreaking history and her glories of romantic fancies, Anne was the very avatar of adventure. It seemed a great injustice to Diana that she should be stuck doing boring old chores like some sort of peasant, when now she knew how grand life could be... *ought* to be. She thought of the dream-lover she and Anne had conjured up between them: tall, dark-haired, with sober eyes and an air of mystery hanging over him. *He* would never find any interest in a girl who washed potatoes and carrots.

"Diana!" Mrs. Barry called from the kitchen door. "Stop dilly-dallying and come back inside. There's work to be done."

Diana sighed heavily and marched back toward the kitchen, her pail swinging against her knees. It left wet splotches on her dress.

"Now peel those potatoes," Mrs. Barry said, the moment Diana appeared over the threshold. "They aren't about to peel themselves."

Diana pulled a stool near the kitchen window and began her duty, dropping the long, ruddy curls of peel into the bucket at her feet. After a few minutes, Mrs. Barry looked up from where she was kneading the bread dough on the flour-covered kitchen table.

"Land's sake, you've only peeled one potato! You're mooning out the window, not working."

"The day is so beautiful," Diana said plaintively. "I can't help but look."

"You were already out playing until lunch-time with that orphan girl the Cuthberts have acquired. That ought to be enough idleness for any child."

"Anne and I aren't idle when we play. We go everywhere... down the brook and along the road and even away back into the woods. It's great fun. And we talk about so many interesting things. Anne is terribly interested in my new dress. I told her all about what it's like to have a fitting by a real seamstress, because she has only ever had Marilla and other benefactors make dresses for her, but I've had seamstress-made clothes so many times before."

"I suppose it was that Anne child's idea that you should have your dress made in flamboyant pink."

Diana looked up from her potato with a guilty flush on her cheeks.

Mrs. Barry sighed with all the burdensome weight of dignity. "I suppose the girl isn't to blame. Waif that she is, I'm sure she has never had the opportunity to learn how to be elegant and becoming."

Diana always did her best to be a proper, well-behaved little girl, but she could put on a display of temper when her ire was roused. Even the angels in Heaven have their limits. It was more than she could bear, to hear her bosom friend referred to in such a derogatory manner. *Waif!*

She dropped her paring knife in the bucket with a clatter. The potato thumped into the bucket, too. "Pink *is* becoming and elegant. At least, it is on me. *I* still have the bloom of youth—"

Her mother's gasp cut Diana short, which was probably for the best. "The bloom of youth," Mrs. Barry repeated with scorn. She wiped the dough from her fingers with fidgety jerks of a sack-cloth towel. "What nonsensical, high-flown words."

Diana suspected it wasn't the high-flown words that had angered her mother so, but rather the unfortunate stress she had placed on the word *I*. She couldn't help it; ever since their conversation in the birch-tree playhouse, Diana had nurtured a scandalous fantasy that Mrs. Barry was, after all, the aging old countess and she, Diana, was her envied, orphaned step-daughter.

"Anne Shirley is a bad influence on you," Mrs. Barry said sternly. "She is teaching you to think and speak in ways good little girls ought never to think or speak."

The front door opened, and Mr. Barry's cheerful hello rang through the house. But neither Mrs. Barry nor Diana responded, caught up as they were in their private confrontation.

"I speak from my own heart," Diana insisted. "I *am* my own person, Mother, whatever you may think."

Mrs. Barry dunked her hands in the wash-bucket so vigorously that water slopped onto her apron. "You are saucing me, Diana, and I won't stand for it."

"Now, what's all this?" Diana's father stepped into the kitchen, glancing with obvious concern between his wife and his daughter.

"Your daughter is full of vinegar, that's what. She has been giving me the sharp side of her tongue all afternoon, and generally being contrary."

"I haven't!" Poor Diana's protest sounded very weak.

"There; you can see for yourself," Mrs. Barry said with steely composure. "I've allowed her to play too much with that wild girl the Cuthberts have taken in. Anne Shirley has had a corrupting influence on Diana's morals."

"My morals haven't been corrupted one bit!" Diana sprang up from her stool and clasped her father's hands, heedless of the wet slurry of potato starch that covered them. "Oh, Father, don't let Mother prevent me from seeing Anne! She's the only dear friend I've ever had."

"Now, now," Father murmured, attempting to soothe Diana's fears even as he tugged his hands away and sought out something to clean them with.

"You have plenty of friends who are good, obedient, perfectly normal girls," Mrs. Barry said, relentless in her righteousness. "What about Jane Andrews? And Ruby Gillis? You like them well enough."

"Jane and Ruby aren't the *same*," Diana wailed. "They aren't like Anne." Oh, how could she ever explain it?

Mrs. Barry issued a hard, level stare to Diana, the kind that meant she had reached the absolute limit of her leniency. "Diana, stop this protesting at one. You've heard my opinion on the matter."

Diana knew she should stop herself, but a fiercely rebellious spirit had bubbled up in her, like a spring bursting from the earth. She lifted her chin to an arrogant angle and said, "I don't care for your opinion on the matter."

The moment the words were out of her mouth, she knew she

had misstepped gravely. Her mother's face set in a mask of stony disapproval. Her eyes were as cold as black ice.

"Go up to your room at once," Mrs. Barry said, quiet with authority. "And for your backtalk, you have forfeited the right to attend the picnic."

Diana's mouth fell open, but nothing came out of it, not even a cry of despair. The cruel blow struck her mute and numb.

"Now, wait a moment, Rebecca," Father said. "You know the Sunday school picnic is an important affair."

"It is equally important for a child to obey her mother."

"Of course, of course. But what will your circle of friends think if Diana isn't there? And the minister's wife... she has been considering Diana for the choir. The picnic will be a perfect opportunity for Diana to present herself favorably to the minister's wife."

Mrs. Barry thawed—only by a droplet or two, but it was enough. "Perhaps you're right. Though I wish you would not interfere in my discipline, George! If you had your way, both your daughters would grow up to be scandalous examples of womanhood. *Somebody* has to raise them properly."

"So... so I may go to the picnic after all?" Diana ventured.

"I suppose," Mrs. Barry snapped. "But you had best exhibit impeccable behavior between now and then, or I shall change my mind. And don't think your father can save your goose a second time, Diana Barry."

Diana lowered her face contritely, but not before catching a conspiratorial wink from her father.

"I still maintain," Mrs. Barry said in a voice thick with dignity, "that Anne Shirley is a dreadful influence on you. I don't trust the girl. Don't try to protest, George; I know my suspicions about that orphan child will be justified in time... to this family's sorrow."

ANNE IS INTRODUCED

THE DAY OF THE SUNDAY SCHOOL PICNIC WAS FINE AND BRIGHT. THE sky was a clear, sweet blue, as of spring-time hyacinths, but the day's warmth was summer at its ripe, fulsome best. The sun coaxed a spicy perfume from the shore of Barry's Pond, a ferny, green-smelling air that mingled in an intoxicating way with cut grass and the roses blooming in the Andrews's garden. Under the shade of a broad, gray-barked willow tree, the Avonlea band played a tune that felt much bigger and bolder than its handful of horns and lone drummer ought to have produced. Everyone from the Methodist church was there, eating potato salad and scones on the patchwork blankets spread about the field, or paddling in canoes and skiffs around the glass-smooth, sapphire lake.

Diana longed to be out on the water. She loved rowing, and loved the stillness at the heart of Barry's Pond (which was so large that it more properly should have been called a lake.) But there was no hope for stillness on the water today; several of the older boys were splashing each other with their oars and rocking one another's canoes. Their laughter was almost as loud as the band's music.

And anyway, Diana couldn't justify rowing in her new blue

dress. Miss Adams had worked a marvel with the powdery blue fabric, so that even if Diana still would have preferred the pink, she could hold her head up high in this present frock. Perfect pintucks ran from neck to waist in an intricate, repeating pattern of varied widths. The elbow sleeves really were becoming. A row of buttons, shining mother-of-pearl, ran down the bodice, and just the right amount of lace peeked out at her collar: not enough to be ostentatious, but enough to inspire a thrill of envy in any girl who looked Diana's way.

"I can be quite proud sometimes," Diana reflected as she stood beside her mother, waiting in polite silence while Mrs. Barry conversed with the ladies of her sewing circle. "I suppose it's a fault in me. But as long as I never *act* proud, or allow my pride to lead me into bad deeds, there simply can't be any real harm in it."

The sewing circle's chatter drifted about her. It was all featureless, inconsequential—monotonous as the droning of bees among lavender. She gazed out across Harmon Andrews's field, and the picnic itself, to see Orchard Slope across the sparkling expanse of the pond. The last of the blossoms had fallen from the apple trees. Now the hill was blanketed in lush green, the branches of the old orchard so thick and profuse that Diana could not make out the foot-path through the trees. The white house stood out distinctly, though, its gabled roof peeking up over the billowing waves of green. The house—her home— seemed curiously far away. For the first time in her life, Diana felt separated from all that she once knew, held apart by a great chasm, though she couldn't say just what had caused that rift, or how deep it ran.

"Does this mean I'm growing up after all?" she wondered. She *did* feel somehow older than she had the day before, in her smart new dress with fashionable sleeves, surrounded by elegant and soft-spoken women. "But surely it's still too soon for me to feel like a real, grown girl. I'm still little; there's no denying that.

Maybe Mother has been right all along to plan for my future." The thought neither cheered nor encouraged her.

Diana caught sight of a flash of copper-red across the picnic grounds, near the refreshment table. She squinted through the bright afternoon sun and... yes! There was Anne Shirley, her braids swinging as she leaned over the table to inspect the offerings. She was trailed by tall, thin Marilla and Mrs. Rachel Lynde, considerably shorter and stouter but of the same dignified age. Whatever Mrs. Lynde lacked in height, she made up for with the grandness of her hat. Dusky violet with a wide, arcing brim and a spray of tall pheasant feathers, the hat's style wasn't precisely out of place at a picnic. But it did seem determined to be the very finest hat on display that day in Avonlea.

Diana fidgeted, glancing nervously around her mother's circle. Not a one of those women paid her any mind... nor had they for an awfully long time, except to compliment her looks and her new dress when she and her mother had first appeared. Would they miss her if she simply vanished from the circle? Would her mother call out shrilly to summon her back, and thereby embarrass Diana beyond what any mortal soul could bear, especially in the presence of Pyes?

Diana ached to run over and play with Anne; they had been separated for two whole days, and Diana felt sure she simply couldn't tolerate that cruelty any longer.

"I'll just have to take the risk," she told herself sensibly. And then, scalp prickling and spine tingling in dreadful anticipation, she edged slowly out of the sewing circle, step by careful step, until she was far enough away that she could turn on her heel and march briskly across the field. She would have run as if her feet were winged, but she feared to draw attention to herself.

She reached the shade-covered table just as Anne straightened with a plate of chocolate cake in her hands.

"Oh!" Anne said in surprise at finding Diana there before her. Then all the startlement left her eyes, replaced at once by a dreamy haze of bliss. "Oh, Diana, I'm so glad you're here. And I'm so glad there's chocolate cake. I have always wanted to try it, but haven't had the opportunity until now. I wanted to avoid any other sweets until after I'd tried the ice cream, because I've longed for ice cream for so many years, and what if it couldn't live up to the bliss of chocolate cake or lemon pie? I might never recover from the disappointment. But Mrs. Lynde said the ice cream must chill in the Andrews's springhouse until three o'clock, so I suppose it is better in the end to sample the chocolate cake now, in case some of these boys eat up all of it and then I don't get to try any.

"Oh, but your new dress! It's perfectly lovely, Diana!"

Diana held out her skirt so that Anne might appreciate the garment in its full glory. "I do wish it was pink, but Mother wouldn't hear of it."

"No, no—pink would look splendid on you, for you have the right coloring to wear any color at all. But *this* dress couldn't be anything but blue... soft, flowery, feather-light blue. I can see that now. Oh, Marilla," –turning to that same lady— "may Diana and I go off alone to talk and play together? You know it has been such a tragically long time since we have walked arm-in-arm and confided in one another."

Marilla's already thin lips thinned even further. She seemed to be holding back a sigh, or restraining herself from rolling her eyes. "Tragically long, indeed," she said drily. "But yes, you may go and play together. Mind you don't get chocolate cake crumbs on your new white pinafore, Anne. The stain will never come out. And hello, Diana," Marilla added pointedly.

Diana's smile was timid. "Hello, Miss Cuthbert, Mrs. Lynde. You both look well."

"Such a well-behaved child," Mrs. Rachel Lynde said to Marilla, as if Diana weren't there at all. "Rebecca Barry did right in raising her daughter, I can vouch for that." (Mrs. Lynde had brought up ten children, all the way to adulthood, and seldom passed up a chance to share her distinguished opinions on the rearing of children.)

"Run along, if you're going to," Marilla said.

Anne linked her arm with Diana's, balancing her plate of cake carefully in the other hand. They scampered off toward the big willow tree. The brass band had finished its final song, and was vacating that prime estate to the applause of the picnic-goers. Diana and Anne hid themselves on the far side of the willow's trunk and sank down to sit among its gnarled old roots.

Anne wasted no more time; she bit into a huge forkful of cake, then closed her eyes in blissful silence. When she had swallowed it, she said, "Diana, it's better than I ever imagined any cake could be. Marilla makes plum cake, of course, for there are plenty of plums and plum preserves at Green Gables. And I like plums just fine, I'm sure, but nothing... *nothing* can compare to chocolate. I don't know how I can look favorably on a bowl of preserves again. And I fear the ice cream is already spoiled for me, but I shall have to endure the disappointment anyhow. Do you want some of my cake? I wouldn't share with anyone else, but I would give you *anything*, Diana."

Diana helped herself to a corner of the cake. It was delicious. "Is Marilla really well?" she asked. "She seemed sort of... subdued. As if something was troubling her."

Anne's narrow, freckled face drooped into a solemn frown. "Marilla and I have had a perfectly terrible time. I felt sure she would send me back to the asylum. And worse, she forbade me to come to the picnic, too! I might actually have died of grief if it had truly come to that."

"What happened?"

"She thought I had taken her amethyst brooch... a very precious heirloom. I didn't take it, though I did play with it a little... pinned it on and pretended I was a rich, beautiful lady. I shouldn't have done even that. It was wicked; I see that now. But I didn't take it. Marilla refused to believe me, though, and she swore she would keep me locked in my room until I confessed to the crime."

"Oh dear!" Diana's heart had actually sped up and was now pounding quite alarmingly. That was how suspensefully Anne wove the tale. "Whatever did you do, Anne?"

"I confessed. What else could I do? I made up an extremely romantic and dramatic story about how I carried myself away with imaginings, and dropped the brooch in the Lake of Shining Waters, where it could never be found again. I thought that would be the end of the matter, but Marilla was so cross I thought steam might actually come out of her ears. She utterly forbade me to come to the picnic, and oh, Diana, my heart was so terribly broken.

"But this afternoon, Marilla found her brooch; it had snagged on her shawl and was simply overlooked. Marilla confessed to me how she had wronged me. She told me it was wicked to make up a story, but fate had backed me into a corner, Diana... I had to do it. I apologized to Marilla, too, and was very contrite, but I don't mind telling you that I still don't think I was *entirely* in the wrong. You won't tell anyone, will you? No, of course you won't... good, sweet Diana!

"So that's why Marilla seems so strange, I suppose. The fragile bonds between us have been sorely tried. She proved herself fair in the end, though. I think she's an awfully good old lady, with a very kind heart, once you find it."

"That explains why your eyes are red," Diana said. "You must have cried terribly over it... poor Anne!"

"Are my eyes very red? I hope I don't look miserable. Because really, I have never been happier in all my life. This is such a beautiful day, and Marilla made a sponge cake for our contribution to the picnic fare and it looks better than anybody else's cake, except for this chocolate one here, and I would hate for anyone to think I were unhappy."

"You needn't worry," Diana reassured her friend. "It's not very noticeable, and anyway, it looks sort of becoming on you. You told me you couldn't wear pink with your red hair, but your eyes look all right in pink."

Both girls laughed over that, and finished off the chocolate cake in good humor.

"Mother was furious with me, too," Diana said, licking crumbs from her fingers. She recounted the story of their fight over the dress, taking far less time to tell it than Anne had taken over her quarrel with Marilla.

"I feel dreadful, that I should have been the cause of any trouble for you," Anne said mournfully.

"Not a bit of it! Mother and I are always arguing. Father says we're like cats and dogs now. He doesn't know what has come between us, and I guess I don't either, except that I don't like the way she bosses me. I know she's my mother, and mothers have a duty to boss, but it seems she could be a little kinder now and then, if she made up her mind to."

"Your dress is glorious, though," Anne said. Those buttons are so dainty. How they shine! You look just like a pearl, and I look like a muddy old pebble beside you."

"No, you don't."

Diana climbed to her feet, then pulled Anne up, too. She looked Anne up and down, assessing her with a critical but fair eye. Anne wore a simple cotton dress, midnight-blue checked with white, and a spotlessly clean pinafore that was glowingly bright in the summer sun. The neck of her pinafore was accented by a row of simple but remarkably neat and pretty ruffles. A straw boater, with a deep-blue ribbon for a band, kept the sun from propagating more freckles on her eager, hopeful face. Her braids were tied with blue ribbons, too. If her look was rather simple and rustic, it was also tremendously becoming. There was no showiness in Anne... Diana sensed that perhaps there never would be, even when they were grown-up ladies in long skirts with their hair worn high. Yet there was still something fantastically attractive about the girl. Other girls might have to work for admiration... dress for it, style themselves, choose their manners and elocution with care. Anne Shirley *compelled* admiration, as if it were hers by nature, by right. She had no need of fancy dresses or affected ways.

"You look just perfect," Diana said honestly. "I wouldn't change a thing about you."

"Oh, look!" Anne said, craning her head to stare past Diana's shoulder toward the Andrews's home. Her braids swung wildly. "They're bringing the ice cream down! Diana, I'm trembling. I feel as if my life is about to change forever. From this moment on, I cannot ever be the same Anne I was before. What should we do?"

"Let's go stand in line," Diana suggested.

The girls eagerly joined the queue, watching with wide-eyed anticipation as Mr. Harmon Andrews and his hired boy carried the big jug up from the distant springhouse. It swayed heavily between them, promising a bountiful reward. As Diana watched the ice cream advance, her mouth watered and she almost began to tremble in anticipation herself, though she had tasted ice cream many times before.

"Who's *this*?" a girl all but sneered near Diana's shoulder.

Diana's joy sank into the pit of her stomach. There was no mistaking that voice. She didn't need to turn around to know that Gertie Pye was directly behind her, almost certainly with her impish little sister Josie in tow. Diana stifled a sigh and tried to fix a friendly smile to her face before she greeted the Pye girls.

Gertie was older than Diana and Anne by two years, but she wasn't especially tall for thirteen. She had chestnut-brown hair that hung in neat, rag-curled ringlets down to her shoulders, and a round, dimpled face that had too mocking an expression to ever look pretty or sweet. She stood, as usual, with fists braced on her hips. Beside her, ten-year-old Josie twirled one of her golden curls around a finger and gazed up at Diana with an impudent expression.

"Aren't you going to introduce us?" Gertie demanded of Diana.

"This is Anne Shirley of Green Gables," Diana said primly, with a small thrill in her middle. It was exciting to be the keeper of such exclusive knowledge. "She is new to Avonlea."

"Diana and I are bosom friends," Anne added.

"You're *what*?" Gertie's dimples deepened; she seemed to be on the verge of shrieking with laughter, but she controlled herself at the last moment. A stony expression, narrow-eyed and chilly, replaced her merriment. "Is that a new dress, Diana Barry?"

"Yes. Do you like it?" Diana looked down at her pintucks and buttons to hide the flush of triumph on her cheeks. So Gertie Pye *was* envious. The day was surpassing all of Diana's expectations.

"We got new dresses, too," Gertie said, declining to offer her opinion. As if on cue, she and Josie both twirled in place so their skirts flared. The smaller girl's dress was of pale lavender, but Gertie's was blushing pink.

"Of course Gertie Pye got a pink dress," Diana thought, her pleasure and pride both temporarily extinguished. "But I really don't think theirs are as fine as mine. They have old-fashioned sleeves, for one thing, and not a hint of lace."

Anne sniffed, lifting her chin with an air of lofty judgment. Her gray eyes swept the Pye girls from head to foot, quite pointedly. "Diana's dress is the nicest *I've* ever seen."

Gertie cut Anne with an especially sour look, but Anne seemed to take no notice at all. She held herself with an air of regal poise, of perfect calm, and Gertie's nasty looks withered and faded, as if stricken by a blight.

"If you're living at Green Gables," Gertie said to Anne, "then you'll be in Avonlea School when the summer's over. If you're to go to school at all, that is."

"Of course I'm to go to school!"

Diana heard a queer shiver in her friend's voice, and she suspected that Anne in fact had no idea whether she would attend school or not. Diana suspected, too, that despite Anne's grand declarations about the importance of ice cream, what she truly longed for was to go to school.

"Mr. Phillips is to be our teacher again next school year," Gertie said. "He's simply awful, isn't he, Josie?"

Josie Pye nodded. "He's terrible mean and cross all the time. He'll switch your hand if you get your sums wrong."

Diana glanced at Anne, noting how pale her friend's cheeks had gone. "I've never seen Mr. Phillips whip anybody," Diana said. "You shouldn't tell falsehoods, Josie Pye!"

Gertie stepped into the breach, defending her little sister. "It's not a falsehood, and you know it, Diana Barry! Mr. Phillips growls at all the students and doesn't have any patience at all. If you miss your spelling he'll stand you up in front of the whole class, where everybody will *stare* and *stare* at you. You *know* it's true, Diana."

"Grumbling and standing up in front of the class isn't the same as whipping," Diana insisted.

"He whipped Moody last year, on a day when you were out sick with a cold. Moody was so hurt that he cried over it, right in front of everybody."

"Moody was probably acting out. He deserved it!"

Gertie shook her head, smiling. "Moody never acts out. He's a model student. He only spelled one word wrong on his test, and Mr. Phillips came down on him something awful, because Mr. Phillips can't be predicted."

Poor Anne was trembling again, but not on account of the ice cream. She stared at Gertie Pye, horror plain to read in her pink-tinged eyes.

"Why don't you spell 'predicted,'" Diana said saucily, "and if you get it wrong, we'll have Mr. Phillips over to whip you. Don't listen to a thing she says, Anne... either one of them. By and by, you'll learn all about Pyes."

"I'm not afraid," Anne said. She had marshalled her fear and now stood proud and defiant before the Pye girls' insidious glee. "I have every confidence that I will meet all of Mr. Phillips's expectations, and learn well enough to please any teacher."

"Any *normal* teacher, maybe," Gertie muttered, turning away with a cruel little laugh. Then she spun back abruptly, as if recalling something important. "Diana, did you hear? Gilbert Blythe will be back in school this autumn."

"Oh!" Diana exclaimed in delight, then immediately wished she had not. Ever since she had taken notice of boys—which was a new development, to be sure—she had thought none of them were nearly as handsome as Gilbert. But she felt a queer, fluttery instinct of secrecy on that count. No one must ever know what she thought of Gilbert... *ever*. Diana couldn't tell just what kind of danger might develop if anyone were to suspect. Death by some vague (but still quite ominous) shame seemed likely. And Gertie Pye would be the very last person in all the world whom Diana could trust with such a delicate, crucial confidence.

She mustered an air of calm. "Oh, how nice for Gilbert Blythe. Is his father better, then?" She turned to Anne, and said for her benefit, "Mr. Blythe has been ill for two whole years, so Gilbert had to leave school and look after their small farm."

At that moment, Charlie Sloane approached with his cap in his hands. "Hullo, Diana. Won't you introduce me to your new friend?"

Several other requests for introductions followed, from girls as well as boys, while the picnic attendees watched the great jug of ice cream opened and waited to receive their portion of the treat in tin bowls and cups. Diana's throat was nearly dry from talking to all her school and church friends, debuting Anne Shirley to Avonlea's curious and gregarious society of small fry.

"Anne doesn't seem to realize how popular she is," Diana thought. "If it were Gertie who was new in Avonlea—or even Ruby Gillis—she would preen and strut from so much attention. But Anne isn't puffed up at all. She just seems happy to make so many new friends. I'm awfully glad she's *my* chum... and don't I feel lucky to have met her first, before she could find another bosom friend!"

When at last they received their scoops of strawberry ice cream, Diana and Anne broke away from the crowd of welcomers, slipping away to the edge of the pond where they could sample the long-awaited bliss without any distractions. They hid themselves behind a screen of reeds; Anne stared down at her dish of ice cream with the air of one going to meet her fate.

"Now that the moment is here, I can hardly believe it's real," she whispered. "I have so many regrets. I utterly repudiate that slice of chocolate cake!"

"Taste it, silly," Diana laughed.

Anne tasted a spoonful. She savored it for a long moment, then suddenly tears sprang to her eyes. She tossed her straw boater aside and leaned her ruddy head on Diana's shoulder.

"Oh, Diana, today has been simply perfect. It was worth all the strife and uncertainty, to find myself here. Even those horrid Pye girls couldn't spoil it. Life is good, after all... and best, I get to share it with my dearest friend."

SCHOOL BEGINS

THE AIR WAS AS CRISP AS THE APPLES THAT SCENTED IT. THE FIRST blush of autumn revealed itself in the changing color of light filtering down through the treetops, where leaves touched with tinges of gold and flame-orange had just begun to overtake the hardy green of summer. Everything was warming to a most delicious, golden-yellow hue in preparation for autumn's full display of splendor.

Anne had hardly paused in her chatter since she first met Diana at the log foot-bridge. The little red-headed slip hadn't even noticed the turning of the first leaves or the slight chilling of the air. It was clear from Anne's agitation—the fidgety way she clasped her primer and lunch basket to her chest, the flush on her cheeks that obscured even her most assertive freckles—that she was both thrilled and terrified in equal measure, too much so to gaze about her in wonder at the turning of the seasons.

"I was very bold with Gertie Pye at the Sunday school picnic," Anne was saying as the girls passed Violet Vale. There were no violets there now, of course, this being early September, so it was just a little depression in the earth, a cup full of bright green and gold-faded grasses at the edge of Mr. Bell's woods. But the red clusters of pigeonberries that peeped over the vale's edges were almost as pretty as springtime violets. "But the truth is, I'm awful afraid of my spelling, Diana, and my reading, too."

"You have nothing to worry about, you goose," Diana said affectionately. "Why, we've been reading together all summer long... haven't we finished seven whole books between us? And you're just as good a reader as I ever seen." She blushed and clapped a hand to her mouth. "*I've* ever seen, I meant to say. I must get out of the habit of talking like a country bumpkin. Mr. Phillips is even stricter about grammar than Mother is, but I can't seem to break myself of it. I don't know how you avoided it, Anne. Did they have teachers to school you in proper grammar at the asylum?"

"Indeed, no," Anne said soberly. "We had no teachers at all. Of course, I was only at the asylum for four months. Maybe if I'd stayed longer, they might have put some schooling into me, to make me more appealing to grown-ups, you know. But I feel terribly lucky they didn't, because if they'd given me any affectations then perhaps Mrs. Spencer wouldn't have picked me out for Matthew and Marilla—they're such dear, sweet, countryish old things. Of course, Matthew and Marilla wanted a boy, not a girl, and Mrs. Spencer was mistaken... but you know all about that.

"No, Diana, whatever modest knowledge I can claim, I have learned from books. The first lady I lived with taught me how to read, because it was the only way she could think to distract me so I wouldn't pepper her with questions. That's what she called it... 'peppering.' I do think that's a funny way of saying it. I couldn't help but imagine all the questions sticking to her skin, like little flecks of pepper on a roasted chicken, and then picturing it made me want to laugh, which would only make her more exasperated. I fear I am an especially exasperating girl, and even good grammar can't make up for it.

"But I'm dreadfully worried about Mr. Phillips. What if he

shouldn't like me? Oh, and Diana, I've just thought...! What if we aren't allowed to sit together? I won't be able to bear it!"

"I guess you'll bear it all right," Diana said. "All the girls at the school are pretty nice. Well... all the girls who aren't Pyes." But Diana, too, felt a twinge of anxiety at the prospect of being separated from her bosom friend for the length of an entire school day. What if Anne should make other, better friends, and forget all about Diana?

"None of the girls can be as nice as you," Anne said stoutly. "I'll sit with them if I must, but I won't..."

Anne trailed into a sudden, weighty silence, a kind that had become quite familiar to Diana through the pleasant weeks of summer. She didn't need to look at Anne to know that her eyes were wide and starry with inspiration, that her mouth hung open in breathless awe. The lane they followed past Violet Vale had entered back under the canopy, but these were not the dark, stately firs of Mr. Bell's woods. This stretch of forest was composed almost entirely of birches, young and slender and white, just like those that encircled Idlewild. But there were dozens of birches here... perhaps hundreds. Autumn had only just begun to touch the leaves with its cold, golden fingers; veils of morning light hung in airy layers all down the length of the path, rippling subtly in shades of green or gold, depending on the shade of the leaves overhead. Here and there, a shaft of unfiltered light burst through an open spot in the birch boughs, and in those dazzling columns, dust motes whirled and glinted like stars drawn down to the earth. The starflowers had long since lost their delicate, pearl-white blooms, but the leaves of the plants still edged the path, glossy and lush. Curls of fern, just beginning to dry as the fall came on, stood up alertly between the white birch trunks.

"Oh!" Anne gasped. "I've never been so far along this path before. What is this place called, Diana?"

"I don't know that it has a real name. We just call it 'Bell's Road.'"

"A place so stirring must have a better name. Can't you feel the magic here? We must call it..."

"Please, can I name it?" Diana asked suddenly. Anne had named all their various haunts, and while Diana liked every name Anne had picked, she felt as if she must contribute *something* to their mutual lore.

Anne nodded at her in encouragement, gray eyes shining, eager to hear what romantic title Diana would bestow on the place. Diana's heart sped in a rather disconcerting way. She hadn't thought this through. Anne had such a talent for romance; Diana would only let her down if her name fell short of the mark.

"We shall call it," Diana said slowly, stalling for time while her mind worked furiously. But she could stall no longer, or Anne would think her silly. She was obliged to say the first and only name that came to her. "The Birch Path."

Anne's hesitation was fleeting; then she smiled at Diana and wrapped one thin arm around her shoulders. But Diana had caught the flicker of disappointment. "I'm not as good at naming places as she is," Diana thought, "but I'm glad she's nice enough not to draw attention to it."

The girls soon left the Birch Path behind. The lane joined the main Avonlea road, which was hot and dusty even in the morning. Fortunately, they had only a short walk along the road until the way forked. Their path led up a spruce-covered slope, blanketed in blue-green shadows, to a whitewashed school at the hill's crest. Anne lapsed into silence again as the girls climbed the hill, but now there was no awe in her... only fear. Other children joined them as they walked—children who came from all directions, from every rustic corner and hidden dell of Avonlea. Their greetings and laughter and general merriness seemed to throw a little light to chase away the shadows of Anne's worry.

They climbed the school's porch steps just as the bell clanged briskly in the yard. A nearly-grown girl of fifteen or sixteen years was ringing it.

"But I thought we had a man for a teacher," Anne said. She paused on the porch to watch as the slender girl with curly brown hair gave the bell's rope a few more solid tugs.

"That's not our teacher," Diana said. She couldn't keep a faint note of disgust out of her voice. "That's Prissy Andrews."

"Is she Jane's sister?" Anne inquired. They had played often with Jane Andrews over the summer, for she was the girls' own age. Jane lacked Anne's wild imagination, and was very plain and steady... but she was always kind and sweet, too, and happy to take part in their adventures, no matter how intricately Anne knotted romance through and around their games.

"No, Prissy is a cousin to Jane," Diana replied. "At the end of last school year, Mr. Phillips started making eyes at her, and some of the boys wrote up his name with hers right here on the porch, in a big 'take notice.' The boys got in terrible dutch for it." Diana leaned close and whispered in Anne's ear, "But all summer long, Mother has heard rumors that Mr. Phillips has started courting Prissy Andrews... or that he intends to start courting her in earnest, when this school year is through. I don't know if it's true or not, but Prissy is definitely Mr. Phillips's pet. He positively worships her."

"It is very intimidating, knowing that the teacher has a pet," Anne said meditatively. "Do you think it's likely to make Mr. Phillips less favorably inclined toward a new scholar?"

The last of the Avonlea School students clattered up the porch steps and crowded through the red-painted door, into the bastion of learning that waited beyond. Anne and Diana were left alone.

"I don't know," Diana said, seizing Anne's hand and pulling her into the schoolroom. "But we'd better not be late to our desks!"

Upon entering the schoolhouse proper, Anne checked and

stared around her in delighted wonder, so that Diana was forced to stop, too, or let go of her hand. The sight of the old-fashioned, hinge-topped desks, standing in orderly rows and separated by stately aisles, seemed to thrill Anne to her very core. And the simple wooden lectern with a clean, dark expanse of blackboard behind it struck Anne mute and still, as a pilgrim who stands before a shrine.

Mr. Phillips was bowed over his lectern, busy with his notes. He looked up, caught sight of Anne, and said, "Ah. And you must be Anne Shirley, our new student. Welcome to our school."

His words were welcoming, but his expression and tone were guarded, even suspicious, as they so often were. Mr. Phillips was still a very young man—Diana guessed him to be twenty-one or twenty-two. He had neatly parted and slicked, coffee-brown hair and a remarkably natty mustache. In addition, he always wore starched collars and brightly colored neck-bows, tied in the stylish "floppy" way. But despite his smart looks, Diana had never been able to make herself like Mr. Phillips. She obeyed him, of course, and showed him the respect a teacher was due. But she decidedly did not *like* him. There was something about him, a faintly stuffy air, that simply refused to be liked.

Diana elbowed Anne, for the latter was staring at Mr. Phillips in pale, trembling silence.

"Yes, sir," Anne finally managed. "I'm Anne Shirley; Anne is spelled with an E."

"You will share a desk with Diana Barry," Mr. Phillips said, gesturing with his pencil to one of the unoccupied, double-bench desks. It was perfectly situated next to a window, which was useful for daydreaming when lessons grew dull.

Diana and Anne squeezed each other's hands in triumph and hurried to their desk.

"I'm so glad," Anne whispered as the girls tucked their primers into the cavernous desk. "I would have gone wild with fear if I had to be parted from you, Diana."

When the classroom was more or less settled, Mr. Phillips cleared his throat to marshal his scholars' attention and stepped grandly in front of the lectern. His hands were clasped behind his back and his mustache quivered as he addressed the school in his most sonorous and authoritarian manner.

"Today we witness the opening of another school year. Now is the time for us all to reflect on our ambitions, to set and achieve worthy goals. The weeks and months ahead promise to bring—"

Diana stifled a sigh; Mr. Phillips never squandered a chance to make a grand speech. Anne's eyes shone with inspiration as the teacher spoke about taking pride in one's work, striving for improvement, and embracing the glories of new knowledge. But Diana allowed her mind to wander… and presently, she allowed her eyes to wander, too. Across the aisle, on the boys' side of the classroom, the seat next to Moody Spurgeon MacPherson remained empty. Diana's stomach sank a little, and some of the day's glowing thrill snuffed itself out, replaced by the dull ashes of disappointment.

A sneering whisper hissed behind Diana. "*You're* looking for *Gilbert Blythe*. You're *dead gone* on him."

It was Gertie Pye. Diana did not turn around to fix Gertie with a withering, offended stare; Mr. Phillips would only punish her for that. But she did snap to attention, focusing on the front of the classroom with her face burning and her heart racing painfully in her chest.

"Gertie doesn't know a thing," Diana told herself. "She's only trying to get my goat."

But Diana could feel the emptiness of the seat across the aisle all throughout the morning. As their lessons progressed, Mr. Phillips paced up and down the aisles like some dignitary in a stately procession, orating as he went. And Diana bit her lip and squeezed her chalk hard in her fingers, concentrating on her slate, resisting the urge to gaze wistfully at Gilbert's vacant seat.

Anne was remarkably focused on their lessons, even though

she struggled tremendously with arithmetic. Diana was glad to help her work out the sums, for numbers had never given Diana any trouble. But in the hour before lunch time, Mr. Phillips instructed the scholars to take their primers from their desks. It was time for the reading exercise... the moment Anne had dreaded.

As the girls laid their primers on their desks, Anne peered uneasily at Diana's book. "You're in the fifth reader," Anne said, tragedy lacing her words. "I thought you would be in the fourth, with me."

"It's only because you've never been to school before," Diana said practically. "You're such a good reader; you shouldn't fret over it. You'll be moved ahead to Fifth in no time."

Mr. Phillips assigned pages to each class of readers; there was a rustling of paper and a general shuffling of bodies as the scholars located their lessons. Then a tense silence descended on the schoolroom as silent reading began. The tension was largely concentrated around Diana's and Anne's shared desk, though, where a red-haired girl, miserable with anxiety, fumbled and fretted through her reading.

Mr. Phillips called students one by one to rise and read from their books, each presenting a single paragraph with their best, steadiest, clearest elocution. The eldest students went first, with Prissy Andrews foremost of them all. She did have a pretty, melodious voice, which was pleasant to hear... but she punctuated every sentence with a coy little giggle, and Diana could barely stop herself from rolling her eyes crudely when Prissy had finished.

Diana acquitted herself well amongst the fifth-reader class. She always felt a bit light-headed and jittery whenever she read aloud, but she was determined to get through the first day of school without attracting any disapproving sniffs from Mr. Phillips, so she took her time and spoke each word with care.

"Good," Mr. Phillips said shortly when she had finished her paragraph. "Though you must work on your presentation, Diana. Speak too slowly and you will put your audience to sleep with boredom.

"Now the fourth readers."

Anne stiffened on the bench.

"Anne Shirley, will you please rise and read the first paragraph from 'The Summer Garden'?"

Anne did not move. She stared fixedly at Mr. Phillips, her face pale and sickly, until Diana squeezed her hand. "Pretend we're only reading to each other at Idlewild," she whispered.

"Anne Shirley," Mr. Phillips said sharply.

She climbed shakily to her feet. "In s... summertime the garden blooms with a var... variety of flowers," Anne read. Her voice, like her poor little frame, shook and shivered as if buffeted by tempest winds. But she soldiered on bravely, stumbling only a few times and mispronouncing only one flower's name.

"Hydrangea," Mr. Phillips corrected her as she finished.

With flaming face, Anne sank miserably back down on her seat.

At lunch time, the fourth- and fifth-reader girls retrieved their bottles of milk from the stream behind the shoolhouse, then arrayed themselves in a circle on the grass. They opened their baskets and commenced the Avonlea School tradition of pooling their lunches, so that everyone might have a taste of each delicious goodie their mothers had made and packed.

Diana passed around her raspberry tarts, so each girl could sample a bite. "I think you did really well at reading, Anne," she said.

"Mr. Phillips didn't think so."

"Oh, he was more impressed than he let on," Jane Andrews said. "He's an awful prickly man. He wouldn't say anything nice about anybody if his life depended on it."

"And I think you did grandly," Ruby Gillis said to Anne as she broke off her portion of raspberry tart. Ruby was a remarkably pretty little girl, with shiny, golden hair and big, twinkling blue eyes. "Really, I never saw anybody do the fourth reader so well. Last year I never read it half as good as you."

"I fear that you are all flattering me just to soothe my pride," Anne said soberly. "But it is nice to be flattered now and again."

"I wouldn't ever guess that you were a wild, uneducated orphan, to hear how smartly you read," Ruby said.

Diana blushed on her friend's behalf. "Ruby, it's not polite to call Anne 'wild' and 'uneducated.'"

"But I didn't mean anything by it," Ruby said, with a hint of a whine. "My mother said you were a wild orphan, Anne, and had no schooling."

"That is true," Anne said. "Well… I had no proper schooling before today. The part about being wild isn't so true, but I sort of like it all the same. It makes me feel like a heroine in a story."

All of the girls laughed delightedly at that, even Gertie Pye, who for once had no hint of meanness in her merriment.

When lunch was over, the students headed back to the schoolhouse to resume their lessons. Anne clung to Diana's arm. "Do you think the girls like me well enough?" she asked anxiously.

"I know they do," Diana said. "Why, you seem really popular, Anne."

"I'm glad they're able to look past my red hair. I was so fearful that they never could, and I do *so* want to make friends. But of course, I have only one bosom friend, and that is you."

"I'm proud to be the bosom friend of such a well-liked girl," Diana said. A soft murmur, deep down in her heart, told her that perhaps she shouldn't be so glad. Perhaps she ought to give in to a sneaking, Pye-like instinct and despise Anne, for she *was* so very popular with the school crowd, and gained their admiration with no effort at all.

"But I never could despise her," Diana reassured herself with decisive calm. "We are bosom friends, after all... sworn by a sacred oath. And I will stand by my friend forever."

THE INCIDENT OF THE SLATE

THE SCHOOL YEAR UNFOLDED AS SCHOOL YEARS DO, WITH THE fresh excitement of the first week settling down into a cozy, steady rhythm. By the third week, the summer's sunny, breezy delights already seemed a lifetime past, and the routine of rising early, dressing for school, and walking with Anne to the whitewashed building on the spruce hill was well ingrained in Diana's habits.

Anne, too, had adapted nicely to her new reality as a scholar. She was often distracted by her daydreams. (Mr. Phillips had been obliged to crack his pointer down across Diana's and Anne's shared desk more than once, thanks to the latter's habit of sighing as she gazed out the window at the Lake of Shining Waters instead of gazing at Mr. Phillips's blackboard lessons.) But despite her wayward wandering through the realms of fancy, Anne still managed to succeed at school. She was already so strong in the fourth reader that all the girls agreed she'd soon be moved up to the fifth, and her arithmetic was so improved that she hardly ever needed Diana's help anymore. Anne seemed to have found her place in the world at last. She was made for scholarly endeavors, and pursued them with a bright-eyed gusto that did her credit.

"Your mother packed your lunch basket," Father said as Diana came down the stairs to the kitchen. It was a Monday morning; the sky outside the kitchen window was still flushed with the golden memory of summer. "She was called down to the Wilsons' early this morning to help old Cousin Francine until her special doctor arrives from Carmody."

Francine Wilson was barely a cousin at all; the old lady's relation to the Barry household was so distant that Diana was sure Adam and Eve were closer kin. But Mrs. Barry was well known throughout the island for her family loyalty. She would certainly never leave a family member in need, no matter how tenuous the relation.

"Is Cousin Francine all right?" Diana asked, peeking in at her lunch as she wriggled into her coat.

Father barely glanced up from his newspaper. "It's only her rheumatism, but her daughter couldn't sit with her this morning, since her baby was colicky all night... or something like that. I don't exactly recall just what your mother said as she was leaving. Anyway, I've made breakfast."

Diana stifled a mischievous giggle. Father had sliced a loaf of bread. A crock of plum preserves stood open on the table beside a roll of yellow butter. It wasn't much of a breakfast—Mother would have fainted dead away at the thought of calling such a rustic spread a meal—but it did look delicious. There was a pail of fresh, creamy milk on the table, too, just brought in by the hired boy. Diana dipped a cupful, careful to catch as much of the rich, frothy cream as she could. Then she spread an immoderate amount of butter on her bread and followed it with a heaping spoonful of preserves.

"I'm sorry to hear Cousin Francine's rheumatism is troubling her," Diana said. Her speech was prim and proper enough to please Mrs. Barry, if she had been there to hear it. But she promptly ruined the effect by biting into her thick bread and painting her cheek with a smear of sticky preserves. "Is there any other news?" she asked, scrubbing at her face with a napkin.

Father scanned the paper without real interest. "Not much to speak of. Oh, the Blythes are back from New Brunswick."

Diana swallowed her mouthful of bread with a gulp, as if it were a boulder in her throat.

"They just got back on Saturday," Father went on, not looking up from the advertisement section. "By now, I suspect young Gilbert will be so far behind in school that his father will think of pulling him out and putting him to work as a farm hand. Perhaps I'll see if Gilbert would like to come and work for us. He's a strong, sturdy boy. He could do quite well, to learn how to manage a farm first-hand."

Diana's heart pounded so hard in her chest that it nearly made the ruffles jump on the bib of her dress. She was glad her father was still engrossed in his paper.

"I... I don't think Gilbert will be behind in school," she stammered.

"He missed three years of schooling when his father was ill and the Blythes went out to Alberta."

"But he's terribly smart," Diana said quickly—too quickly. Father looked up from his paper with a curious expression, and he didn't fail to note the hot flush on Diana's cheeks.

"Ah," he said with a knowing, comforting smile. "Perhaps I won't ask young Gilbert to work for me after all. If he wants to take up as a hired boy, I'm sure there are plenty of farms in Avonlea who would be glad to have him."

"He won't," Diana muttered, studying her cup of milk so she wouldn't have to meet her father's eye. "He'll be a teacher or a lawyer or a doctor someday, I'm sure of it."

Just thinking about Gilbert Blythe made her feel prickly and wobbly. Talking about him was even worse. Diana had never felt so unnerved before, merely by the thought of a boy... a *boy*, of all creatures! It certainly was strange, being eleven years old.

"I must go now." Diana drained the last of her milk and jumped up from the table before she could babble on and betray more of her thoughts to her father... thoughts she herself didn't fully understand.

Father smiled a little ruefully as Diana took her felt tam and scarf from the peg beside the stove. "Your secret is safe with me, darling."

"Secret?" Diana thought, half-furious with her father. "There is no secret." But she suspected that there was a secret, buried so deep down in her heart that she hadn't quite found it herself.

Outside, the morning was crisp and bracing. Each tree of the orchard was robed in magnificence: rich scarlets, flaring orange, mellow gold, and dark, royal purple for the plums. Most trees of the countryside hadn't yet given up all of their summery green, but the gnarled old apples and pears loved to display their autumn finery as early as they could manage. It was one of the things Diana loved best about the orchard. But as she hurried down the long, sloping foot-path toward the Cuthberts' farm, she hardly noticed the colorful display.

Anne was waiting for her at the log bridge, as ever. Diana hoped Anne would take the color in her cheeks for the rosy tint of autumn's chill, or the exertion of running. She prayed desperately that Anne would not be as observant as her father was.

"Isn't it a lovely day?" Anne said ecstatically. "Of course, springtime is my favorite, because all the flowers are so sweet and gay, and the whole world seems to be waking up, fresh and new and ready to make the best of itself. But I think fall is second-best. It's as if the whole of creation is having one big, grand party to celebrate how well the year has gone, and all the beauties that have passed through it. Oh, Diana, look at that big plum tree! Its leaves are so glossy and red. It looks like a fine old queen wearing a thousand glittering rubies. And see these maple leaves on the path? If I were an autumn fairy, I would make my dresses out of maple leaves. Their edges are as pretty as the finest lace, but orange and gold veined with green is so much prettier than plain white. Yesterday I went for a walk over the Lake of Shining Waters, and I looked down from the bridge and watched the fallen maple leaves drifting on the water's surface. They were so beautiful against the velvety black of the water that I sort of hurt inside, but in a very pleasant way, and I actually got tears in my eyes, Diana."

Anne went on chattering about her seasonal bliss as the girls walked down to Violet Vale and the Birch Path beyond. The bright, biting feel of the morning air reminded Diana of tart-skinned apples. That made her think of how good the strawberry apples were from the Blythe orchard, and all at once the morning's turmoil rushed back into her mind. She *had* to tell Anne about Gilbert... had to say something, or she feared very much that she would burst open.

"I guess Gilbert Blythe will be in school today," Diana said suddenly, when Anne paused in her litany to draw a deep breath. "He was in New Brunswick all summer long, visiting his cousins, but he came home Saturday night."

Anne looked at Diana... just that, nothing more. But the *way* she looked caused Diana's heart to flutter frantically. Anne's red-gold eyebrows were arced up in an unspoken question. It was plain that Anne could read some difference in Diana... a difference Diana didn't yet fully understand.

"He's *awfully* handsome, Anne," Diana said, trying to explain. "And he teases the girls something terrible. He just torments our lives out!"

Anne sniffed and lifted her chin to a haughty angle. "Gilbert Blythe? Isn't it his name that's written up that's written up on the porch wall with Julia Bell's, and a big 'take notice' over them?"

"Yes," Diana admitted. She had seen the aforesaid "take notice" on Friday afternoon. She'd been sure Julia had written it herself when no one was looking, and how she had longed to scribble it out! She would have done it, too, if so many other children hadn't been around to see. "But I'm sure he doesn't like Julia Bell so very much. I've heard him say he studied the multiplication table by her freckles."

Anne bemoaned her own freckles then, which Diana thought were perfectly adorable in a sunny, innocent sort of way, even if freckles weren't in fashion. They talked of inconsequential things —Anne's speckled nose and boys both liked and despised—until at last they reached the school. There, Diana paused beside the bell and looked around tensely for Gilbert. There was no sign of him. She was glad of that; she wasn't sure how she might react when she first saw him again. It had been so long!

"You'll have Gilbert in your class," Diana said to Anne. "He's used to being head of his class, Anne, I can tell you. He's only in the fourth book although he's almost fourteen. But four years ago his father got dreadfully sick and had to move to Alberta for his health. Gilbert went with him, and for three years he barely had any schooling at all. But he's awfully smart and, as I said, he likes to be first in everything. I'm afraid you won't find it so easy to keep head of the fourth readers after this, Anne."

Anne professed gladness, saying she couldn't feel proud of keeping ahead of little boys and girls. Josie Pye was her biggest competition, and both girls agreed that keeping ahead of a Pye was about as difficult as outsmarting a chicken. They filed into the schoolhouse with the other students, Diana with her eyes on the ground and a burning in her cheeks, Anne with her gray eyes narrowed, looking around boldly for the new challenger.

Gilbert Blythe's seat certainly was not empty now. Diana never looked directly at him, yet she was as much aware of his presence as if he stood directly in front of her. From the corner of her eye, across the aisle that separated them, she could see his new, pale blue shirt and his dark suspenders, and the shine of his new leather shoes. He had grown taller—quite a bit taller. Even sitting at his desk, she could tell how much he had sprouted up. He was about as tall as a man now, a fact which made Diana feel rather dizzy and bewildered. His hair was still the same, though, dark brown and curly, and tousled from his habit of running his hands through it. Gilbert never could keep his hair combed straight.

Mr. Phillips gave his usual morning oration, then wrote assignments on the blackboard. As he drifted back to the rear of the schoolroom (where Prissy Andrews waited, her dainty white hands folded charmingly on her desk) Diana leaned close to Anne and whispered, "That's Gilbert Blythe sitting right across the aisle, Anne. Just look at him and see if you don't think he's handsome." Diana herself could not look directly at him, but then, she had no need to verify her own opinions of Gilbert Blythe.

Anne peered at Gilbert with a scrutinizing air. She wrinkled her pretty, pointed nose in consideration. Gilbert, lounging rather than sitting in his chair, was engaged in mischief. There was a superfluity of girls that year at Avonlea School, so the classroom could not be divided evenly down the middle, and some of the girls—namely, Ruby Gillis and Jane Andrews—were obliged to sit on the boys' side of the room. To maintain propriety, they were kept in the front row, which provided an illusion of separation from the male scholars. Unfortunately for Ruby and Jane, though, this arrangement also kept them in the convenient reach of Avonlea's prank-players. The end of Ruby's long, golden braid had landed, by some great misfortune, atop Gilbert Blythe's desk, and he was engaged in quietly but firmly fixing that braid to his desk-top with a long pin. Anne gave a quiet gasp of horror. She seemed about to warn Ruby, but in that very moment, Mr. Phillips called Ruby over to show her sums. The poor girl popped up at once, then fell back into her seat immediately with a shriek. In the commotion, Gilbert plucked his pin from desk and braid, unnoticed by anyone but Anne and Diana. He casually turned a page of his history book and gazed down at it as if he were studiously reading.

Ruby Gillis, of course, began to cry, and all the harder when Mr. Phillips gave her a stern, vexed stare. Anne gaped at Gilbert Blythe, shocked by his mean teasing, while Diana's stomach turned over with a queer mixture of excitement and dismay. As the class laughed at Ruby's plight, Gilbert looked up from his book, caught Anne's indignant stare, and winked, smiling like he owned the whole place: schoolhouse, yard, and every student in it.

Anne looked frostily away from Gilbert. "I think your Gilbert Blythe *is* handsome," she whispered to Diana, "but I think he's very bold. It isn't good manners to wink at a strange girl."

Diana's mouth felt quite dry. Gilbert had never winked at her. And oh, wouldn't she love it if he would! Well… no, she wouldn't. It really was a terribly bold thing to do. But she would like to see him smile at her the way he'd smiled at Anne.

The morning passed slowly. Diana found it more difficult than ever to concentrate on her lessons, with Gilbert sitting so near. And worst of all was the fact that he hadn't so much as *looked* at Diana the whole day, let alone teased her or winked at her, as he'd done to the other girls. What Diana wouldn't have given to be called 'crow,' like Gilbert used to do, and have her black curls pulled! She would pretend fury and stamp her feet, but wouldn't it be nice to know that he had at least noticed her!

At lunchtime, Diana decided she couldn't bear it any longer and asked Anne to switch places with her when they returned to their desks. "I want to look out at the pond today," Diana said. "It's such a pretty day. The sun is just like diamonds on the water. We might not have more sunny days after this."

Anne cheerfully agreed, and duly took her place on the aisle side of the bench seat when lessons resumed. With Anne as a buffer between herself and Gilbert, Diana found it somewhat easier to tend to her learning. But Diana didn't fail to note the special effort Gilbert went to, trying to attract Anne's attention. He twisted paper into tiny balls and flicked them at Anne's head. He drew pictures on his slate and flashed them in Anne's direction whenever Mr. Phillips wasn't looking. He even made a few snuffling, barnyard-animal noises softly, so quietly only Anne and Diana could hear, in an attempt to make Anne laugh.

Anne steadfastly ignored him. She watched Mr. Phillips with unfailing focus, worked problems steadily on her slate as if she weren't being assailed by a barrage of paper balls, and generally treated Gilbert Blythe as if he didn't exist at all. Diana couldn't understand it. How could Anne remain so perfectly unaffected by such a handsome boy? How could she so thoroughly ignore him? Gilbert's pestering was an irritant, of course. But he was so *charming*. That more than made up for all his annoyances.

Just when Diana was convinced that Anne's composure was entirely unassailable, Gilbert found the chink in her armor. In a final attempt to ruffle her feathers, he reached across the aisle, picked up one of Anne's braids, and whispered, "Carrots!"

Anne's attention fell on Gilbert so hard and fast that the color actually drained from his face. Diana couldn't see Anne's face from where she sat, but she could see Gilbert's, and his expression told her everything she needed to know. Gilbert gaped at Anne in surprise, his hazel eyes wide and startled, so Diana felt sure that Anne's gray eyes must be positively *blazing* with fury. She reached out a trembling hand to try to restrain her friend, but it was too late. Anne sprang to her feet.

"You mean, hateful boy!" Anne shrieked. Everybody in the schoolhouse looked up from their lessons with a thrill of excitement.

Diana alone was not delighted by the scene. She could hear tears in her friend's voice. She reached out again, trying to pull Anne back down to her seat before Mr. Phillips could descend upon her, but Anne darted like lightning, seizing her slate from the desk-top. She raised the slate high above her head and —*crack!*—smashed it down, right on Gilbert Blythe's head.

The girls screamed. The boys released a collective groan of sympathy. A moment later the school erupted into chaos, with boys jumping up from their desks to point and laugh at Gilbert, and girls hugging each other in fits of hysterics. Ruby Gillis started to cry again. Through it all, Anne stood stock-still with her fists balled at her sides, trembling and glaring at her tormentor. Gilbert looked up at her rather blearily, slumping at his desk with pieces of cracked slate scattered about him.

Silence returned to the room when Mr. Phillips laid hold of Anne by one thin shoulder. He scolded Anne roundly, but Gilbert stood up from his desk, swaying slightly.

"It was my fault, Mr. Phillips. I teased her."

Diana goggled at him. Gilbert had never admitted to teasing any girl before. She thought it was extremely gallant. But Mr. Phillips was unimpressed by Gilbert's admission.

"I am sorry to see a pupil of mine displaying such a temper and such a vindictive spirit," he said sternly. Then he directed Anne to stand at the front of the room, right in front of the blackboard, for the remainder of the school day.

Diana writhed with sympathy. It was the worst thing she could imagine, to be stood up on the platform, with every student's eyes upon you. "Oh, Anne," she said under her breath.

Anne went resolutely to her doom. She stood straight and stiff on the platform, her small white face fixed on a point above all the students' heads so she would not have to meet any of their eyes... not Gertie and Josie Pye, not weeping Ruby Gillis, and certainly not Gilbert Blythe, who was by now blushing with remorse. Anne would barely even glance at Diana, who brimmed over with such powerful sympathy for her friend that she thought she might weep.

Mr. Phillips stalked up to Anne and snatched a piece of chalk from the tray. He wrote above her head, "Ann Shirley has a very bad temper. Ann Shirley must learn to control her temper." Then he read the sentences aloud so there could be no mistake about it.

Anne glanced up at the blackboard once, then turned to glare out over the class again, pressing her lips together in a furious white line. Mr. Phillips had spelled her name without an E: an unbearable insult added to injury.

A GRAVE INJUSTICE

THE FOLLOWING DAY FOUND AVONLEA MUTED BENEATH A BLANKET of gray cloud. September was releasing its last hold on the soft greens of summer; trees and hedges blazed with autumnal glories as October prepared to make her grand entrance, and the morning air was sharp with the promise of early frosts to come. Anne was unusually quiet as Diana walked with her to school. A hectic flush darkened her complexion, telling Diana all she needed to know about the thoughts tumbling unchecked through Anne's mind. Anne was so distracted by her anger—and the humiliation she'd been forced to bear the day before, standing up before the entire class—that she never remarked once on the crisp, delicate beauty of the season. Nor did she seem to notice the rabbits that darted across the Birch Path as the girls made their way through the woods.

After a few unsuccessful attempts to engage Anne in light-hearted conversation, Diana clutched her friend's arm in desperation and wailed, "Oh, I wish you wouldn't be so angry! You can't go on hating Gilbert forever."

Anne stiffened, lifting her pointed chin, staring straight ahead with icy resolution. "You know how I feel, Diana. My mind is made up. I cannot ever forgive Gilbert Blythe for the awful thing he said to me. I shall be forever set against him. We are mortal enemies, from this day forward. No... from yesterday forward. It's *history* now, Diana—a grave history between us. One can't ever undo what is in the past."

"But one can forgive." Imploringly, Diana pulled Anne closer. And all the while, as she tried to convince Anne to grant some leniency to Gilbert Blythe, a tiny voice shrieked at her from inside her head. "Don't stop this," the voice cried. "Let Anne be cross with Gilbert forever. That way you will have a chance someday to catch his eye."

Diana ignored the voice—or tried to. She had no desire to set her heart against Anne, the only true and loving friend she'd ever had. The very last thing she wanted was for things to spoil between herself and her bosom friend, for Anne to become as distant and disagreeable to her as was Gertie Pye. "If I let jealousy rule me, I shall hate Anne," Diana thought morosely. "For there's no one more popular in school or in town, no girl as well-liked. She may have started life as an orphan, but she has won every heart in Avonlea. Even Gilbert Blythe's. If I am not to be her friend, then I must be her enemy, like the Pye girls... and I don't want to feel spiteful and bad-tempered like them."

(It must be stated here that Diana Barry was remarkably clear-headed for a girl of only eleven years!)

But Anne would hear no more on the subject of Gilbert, and now refused even to speak his name. Diana was forced to let it drop, for fear that Anne would grow angry with her, too. An uncomfortable, heavy silence accompanied them the rest of the way to the schoolhouse. They reached the yard before Prissy Andrews appeared to ring the bell. Diana embraced Anne impulsively beside the stout little bell-tower. "You are still my friend, Anne Shirley, no matter what. I do hope that someday you'll forgive... *that person*... but even if you never do, I will always treasure you."

Anne stared at Diana, her soulful eyes wide and shining with emotion. "Diana. I treasure thee more than silver and gold and heaps of pearls and rubies and sapphires."

Diana smiled cautiously at this. She always found it secretly amusing when Anne used poetic language, but she never dared to laugh about it. The merest hint of affection could send Anne off in a bout of starry sentimentality.

"We must never be separated," Anne went on passionately, clinging to both of Diana's hands. "Never, never! Now that I've found a true friend, I cannot bear to spend my days apart from thee. It's a good thing we go to school together, or else I am fairly sure my heart would break and I'd waste away from lonesomeness."

"There's Prissy, about to ring the bell. Let's go in to our desk now."

"All right, but you must hold my hand to guide me. I will have to shut my eyes so I won't see *that person.*"

"Really, Anne, I think it's safe to walk with your eyes open. If you see Gil... I mean, *that person*, just look away quickly and it will be the same as if you'd never seen him at all."

Anne drew a very deep breath, as if steadying herself for a charge into battle. Mind made up, she let the breath out again in an explosive rush. "All right. I will keep my eyes open. But you must sit on the aisle side. He mustn't be able to touch my hair again. Just *thinking* about what he said makes me wild with indignation!"

Anne weathered the morning lessons without her indignation boiling over, though Diana, seated between her and Gilbert Blythe, could feel her friend quiver with anger whenever Mr. Phillips called upon her hated enemy to deliver an answer or spell a word. Poor Diana felt torn between her loyalty to Anne and excitement at being a few feet closer to the handsome Gilbert. For his part, Gilbert, who had apologized the previous day after school had let out (even though his head was no doubt still smarting from Anne's slate), kept casting surreptitious glances across the aisle at Anne. His face was full of remorse. He even attempted to whisper more apologies while the teacher was distracted, but they fell on deaf ears. While Mr. Phillips wrote on the blackboard with his back turned to the class, Diana caught Gilbert's eye and offered him a sympathetic smile. He smiled sheepishly back, and the glow it ignited in Diana's chest stayed with her until lunch time.

That day, Mr. Phillips announced to the class that he must return to his home for the dinner hour. He had some business there which needed urgent attention. "But I shall return at the end of the hour," he admonished, "and I expect to find all of you in your seats when I do return. Anyone who comes back late will be punished. Am I understood?"

The class murmured their assent, and Mr. Phillips dismissed the children to their free hour.

Now, without a shepherd to guide them toward more sensible pasture, the children embarked together for Mr. Bell's spruce grove, skipping and singing and tussling as they went. The spruce grove was a favorite gathering place for Avonlea School pupils. Occasionally, in the earliest weeks of the school year and later, when spring began to give way to summer, the teacher would indulge his students' restlessness and arrange for outdoor lessons. Then the children would sit on the springy, loamy ground beneath the trees, on cushions of fallen needles that smelled of green sap amid cool, soothing shadows. Mr. Bell had no objection to the scholars roaming about his spruce grove with proper supervision. However, an entire school of children left to their own devices was another matter altogether. The children knew they risked Mr. Bell's ire if they made too free a use of his grove. Whenever they played in the grove, they always intended merely to pick golden nuts of spruce gum from the branches, chew them to savor the earthy, refreshing taste, and then return to the schoolhouse like good boys and girls. Yet somehow their best intentions never managed to hold. The enchantment of the grove was too strong for them. Before long they were ranging far and wide beneath the blue-green, shadowy boughs, wandering down the hill toward the road, and even climbing up into the spruces.

Diana picked a nut of gum quickly and popped it into her mouth, then joined Anne on the far edge of the grove. Anne had found a patch of rice lilies, tricked into an autumn bloom by the warmth of the preceding weeks, growing down among the dainty feet of the tall ferns. Together she and Diana plucked up the nodding, checkered-brown blossoms and wove them into a crown, along with a few newly opened, pale-purple asters, the heralds of October.

"These brown lilies will look real pretty with your hair," Diana said. "Brown is your color."

"Do you think so?" Anne had left her straw hat back in the schoolhouse; she set the crown of lilies gently atop her ruddy head. "Brown is a good, sensible color, I suppose, and I should be glad it looks good on me, because it can be very elegant. But it's only really elegant on older ladies—the kind who are grand dames with mantles of dignity—isn't it? It's not a very good color for a girl."

"Any color is a good one," said sensible Diana, "as long as it brings out your best."

"Pink would be so delicate and sweet, though," sighed Anne. "Or a soft, pale purple, like these asters here. You're lucky you have such dark hair, Diana. You can wear any color you please. And Ruby... what I wouldn't give for hair like hers! Hair like strands of golden floss, spun on a fairy's spindle. Ruby can wear any color she likes, too. I try not to be ungrateful, because I know I am very fortunate now that I'm here in Avonlea and not in the asylum anymore, or in Mrs. Hammond's care, so I shouldn't complain about anything. But if pink looked becoming on me I do think I could finally manage to be rapturously happy all the time, and never feel dismayed about anything."

"Not about *anything*?" Diana teased.

"Nothing. Because if pink were my color, then I wouldn't have red hair, and then the last of my sorrows in this world would be undone." Anne narrowed her eyes, glaring across the spruce grove at Gilbert Blythe, who was swinging by his hands from a spruce bough. She muttered hoarsely, "*Carrots!*"

Diana sighed. "You must let it drop someday, Anne."

"I must not! And I never will. Just try me, Diana." Anne folded her arms stubbornly across her chest. With her crown of delicate rice lilies and her pale, pointed face, she looked like the most determined fairy-queen the woods had ever seen.

"Some spruce gum will make you feel better. It's impossible to be cross when you've got a chew."

"I've never had spruce gum before."

"It's delicious," Diana promised. "I'll go pick you a nice fat piece. Mine has already lost its flavor anyhow, so I need another. Wait here; I'll be back before you know it."

Diana skipped off into the depths of the grove, among the circles of playing children. She busied herself with inspecting the trunks of the trees, looking for two good pieces of gum, just the right size to soften and chew easily, and of the amber-gold color that meant a pleasant, piney taste. As she broke off a few pieces and picked the bits of bark and needles from their surface, someone sidled up to her with a hesitant, shuffling gait.

"Hello, Diana."

She looked up in surprise, her heart thumping. It was Gilbert Blythe. She didn't know what to say to him, and wasn't sure she could trust her tongue to function properly anyhow, so she only stared at him, wide-eyed.

"You're Anne's closest friend. Is she really that cross with me?"

"She's awful sore, Gilbert," Diana said, finding her voice at last. "You shouldn't have twitted her about her hair."

"I know that now." He grinned ruefully and rubbed his head in exactly the spot where the slate had cracked down. "Don't you think you can talk to her for me? Make her see that I'm sorry?"

"I've already tried. She's dead set in her ways. She's determined not to like you now, and I don't think there's anything in all the world that can make Anne Shirley change her mind once she's set it."

Gilbert's grin slid away. He gazed across the grove at Anne, who drifted among the ferns with a distant, dreamy expression on her face. Now and then she bent to pluck up a flower, and her lips moved rhythmically, as if she were singing to herself, lost in her world of rosy fancy.

Diana bit her lip, glancing at Gilbert from the corner of her eye. "I'll... I'll try to convince her," she said. "Maybe I can—"

At that moment, a panicked shout rang out from high above. "Master's coming!" Jimmy Glover, perched high up in the nearest spruce like a crow on a rooftop, was sounding the alarm.

"Oh, dear!" Diana spun this way and that as the children ran past her, emerging from all directions. Like a herd of frightened deer, they sprang out of the shadows and thicket-veiled dells, running as fast as they could go toward the schoolhouse. In the chaos, Diana ran with the other girls, never thinking to stop and wait for Anne.

It wasn't until she was back on the schoolhouse porch, panting and gasping, that she realized Anne was not among her other friends. Diana clutched her hand tight around the spruce gum and stared back toward the grove. The girls, who hadn't climbed up into the trees, made it back to the school with enough time to spare—but the boys were not so fortunate. They had lost precious time in scrambling down from their perches, and now ran as one frantic mass toward the schoolhouse. And there among them, white and frail-looking in her calico dress, was Anne. She had wandered too far in her private musings; she was stuck with the rowdy, hooting, shoving band of boys.

"Come on, Diana," Ruby squealed. She seized Diana by the arm and dragged her toward the door. "Mr. Phillips will punish you if you're caught out of your seat!"

Diana could see Mr. Phillips now, coming up the lane with a terse, angry stride. No doubt he had noted the stampede of boys as they thundered up from the spruce grove.

With a sob of remorse, Diana followed Ruby into the school-house and dropped numbly into her seat.

Mr. Phillips burst into the room a moment later. The girls rustled in their seats, like hens in a coop when the fox has slipped inside. The schoolmaster stared silently around the room, his mustache quivering with the words he only just managed to hold back. He hung his hat on the peg beside the door and strode grimly to the platform at the front of the room.

Just as he reached it, the door flew open and a fountain of boys poured into the room. And there in their midst, flushed and winded with her tousled hair pulling itself right out of her braids, was Anne.

Anne fought her way up the aisle to her desk. She fell into the seat beside Diana and huddled down, trying to avoid Mr. Phillips's eye. But she was to find no mercy at his hands. He couldn't mete out the promised punishment on every boy in the classroom—half of Avonlea School! Instead he let the full force of his wrath fall upon Anne's narrow shoulders.

"Anne Shirley," he said coldly, "since you seem to be so fond of the boys' company, we shall indulge your taste for it this afternoon. You will sit with Gilbert Blythe. And take those flowers out of your hair."

Diana gasped. To sit with the boys was scandalous enough, but for Anne to be relegated to Gilbert's seat...! She knew how her friend must burn with helpless fury. But there was nothing to be done now, except follow Mr. Phillips's command. Diana gently removed the wreath, which was falling apart by now, from Anne's hair.

Anne did not move. She only stared at the schoolmaster, blank with shock or anger or both.

"Did you hear what I said, Anne?" Mr. Phillips said.

"Yes, sir," she replied in a small, perfectly controlled voice. "But I didn't suppose you really meant it."

"I assure you I did." Mr. Phillips sounded so sarcastic, so puffed up, that Diana fought the urge to poke out her tongue at him. "Obey me at once."

Anne stiffened; Diana was sure she would defy Mr. Phillips, and then... oh, what horrible further punishment might await her! But after another moment, Anne thought better of her rebellion. She rose slowly and gracefully, with a splendidly arrogant poise despite her disheveled appearance. Then she stepped silently across the aisle, and without looking once at Gilbert Blythe, she sat down beside him, on the very edge of the seat.

There her icy control met its limits. Anne's face flushed an alarming shade of pink; Diana, with a lurch of sympathy in her stomach, felt certain Anne would cry. Anne folded her thin arms on the desk, dropped her head down on her arms, and refused to look up for the remainder of the day.

When the afternoon finally came to its merciful end, Anne stood abruptly from Gilbert's desk, turned her back on *that person* with eloquent disdain, and opened the desk she normally shared with Diana. Whereupon she piled up everything she had kept inside—books, pen, ink pot, and even the cracked pieces of her slate—and gathered the bundle in her arms.

"What are you doing, Anne?" Diana asked. "Why are you taking all those things home?"

"I am not coming back to school anymore."

Diana gasped, stung right to her core. "Will Marilla let you stay home?"

"She'll have to," Anne said as they marched out the door and found their way down toward the Birch Path. "I'll *never* go to school to that man again. He is *insufferable*."

"But what about those things you said this morning, Anne? About how we must never be parted?" Diana felt tears welling up in her eyes; she blinked them away, determined not to cry, but she was quickly losing that battle. It had been such an emotional day! "I do think you're mean. What shall I do? I'll be made to sit with Gertie Pye!"

Anne's sensitive little face turned down toward her boots. She watched over the heap of supplies in her arms as her own feet marched along resolutely. "I'd do almost anything in the world for you, Diana. I'd let myself be torn limb from limb if it would do you any good. But I can't do this, so please don't ask it. You harrow up my very soul."

Diana tried in vain to convince Anne of her folly. She brought up every delight the school year promised: building a new playhouse down by the brook with the other girls—a private spot where they could all share their lunches in peace, without any interference from the boys. Also the ball games they were to learn the following week, and the songs Jane Andrews promised to teach the girls, and the story book they had planned to read together. But nothing could divert Anne from her path.

They parted ways sadly at the foot bridge. Diana was sniffling, miserable with the effort of holding back her sorrow. "I suppose this is good-bye," Diana said softly. "Not forever, I hope."

"Of course not, dear Diana," Anne promised. But she didn't sound reassured by her own words. After all, now that school was in for the year and the days were growing shorter, they would find little time to play and to share their idles. The long, sweet days of summer were behind them.

Diana trudged up the hill of Orchard Slope, and the weight of all her woes seemed to drag behind her like an anchor chain. That weight only grew heavier when Diana entered by the kitchen door.

Mrs. Barry there in her green-striped apron, stirring a pot on the wood stove with a tense air of triumph. Her expression when she looked up at Diana was somewhere between a scowl and a grim smile.

"I saw the Pye girls not five minutes ago," she said. "Their father picked them up from school in his buggy, since they must all go down to Carmody. And do you know what Gertie Pye told me?"

Diana said nothing. She felt her face drain of all color.

"She told me that Anne Shirley was punished today for consorting with boys!"

"That's not so," Diana wailed. "Mr. Phillips was cross and was looking for someone to take it out on. You can't believe anything a Pye says!"

"Diana Barry, your tone is too pert by half."

Diana didn't care if she was being pert. The many injustices of the day seemed to fall upon her like an avalanche. "It *wasn't* like Gertie says. I was there, Mother; I know!"

"Any girl who runs about with boys like some wild thing is not fit company for you. I suppose I must speak to the schoolmaster and see to it that you're kept apart from Anne Shirley from now on."

"No, you can't!" Diana still didn't quite believe that Anne would really remove herself from the school; the very thought of being in the same room with Anne, but forever separated by the unseen but still impenetrable barriers of grown-up authority, cut Diana right to the very center of her tender little heart. "You can't, Mother, I won't let you!"

"That is enough of your backtalk," Mrs. Barry said in a dangerous tone.

Diana knew she should heed that warning, but her grief, and her sense of injustice, carried her on. "You *can't* keep me from Anne. You can't, you can't! She's the only one in all the world who understands me. If you try, I'll... I'll simply disobey you! I'm big enough now that you can't stop me from doing anything I please!"

Mrs. Barry set her spoon aside on a trivet, crossed the room in three quick, measured strides, and then struck a stinging blow right across Diana's cheek.

Diana gasped, wordless with shock, fear, and pain. She stared at her mother for a long moment. Through the tears in her eyes, Diana could see a flash of remorse and grief cross her mother's features. But then Mrs. Barry's mask of stern poise and perfect control returned.

With a great cry of sorrow, Diana turned and ran from the kitchen, out into her garden. She crumpled down among the dead stalks of her tiger lilies, wiping tears from her cheeks. But more tears fell, faster than she could brush them away. Never in her life had she felt so lonesome, so "harrowed up," as Anne would say.

"Oh, it's terrible growing up," Diana sobbed to the empty, autumn-brown garden. "It's more terrible and lonely than anyone can understand!"

AN UNEXPECTEDLY POTENT CORDIAL

OCTOBER ARRIVED TO BLESS AVONLEA WITH COLOR AND SALT-laden winds, and with the cozy, heart-warming smell of wood smoke. The last fruits of the harvest hung heavy on orchard boughs, and the final cutting of hay was gathered up in Mr. Andrews's field, leaving only dry, pale stubble behind.

Ordinarily Diana loved this time of year, for the early sunsets and the snuggling down into thick woolen sweaters appealed to her quiet, thoughtful nature. Now, however, the grayness and dullness of the world seemed to emphasize how very alone she felt. True to her prediction, Mr. Phillips made her sit with Gertie Pye in school, and Gertie was a terrible sneak who was forever peeking at Diana's work and copying it on her own tablet. The girls of Avonlea school soldiered ahead with their songs and stories and play-houses, just as they had planned, but without Anne by her side, Diana felt as if she existed only on the fringes of their frolics, never quite welcomed into the heart of the group. And her walks to and from the schoolhouse, which had previously been full of fun and the sparkling of crystalline imaginations, were now nothing more than rote, joyless trudges through a landscape that was cold, colorless, and muddy.

Diana still had Saturdays with Anne, for which she was grateful. Together they rambled along hedges and lanes, tucking sprigs of bright berries into their hair and reading to one another from the story books Diana borrowed from school.

She longed for those Saturdays with the all-encompassing hunger of a starving person. Being deprived of Anne's company had only made the red-haired girl all the more fascinating and wonderful in Diana's estimation. Now Anne's life seemed positively glamorous, for she existed outside of the common sphere of everyday little girls. *She* no longer went to school, and so her daily routine sparkled in Diana's imagination with the splendor of a faceted gem.

It was true that Anne's day-to-day existence was now given over almost entirely to chores. Plain, ordinary, workaday chores; female creatures up and down the length of Prince Edward Island devoted themselves to those same tasks from sunrise to sunset. Even so, for Anne to perform them as if she were the mistress of a household filled Diana with awe.

"I wash all the dishes in the house, after every meal," Anne confided, showing Diana how pink and chapped her hands had become. "I think Marilla secretly hates dish-washing and is glad to have someone else to do it. I don't like it, either, but seeing as how she dislikes it so, I am glad to relieve her of the burden, since she has been so kind in taking me in. I think I would find the washing-up very tedious, Diana, except that I can stand beside the window while I do it, and oh, it is so nice to look out at the world and imagine romantic things about it. Just this morning, while I was washing up after porridge and bacon, I was thinking how nice it would be if I were the daughter of an exiled baron, and I had to be hidden away in a quaint countryside farm where no one would suspect my true identity while the war raged on in my homeland. And just as I was about to be discovered by villains, word would arrive that we had won after all, and my father would come sweeping over the hills in a grand sleigh—for you know, such a story would have to take place while it's snowing; snow is so much more dramatic than autumn fields—and he would be dressed in all his finery, and would reveal me as a noble lady before the whole village, and then the Pyes would repent of ever having used me ill.

"That's the sort of daydream you can have while you're washing dishes. It's easy to let your thoughts wander, since you don't have to pay attention to much, other than being sure you don't drop a dish and break it. I've gotten pretty good at getting all the dishes cleaned by feel alone, so I hardly ever have to look away from the window. At least, Marilla doesn't complain that I've left spots on them."

"What else do you do?" Diana asked. "Dishes can't take up the whole day."

"No... I collect the eggs for Marilla and rake the hen yard and sweep the floors—and wash them, too, for you know she likes the floors washed every third day. She is terribly neat, though I suspect some ladies in Avonlea feel she isn't neat enough, and believe floors ought to be washed every second day if a home is to be properly kept. And I help with the washing, though she doesn't trust me to do it all by myself yet, so I mostly hang things up to dry. That, at least, I can manage on my own. It does make my arms sore and tired, though. Wet laundry is heavier than you might think."

"And what do you imagine while you're hanging laundry?"

Anne wove fanciful tales of her dream-wanderings—stories about lost princesses and spurned lovers—about benevolent house-sprites helping the unsuspecting old dears, Matthew and Marilla Cuthbert, and about tragic step-daughters ruthlessly enslaved to cold-hearted, villainous women. The stories thrilled Diana's heart and set her to sighing. Anne's imaginings always made things seem so much grander than they really were. Avonlea would surely never be the prosy old village it once had been, not ever again... not now that Anne was here. Now it was a world wreathed in gossamers of fancy.

On one Saturday in particular, when a welcome clear sky reigned over the valley with a deep wash of regal, sapphire blue, Diana was engaged in her own bout of dish-washing. She was trying in vain to summon up Anne's dancing, delightful imaginings, with the hope that she might apply a veneer of romance and adventure to her very dull and uninspiring chores. She sighed as she gazed out the kitchen window, down the slope toward Green Gables. She could see the deep, hunter-green peak of the roofline clearly through the trees, and the white sides of the old farmhouse, too, for the orchard and the birches that grew along the book had lost most of their leaves to a fierce wind the night before. No fancies would come to her as she splashed and slopped in the wash bucket, but she did catch sight of something not a fancy at all... something altogether real, and entirely welcome. It was a small figure dashing excitedly over the field toward the foot bridge, with red braids flying out behind.

Diana stacked the last dish in the drying rack and patted her hands quickly on a towel. "Mother," she called into the parlor, "Anne is running over from Green Gables."

There was a faint rattling of wooden rings in the parlor, as Mrs. Barry drew back the curtain to have a look. "Land sakes. Do you think there's trouble at the Cuthberts' place?"

Diana didn't think so. Even parted by cruel fate (except for on Saturdays), she and Anne shared such a perfect bond that she felt certain she would know if anything was amiss. She would be able to *sense* the danger. There was no aura of worry hanging over Anne... only excitement. Diana hung up her apron and did her best to smooth the wrinkles from her skirt, and presently a rapid tap sounded at the kitchen door. She hurried to open it.

Anne's cheeks were flushed from the October cold, and from her barely suppressed joy. A light of pure delight sparkled and glinted in her eyes, but she didn't burst out with her news. She drew herself up to her fullest height, lifted her chin proudly, and pronounced with exaggerated dignity, "Diana, Marilla is going away to Carmody and won't be back until after dark. She said I may invite you to afternoon tea. Won't you please join me?"

Diana's mouth fell open. She heard her mother's footsteps behind her, and prickled with worry. Mrs. Barry was not likely to permit it, Diana knew. She was convinced that Anne was an influence for mischief, and only grudgingly allowed their Saturday rambles only because she felt that walking with an urchin of questionable morals was, when weighed in the balance, only slightly better than mooning around the parlor with one's nose pressed in a yellow novel.

But what trouble could two girls get up to in an old country farmhouse, quietly conversing over tea? Why, Green Gables was even quainter than Orchard Slope, if such a thing were really possible. Clinging to that slim hope, Diana turned slowly and gazed at her mother with questioning—pleading—eyes.

Mrs. Barry's mouth thinned. She looked long and thoughtfully at Diana, though she spared only the most fleeting and dismissive of glances for Anne. Her eyes seemed to linger on the cheek where, a few weeks before, she had struck Diana in anger. Again Diana saw the faint trace of regret cross her mother's features.

"Very well," Mrs. Barry finally said. "Since Anne was kind enough to invite you…" *in such an unexpectedly civilized way,* her expression seemed to say, "then I see no harm in it, as long as you are home before sunset."

Anne and Diana stared at one another, struck silent with disbelieving wonder. Then they threw themselves into each other's arms. Neither could restrain herself from hopping excitedly from foot to foot.

"Now, now," Mrs. Barry scolded—but it was a very mild scolding.

Anne broke from the embrace first. "I must go back home and get dressed. It's such a *special* occasion. I want to look my best, though of course my best isn't especially fine."

"I'll get dressed up, too," Diana said.

"You certainly will not," Mrs. Barry interjected. "Nothing nicer than your Sunday dress. It's only tea with a neighbor, after all. It's not as if you were off to Ottawa to dine with the Premier."

Anne departed with grave solemnity, and Diana hurried up to her bedroom. She sorted through her closet until she found just the right dress for the occasion: a deep blue velveteen with dear little ruffles at the shoulders. When she had dressed, Diana stood before her tiny mirror for some time, fussing with her hair. Should she wear it in braids? She had some blue ribbons to match her dress... but no. Braids were a very girlish style, and not nearly fancy enough for an occasion as fine as a private tea between two bosom friends. She peeked surreptitiously out her door and, finding the upstairs hall empty, quickly twisted her hair up into a bun on the back of her head. She secured it with a few pins and then studied herself for a long while. It was a hairstyle only grown-up ladies were supposed to wear, and Diana had never tried it before. At first she thought she looked entirely too awkward with her hair up, for her neck was so obvious and pale. She despaired of ever being pretty. But the longer she watched herself, the more the style became her. She tilted her head this way and that, delightfully shocked by the exposure of her ears and the corners of her jawline.

"Why, Diana Barry," she told herself happily, "there might be hope for you after all."

Then she thought of Gilbert, the smile sliding off his face as he gazed desperately across the spruce grove toward Anne, and with an angry shake of her head she pulled the pins from her hair. Her black curls tumbled down to cover her soft, white skin.

"You are a very silly girl sometimes," she scolded her reflection. Then she pulled back a few locks at her temples, as she always did, and tied them behind with a simple bow.

～

DIANA KNOCKED on the green-painted front door, sheltered from the October sun by the slant of the Green Gables porch roof. She had never used the front door when visiting the Cuthberts, as they never used the front door at Orchard Slope. Front doors were so formal, and such close neighbors had no need for stiff formalities. This tea, however, was special.

Anne must have been waiting beside the door, for she swung it open almost immediately. She had on her pearl-gray dress, one she often wore to church, and Diana was glad to see that she had fixed her hair in the same style, pulled back at the sides and tied with a ribbon behind. It was the most grown-up hairstyle two girls of eleven might reasonably aspire to. Diana thought it gave them both a regal, refined appearance.

A thin, pale hand reached out to Diana. Diana took it, shaking graciously, just as if it were the first time she'd met Anne Shirley.

"Won't you please come in?" Anne asked, and stepped aside with a grand, welcoming gesture. Diana was escorted upstairs to the east gable room, which was Anne's very own.

"Marilla told me I ought to let you lay off your hat in the sitting room, but I didn't feel that was quite special enough. We couldn't enjoy a real tea with your hat sitting right there on the sofa as if this were any ordinary day, could we?"

"Certainly not," Diana said. She looked out Anne's window, and there was Orchard Slope, grandly white and brilliant against the majestic, spotless sky. She could see her bedroom window clearly, a square of reflected blue glinting above the tallest treetops. And there on the table before Anne's window, held in an old brass candlestick, was the candle stump which Anne used for signaling. The girls had worked out an ingenious code of candlelight flashes, which could be read clearly between their two widely separated bedrooms.

With formalities observed, the girls returned to the sitting room, where they engaged in sedate, ladylike discussion of their families' farms and crops, until Diana raised the subject of apples. That made Anne start up in her chair with a jolt of delight. "Let's go out to the orchard and get some of the Red Sweetings."

The Red Sweeting apples, and the orchard itself, proved an irresistible distraction. Anne and Diana quite forgot their dignity and played for hours in the Green Gables orchard, picking the last delicious apples straight off the leaf-bare boughs and lounging in the last lingering patch of green grass behind the shed. The sun was warm and glorious, caressing their rosy cheeks with a benevolent touch, and shining brightly on the apples they had gathered in their skirts.

"Tell me everything about school," Anne implored. "I do miss it, you know, though I'd never admit it to Marilla, because then she'd make me go back, and this has become a matter of honor for me."

Diana spun out every tale she could recall of school goings-on: Whose name was written up with whose on the porch wall, and which girls had been unkind to the others. She told all about Gertie Pye—what a torment it was to sit with her day after day!—and the airs that were put on during lunch hours, the games and jokes that were played. Both girls doubled over with laughter when Diana told how Mr. Phillips had whipped Sam Boulter for backtalk, only to be confronted the next day by Sam's father, who barged into the schoolroom and shouted at Mr. Phillips, and *dared* him to so much as *touch* one of the Boulter children ever again. Diana's impression of the look that had fallen over Mr.

Phillips's face had Anne so helpless with laughter that she could scarcely breathe.

But when Diana tried to bring up Gilbert Blythe—and oh, didn't she just want to talk about Gilbert with her dearest friend! —Anne sprang up, letting the last of her apples roll off her lap and tumble across the grass.

"What if we go in now and have some raspberry cordial?"

"I'm awful fond of raspberry cordial," Diana said, climbing to her feet more slowly than Anne had done. She was reluctant to halt their chatter, for it felt so nice to be chummy with Anne again, to laugh and share their secrets, to be carefree. Best of all was that it was just the two of them... Diana and Anne alone together, without Mrs. Barry or Marilla looming over them, without the school-master glaring at them or even the well-meaning but still judg-mental gazes of their peers. In one another's company, as nowhere else in the world, Anne and Diana could truly be Anne and Diana.

But on the other hand, this was supposed to be a real, grown-up tea. Diana supposed it was only fitting that they go about it the right way.

Back in the sitting room, Diana settled on the sofa, sitting primly upright with her very best posture, while Anne vanished into the pantry. Diana could hear a rustling and bumping as her friend searched for the bottle of cordial. Diana's mouth watered with anticipation; Marilla Cuthbert was famed for every kind of preserve, including the refreshing drinks she made each summer when the berry canes back behind Green Gables were heavy and ripe. A taste of real summer raspberries would be welcome now, with autumn so persistent in the air.

Anne reappeared, triumphant, with an uncorked bottle of red liquid in one hand and a tumbler in the other. She set them before Diana on the little tea table. "Please help yourself," she said. "I fear I ate so many apples that I can't have any, myself, not just now."

Diana poured and tasted. She leaned back in surprise, gazing down at the drink in her tumbler. The taste was far more complex than any cordial she'd ever had before, with a strange, almost vinegarish bite. Even after she swallowed, the feel of it seemed to linger in her nose as she exhaled, rather like a strong perfume.

"That's awfully nice raspberry cordial, Anne. I didn't know raspberry cordial could be so nice."

Anne encouraged Diana to have all the cordial she pleased while she, Anne, tended to the kitchen stove. She was tasked with having supper ready for Matthew and his hired boy when they returned from town, where they had gone to sell the potato harvest. Anne wandered into the kitchen to see to her work, but she talked as she went, as was Anne's habit, of course. Diana listened with half an ear while she drank down more of the cordial, wondering at its earthy, luscious flavor.

She finished the glass more quickly than she'd intended, then sit it aside on the table and stared at it rather blearily while Anne went on talking.

"It's strange," Diana thought. "I've never tasted anything quite like that before." A queer little twist of fear in her stomach told her perhaps she ought not to have any more of the cordial. But the cordial itself was also very compelling. It sat there in its tall, slender jar, sparkling in a most inviting way when a shaft of sunlight fell through the window and lit up its ruby insides. Finally, Diana decided, "One more cup can't hurt me. It's only cordial, after all." She poured another.

Anne returned from the kitchen, talking rapturously about a most pathetic and affecting tale she had imagined while her chores. It had something to do with smallpox, and Anne nursing Diana when no one else would go near her, which didn't sound very grand to Diana at all, but she was so enraptured by her second tumbler of cordial that she raised no objection to Anne's story.

Before Diana knew it, she had drained her second cup. A hiccup seized her chest and came out of her mouth in a terribly undignified, backwards squeak.

"'Scuse me," Diana said. Her tongue was thick and tingling. It moved more slowly than she liked.

"Here, now, have another glassful if you'd like," Anne said, tilting the cordial bottle eagerly toward Diana. "Marilla said we may finish it off."

By now, Diana could think of no reason to object to the cordial. Her head felt pleasantly light; her arms insisted that they were floating, although she knew they were not because she could see them behaving just as arms ought to behave. The outlines of whatever she looked at did seem a bit fuzzy, though. She lifted her cordial cup so energetically that she nearly spilled it on her velveteen dress. Then she drank it... and drank... and drank, unable to stop herself from gulping down the whole tumbler in one long draught, though she knew it was a very unladylike thing to do. The cordial was just so *good*. It refused to be ignored!

"I meant to cover it just as much as could be," Anne was saying. Her voice sounded strangely bubbly and slow, as if Diana were listening to her from the bottom of Barry's Pond. "But when I carried it in, I was imagining I was a nun..."

"Cover what?" Diana said. Her tongue stumbled worse than before.

"The pudding sauce, of course."

Diana thought dizzily, "Oh... the pudding sauce. Of course." Anne had been recounting some funny tale about a plum pudding gone wrong. Diana blinked heavily, trying to sort out the details of the story.

"I thought to cover it the next morning," Anne said, "and ran to the pantry. Diana, fancy if you can my extreme horror at finding a mouse drowned in the pudding sauce!"

Diana stared at Anne in sluggish disgust. She couldn't think of anything worse than scampering mice, unless it was a dead mouse floating in a perfectly good pitcher of pudding sauce. Her stomach lurched at the thought. Anne continued with her story, telling of how her distractibility led her to neglect the tainted sauce until Marilla's guests from Spencervale very nearly ate it.

The thought was too much for Diana. She clutched at her stomach, and as she did so the room lurched and whirled around her. Groaning, she shut her eyes tightly, but the dizzy, disorienting sensation did not abate.

"Why, Diana, what is the matter?"

Diana was sure she couldn't speak. If she opened her mouth at all, she feared nothing would come out of it but sick. She tried to stand, but her legs were as wobbly as aspic. She sank back onto the sofa again and clutched her head with both hands. "I'm... I'm awful sick. I... I must go right home."

"Oh, no, no!" Anne cried in distress. "You must have your tea, Diana... think of our tea! Wait here. I'll go and start it off this very minute."

Diana tried unsuccessfully to rise again. "I must go home," she insisted thickly.

Anne tried to press food on Diana, which only turned her stomach all the more. Diana shook her head weakly and squeezed her eyes shut, refusing to look at the fruit cake and cherry preserves that Anne offered up with trembling hands.

"Oh, Diana," Anne wailed, "do you suppose it's possible that you're really taking the smallpox? If you are, I'll nurse you. You can depend on that. Even if I die from it... I'll never forsake you. Where do you feel bad?"

"I'm d..." Diana gave another tremendous hiccup. "I'm dizzy, Anne. Awful dizzy."

Pale with worry, Anne pulled Diana to her feet. Diana tottered and swayed in a most alarming way. The sitting room spun around her, a whirl of the dark, sober colors, serviceable furnishings, and meager doilies favored by the staid Marilla Cuthbert. The room seemed to press in upon Diana; she felt quite confined, on the verge of suffocating. She would have run from the room, but her feet would not move with any reliable speed. She clung to Anne's arm, gazing about her in thick confusion.

"Outside," Diana muttered. "I must go... outside."

"But what if you catch your death?" Anne shrieked, though there was no real danger of Diana catching her death, for the October afternoon was still quite mild and sunny.

Diana's stomach lurched. She choked back a most unladylike heave. That inspired Anne to propel her outside with all haste; Diana staggered along until she found herself on the Green Gables porch, where Anne eased her down on a wicker seat to wait while she fetched Diana's hat from the east gable room. Anne returned and set the hat on Diana's head, but it kept sliding down over one ear as Diana's head wobbled weakly on her neck. It seemed she couldn't keep herself straight—couldn't even look straight at the tilting, shifting world.

"Home," she pleaded with her friend.

"Oh, all right," Anne gave in at last. "But if you are truly sick I shall never forgive myself for abandoning you."

It took some doing for Diana to descend the unexpectedly treacherous steps of the front porch. The walk across the field to the brook was longer and more laborious than it ever had been before. With ever step, Diana's stomach churned. She felt decidedly precarious, even with Anne supporting her.

When they arrived at the foot bridge, both girls paused and gazed up the hill to Orchard Slope—Anne desperately, Diana blearily. Diana could see the dark shape of her mother standing at the kitchen door. Even through her curious fog, she could read the tension in Mrs. Barry's stance.

"I'd better go on alone," she managed to say. "Mother looks awful cross."

"No, Diana, you mustn't! Let me help you. What if you were to fall?"

"Let me go, Anne... let me go!"

Diana hadn't meant to speak so sharply to her friend, and the pained look that crossed Anne's features wasn't lost on Diana, even in her present state. She wanted to apologize, but she now feared that if she said anything at all, she would be sick all down the front of her dress. She turned as quickly as she dared and staggered away from Anne, over the bridge and up the sunlit hill to where her mother was waiting. Anne's cries of, "I won't abandon you, Diana!" followed her up the path below the orchard boughs.

MRS. BARRY TELLS A FALSEHOOD

"For the land's sake," Mrs. Barry exclaimed when Diana came woozily through the garden gate. "Diana Barry, what is the matter with you?"

Diana tried to reply, but there were suddenly two images of her mother standing before her, both furry and indistinct around the edges. The dual Mrs. Barrys were more than she could bear. She groaned and clutched at her stomach, struggling valiantly to keep herself from vomiting.

Mrs. Barry rushed forward to catch her daughter, frightened that she was about to fall. When she drew close, though, she stiffened with sudden affront. Then she sniffed the air around Diana, wary as an old hound, not quite believing what her nose was telling her.

"You're... you're *drunk*," Mrs. Barry said, caught somewhere between fury and wonder.

Despite her sick stomach, Diana laughed at that. It was such a silly proposition. "No, Mother, I... I can't... be." She punctuated her statement with an enormous hiccup.

"By every angel in the heavens," Mrs. Barry said darkly. It was as close as she ever came to swearing. Then she dragged Diana roughly into the house. Diana, hauled along like a kitten in a sack, could only mewl weakly in protest.

Mr. Barry was seated at the kitchen table, having his afternoon tea. He stood at once, for it was clear from his wife's indignant quiver that something was terribly wrong.

"Your daughter," Mrs. Barry said in cruel triumph, "has been set drunk by that orphan girl... that *child* the Cuthberts have taken in. Drunk, George! Of all things!"

"Diana!" Father rushed to her side, lifting her face gently to peer down at her in concern. He looked carefully at her eyes (which were, it must be said, quite red-rimmed), and turned her this way and that to examine the flush on her cheeks. He, too, caught the unmistakable scent and turned a frown of reluctant agreement on his wife.

"This is the end, George, the very end! Even you can't deny it now: That Anne girl is a bad influence on our Diana. I won't have her around any longer, nor let Diana or Minnie May associate with her. I *will not* permit it!"

"No," Diana protested. "Anne never... I didn't...!" But she couldn't form a clear thought, couldn't find the words to express her innocence or her parents' injustice.

"I suppose you are right after all, Rebecca," Father said quietly. "I had hoped the girl would be a good play-mate for Diana, but I suppose it's true, what Mrs. Lynde said. Perhaps orphans really can't be trusted." He didn't sound as if he *actually* agreed with Mrs. Lynde's low opinion of orphans, but before Mrs. Barry's towering fury, there was little he could do. "If you think it's best to keep the girls separated, I won't interfere."

Mrs. Barry gave a sharp sniff, one that said, "Perhaps next time you'll listen to me *before* your daughter turns up intoxicated" with an economy of sound. Then she seized Diana by the arm again and marched her upstairs to her bedroom.

"Really, Diana," Mrs. Barry said as she undressed her tottering, swaying daughter. "Of all the unladylike things. Of all the foolhardy, wild, reputation-destroying things you could have done... *this* truly takes the cake!" She found a night dress and pulled it roughly over Diana's head, then led her to the iron-framed bed and stuffed her under the covers. "I'm only grateful that no one saw you but that Anne girl. No one else saw you, I trust? Good. That is one indescribably small mercy in this whole mess. If word got around town that you were as drunk as a tramp, why, there would be no hope for you, not in a hundred years! Don't you understand, girl? I do all this for you. I guard you and protect you because it's a mother's duty... because I want for you what I—" She cut herself off abruptly, shaking her head and turning away, unwilling to say those words. After a moment, when her anger was better controlled, she resumed her lecture with ice-cool calm. "Diana, I know you are very young, but still you have a future to think of. We all must think of your future. You're only a girl now, but you will be a woman sooner than you think. The best life for a woman is one of quiet dignity... married well to a man of standing, keeping a home in fine order, and raising well-behaved children who do their mother credit. Any other life, any other path, would be below you. Less than you deserve. Do you understand?"

Diana blinked back tears. She understood all too well... and she wanted nothing of the life her mother described. Oh, it would be fine to be a wife and a mother someday. She hoped she would. But a man of standing? Her mother meant a plain, dull, uninteresting man. Not a handsome one. Not one whose eyes sparkled with mischief and adventure. She turned her face away and tried not to think about Gilbert Blythe. She wouldn't think of him now... not now, when her head was already so mixed up that she couldn't even see straight.

There was a gentle tap at her door. A moment later Diana's father entered, carrying a wide porcelain basin. He set it on the floor beside her bed.

Diana wanted to ask what the bowl was for, but all at once her stomach heaved, and she leaned instinctively over the bowl. As she retched up her lunch—and the raspberry cordial with it—her mother sighed deeply and pulled Diana's black curls back so they wouldn't be fouled. Mrs. Barry rubbed Diana's back with a surprisingly gentle hand.

"We have your future to think about," she murmured, again and again, until Diana's stomach was as empty as it could be.

When Diana sank back on her pillows with a shuddering sob, Mrs. Barry covered the basin with a towel and stood, stiff and resolute once again. "Make no mistake. You will never see Anne Shirley again." Then she swept out of the room like a cold winter wind.

Diana felt too sick and wrung-out to argue.

SHE WAS PERMITTED to stay home from church the next morning, though Diana couldn't be sure the previous day's sickness had anything to do with her vacation. She suspected her mother was afraid to risk her safety too soon: The Cuthberts would certainly be there for the morning's sermon, sitting in their usual pew with Anne beside them. Mrs. Barry wouldn't allow Diana and Anne to come under the same roof until she could be entirely assured of keeping the two girls separate. It was all one to Diana. She hadn't the heart to tell Anne that she had been entirely forbidden to see her again... not yet.

"I suppose I'll have to tell her sooner or later," Diana mused darkly, staring out her bedroom window from the quiet shelter of her bed. "But I can't face her now. It's all so unfair, and Mother is so mean! She doesn't understand at all. Anne never harmed me. And I wasn't drunk. How could I be? Raspberry cordial never set anybody drunk."

She no longer felt ill, though her head did ache a little, and she was so thirsty that she drank in one draft the tall glass of water her father had brought her before he and Mrs. Barry and little Minnie May had departed for church. Orchard Slope was enshrouded in silence. Even outside her window no birds sang, for autumn had driven them all away with its cold, hard stare. The world seemed very bleak to Diana now. She slept through the hours of the church service, grateful that she could sleep, that she could retreat from her troubling, heartbroken thoughts.

She woke shortly before the family was due to come home. Resigned to her fate, Diana climbed out of bed. She was groggy from too much sleep, and her eyes stung as if she'd been weeping in her dreams. But she dressed in her Sunday best and did what she could to put herself in order. Mrs. Barry would expect help with dinner. Diana supposed there was nothing to be done but pitch in and act the part of the complacent, perfect little girl.

A familiar clop of hooves sounded in the yard below. Diana looked down from her bedroom window to see the buggy swinging into the yard—Father driving, Mother sitting straight and motionless beside him, and Minnie May kicking her feet on the bench seat in the back. The buggy paused in front of the porch. Mrs. Barry stepped delicately down, then lifted Minnie May out of the buggy and turned her loose to run up into the house on her own. Father drove on toward the barn.

Mrs. Barry should have gone straight into the house, but she paused, looking back down the lane that led to the road. At first Diana couldn't see what she was looking at, but just as she was about to leave the window and go downstairs to greet Minnie May, a familiar tall, gray figure appeared from the russet curve of the lane. It was Marilla Cuthbert.

Diana gasped. Suddenly her whole body was tingling with a tense, nervous energy. She pulled her curtains down from their iron tie-backs to hide her face, then wedged her fingers beneath her window and cautiously pried up the sash, just far enough that she could hear the goings-on in the yard below.

"Good afternoon, Miss Cuthbert," Mrs. Barry said stiffly. "Though I must say, I am surprised to see you here."

Marilla hesitated a moment before answering. "Good afternoon. I thought it only right to pay you a call, seeing as how—" here an unaccustomed edge of hardness suddenly formed in Marilla's voice— "I've just been speaking with Rachel Lynde."

"Oh?" Mrs. Barry seemed unconcerned, even airy. It made Diana grit her teeth.

"Mrs. Barry, Rachel Lynde tells me you paid her a visit yesterday evening and you told her that my Anne *intoxicated* your Diana."

Mrs. Barry drew herself up to her full height, which wasn't a patch on Marilla's tall, imposing stature. "That girl of yours *did* intoxicate Diana. The poor child was sick, and has been sleeping it off all day, as if she were some kind of hardened degenerate! I don't know what you're thinking, keeping a wild thing like that under your roof. No good can come of it, Marilla, and you'd be wise to listen when your neighbors tell you so."

Marilla clenched her fists and trembled slightly. She seemed to be wrestling inside herself, struggling valiantly to control her temper. Finally she said, slowly and evenly, "It was nothing more than a mistake, Mrs. Barry. I told Anne she could serve raspberry cordial for tea, and the poor girl didn't know which bottle was which."

"What do you mean, which bottle was which?"

"She got out my currant wine by mistake. Having no experience with such things, Anne can hardly be blamed. It's not as if she made Diana drunk intentionally."

Mrs. Barry wagged her finger right at Marilla; Diana was so mortified to see it that she wanted to sink down into the floorboards. "That currant wine of yours! You know I've long objected to your making it. As have many others in Avonlea—oh, yes! None of us approve, yet you go on making it year after year. It isn't

Christianly, Miss Cuthbert. Ladies have no place *drinking* spirits, let alone brewing them up in their kitchens!"

"Currant wine can hardly be called 'spirits,'" Marilla objected smoothly. "And in any case, I haven't made a drop of currant wine in three years, not since I found out the minister didn't look kindly on it. Though *he* has enough manners to be *polite* about his disapproval."

Diana couldn't help but smile at that. If anyone was more than equal to Mrs. Barry in the fullest of her wraths, it was good old Marilla.

"I kept that bottle of wine for treating sickness," Marilla went on.

"Well, now it has *caused* sickness. That goes to show you!"

"My wine didn't cause your child's illness," Marilla returned, with more than a hint of sauce. "I dare say it was common greed. Even if that bottle had contained innocent raspberry cordial, three glasses of it would have sickened any child, purely from too much sweetness."

"A sick stomach from too much sweet is an entirely different matter from sickness due to *wine*, Marilla. Wine! Of all things! I'm not the kind to speak my mind so frankly, but I feel I must now. You've never been one to follow the order of things, to do what ought to be done. And I have always known that your ways would sting you in the end. But now they have stung us, too, Miss Cuthbert. I hope you will reconsider your choices. It's too late now for you to marry and settle down, as is proper—" at this, Marilla gave one loud, sharp laugh— "but at least you can be more sensible when it comes to that girl you've taken into your home. For my part, I must draw the line. Diana will never see Anne again. It's clear that the child is dangerous, and you should heed the warning while you still can."

"Perhaps *you* should heed the warning," Marilla said, coldly dignified. "Currant wine wasn't meant to be drunk three tumblerfuls at a time, and if any child I had to do with was so greedy, I'd sober her up with a right good spanking."

Diana's face burned, but even in the midst of that humiliation she gaped in delighted awe at Marilla as the woman turned on her heel and walked away. Mrs. Barry quivered helplessly, alone in the yard, watching her neighbor saunter off like a cat with its tail in the air. Then she spun, too, and stormed into the house. Diana shut the window quickly. She knew it was long past time she was down in the kitchen, helping her mother prepare dinner. But how would she ever keep the secret smile of mischief from her face?

LATER THAT EVENING, supper was tense and quiet. Neither of Diana's parents said much, for offense and anger were rolling from Mrs. Barry in waves as cold as the ocean's swells. Diana confined herself to conversation with Minnie May, who, at three years old, was not exactly an elocutionist. But at least the little girl was unaware of the ill feelings that were drawn up like a hunter's net around the Barry table. She chattered on sunnily about the flowers she'd seen in the frosted autumn dells on the drive home from church, and about the story books she wanted Diana to read to her that night. Her dear, innocent face was so charming and sweet with its bright, rosy cheeks... thanks to her gay little sister, Diana nearly convinced herself that nothing had gone wrong in the world.

But then, as Mrs. Barry stood to carry a load of dishes into the kitchen for washing, all rudiments of joy were swept away. Mrs. Barry drew in a sharp, hissing breath through her nose as she stared out the window toward Green Gables, bristling like a cat. She flashed a swift, commanding glance at Diana. "You, up to your bedroom, and don't make a peep. Take Minnie May with you."

"But Mother, I—"

"Do not argue, Diana. And George," Mrs. Barry added, narrowing her eyes at her husband, "leave this to me. Remain in the parlor, please, until I've handled it."

What *it* was, Diana could not begin to guess. But she figured it was neither safe nor wise to test her mother's patience tonight. She took Minnie May by the hand and hustled her upstairs. When they safely shut up in Diana's bedroom, she sat her sister on the bed and said sternly, "Now, you heard Mother. Don't make a sound." She handed Minnie May a book, a volume of fairy stories with beautiful painted illustrations, to keep her distracted and quiet. Then she crept to her window for a repeat performance of the afternoon's subterfuge.

The curtains were still down. Diana barely parted them with one finger, and squinted past the lace and ruffles to the world outside. A purply-gray dusk was just setting in, lit palely by a low western moon. Tints of silver and white hung about the orchard, picking out bare branches and the occasional dull orb of an overlooked apple high up in the skeletal branches. Something moved on the slope. A lone, forlorn shape was making its way up the orchard path, moving with hesitant, dragging steps as if it went to a gallows. A russet-red coat was pulled tightly about the little figure's thin shoulders, shielding her against the evening chill, and where a good stout cap should have been pulled down to cover her ears, there was nothing but a crown of fiery red, exposed to the cold.

"Anne," Diana whispered. Her heart gave a great, painful lurch. Carefully, she eased up the sash so she could hear what would transpire below.

Anne went right to the front door, not to the kitchen, for her business was serious and formal. She disappeared under the porch roof, but Diana could hear her slow, hollow footsteps, and then the timid knock on the door below. Then there was the squeal of hinges as Mrs. Barry opened to confront Anne.

"What do you want?" Mrs. Barry's voice was stiff and loud enough to carry up to Diana's bedroom window.

"Oh, please, Mrs. Barry, please forgive me." Anne's words were earnest, her voice thick with emotion. "I did not mean to—to—intoxicate Diana." Anne went on to plead her case in the most heart-rending and moving terms, imploring Mrs. Barry to imagine herself in Anne's position: an orphan without a friend in the world, except the kindly folks who had adopted her. "If you had just one bosom friend in all the world, do you think you would intoxicate her on purpose?" Anne said. "I thought it was only raspberry cordial. I was firmly convinced it was raspberry cordial. Oh, please don't say that you won't let Diana play with me anymore. If you do, you will cover my life with a dark cloud of woe."

The speech brought a tear to Diana's eye. She was obliged to let her nose run, for if she sniffled she might be heard down on the porch, or Minnie May might pipe up, and she was now so conveniently absorbed in the fairy book.

Mrs. Barry answered Anne at once, without even pausing to consider her moving plea. "I don't think you are a fit little girl for Diana to associate with," she said coldly. "You'd better go home and behave yourself."

"Won't you let me see Diana just once, to say farewell?" Anne all but wailed.

"Diana has gone over to Carmody with her father." Then the door closed abruptly, cutting Anne off from the Barry household forever.

Diana gaped out at the purple dusk and the silvery moon, seeing none of it in her shock and hurt. Her mother had lied. Mrs. Barry *never* lied, as far as Diana knew, and certainly did not permit her daughters to tell any falsehoods—not even Minnie May, who only made up stories in fun, as little children do, and who meant no wickedness by it. The very thought that her mother could lie so smoothly and easily stunned Diana to her very core. Mrs. Barry was not the paragon of virtue Diana had always grudgingly thought her to be.

Her eyes flooding with tears, her lip trembling with uncontained feeling, Diana watched as Anne stumbled blindly back down the porch steps and trudged slowly back toward Green Gables. As she passed through the orchard gate, a gust of wind caught at her coat and lifted her red braids, but Anne seemed not to notice. A desultory swirl of dry leaves gusted across her path, but she didn't turn to watch their flight with her usual star-eyed fancy. She only walked, head down and steps dragging, as if all the hope had drained right out of her world.

"Anne," Diana said plaintively, causing Minnie May to drop her book and look around. "Oh, Anne, is this to be the end of our friendship forever?"

There was no answer but the wind howling around the eaves of the old white farmhouse.

THE REALITIES OF TRAGEDY

THE NEXT AFTERNOON, DIANA WORKED HER ROSY-CHEEKED CHARM on her highly susceptible father, and he pled the case to Mrs. Barry on Diana's behalf. Diana knew there was no hope of her mother relenting and allowing Diana and Anne to play together again. She did not even attempt to win the unwinnable fight. But she did manage to gain her mother's permission to say a proper farewell to Anne.

"You have ten minutes exactly," Mrs. Barry warned, stern-faced and hard-eyed. "I shall be timing you by the kitchen clock. If you are back even one minute late, Diana, there will be consequences."

Her heart pounding with mingled hope and despair, Diana flew down the hill to the back road and along it to the little fern-fringed spring the girls had named the Dryad's Bubble. There was an unobstructed view of Green Gables from that point. It being situated in the little hollow halfway between the two farms, Diana supposed the location would give her and Anne the most time together. She stood beside the spring, which was matted and clogged with brown oak and maple leaves, and waved desperately toward Green Gables. Time was winging by, and Diana was beginning to feel desperate. But presently Anne appeared on the back porch, capped and scarfed and running as fast as she could go toward the hollow.

Diana could see the bright gleam of hope in Anne's eyes before she even reached the Dryad's Bubble. She was sorry to extinguish that hope with a forlorn shake of her head.

"Your mother hasn't relented?" Anne said.

"No," Diana replied tragically. "And oh, Anne, she says I'm never to play with you again. I cried and cried and told her it wasn't your fault, but it wasn't any use. She gave me only ten minutes, and if I'm not back exactly on time she won't be happy."

Anne's eyes filled with tears. "Ten minutes isn't very long to say an eternal farewell in."

"I know," Diana answered miserably.

The girls fell into each other's arms, sobbing and sniffling. It really was the greatest tragedy either of them had ever witnessed, and all the more poignant because they stood at the very center of it. No romantic novel had ever offered such an affecting, heart-piercing, utterly hopeless scene.

After a moment, Anne pulled back, holding Diana firmly by the shoulders. "Oh, Diana, will you promise faithfully never to forget me, the friend of your youth, no matter what dearer friends may caress thee?"

Normally it amused Diana when Anne spoke so loftily, but there was nothing funny in it now. She sobbed all the harder, wiping her nose on the sleeve of her felt coat. "Indeed I will." Diana could hardly choke out the words. "And I'll never have another bosom friend. I don't want to have one. I couldn't love anybody as I love you."

Anne clasped her hands, her face paling with awe. "Oh, Diana! Do you *love* me?"

Diana scrubbed the tears from her cheeks. "Why, of course I do. Didn't you know that?"

"No. I thought you *liked* me, of course, but I never thought you *loved* me. Why, Diana, I didn't think anybody could love me. Nobody ever has loved me since I can remember. Oh, this is wonderful! It's a ray of light which will forever shine on the darkness of a path severed from thee, Diana. Oh, just say it once again."

Diana smiled through the fresh welling tears. Anne was a funny creature sometimes, but Diana adored her all the more for her strangeness. "I love you devotedly, Anne," she said, quite truthfully, "and I always will. You may be sure of that."

Anne reached out her slender, white hand between them. Diana clutched it hard, knowing that in only a few cruelly short minutes, Anne would be torn from her grasp forever. "And I will always love thee, Diana," Anne said. "In the years to come, thy memory will shine like a star over my lonely life. Just like in that last story we read together. Wilt thou give me a lock of thy jet-black tresses in parting, to treasure forevermore?"

"Have you got anything to cut it with?" Diana pulled a lock of her hair out of the red ribbon that bound it.

Anne did have her patchwork scissors with her, as it happened, for she had been engaged in sewing when she'd seen Diana beckoning to her from the Dryad's Bubble. She carefully clipped one of Diana's black curls and wound it around her finger.

"Fare thee well, my beloved friend," Anne said solemnly. Henceforth we must be as strangers, though living side by side. But my heart will ever be faithful to thee."

"I have to go now," Diana said. "I don't want to, Anne, but Mother will be so cross with me if I'm not back exactly on time."

Anne nodded in silent acceptance, but her chin quivered with the promise of several noisy sobs to come. Diana turned and fled before she could see or hear Anne crying afresh. She wanted to return home in full control of herself, like a grown-up lady, like a heroine from a book, overcoming all the tragedies of life.

"But how do the ladies in books stand it?" she thought as she hurried up the orchard path. "Tragedy is so much harder to bear in real life than when you read about it on the page. I suppose the ladies in books can bear it because they aren't real at all; they're just made up for the stories. But I *am* real, and I'm sure my heart is broken forever!"

Diana made it back to the house with half a minute to spare. Her mother only raised her eyebrows in mute acceptance, and Diana was glad she was not expected to talk. She knew she couldn't trust herself to speak without crying like a helpless little baby, and she didn't want to relinquish her dignity now.

She took herself up to her bedroom and threw open the curtains to let the weak, sideways light of late October spill in. Then she stood before her mirror and shook down her hair from its ribbon. The shortened lock hung awkwardly beside her cheek. Diana plucked at it with trembling fingers, pensive and wondering.

"Nothing has ever hurt me as much as this," she thought. "Losing Anne. She was my truest friend, the very best friend I ever had. She is still my friend, no matter what Mother says, even if I may not play with her. She will forever be in my heart."

But there was something else in Diana's heart, too—something quietly warm and softly glowing. It was the first blush of a hope renewed... a hope Diana hadn't even dared to confront or acknowledge until that moment.

"Is it..." she wondered haltingly, "may I... is it all right now if I like Gilbert?"

It had been plain to Diana that Gilbert only had eyes for Anne, from his first day back at school. But Anne had quit school forever, and after more than three weeks of staying home, Diana supposed Anne was as serious as could be about her vow never to return to Mr. Phillips's class again. Gilbert had little opportunity to see Anne now, and maybe, just maybe, sitting across the aisle from him, as she did... perhaps he would finally turn his attention to Diana. Of course, she couldn't chase him—*wouldn't* chase him, even if she were a girl of seventeen, when chasing boys was understandable and occasionally acceptable. Even if she were as much as hoyden as her mother now thought her to be, the very idea of chasing a boy made Diana blush to the roots of her velvet-black hair.

No, she would never chase after Gilbert Blythe. But she could do her best to make him notice her. And now that Anne was to be forever parted from her side, Diana felt for the first time that she might actually have some hope of catching Gilbert's eye. It was a very thin and tarnished silver lining to the cloud that hung over her heart, but even the smallest glint of silver gives reason for hope.

Diana combed out her curls before her mirror, then lifted and twisted her long, thick tresses up into a grown-up hairstyle, as she had done before. She tied and pinned it all in place, and this time she didn't shy away from the sight of her exposed neck and ear lobes. She liked the way she looked, and she thought that in a few years, when she was truly a grown-up girl ready for courting, she could see her way clear to ensnaring Gilbert's heart. But she would have to start now, while the opportunity to stand out was still there.

"A ray of light which will forever shine on the darkness of a path severed from thee," Diana muttered, repeating Anne's pretty words. And she was just beginning to feel that it was a ray of light indeed—that the future held a few bits and bobs toward which she could look with pleasant anticipation—when she caught sight of the shortened lock, swinging beside her cheek. Diana tried to pin it up into her fancy, grown-up hairstyle, but it refused to obey. It swung down again no matter how she twisted and arranged it.

Finally, she sighed, and let all her hair fall back to her shoulders. It was no use looking forward to the future just yet. The present was still too near, and far too painful. She pulled the curtains closed with a peeved flick of her wrist, unable to look upon Green Gables standing solemnly beyond the treetops.

∿

THE FOLLOWING WEEK began with a cold, subdued Monday. Diana's breath hung in the air in soft, white clouds as she walked alone to school. In the weeks since Anne's departure from school, Diana had mostly grown used to the lonesome way. But no matter how routine the unaccompanied walk became, she never quite shed the small ache of remembrance, the memory of warmer days on those paths and roads with Anne talking dreamily beside her.

Now her boots crunched on the frozen surface of the Birch Path. No snows had yet fallen on Avonlea, but the world was whitened and hardened by frost. Everywhere Diana looked, she saw the cold kiss of winter and felt the promise of deeper chills to come. Every twig that arched above the path, every fern in vale and hollow, every lone leaf that clung to the black forest boughs, was rimed in a delicate white lace. The air smelled brisk and damp, when it did not smell of slow-drifting wood smoke from the farms Diana passed. And her cheeks and eyelids and snubbed little nose tingled with the touch of winter.

The whole island, indeed the whole world, seemed bedded down and resigned to the bleak onset of the season. And so it gave Diana the warmest, thawing thrill, and an uncurling of hope like a springtime seed sprouting, to see Anne, of all people, sitting at one of the desks inside the schoolhouse.

Anne's return to the Avonlea School caused a real sensation, the likes of which the children had not seen since Charlie Sloane hid a big, hairy-legged spider in Ruby Gillis's desk two weeks before. Anne sat very straight and sober at her desk, with her hands folded neatly before her, the picture of a model student, while girls and boys alike flocked around her, welcoming her back with all enthusiasm. Anne was such a charming and spirited girl that her presence had been sorely missed. After all, she had provided such great entertainment, the day she broke her slate over Gilbert's head. Everyone hoped more such demonstrations might be forthcoming; Mr. Phillips was so very dull and the school routine already felt old and worn out, with weeks still to go until Christmas vacation. Anne received each greeting politely, turning to every school friend in turn with a show of warmth and interest, but she did not lapse into any of her wide-eyed raptures, nor did she stir from her desk. She seemed determined to be the pattern of perfection, to take school as seriously as Mr. Phillips himself took it.

Diana wanted desperately to go to Anne, too, and throw her arms around her and weep relief against her shoulder. But she knew if she did, word would get back to her mother. She had no choice but to hold herself apart from Anne, to pretend the brilliant little red-head didn't exist at all. It was terribly unfair. She watched with envy as Jane Andrews sat beside Anne, and the two girls whispered together while pulling their slates from their shared desk for the arithmetic lesson, which was always first thing in the morning on Mondays. Gertie Pye was already squeaking her pencil atrociously beside Diana. She edged a little farther down the bench, wishing against all hope that Anne could sit beside her once more.

Gilbert Blythe sauntered into the school room just as the bell was ringing. He dropped into his seat across the aisle from Diana, gave her a rakish but not especially meaningful smile, and then, as one of the girls called out Anne's name so that she could toss her a plum as a welcome-back present, he sat up as if stung by a bee and looked around eagerly. Anne was two rows in front of him and across the aisle. Gilbert's eyes fastened on the back of her red head, with its neat part and two hanging braids, tied with green dotted ribbons. And by the persistence of his gaze, Diana saw that it would be a very long time before Gilbert looked away from Anne again.

Sighing, she sank down miserably in her seat, only to be elbowed by Gertie as the latter rummaged in the desk for her slate.

The lessons unfolded, with Mr. Phillips making no great fanfare over Anne's return. But the students kept up their simmer of excitement. As the day progressed, girls passed Anne notes with verses or drawings on them, and Ella May MacPherson gave her a yellow pansy she'd cut from the cover of a seed catalogue. More little presents followed, the kind of treasures school children prized: a pretty glass bottle to hold Anne's slate water, the instructions for knitting a new kind of lace, and more sweet fruits pulled from farm cellars all across Avonlea. Diana felt terribly conflicted over the show. She loved Anne dearly, and just to be near her again was a treat she had never expected to enjoy. But she was more than a little jealous of all the attention the other girls showered on *her* Anne, her own bosom friend... and she envied the girls, too, for they were free to talk to Anne and play with her at break times, while Diana was forever barred from her company.

And, of course, there was the matter of Gilbert Blythe. After the lunch hour (during which Mr. Phillips took Anne aside and re-assigned her a seat beside Minnie Andrews, who was too prim for words, but whose staunch presence would discourage all the excitement that now hung around Anne) Diana went inside the school house early. She had eaten her lunch alone, hiding out on the back side of the school, seated at a rickety old picnic table under the bare branches of a huge oak. None of the other girls were yet ready to part company with the prodigal scholar, so Diana was doomed to a solitary state. (Though at least she was obliged to share her apple tarts with no one.) She returned to her desk and would have dropped her head on her arms, to stew in her misery until the classroom filled up again, but she heard a cheerful "Hullo, Diana" from the doorway.

She turned quickly to see Gilbert, tossing a big, red apple and catching it again in his palm. He winked at her, and Diana's heart skipped several beats... but just when she thought he might say something more to her... just when she thought perhaps she had managed to catch his eye after all, and despite the electrifying presence of Anne in the classroom, he sauntered to Minnie Andrews's desk and set the apple carefully atop it.

Diana sighed and looked away, all her glad hope withering. So Gilbert had overheard Mr. Phillips changing Anne's seat, too. The world really was a dull, dark place after all, and the cold of the season had truly set in. Set beside the popular and worthy Anne, Diana felt she had as much hope of shining as the weak winter sun behind a shroud of storm clouds.

THE SECRET LETTERS

WINTER TIGHTENED ITS GRIP ON THE ISLAND, DRIFTING SNOW OVER the little hollow of Violet Vale, collaring the Dryad's Bubble in ice, and gowning field and forest alike in a glitter of diamond-white purity. Avonlea was quiet and still, by day and by night. The weight of snow and heavy, dark cloud muted the life that still stirred beneath the ground in dark burrows and secret caves, and all who dwelled in the pretty farm houses, too—those quaint, charming homes whose roofs were capped by snow and whose windows glowed golden-orange with warm, welcoming light.

The silence of winter made Diana feel like an island herself, separated from everyone and everything by a gulf of introspection. And the waters that isolated her were white-capped and wind-tossed, agitated by the feelings that howled about inside her soul like the most unpredictable of storm winds. Diana honestly wanted to be good and obey her mother, for she sensed instinctively that she would never know any peace within her heart if she and Mrs. Barry were forever at odds. But it is so difficult to go along when a parent's command is unfairly given. Even the best, most dutiful child finds it grating to acquiesce to an oppressive rule.

And so, knowing herself to be an island—a girl apart—Diana braved her mother's wrath one Tuesday and passed Anne a note in class. She did it when Mr. Phillips was in the back of the room, sitting beside Prissy Andrews and too absorbed in her essay to pay any heed to the goings-on at the front of the class. Diana had written her note that morning in her bedroom, and folded it intricately into a star shape so that no one could tamper with it while it passed from hand to hand to reach Anne's new desk. The message was far too important for Diana to risk alteration or sabotage. She also sent along a little present for Anne, since she hadn't yet had her chance to offer up a "welcome-home" gift.

She watched eagerly as Anne unfolded the star and read the contents of Diana's note.

Dear Anne,

Mother says I'm not to play with you or talk to you even in school. It isn't my fault and don't be cross at me, because I love you as much as ever. I miss you awfully to tell all my secrets to and I don't like Gertie Pye one bit. I made you one of the new bookmarkers out of red tissue paper. They are awfully fashionable now and only three girls in school know how to make them. When you look at it remember

Your true friend

Diana Barry

Anne planted a rapturous kiss on the pretty, folded-paper bookmarker which Diana had given her. Then she whisked a sheet of paper from her desk and bent over it with her pencil—a new, beautifully striped one, which one of the boys had given her on her return to the school. It certainly was an enviable pencil.

Forthwith, Anne's reply was passed from one desk to another until it reached Diana's hand. Anne hadn't folded it into a star—not many girls knew that trick, either—but it was creased into a neat little square, which Diana unfolded as quickly as her fingers could manage it. She was trembling with hope and happiness by the time she read Anne's letter. Anne promised she wasn't cross because Diana had to obey her mother. And oh, she declared herself still Diana's bosom friend (though "bosom" was misspelled.) She affirmed that even if they couldn't talk face to face, their spirits could commune. That sounded so pretty and poetic that it gave Diana a proper thrill right up her spine.

And thus began the communing of those two kindred spirits, which sustained Diana throughout the long, dreary, dark weeks of winter. She was always careful to write her notes in the early mornings, when Mrs. Barry was occupied with Minnie May and unlikely to burst into Diana's bedroom and catch her in the act. She did often worry that word might make it back to Mrs. Barry that Diana had become a habitual note-passer, and of course Mrs. Barry would know at once exactly who was receiving her daughter's missives. But she was always as cautious as could be, leaving her notes safely in her pocket until Mr. Phillips was thoroughly engaged in the back of the classroom and the danger of her being discovered was minimal. In any case, note-passing was a popular vice in the Avonlea schoolhouse. Letters of all sorts circulated surreptitiously around the room, and Diana was no more guilty than any other scholar.

Those notes to and from Anne were a balm to Diana's soul. For no other girl offered her the kind of friendship Anne did—deep and loyal and devoted, without a hint of the childlike fickleness that marked Diana's friendships with her other schoolmates. To Anne alone could she trust the dearest secrets of her heart. It made her feel better, less "harrowed up" inside, to write out all her dreams and frustrations, and even to describe the wonderful things she'd seen or the little joys she'd had, knowing that Anne would read every word with sympathy and fellow-feeling. It was good to have a friend who truly loved you, who really cared about what was in your heart and didn't just pretend to care. It made the world a less wintry sort of place.

Anne never failed to write a response. Her notes were often long and rambling, as was her conversation, but they were also just as brightly colored, just as stirring. Diana could even look past Anne's creative spelling—which was honestly improving, day by day. She kept and re-read every letter Anne sent.

My dearest Diana,

(one note read)

I was so happy to recieve your last letter, and I am gladened to know that relations are better between you and your mother. I hope they stay that way, for there is nothing in the world I want more than for you to be happy, my sweet busom friend! Many a night have I wept bitter tears for knowing that I was the cause of the strife in your household, tho' of course I didn't mean to be, and I still maintain that an orphan shouldn't be expected to know the difference between wine and rasberry cordial. I think I would actually perish from grief if your mother never gave you a smile again. I know we must remain quite without any hope that she will relent and allow us to play together someday, but I did have a comforting thought last night while I was laying in bed thinking about you, and here is that thought: Someday we will be grown up and then your mother won't be able to tell us what to do any longer. I suppose that goes for Marilla, too, tho' she is not as strong-willed as your mother, and I am surprised to find myself writing this, but I believe Marilla is not as "prickly" as your mother either. Marilla is a very "prickly" woman, tho'. But her heart is good. I think your mother's heart is probly good, too, but her mind gets in the way of her heart and then she "fouls her own traces," as Matthew says. I am not sure what fouling one's traces means, but I think it has something to do with plow horses or possibly with harvesting potatos. Do you know?

Tho' our hearts sorrow in our seperation, dear Diana, we may look forward to the gloryous day when we are real ladies grown up, making our own way in the world and no longer under the thumb of older ladies who have the charge of caring for us and seeing that we are brought up proper. It is almost Febuary, which is your birthday month, and then March, which is mine, and then we will both be twelve, and that makes it five more years until we are grown up enough to be our own ladies. Five years does seem like a terrible long time to wait, but Matthew says five years goes by in a blink and Matthew is usually right about things. He is very observant, Diana, and knows so much about everything, even tho' he doesn't talk much. So we have only "a blink" until we are big and then your mother can't infloo (crossed out) *influence our lives any longer. I hope that she will repent of her hard cruelty, but I also pray that it will not take any great tragedy to make her repent. Just the passidge of time.*

When we are seventeen and grown up I am going to wear my hair up like the lady on the catalog that Julie Andrews has in her desk today. You should ask her to see it at break time. That lady looks ever so fashionable, but I am going to dye my hair raven black, like yours, before I put it up, even though some people say it's a sin for a woman to dye her hair, but I'll do it anyway because really there is no point in putting up hair that is red. No point at all.

Until we may embrace again in friendship everlasting, I am
Yours eternally
Cordelia F. Shirley, also known as Anne

Anne's suggestion that their grown-up futures were not so very far off inspired a flutter of hope in Diana's breast. That night she read the note again by the light of her little brass oil lamp, then tucked it under her pillow and imagined the dazzling cosmopolitan life she and Anne would enjoy together when they turned seventeen. No more sleepy Avonlea for them! They would have fabulous dresses made, in the most current styles, and go together to Charlottetown or perhaps even to Halifax. There they would enter into glamorous careers—Diana a celebrated singer, Anne a poetess—and they would pool their earnings to buy a grand house like the one Aunt Josephine lived in. In that house, which Diana's imagination and ambition furnished with the richest velvet drapes, the plushest Persian rugs, and the most fine and delicate settees, the two girls would entertain company from the heights of society, and hear the pleas of hopeful suitors, whose proposals they would turn down with words so charming and gracious that the men would never hold a grudge against them, and would go away still entirely besotted with the wonderful Anne Shirley and the scintillating songbird Diana Barry.

"It's such a lovely story," Diana thought, yawning on her pillow. "I should write it all out in a letter to Anne."

Anne would, no doubt, find the whole idea thrilling. But Diana snuffed her lamp and lay back with a stormy sigh. What if Anne replied wishing to know what these imagined suitors looked like, talked like? There was only one boy Diana could picture in the role of the gentleman on bended knee with his hat in his hand, waiting in tense, manfully stoic silence for Diana's answer.

But Diana never wrote of *him* in her letters to Anne. Anne simply wouldn't suffer to read that boy's name.

DIANA DID SEE that very boy several days later, and had occasion to talk to him, too. She and Anne had worked out a new method of communication. Concerned about potential meddling from the Pye camp, Diana and Anne agreed to use the oak tree at the back of the school yard as their private mail depot. It had a hollow about shoulder height, with a small opening just big enough for a girl's hand to fit through. The space inside remained dry throughout the winter. Diana was lurking around the oak after school had let out, retrieving Anne's most recent correspondence and depositing something of her own: the cover of a pattern catalogue, which she had pilfered from the bottom of her mother's sewing basket. The cover featured several dresses with puff sleeves, and Diana knew what a passion Anne had for the style. She didn't know that Gilbert Blythe had also lingered after Mr. Phillips shut up the school house, and was watching her curiously from the porch railing.

"Hullo, Diana," he called, just as Diana withdrew her hand from the oak trunk.

Diana jumped guiltily and turned to glare at him. "Gilbert, whatever are you doing? Everyone else has gone home."

"I should ask what you're doing," he said, cheekily leaning against one of the shingled posts that held up the porch roof. "But I already know."

"Oh, do you? Aren't you smart," Diana returned saucily, as was the custom when a boy and girl confronted one another in the schoolyard, about any subject.

"You're passing notes to Anne Shirley," Gilbert said.

Diana shoved her hands, one of which held Anne's note, deep in the pockets of her winter coat and said nothing. She could feel the flush rising to her cheeks, though. "I can't let him get the better of me," she told herself, even as her heart raced. "I must be as bold to him as Anne ever was." Though, she reminded herself, she ought to stop short of breaking a slate over his head.

"What do you know about it?" she said, and turned away with a toss of her head. She made briskly for the Birch Path.

"Wait, Diana," Gilbert called. He dashed down the porch steps and fell in beside her. "Don't be mad now. I won't tell anyone."

Diana eyed him dubiously as they walked.

"I *promise*," he said with solemn emphasis. Then he brightened. "Say, how about if I walk you home? You always go by the back way, don't you, instead of the road?"

Diana bit her lip so she wouldn't grin too broadly, thereby ruining her poised demeanor. No boy had ever offered to walk her home before. And for the first one to be Gilbert...! "All right, I suppose," she said airily, as if she was used to being accompanied by boys every day. "But you mustn't tell anybody about the tree. It's the only way Anne and I can be friends now. If Mother ever found out, she would forbid me from going anywhere near that tree, and she'd be ever so cross with me, and everything would be ruined."

"You and Anne aren't allowed to be friends?" Gilbert asked as they left the spruce grove behind and crossed the Avonlea Road. The Birch Path stretched before them. The birch trunks were palisades of the purest silver, gleaming faintly in the last pale light of afternoon.

"Not since... well..." Diana hesitated, lowering her face to watch her own feet tread the frosty ground. What ought she to say? Gilbert was a nice boy most of the time, but he did have a penchant for mischief. She was lucky that word of her disastrous brush with the "raspberry cordial" hadn't escaped to circulate around the town. She aimed to keep it that way. "Not since Anne accidentally made me sick. But I wasn't very sick; I was better by the next day. Mother thought Anne did it on purpose, though, and she absolutely *forbids* us to be friends. It's terribly unfair, Gilbert. I've never had a friend like Anne before."

"She is... well... different, isn't she?"

Diana heard the somewhat wistful note in Gilbert's voice. She glanced up at him and saw that his eyes were distant, his smile strangely hopeful. It was clear he didn't mean "different" as an insult.

"I've never known anyone like her," Diana admitted quietly.

"You don't talk to her at all anymore?" Gilbert said.

"Only in our letters. It's the only way I can manage, without Mother hearing about it and coming down on me."

"Does she ever... well... has she ever mentioned me in her letters, Diana?"

Diana laughed. "Indeed, no! She's furious with you, Gilbert."

"All because I twitted her about her hair." He sounded regretful. "Do you think she'll ever forgive me, Diana?"

Diana didn't know what to tell him. Anne's passions were vast, impressive things, just as whole-hearted and all-encompassing as the loves and hatreds of the most romantic heroines in the grandest of stories. Diana thought it entirely possible that Anne could carry her dislike of Gilbert Blythe to the grave.

"Well, she must forgive you at some point," Diana replied practically, though she wasn't at all convinced, herself. "After all, it was just a comment about her hair. No one can stay mad over such a thing forever, can they?"

"You're so steady and thoughtful," Gilbert said suddenly, beaming at her as they passed Violet Vale and skirted the snow-drifted hay fields. "That's what I like about you, Diana."

Her cheeks flamed, and she looked away quickly so he wouldn't see her blush. She wanted to say, "Do you really *like* me, Gilbert?" But no words would come.

"Seeing as how you are so steady," he continued, kicking a rock down the lane, "maybe you can write to Anne and tell her she ought to forgive me. She'll listen to you; I know she will."

The blush faded from Diana's cheeks, replaced by the sting of winter cold. So the talk had come around to Anne again. A painful weight had settled in Diana's stomach. She loved Anne and missed her terribly. But... why couldn't Gilbert like Diana for her own merits? "Even without Anne beside me," she thought miserably, "I am still in her shadow." It was clear now to Diana that she had no chance of catching Gilbert's eye with Anne as her best friend.

They reached the foot bridge, nestled in the gray-and-white division between Orchard Slope and Green Gables. Gilbert turned to look at the neighboring farm, the stout white house with its dark-green roof peak standing out sharp against the dimming clouds. There was a golden light twinkling in the window of the east gable—Anne's room, though Gilbert didn't know that. He turned to Diana with hope sparkling in his hazel eyes. "Please say you'll write to Anne," he implored. "I'll owe you a favor if you do, and I'll be so grateful."

Diana offered a tremulous smile, but she really wanted to frown and even to cry. She was grateful that the cold made her eyes dry; otherwise she might actually have burst into tears. "He is so handsome," she thought angrily. "Why is it so hard to say 'no' to a handsome boy?"

"I'll... I'll write to her," Diana faltered. "Maybe I can convince her."

Gilbert's grin broadened. "Thanks, Diana. You're a real friend. Well... good night." He tipped his cap to her, then sauntered away toward the long bridge that crossed Barry's Pond. Beyond lay the eastward bend of the Avonlea Road, and the Blythe homestead tucked away in the sleeping, barren fields.

Diana watched him go in a pinched, pained silence. "Anne was all he talked about," she said to herself. "All *we* talked about. She had bewitched us both, I suppose. There isn't any hope for me if I can't get out of her shadow... none at all! What am I to grow up to be, if I can't stand out and make a way in the world? Why, I'll be just *no one* forever. Forgotten and ignored. No, I won't write to Anne... about Gilbert or anything else. I won't leave any more presents in the oak tree, either. I must make other friends, find other girls to be my chums. I want friends who are nice and fun, like Anne, but who will still give me a fighting chance."

Thus decided, Diana cast one lingering look at the light in Anne's window. Then she trudged up the hill to Orchard Slope. But no matter how quickly she walked, she couldn't outpace the weight of regret that dragged along behind her.

DIANA DARES

CHRISTMAS CAME AND WENT IN A BRIGHT FLURRY OF HOLLY AND IVY and evergreens, and candles glowing merrily at every window-pane in Avonlea. Diana always loved Christmas-time, not least because her mother loved the season and always drifted through Christmas in a splendid mood.

Mrs. Barry spent the two weeks of Christmas vacation flitting about a kitchen that was always warm from the prodigious amounts of baking that determined lady undertook. The whole house smelled richly of cinnamon and cloves and fresh-made breads. Diana was glad to join her mother in the kitchen, lending a hand with the cookies and pies and delicious roasts Mrs. Barry prepared. They sang songs of the Nativity as they worked side by side, and not once did a quarrel arise between them, even when Mrs. Barry's considerable talents in the kitchen were taxed to their limits by the rigorous schedule of parties and visits and cake exchanges with her sewing circle and society friends.

Diana and Minnie May were each given new felt coats and hats with matching mittens and scarves. They looked as charming as could be, dressed alike and standing side by side in the snow to wait for the sleigh that would take them on a ride across the frozen fields. That Christmas was the happiest time Diana could recall in many months. She hadn't felt so glad in her heart since she and Anne had first initiated their friendship. And the busy, bright whirl of the season swept thoughts of Anne away from Diana's mind... most of the time... so that she didn't always feel the confusing ache in her heart that arose whenever she thought too much of Anne and Gilbert and the letter he so desperately wanted Diana to write.

Those thoughts only came at night, when, brushing out her long, dark curls at her small mirror, Diana would catch sight of the light flickering in the east gable across the fields. Then she would remember the good times she'd had with Anne before... in a time that felt "long, long ago," as stories often say. Sometimes she only sat and gazed out her window toward Green Gables, which now seemed to reside beyond an uncrossable gulf. Sometimes she repented of her decision to cut off communication with Anne, and got out paper and pencil, determined to write and spill out the jumble of her feelings. But she never made a single mark. Diana didn't know what she could possibly say now, nor where she might begin.

Sometimes the light in the east gable would blink out the rhythms of the secret code Anne and Diana had developed, a signal to summon one another to the Dryad's Bubble to exchange secrets that were too exciting to keep. In those moments, Diana would watch Anne's lamp flare and darken and flare again. It was a like a hand reaching out through endless dark, desperate for a friend's touch, yearning for an end to her isolation. But Diana could never quite convince herself to signal back.

The Christmas vacation came to a close and the Avonlea School opened its doors once again, welcoming its young scholars back refreshed and invigorated from their celebrations. Minnie May had caught a fearfully bad cold, and Diana was afraid she'd take it, too, and miss the first days of school. She was determined to re-enter Avonlea School society and venture whole-heartedly into new friendships.

In the schoolyard she caught sight of a bright bit of something protruding from the hole in the old oak tree, and all her conflicted feelings about Anne came rushing back to her at once. She approached the tree cautiously when she was certain no other children were watching. Inside was a small parcel wrapped in red paper and tied with a bit of pink ribbon. Diana pocketed the gift and went inside, as Prissy Andrews had begun to ring the bell with vigor. But all day long, Diana found it impossible to concentrate on her spelling and history. She was aware of nothing but the small gift in her skirt pocket; the temptation to open it then and there was great, but Diana knew it would only attract attention from the other children—perhaps even from Mr. Phillips.

At last the school day ended. Diana raced home, her hands tingling with the desire to open the gift and learn what Anne had to say to her... if indeed Anne had sent along a note at all. She hung up her new coat and scarf on the peg beside the kitchen stove, then rushed up to her bedroom and shut herself away. Diana flung herself across her bed and examined the parcel carefully, admiring the way Anne had folded the red paper so neatly, the simple prettiness of the pink bow.

She untied the bow and let the red paper fall open. It revealed a match box, decorated with a stamped scene of horses pulling a sleigh. Diana slid the box open. Inside was a slender bracelet made of braided, multi-colored thread and decorated with a single blue glass bead. And beneath the bracelet was the neat, square fold that always identified one of Anne's letters.

Diana pulled the letter from the box, unfolded it, and read eagerly.

Dearest Diana

How I miss you and your letters! I walked up to the schoolhouse almost every day during Christmas vacation to see if you had left anything for me to find in our tree. I do not know why you no longer write to me, but I suppose your mother found out and won't let you. I hope it is only that. I don't want to think that you have decided you don't love me after all, or even like me, and that you've given up on the dream that we may still be true friends one day. But most of the time my imagination gets the better of me and I think exactly that. O, Diana! If I have done anything to hurt you, I am tremendously sorry and will carry the shame and regret with me all of my life, even unto my grave, for you are the last person I would ever wish to upset. I never had a friend until you. Maybe I am not very good at tending friendships because I had so little experience to begin with, and made a mistake that most girls would have known to avoid. If so, I beg you to forgive me and to grant me another chance to prove myself worthy. To be without you, even as my secret friend of letters, is a misery that CRUSHES me under a weight of sorrow. The other girls in school are nice to me, but they all think I'm queer and don't understand or appreciate my fancies like you do, dear Diana. I can't be myself with anyone but you. And I don't want to be myself with anyone else, for the truest and best Anne is the Anne who has her Diana beside her.

Aside from being in the depths of despair, Christmas was fairly jolly. One of Marilla's and Matthew's cousins came to visit, an old lady from Halifax. She was not as thrilling as I imagined a real Haligonian to be. I thought because she came from a city, there would be something dazzling and splendid about her, because just the idea of a city is so thrilling all by itself. But she seemed like the kind of person who would fit right in here in Avonlea. She didn't have any good stories about the city, and mostly talked about her aching joints and how bad the boat ride was to P.E.I. and how bad the trains were. I got the impression that it is a fearful nuisance to travel when you are an old lady. I made up my mind that I will do all my traveling while I am still young, so I will have plenty of interesting things to say about it when I go on visits and talk to younger people about where I've been and what I've seen. I do want to travel someday, but I also don't *want to leave the island because it is so pretty and pleasant and comfortable here. Sometimes I think there can't really be anywhere as nice as our island, even though great cities like Paris and Boston have such glamorous reputations. Anyway, I got some good new stockings and a felt cap from Marilla for my Christmas present, and Matthew gave me some nice peppermints and some pretty pencils. I am so grateful. It's nice to be given presents, isn't it? It makes you feel so warm and cozy on the inside, to be remembered with something special, even if it is only pencils with striped paper on the outside. I am using one of my new pencils to write this letter. It is green with pink stripes, very fetching. I'll be sorry when I've used it all down to a stub.*

I made this bracelet for you out of Marilla's leftover embroidery thread. She says I am hopeless at embroidering things so I might as well do something else useful with the thread instead of tangling and knotting it all up trying to make a proper sampler. (I don't understand the point of samplers anyhow.) So I braided it and used this bead, which one of the girls gave me when I got back to school, for a fastener. I think it will fit your wrist perfectly because I remember exactly what you look like and how big you are, even though circumstances have held us far apart. I hope that you will wear it, dearest Diana. It is a symbol of my everlasting devotion to you. But if you don't wear it, I won't be mad at you. I never could be mad at you for anything, and that's why I hope I haven't offended you with some unintended slight.

Until we may meet in friendship again, I am
Despairing but ever hopeful,
Anne Shirley

As soon as she finished reading the note, Diana pressed her face down into her pillow and wept. The guilt that had formerly dragged behind her now hung as heavy on her as a cape made of lead. "Anne," she thought passionately, "I'm so mixed up inside! I don't know whether to be angry with you or not, and if I am, I don't know why, exactly, or how to make myself stop feeling this way!" Diana suspected very much that it had been a grave mistake to stop writing her letters to Anne, not because Anne was now heartbroken—which was tragic enough to contemplate— but because she herself felt lost and disoriented in the tangled forest of their relation. How did one rekindle friendship's flame when cold, bitter winds had snuffed it out?

"I'll write to her," Diana decided, "and explain everything, as best I can."

She went at once to the little table beside her window, where her flower-covered writing box stood ready beside the little brass lamp. But even though the paper was smooth and inviting, and even though her pencil was sharp, Diana stared helplessly at the blank page, never knowing how to begin. After many fruitless minutes, she rose from her table in consternation and rummaged around her room until she found some small gifts of her own: a piece of saltwater taffy wrapped in wax paper, a square of pretty fabric for patchwork, and the new green hair ribbons she had received for Christmas. Green always looked very pretty in Anne's hair. These she bundled up in a tiny linen bag. She would leave them in the oak tree for Anne to find first thing tomorrow morning.

On the paper, she wrote the simplest of messages: "Love always, Diana." The message was short, and perhaps it was an inadequate response to Anne's heartfelt letter. But the words were also true, even if Diana wished they weren't.

JANUARY WOULD HAVE BEEN a dull disappointment of a month, if not for the fact that the Premier had taken it into his head to visit sleepy little Prince Edward Island on his big political tour. The whole of Avonlea was in an uproar. Most folks thought it likely that nobody in the town would ever have a chance to see a real, live politician at close quarters again, and so everyone who was anyone planned to attend the mass meeting in Charlottetown, thirty miles away, whether they agreed with the Premier's political stances or not.

Mr. and Mrs. Barry were in a grand bustle for days before the event. They flitted and dashed around Orchard Slope making preparations for their departure and absence—for the meeting was at night, so they would be obliged to take a room in Charlottetown and return the morning after. Diana was terribly excited, too. She was not to go with them, which was all right by her, for a political meeting sounded impossibly dreary. She would have liked to visit Charlottetown, for she always enjoyed the island's biggest city on the few occasions when she'd been allowed to accompany her parents there. However, remaining at home with Orchard Slope to herself... more or less... was the next best thing to visiting the city.

I say "more or less" because Diana was not quite old enough, at eleven years of age, to be left entirely in charge of home and hearth. She was a good, responsible girl, but there are situations even the best of little girls can't be expected to handle on their own. Mrs. Barry had employed Mary Joe, a wonderfully plump and stoic French girl from the creek, to look after things at Orchard Slope while she and Mr. Barry were off enjoying the meeting. Mary Joe was fifteen and had a reputation for steadiness that did her service. No turn of events ever unsettled her—she was known to be quite unflappable—which made her the perfect candidate to oversee Diana and little Minnie May for the night.

Mary Joe arrived just as the sun was beginning to set. She set her bag of overnight things on the little, plain sofa beside the kitchen stove and hung up her hat and scarf, which she did indeed do a steady, unflappable, business-like way. Diana didn't mind having Mary Joe about. She spoke English well enough to get by, and although she was never any fun she also didn't meddle with Diana or Minnie May, as long as they behaved themselves.

"So good of you to come," Mrs. Barry said to Mary Joe. "The girls won't give you any trouble tonight, but it gladdens me to know they are in your capable hands."

At that moment Minnie May, who had been lounging rather listlessly on the sofa as close as she could get to the warmth of the stove, set up a rackety cough. Mary Joe paused, eyeing the three-year-old with a worried expression.

"She caught a cold in the chest two weeks back," Mrs. Barry explained. "It hasn't left her yet, the poor mite, but she'll be all right."

"Are you sure, Missus Barry?" Mary Joe asked. "Dat sound like de croup to me."

"Nonsense, my dear," Mrs. Barry said with a light-hearted laugh. "It's only a cold. She's nearly over it now. She'll be just fine, won't you, darling?"

Minnie May, pale-faced and with violet rings shadowing her sad, dark eyes, looked up at her mother in solemn silence. Then she sniffled noisily.

"Just put her to bed early. She can have some chamomile tea. The steam will soothe her. There's George driving up with the sleigh. We're on our way to Charlottetown. You be perfect, Diana, and help Mary Joe with anything she needs."

"Yes, Mother," Diana said. But she didn't look at her mother as she hurried out the door and climbed into the sleigh. Diana couldn't take her eyes off her little sister. There was something wilting and frail about Minnie May's demeanor... something Diana hadn't seen in the girl for all the long weeks she had nursed her fearful cold. As the sleigh glided away down the snow-covered hill, the bells on the horse's collar fading into the distance, a shiver of fear crept up Diana's spine.

AN HOUR LATER, Diana's shiver of fear had turned to a constant, cold clutch of the purest, most hideous dread. She and Mary Joe had tried fruitlessly to get Minnie May to take her supper, a wholesome and tasty chicken stew. But Minnie May murmured and whined and turned her face away, and couldn't be convinced to try so much as a bite.

"This isn't like her at all," Diana said quietly to Mary Joe. They watched Minnie May sag at the kitchen table, drooping down to rest her curly little head miserably on the tabletop beside her untouched bowl of stew. "She always eats her supper, every bite. Oh, Mary Joe, I'm awful scared. What if she's really, truly sick?"

Mary Joe shook her head soberly. "I still say it's de croup. I seen babies wit' it before. Always sound de same."

As if to punctuate Mary Joe's assertion, Minnie May sat suddenly straight on her chair and began to cough. It was a cough like nothing Diana had ever heard before: harsh and barking, wild and fierce, as if some terrible beast had possessed Minnie May from the inside. The poor child hacked and shook with the force of the spasm. Her face darkened; she gasped for air between coughs with a desperate, frightened look in her glazed, tearful eyes.

Diana started back, horrified. "Mary Joe! What's happening?"

"Oh, Lord have mercy!" Mary Joe's hands flew up to clutch at her own broad face. "Dat's a bad case, Miss Diana! What are we to do?"

"I thought you would know," Diana moaned.

"Merciful Heaven," Mary Joe said, staggering uselessly across the kitchen and then back again. "Merciful Heaven, save de baby!"

Diana caught Mary Joe by the arm and pulled her around to face her. "You must think, Mary Joe! Don't lose your head now! How do we treat croup?"

"I don't know, Miss Diana, I don't know!"

"You said you've seen babies with it before!"

"But I never treated dem, Miss Diana! We need a doctor, dat's what."

Diana felt quite sick with fear. A slow, cold realization flooded her limbs and made her tremble with hopelessness. "Mother and Father have taken the sleigh to Charlottetown," she whispered.

"De roads too icy for a buggy," Mary Joe said, just as softly. Her eyes were wide with terror. "And de doctor is miles away. Even if you ran de whole way, it would take hours, Miss Diana... hours!"

At that point, Mary Joe let out a great wail of grief and caught up Minnie May (still coughing and choking piteously.) She clutched the little girl in her arms, a useless gesture, but it was the only expression the poor thing could find for her fear.

"Oh, Mary Joe, this is useless," Diana shrieked. "We must do something. We can't just let her..." She couldn't finish that bleak thought.

"But what, Miss Diana? What can we do?"

Giving in to nervous energy, Diana twisted the bracelet on her wrist. The thread bracelet, braided and beaded. Suddenly she knew exactly what she must do. The Barrys' only sleigh was gone, but Diana knew where there was another close by.

She whisked a shawl from the peg beside the stove and tied it hastily around her head and neck. "Wait here," she said to Mary Joe. "I'm going to run for help."

"No," the French girl protested, her face pale with fright. "Don't leave me 'lone, Miss Diana!"

But there was no time to explain. Diana flung herself through the kitchen door and down the porch steps. The moon was beginning to rise, glowing faintly through the dark net of bare orchard branches. Her icy, treacherous path was poorly lit, and the world around her was disorienting in its patched cloak of moonlight and shadow. But Diana ran as fast as her legs could carry her, down the snowy slope and over the footbridge toward Green Gables... and, she fervently prayed, salvation.

A NIGHT OF DESPERATION

Never had the great stretch of field between Orchard Slope and Green Gables seemed so impossibly vast. Every ragged breath of night air burned in Diana's throat and chest with a vicious, brutal cold. The snow had crusted and frozen over, so that each step held a moment on the glittering surface before cracking and breaking underfoot. Her legs were sore and tired from that faltering, falling gait long before she reached the green-peaked farmhouse... long before she even reached the end of its pastures.

But after what seemed an eternity, Diana struggled up the last bit of hillside and wrestled with the pasture gate. It was coated in ice that stuck to her palms as she forced it open against a drift of snow. When she pulled her hands away, the ice scraped alarmingly against her skin. She was nearly there now. Green Gables was close, and behind her, the Orchard Slope farmhouse was distant and small. A single, wan light burned in the kitchen, where Mary Joe was no doubt still clinging uselessly to Minnie May. By contrast, the lights in Green Gables were like beacons of hope and welcome. Orange light spilled out across the shapeless mounds of the snow-covered kitchen garden. The sight made

Diana weep afresh, but whether from fear or relief... or both... she didn't know.

A portion of walkway had been shoveled clear; it led from the silent garden to the kitchen door. Diana could finally run in earnest when she reached it, and she did run, straining her legs against the pained protest of her muscles. She flew up the steps and along the covered porch, and didn't bother to knock on the green-painted door. She flung it open and hurtled inside, gasping and sagging against the door frame.

Anne was the first person Diana saw, and never was a sight more welcome. The red-haired girl had just emerged from the cellar entrance nearby, carrying a plate of russet apples and in one hand and the stub of a lit candle in the other. Anne's mouth dropped open in shock when she saw Diana, so close and so unexpected. Apples and candle alike fell from her hands and tumbled down the cellar steps with a crash.

"Whatever is the matter, Diana?" Anne exclaimed. Her eyes widened with sudden hope. "Has your mother relented at last?"

Diana had no time to address Anne's hope. "Oh, Anne, do come quick. Minnie May is awful sick. She's got croup, Mary Joe says. And Father and Mother are away to town and there's nobody to go for the doctor. Minnie May is awful bad and Mary Joe doesn't know what to do, and oh, Anne, I'm so scared!"

Matthew Cuthbert dropped the newspaper he had been reading on the kitchen sofa. He took up his coat and hat, bundled himself with urgency, and slid silently past Diana and out the door.

Anne gazed after him admiringly for a moment, then she snatched her own coat from its hanger. "He's gone to harness the sorrel mare to go to Carmody for the doctor. I know it as well as if he'd said so. Matthew and I are such kindred spirits, I can read his thoughts without words at all."

Diana choked back a sob. Everything felt so hopeless, so frightening and desperate! "I don't believe he'll find the doctor at

Carmody," she said, trying her best to remain calm but failing. "Dr. Blair went to town to see the Premier, and I guess Dr. Spencer would go, too. Mary Joe never treated anybody with croup."

"Mrs. Lynde had ever so many children. Surely she has seen croup before."

"But Mrs. Lynde is away, too! Oh, Anne!"

Anne hooked her arm through Diana's. Her demeanor was impossibly cheerful. "Don't cry, Di. I know exactly what to do for croup. You forget that Mrs. Hammond had twins three times. When you look after three pairs of twins, you naturally get a lot of experience. Oh—I should get the ipecac bottle, in case you don't have any at your house." She flashed off into one of the back rooms, and returned with the medicine bottle clutched triumphantly in her white little fist. "Come on now."

Off the two little girls went, over the snowy pastures and through the narrow band of trees that sheltered the brook. The way was as difficult as it had been for Diana alone, but somehow it didn't seem so now, with a brisk, confident friend beside her. And not just any friend... Anne, her truest and dearest companion. It wasn't only Anne's surety about treating croup that put Diana's mind at ease. It was Anne herself, intelligent and focused, ready to face whatever challenge lay ahead with a brave heart. Anne gave Diana great comfort; by the time they were beneath the orchard boughs, with the moon and stars shining diamond-bright above, Diana had stopped her crying. And when she re-entered the Orchard Slope kitchen, she was calm and steady, fully prepared to tend to Minnie May with all her might and mean.

Minnie May lay on the sofa, near the stove, covered by a pair of afghan quilts which Mary Joe had retrieved from one of the bedrooms. The little girl's breathing was loud and hoarse. She sounded on the verge of death, but Diana looked to Anne and saw no fear of death in her face—only business-like practicality.

"She has the croup, all right," Anne said. "She's pretty bad, but I've seen worse."

Anne set right to work, directing the formerly unflappable Mary Joe (now entirely beside herself with helpless terror) to stoke up the fire in the stove and to boil a kettle of water for the steam. Then she and Diana undressed the unprotesting Minnie May and carried her to the nearest bed, which belonged to Mr. and Mrs. Barry. Anne's demeanor was one of brooking no nonsense, either from Minnie May or from Mary Joe. She marshalled and directed her ragtag legion with all the confidence of a general.

"Why, she's wonderful," Diana thought as Anne firmly persuaded Minnie May to swallow yet another spoonful of the hated ipecac. "Why did I ever snub her? And all over a boy!"

What did boys matter, after all, Diana wondered as she watched Anne care for Minnie May. There were certainly more important things in this world. Diana was determined to focus on what truly mattered from that moment on.

Their struggle with Minnie May stretched on for hours. Anne administered the ipecac every quarter of an hour, and the poor little creature who moaned and shivered beneath the blankets often retched miserably into the flannel cloths Diana held up to her chin... but the phlegm in her chest remained stubbornly in place. As the hours stretched on, Minnie May's breathing grew ever more terrible to hear, rasping and grating and often seizing her with coughing fits that left her so weak and breathless she couldn't even hold up her head.

"She's getting worse," Diana murmured once, clutching Anne's hand in a tight, fearful grip.

But Anne smiled at Diana with perfect placidity. "Don't fret, Diana. I've seen this all before. Now, Mary Joe, bring us that kettle. It's time for another steam treatment."

Diana propped Minnie May up and held her over the billowing steam while Mary Joe, mittened with thick pads of wool, proffered the boiling kettle with her stout, strong, farm-girl arms. Anne fanned the steam into Minnie May's face until it had all died away. She glanced at the clock on the Barrys' dressing table. Diana followed her gaze, and realized to her astonishment that it was nearly three o'clock in the morning. Neither Matthew nor the doctor had appeared. Diana, Anne, and Mary Joe had been at it all through the night, yet Minnie May was no closer to relief... and each spasm of coughing seemed to drain more of her life away.

"Anne," Diana whispered fearfully.

"Give me the ipecac bottle, Di," Anne said, stoic and calm.

"It's nearly empty, Anne. There isn't more than a spoonful left."

"And down her throat it will go."

Anne made good on her word. When the last of the ipecac was gone, she sat back on her bedside stool with a long, drawn-out sigh. Diana could see how weary Anne was; hollows hung below her gray eyes and her lips were pale as she pressed them together. "She's as worried as I am," Diana realized, "but she hates to show it."

Suddenly, Minnie May lurched up with a surge of her fading strength. She gave one loud, desperate choke, and then Anne was on her feet, sweeping Minnie May out across the bed so that she hung chest-down.

"The cloths, Diana," Anne directed.

Diana placed the last of their flannel cloths below Minnie May's face. The little girl heaved and sputtered and with one tremendous cough she spat out an impossibly large ball of phlegm.

Diana stared at Anne in wonder and delight. Anne eased Minnie May back onto the pillows and pulled the covers up to her chin. The little darling fell asleep almost at once, wrung out by her terrible ordeal... but her breathing was peaceful and clear.

Anne found a kerchief in the night-stand and gently brushed

beads of sweat from Minnie May's brow. "She'll be all right now, I dare say."

"Anne! Anne, you were wonderful!" Diana caught her friend in a tight embrace, weeping with exhaustion and relief against Anne's shoulder.

"And so were you, dearest Di. You were so brave... just like a heroine from one of Charlotte Morgan's stories!"

"I wouldn't have been so brave without you beside me," Diana said shyly.

Heavy bootsteps sounded on the porch. A moment later the front door opened and the girls heard men's voices coming down the hall.

"The doctor," Anne said, as Diana bundled up the soiled cloths.

The man who strode in beside Matthew Cuthbert was no one Diana recognized.

"I'm Doctor White, from Spencervale," he said to the girls, though he never took his eyes off of Minnie May.

"I... I had to go clear to Spencervale to find him," Matthew muttered, shy as ever. "The rest had all gone down to see the Premier."

"You were wonderful, Matthew," Diana said warmly, which only made Matthew blush and look away. "What a good neighbor you are, to drive all night for my baby sister!"

Dr. White had retrieved a long, trumpet-like device from his bag. He placed its bell over the sleeping girl's chest and set his ear against the opposite end. After a few moments he straightened and smiled encouragingly at Diana and Anne. "Her breathing is quite clear now. She's over the worst of it, and should sleep soundly for many hours. There is little for me to do here, except to leave you with some medicine in case she relapses. Tell me, girls: How did you do it?"

Diana stepped back and allowed Anne to explain—and certainly Anne had no lack of words. She told of the ipecac and the steam, and even admitted that at the very last, she had lost all hope. But then Minnie May turned the corner. "You must just imagine my relief, Doctor," Anne said, "because I can't express it in words. You know there are some things that cannot be expressed in words."

Matthew laid his hand gently on Anne's shoulder. She took his unspoken cue, turning to look up at him with an acquiescent nod.

"I must go now," she said to Diana and the doctor. "It has been a terribly long night, hasn't it? My nice, warm bed is calling to me!"

Diana left Minnie May to the doctor and followed Anne and Matthew out onto the front porch. Anne paused, gazing at Diana with full, grateful eyes as Matthew pulled the sleigh nearer.

"Anne, how can I ever thank you?"

"Why, there's no thanks needed, silly Diana. You know I would do anything for you."

Diana wrapped Anne in a long embrace. "We'll be friends forever," Diana vowed, "and nothing will ever come between us again. Nothing! Not even my mother. Not even Gilbert."

Anne stepped back from the embrace, eyeing Diana with a glint of amusement. "Why did you say *that*, of all things?" But there was something else in Anne's look besides amusement... something sharp and suspicious, but so fleeting that Diana wasn't entirely certain she'd seen it at all.

Diana laughed lightly. "It's been such a long, tiring night. I don't even know what I *did* say, dear Cordelia Fitzgerald, also known as Anne."

"We'll be friends again, won't we?" Anne asked soberly, her eyes lit with longing. "You'll write to me again?"

"Every day," Diana promised. And she meant it.

MRS. BARRY MAKES AMENDS

Diana slept so soundly that even the loud morning trills of the robins, perched in the apple tree just outside her window, couldn't wake her. Nor could the bright, forcefully white light of a sun-soaked winter morning. Consumed by exhaustion, she slept nearly till the afternoon, and only wakened when her stomach, unbreakfasted and surly, rumbled her into action. She lay quietly under her covers for a long time despite her hunger, listening to the gleeful twittering of the birds, who rejoiced in the clear skies and the warmth of the fleeting winter sun. The late-morning light made Diana's lace curtains glow like beams of glory. It was such a pretty morning, such a cheerful day... and all the more because Minnie May was safe, and Anne and Diana were unquestionably good friends again.

Gradually, Diana became aware of another sound, growing louder and louder until the birdsong could no longer mask it. It was the crunch and clop of a horse's hooves in the hard snow, and the hiss of a sleigh's runners. She rolled out of her bed and peeked through the curtains to the yard below. Dr. White had returned, driving his remarkably smart sleigh, pulled by a big black horse, all the way from Spencervale. No doubt he had come to check on Minnie May's progress.

Diana was eager to hear what he had to say, but there was not enough time to dress and neaten up her hair, which looked like a rat's nest after her long sleep. She could listen from the top of the stairs, though, without being seen... and that was exactly what she did, creeping in her stocking feet down as far as the first landing, where she knew she would not be seen from the rooms below.

Mrs. Barry gave Dr. White an effusive welcome. Diana, satisfied that Minnie May was past the point of danger, had gone up to bed before her parents returned from Charlottetown, but she supposed Mary Joe had informed them of the long, terrible night and of the part Anne Shirley had played. Diana leaned as far as she dared over the rail to listen.

"Please, Dr. White, sit down," Mrs. Barry said from the parlor.

"How has your littlest girl fared through the night?" the doctor said.

"Very well. Her breathing sounds fine, just fine. Oh, Doctor, I am such a fool. The French girl tried to warn me that Minnie May had the croup, but I didn't believe it."

"Now, now, Mrs. Barry. You mustn't blame yourself. These attacks can come on quite suddenly."

"But oh, I never should have gone off and left my children with one of them so sick! I'm only grateful that Diana had the presence of mind to run to the Cuthberts' for help."

There was a pause, and then Dr. White said wonderingly, "That little redheaded girl they have over at the Cuthberts' is as smart as they make 'em. I tell you she saved that baby's life, for it would have been too late by the time I got here."

Silence again. Mrs. Barry seemed to be digesting the doctor's words. Finally, in a subdued tone, she invited the doctor into the room where Minnie May slept so that he might examine her.

The doctor's visit was brief, for Minnie May really had made an astonishing recovery. Her color was good, her breathing easy, and she slept like one who is determined to wake up fully refreshed and renewed. When Dr. White had driven away, Mr. Barry joined his wife in the parlor.

"What a terrible lout I've been, George," Mrs. Barry said, so quiet with regret that Diana could hardly catch her words.

"Now, Rebecca..."

"It's true. Oh, I was too hard on that child... little Anne. I suspected her of mischief simply because she is an orphan. Didn't the Lord say to love the little children, and to help those who are less fortunate than we? I must forgive Anne Shirley... and apologize, too... ask her forgiveness in turn. It's the right thing to do. Oh, why was I ever so hard on her?"

"Perhaps," Father said cautiously, "you have been rather hard on Diana, too."

Diana stiffened in surprise at those words, and listened all the more keenly.

"It wouldn't go amiss to be softer with Diana," Mr. Barry went on. "She's a good girl, Rebecca... obedient, most of the time, and bright and kind-hearted. She doesn't need such a watchful eye, nor such rigid shepherding. Some girls do, but not our Di."

"She is a good girl," Mrs. Barry agreed with a faint laugh that sounded rather bitter. "But so was I when I was her age... or close to her age, a little older... and yet my goodness didn't save me from nearly having my reputation ruined."

"Ruined?" Mr. Barry said, startled. "Come now. That can't be true."

"It is true. I was too full of imagination and romance in those days, too apt to chase after adventure instead of pursuing more suitable things, more ladylike and sedate things. I was properly wild, George! I didn't realize it at the time, but looking back now —now that I am a mother with two daughters to care for—now I can see that I *was* wild."

Diana bit her lip. It was flatly impossible to imagine the staid, proper Mrs. Barry in any conceivable posture of wildness.

"I had imaginative, pert friends like Anne Shirley, oh yes, and they led me into adventures I was better left out of. It wasn't long before I was known as... well, before I was thought most definitely *not* a lady, and soon everyone had decided it was quite impossible for me ever to become one. I was lucky to make a match with you... and then only because you didn't know anything about my reputation."

"Why, you're the very best woman I know," Father said, disbelieving.

"With you, I had a chance to transcend the stories that were told about me, to make myself anew," Mother said with an unexpected note of warmth in her voice. "Oh, George, I don't want Diana to go through the same. I want her to make a good match and have a happy, proper life. She is precious to me. My firstborn. I would do anything to ensure her life is one of joy and respect and ease. I would even be so strict with her that I make her hate me, if I must. Her future and her happiness mean that much to me."

Diana leaned against the wall, her heart fluttering with a strange new emotion. She had never realized before that her mother loved her so much. Truthfully, she had always thought her mother somewhat incapable of love... all prickles on the outside with nothing warm in the center. "Why, I almost feel as if I could forgive all her sternness, knowing where it comes from. I almost feel as if I ought to really try and live up to her high expectations." Almost.

There was a faint creak as Mrs. Barry stood resolutely from the parlor sofa. "I must get my hat and coat. It's time I went down to Green Gables and apologized to that little red-haired waif. I've been miserably cruel to her, but she saved my baby's life, and I owe her friendship and understanding from now on."

"Do you want me to come with you?" Mr. Barry asked.

"No," Mrs. Barry said decisively. "This is a task I must do alone."

~

As it happened, Anne was still sound asleep when Mrs. Barry presented herself contritely at Green Gables. Marilla wouldn't wake her, fearful that exhaustion from the long night would sicken the girl. But Mrs. Barry did humble herself in an eminently satisfactory way before Marilla and Matthew.

"Please tell Anne when she is awake that we would be honored to have her up for supper," Mrs. Barry said to Anne's sober, gray guardians.

And accordingly, once Anne had risen from bed and seen to some of her chores, she was given the news that she was to be the guest of honor at the Barrys' for supper. Diana was out in her garden in red cap and long scarf, watching eagerly as Anne came flying across the fields like a bird freed from a snare. The two girls caught each other in a long hug, and whirled together among the drifted flower beds like two snowflakes borne aloft on a happy wind.

When Diana led Anne into the house, Mrs. Barry was there to greet her, wringing her hands anxiously.

"Anne, I treated you terribly, and I am sorry for it," Mrs. Barry said earnestly. To Diana's shock, tears flooded her mother's eyes. She continued in a quavering voice, "I can never repay you for the kindness you did this family. Minnie May is alive because of you. Will you please forgive me, Anne?"

Anne's face turned as red as her braids. But she said calmly, "I have no hard feelings for you, Mrs. Barry. I assure you once and for all that I did not mean to intoxicate Diana. Henceforth I shall cover the past with the mantle of oblivion."

Diana shot a swift look of warning at her father, who covered his mouth—and his startled smile—at Anne's lofty words.

But Mrs. Barry didn't mind Anne's over-dignified speech. She bent and kissed Anne on her freckled cheek, leaving a grateful tear behind.

THE WINTER CONCERT

FEBRUARY SAW THE ORCHARD HUNG ALL ABOUT WITH DELICATE fringes of icicles, which charmed and sparkled from every branch and twig. Barry's Pond—or the Lake of Shining Waters, as Anne still insisted it be called—had thawed at its dark center and then re-frozen when a cold snap blew in across the Gulf waters. Now the pond's surface was a powdery white, with here and there great circles of the deepest blue-green to show where the ice had rotted. Winter was having her last hurrah, displaying all the crystalline beauty of her many diamond facets before springtime returned in earnest, with its flush of new, green growth and its gradual warming of the days.

Diana was pleased that winter still held on for yet a while longer, for it was her twelfth birthday, and she was to celebrate in high style. The Debating Club was hosting a concert and recital at the meeting hall, and various Barry relations were coming over from Newbridge for the occasion. Thanks to the fresh fall of snow and the convenient re-freezing of Avonlea and its surrounds, the Newbridge folks were to arrive in their biggest and finest pung sleigh. Diana couldn't think of a jollier way to spend one's birthday than on a sleigh ride.

Of course, her birthday was not such a spectacular occasion that it warranted her cousins' attendance, but the concert was rumored to be the most exciting show of the season: Singers and elocutionists from all across the island were to put on the best material from their repertoires. Happily, the date coincided with Diana's birthday, and so she was able to pretend that the whole affair was entirely in her honor. Her secret fantasy added to the sweetness of anticipation as she and Anne prepared.

After much careful negotiation with Marilla, Anne had won permission to come home from school with Diana that Friday. The two girls had spent the whole afternoon before Diana's mirror, trying on every one of Diana's prettiest dresses and fixing their hair in every conceivable style, breaking only to have their tea, which they ate as quickly as Mrs. Barry would allow. Then back up the stairs they dashed to finalize the all-important decisions of dress and hairstyles.

Diana fixed the front of Anne's hair up in a high, red-golden pompadour. She would have liked to do all of Anne's hair that way, for the fashion really would have shown off her slender neck to perfection, but everyone would think it ridiculous on a girl who hadn't yet turned seventeen, and Mrs. Barry would never let them out of the house so overly made-up, besides. Instead she fashioned a smart little pull-back that left Anne's loose red waves tumbling down across the backs of her shoulders.

"That really does look becoming on you," Diana said, pulling Anne close so they could both examine themselves in the mirror.

"I'm not sure any style can make red hair look becoming."

"Nonsense," Diana laughed. "Why, there are plenty of people who think red hair is pretty. One day it'll come back in fashion, and then you'll be the envy of every girl in Canada."

"Which dress should I wear?" Anne said, turning away from the mirror. Her red hair really did vex her, for reasons Diana simply couldn't understand. Anne and Diana were both wearing nothing but their shifts and stockings, for neither could settle on a dress.

"Wear this white," Diana said, pulling one of her dresses from the pile on the bed. "It really does look best on you. It'll make such an impression with the snow all around, and the moon will be shining by the time we get to the hall, so you'll positively glow, like something ethereal."

Anne's eyes shone at the thought. "I would dearly love to be thought 'ethereal,' Diana."

"But the waist is too big on you," Diana said a little sadly as Anne pulled the dress on over her shift. "I'm going to keep getting fatter and fatter until I burst; I just know it. I'll be as roly-poly as my mother someday."

"Your mother is a very handsome lady," Anne replied, "and you are the prettiest girl on the island, with your perfect black curls and your dimples. You don't know how I long for dimples, Diana! Besides, I've seen how the boys look at you when you aren't looking at them. When we're finally old enough to go to dances, your card will always be full."

"Well... I'll get you a sash, anyway. That will keep the waist in."

Diana had a marvelous collection of sashes. She settled on one of a smoky, grayish lavender shade to cinch about Anne's waist. "See how nice it looks with your eyes," she said as she tied it in a great, fluffy bow behind Anne's back.

"You have a real eye for pretty things," Anne said appreciatively. "It's a talent with you, Diana. Just look at my hair and my dress! I've never looked so nice or so grown-up in all my life."

Diana did look at Anne, accordingly. They had known each other for almost a year, and in that time Anne had only grown prettier. With her critical, evaluating eye, Diana could clearly see the splendid woman her friend would someday become— willowy, graceful, with a face fashioned on classically beautiful lines. While she, Diana, looked into her own future and saw nothing but a plain, round dumpling. She was fearfully tempted to be jealous over Anne's good looks, but with an effort she stamped those feelings under her heel. She chose instead to be glad of the compliment Anne had paid her. Diana *was* good with clothes and hair—and other pretty things, too, like flower arranging and icing cakes. "I ought to be glad of the good things in my nature," she thought resolutely, "and not pity myself for the things I lack." After all, everyone lacks something. Even those who seem the most fortunate may nurse deep and secret wounds.

Diana turned the subject as she dressed in her own outfit of cranberry red with a creamy white sash. She spoke happily of the excitement in school that day, for almost every scholar would attend the concert to watch older brothers and sisters recite. The children had talked of nothing else all day long. Some had even made bets as to who would recite which poems, and who would stumble over the more difficult words.

"I heard that Mr. Phillips is going to give a recitation," Diana said, tying her sash as snugly as she could to emphasize what little waist she still possessed. "I suppose it will be some awful love poem he picked out just for Prissy. Did you *ever*? And everyone knows Prissy is going to do 'Curfew Must Not Ring Tonight,' and I expect it'll be ever so good. I may not think much of Prissy, but she is very good at concerts. And then I heard Gil—"

Anne cut her off by dashing to the window. The panes were frosted with delicate stars of ice, but they did not prevent Anne from seeing the magnificent, six-seat pung sleigh as it swept up the hill and into the yard below. "Oh, Diana! Your cousins are here. I've never ridden in a sleigh before... well, except for Matthew's old one, but it hardly counts because it's just a farm sleigh and there is nothing fancy about it. I'm so nervous!"

"There's nothing to be nervous about, you dear, silly thing!"

"I don't feel grand enough to deserve such an honor." Anne did seem honestly vexed by the sudden confrontation of the sleigh. Her face was as pale as her white-wool dress, and she had the tinge of greenish-blue about her mouth that always meant she was harrowed up inside.

Diana linked her arm through Anne's. "Come on, you goose. I'll be with you the whole time. And you look real nice, Anne. Nobody will think you don't belong."

Downstairs, the girls dressed in their coats and hats, accepted a kiss on the cheek each from Mrs. Barry, and then headed outside to greet the cousins from Newbridge. They were a merry group, though all of them were older than Diana and Anne. Still, they made the young girls feel welcome and made ample room for them in the sleigh.

Diana and Anne bundled up warmly in fur robes, and then Cousin Jeremy, who was driving, cracked his whip in the air. The horse was fresh and eager, despite having come all the way from Newbridge; when the sleigh reached the flat, smooth, open road, the whip cracked again and the horse sprang into a flying trot. The sleigh skimmed over the snow as easily as a fish through water. The Avonlea Road climbed the easy slope of the northern hills and the gulf was revealed below, a deep curve of brilliant blue just beginning to reflect a fiery sunset. Snow-covered hills warmed with the blush of the sinking sun, and the air was full of the rhythmic, dancing chimes of the sleigh bells. It was one of the prettiest evenings Diana had ever beheld... and was all the more special because it was her birthday, and her dearest friend was by her side.

In time, they arrived at the hall. The girls all clambered out while Cousin Jeremy took the sleigh away to tend to his frisky horse. Anne gasped and clutched Diana's hand at sight of the hall —and what a lovely sight it was. A walkway had been cleared through the snow, down which ladies and gentlemen drifted arm in arm, neat in their winter coats with frosty breath rising in clouds all around them. The walk was lined with paper luminarias, glowing softly in shades of pink, orange, and blue, casting their small spheres of fairy-light on the gentle breast of the snow.

The girls found seats as close as they could get to the podium where their peers and neighbors would perform. At last the show began, and truly the island's residents had saved their finest recitations for this night. Every poem and song, every Shakespearean monologue, was as grand and moving as one could hope to see in the finest concert halls of the mainland. Each piece seemed the height of all thrills, until the next performer proved himself or herself just as adept as the one who had gone before.

When Mr. Phillips finished his rendition of Mark Antony's great speech—not the love poem Diana had predicted—Diana and Anne peeked at their shared program to see who would be next to mount the stage.

"Gilbert Blythe is next," Diana said. "I don't know he's going to recite."

Anne sniffed loudly. She turned to Rhoda Murray, seated beside her, and indicated the little book of recipes that lay at Rhoda's feet. "May I?" she asked sweetly. Rhoda gave Anne a queer look, but nodded. Anne lifted the book up in front of her face so she could not see the podium.

"Oh, honestly, Anne," Diana said in exasperation.

"There's no use talking me out of it," Anne muttered, so only Diana could hear. "I won't even *look* at that person, as you well know. It's bad enough that I shall have to hear his hateful voice. Now please, Diana, leave me to the comfort of oblivion."

Gilbert took the stage with a confident, almost jaunty step. He looked exceedingly smart, in new wool trousers and suspenders with shiny clips. His dark, curly hair was oiled and combed in a way Diana had never seen it before. Its arcing wave over his brow seemed to accentuate the twinkle in his laughing, hazel eyes and the slow, easy curve of his smile. Despite her firm decision not to have her good sense muddled up by a boy ever again, Diana's heart skipped several beats as he struck his recitation pose and began to speak in a clear, carrying, terribly moving voice.

He gave "Bingen on the Rhine," a poem which Diana had

always found wrenching in the best possible way. But she had never heard it delivered quite like this before. She had seen Gilbert recite a few times, and of course she'd heard him read aloud in class, but she had never before seen him *like this*. He seemed to pour every last drop of his soul into the poem, baring a vulnerability that Diana found oddly attractive.

And if a comrade seek her love

Gilbert said, with grand sweeping gestures toward his own heart,

I ask her in my name,

To listen to him kindly, without regret or shame,

And to hang the old sword in its place (my father's sword and mine),

For the honor of old Bingen—dear Bingen on the Rhine.

Gilbert hesitated in the rhythm of his poem, a pause just long enough that everyone in the hall sat suddenly forward on their seats, waiting. Everyone save for one audience member, who was still engrossed in the recipe book.

There's another—not a sister,

Gilbert went on. And he looked straight at Anne—or rather, at the spine of the recipe book, which was all he could see of Anne from the stage.

In the happy days gone by,

You'd have known her by the merriment that sparkled in her eye...

Poor Gilbert got no reaction whatsoever from Anne, but when he finished the poem and struck his final pose, the hall erupted in applause and cheers. Diana clapped loudly enough that she might as well have been applauding for herself and Anne at the same time.

~

IT WAS ELEVEN by the time the girls came home, creeping in on tip-toes so as not to wake the whole house. But they whispered excitedly as they went down the darkened hall of Orchard Slope to the parlor. Anne was to stay the night as a special birthday treat for Diana, and that meant they were to have the use of the spare room, which had a bed large enough for two. Anne was nearly as thrilled and intimidated over the spare room as she had been over the sleigh.

Embers still glowed in the parlor hearth; the room was furrily warm and perfectly cozy. At one end of the parlor, the door to the spare room stood open and ready to receive them.

"Let's not go up to my room to undress," Diana said. "Let's just do it here, and sleep in our shifts. We can put our dresses here on the sofa. It's so cold on the stairway at night, but it's just perfectly warm and pleasant here in the parlor."

"Hasn't it been a delightful time?" Anne whispered. "It must be splendid to get up there and recite. Do you think we will ever be asked to do it?"

"Certainly, someday. They're always wanting the older scholars to recite. I guess it reflects well on the school and proves we're learning something worthwhile. Gilbert Blythe recites a lot, and he's only two years older than us."

At mention of that name, Anne turned sharply away, folding her thin arms across the front of her shift.

"Oh, Anne," Diana pleaded in a strained whisper, "how could you pretend not to listen to him? When he came to the line, 'There's another, not a sister,' he looked right down at you."

Anne shook her head with weary resolve. "Diana, you are my

bosom friend, but I cannot allow even you to speak to me of that person." Suddenly she brightened. "Are you ready for bed?"

Diana nodded.

"Good. Let's run a race and see who'll get to the bed first."

Diana counted down from three and the girls were off, running down the length of the parlor, bursting through the spare-room door at the same instant, and flinging themselves onto the bed.

Diana knew at once that something was terribly wrong. Instead of the softness of the feather mattress, she landed full force on a long, hard, positively *bony* object—an object which gave a startled cry and then sat up beneath the quilts.

"Merciful goodness!" came the distinctive voice, half grating, half shrill.

Even in the dark of the unlit spare room, Diana knew exactly who it was. Only one person in Diana's world sounded that way: Aunt Josephine.

ANNE TAMES AUNT JOSEPHINE

A<small>UNT</small> J<small>OSEPHINE</small> <small>DID NOT APPEAR AT BREAKFAST THE NEXT</small> morning, preferring to remain stiffly sequestered in the spare room—this time with the door firmly closed. Anne scampered back over the snowy fields to Green Gables, and Diana was left alone with the little knot of mischief and anxiety in her stomach.

The old lady did not emerge from her den until late in the morning, whereupon she complained loudly of the poor sleep she'd had and then gestured to her bags—all of them packed, though the Barrys had expected her to stay for a month at least.

"But we were so looking forward to your visit," Mrs. Barry said, trying to soothe the old lady's temper.

"I won't stay another day. I'm going right back to town tomorrow, even if it is the Sabbath. I'd leave today, this very minute, except George must take the buggy to Carmody and by the time he's back it will be too late to catch the train to Charlottetown. Too late, I tell you!"

"But whatever is the matter?" Mrs. Barry said, honestly perplexed.

Aunt Josephine's dark, peevish eye fell sharply on Diana, who stood with her head ducked, shuffling her feet just behind her mother. "You'd better ask that daughter of yours."

"Diana?" Mrs. Barry turned to Diana with a clear note of warning in her voice.

"We... that is, I..." She took a deep breath, then let it all out in one contrite rush. "I jumped on the spare-room bed last night while she was sleeping in it. Oh, Aunt Josephine, I didn't mean to! I didn't know you were there. I thought you weren't to come until Monday, so I didn't expect you to be lying in the bed when we jumped on it. Honest, I never would have done it if I knew you were asleep in the bed!"

"Well!" Mrs. Barry exclaimed, her face going pale. "This is shocking, Diana. *Shocking.* How many times have I admonished you to behave like a lady?"

"Like a lady?" Aunt Josephine gave a rough snort, which, it must be said, was not particularly ladylike. "This child of yours is a regular tomboy, Rebecca Barry."

Both Diana and her mother blushed at that accusation.

"I was going to offer to pay for her music lessons," Aunt Josephine went on, rather acidly, "but rest assured, I shan't waste the funds on a little hellion. She needs proper bringing up before she's ready for any kind of refinement. I'm afraid she's simply not there yet. Perhaps in three or four more years..." she added in a dark, trailing way that suggested she really entertained no hope for Diana's refinement.

Mrs. Barry rounded on Diana, thrust her hand through the latter's black curls, and gave her ear a sound pinch. Diana bit back a squeal of pain and surprise.

"This really is the limit, Diana, the very limit! March up to your bedroom and do not come out again until suppertime."

"But I didn't mean it," Diana pleaded in vain. "I'm ever so sorry, Aunt Josephine!"

"I said, march!"

Diana did ascend to her bedroom, and considered giving the

door a satisfying slam behind her. But she checked herself in time. Slamming doors was unladylike, after all; it wouldn't help her case and would only set Aunt Josephine and her mother more firmly against her. Through the floor boards she could hear the back-and-forth murmur of her mother and her great-aunt in urgent conversation, but she could make out not words. Throwing up her hands in despair, Diana fell face-first across her bed and lay there, fuming into her pillow.

"Oh, why do I have to be a lady all the time?" she wondered helplessly. "Won't it ever be enough to just be *me*? It seems I must always put on a show for somebody or other... must always pretend to be someone I'm not."

In the afternoon, Diana was summoned down from her confinement, but not to appease Aunt Josephine. That affronted lady was holed up once more in the spare bedroom. Instead, Diana was set to her most hated of all tasks: peeling potatoes. Her mother worked over the stove in frosty silence, and Diana did her best to work efficiently so that she would draw no more of her family's ire. But she felt terribly rebellious over the whole affair, and often cast her mother narrow-eyed glares when she was sure Mrs. Barry wasn't looking.

When the last of the potatoes was peeled and soaking in a cool bath, Diana rose from her work stool and picked up her pail. "I'll just go throw the peels to the pigs," she said, and stepped out the kitchen door.

To Diana's surprise, there was Anne in the garden, making her way toward the farmhouse. Diana hooked her arm hurriedly through Anne's and pulled her along to the pigpen before Mrs. Barry could see.

"I've just been to see Mrs. Lynde," Anne said. "Your mother

spoke to her earlier today, and oh, Diana, your Aunt Josephine is very cross, isn't she?"

"Yes," Diana said with a little laugh. She flung the slops over the fence and glanced uneasily at the house. The spare room window looked out over this section of the farm, and Diana was afraid Aunt Josephine might even now be peering out through the curtains at her, dark-faced with malice. "She was fairly dancing with rage. Oh, how she scolded! She all but said I was the worst-behaved girl she ever saw and that Mother and Father ought to be ashamed of the way they brought me up. She says she won't stay, and I'm sure I don't care. But Father and Mother do... Mother especially." Aunt Josephine's fortune was important to Mrs. Barry. It represented the kind of life she might have had for herself, if she had only married better.

Anne gazed at Diana in bewilderment. "Why didn't you tell them it was my fault?"

"It's likely I'd do such a thing, isn't it? I'm no telltale, Anne Shirley. And anyhow, I'm just as much to blame as you."

Anne started toward the kitchen door. "I'm going in to tell her myself."

"You'd never! Why, she'll eat you alive!"

Anne turned to look at Diana over her shoulder, and Diana could see that she was shivering a little. But she never stopped walking. "Don't frighten me any more than I am frightened. I'd rather walk up to a cannon's mouth. But it was my fault, and I've got to confess. Fortunately I have had practice at confessing."

Diana followed Anne inside—Mrs. Barry had gone off to another room, so she wasn't there to see the two girls slinking through the house—and went with her as far as the sitting-room door.

"This is where I leave you," Diana whispered ominously. She pressed herself against the paneled wall while Anne knocked timidly on the door.

Aunt Josephine admitted Anne with a sharp command.

Diana listened breathlessly while Anne introduced herself in rather weak and shivery tones, then claimed it was she who'd had the idea of jumping on the spare-room bed. That was true, but Diana knew she herself was fully complicit, and she felt more than a little guilty at allowing Anne to face the heat of Aunt Josephine's ire.

"Diana is a very ladylike girl, Miss Barry," Anne said with firming confidence. "So you must see how unjust it is to blame her."

"Oh, I must, hey?"

Diana blinked in astonishment. Was that a hint of amusement she detected in the old lady's voice?

"I rather think Diana did her share of the jumping, at least," Josephine went on. "Such carryings on in a respectable house!"

Anne continued to plead her case in ever more moving tones.

"I don't think it is any excuse for you, that you were just in fun," Josephine insisted. "Little girls never indulged in that kind of fun when I was young."

Diana stifled a giggle at that. The idea of Aunt Josephine as a young girl was just too much.

"You don't know what it is to be awakened out of a sound sleep, after a long and arduous journey, by two great girls coming bounce down on you."

"I don't *know*," Anne said at once, "but I can *imagine*. Have you any imagination, Miss Barry?"

At this, Diana gasped nearly loud enough to be heard inside the spare room. It was an audacious thing to say to the grand and dignified old lady. Diana fully expected Aunt Josephine to unleash her fury.

"If you have," Anne said, "just put yourself in our place. We didn't know there was anybody in that bed. You nearly scared us to death. And then we couldn't sleep in the spare room after being promised. I suppose you are used to sleeping in spare rooms, but just imagine what you would feel like if you were an orphan girl who had never had such an honor."

Diana shook her head, caught somewhere between wonder and fear. Any moment now, Aunt Josephine's temper would burst.

But then the queerest thing happened. Diana heard a sound she'd never heard before—a low, gravelly, grudging sound, that somehow had the bubble of merriment in it. Astonished, she realized that Aunt Josephine was *laughing*. The next moment, she implored Anne to sit down for a friendly chat. "Can that be the same Aunt Josephine I've always known?" Diana wondered, feeling rather faint and disoriented.

"I am very sorry I can't stay to talk," Anne said. "I would like to, because you seem like an interesting lady, and you might even be a kindred spirit, although you don't look very much like it."

Again the rough laughter sounded from the spare room.

Anne hurriedly told of Marilla and Matthew, and explained her duties to those two good souls. She had already been away from Green Gables for too long. "But before I go," Anne added, "I do wish you would tell me if you will forgive Diana and stay just as long as you meant to in Avonlea."

"I think perhaps I will, if you will come over and talk to me occasionally," Aunt Josephine said.

DIANA SAW ANNE OFF, with many exclamations of astonishment. "You've done what no one else ever has," she said to her glowing friend. "I never saw the beat of you, Anne Shirley."

Then she took up her egg basket and went out to the coop to collect the day's newly laid eggs. The sun was sinking warm and golden over snow-frosted firs; long shadows stretched blue and silver along the curve of the hill and pooled around the feet of the old white farmhouse.

Diana looked up from her task and then straightened in surprise. Aunt Josephine was coming toward her over the snowy yard, just as blue and silver herself as were the long fir shadows. She was wrapped in a long coat of dark, warm seal, and a matching hat covered her silvery-white hair bun. The cold had raised a tint of color to her sallow, wrinkled cheeks—enough color that for a moment Diana thought she could actually picture what Aunt Josephine must have looked like as a girl of twelve.

"Well, it has been quite a visit already," the old lady said.

Diana lowered her face. "I *am* awfully sorry, Aunt Josephine. I never intended to be so wild."

"No, I dare say you didn't." Her thin, old face warmed with an unexpected smile. Diana couldn't help but smile back; Aunt Josephine had a remarkably friendly smile, on the very rare occasions she chose to use it. "That little redheaded friend of yours is something new under the sun."

Diana could think of no response but half-nervous laughter.

"I believe I was too hard on you, child, and I said things I regret."

Diana looked up suddenly at her great-aunt, wide-eyed and startled.

"I know I don't look it, but I was a girl once, just like you. I do still remember how hard it can be."

"How hard what can be?"

"Why, being a girl, of course. So many... expectations." Aunt Josephine sighed. "So many people to please... your parents, your teachers, your friends. And suitors, later, when you're older. Oh, I know I'm an old maid, but I did have my share of suitors in my time. Everyone thinks girls are all lace and frills and sweet smiles. And believe me, the expectations don't change when you grow to womanhood. If anything, they only grow heavier and harsher.

"But we are more than that, Diana, though the world will never allow you to see it. *You* are more than that." She reached out a hand and laid it gently on Diana's shoulder. "There is a good spirit inside you; I can see it. And it's a hard row to hoe, to find that balance between making others happy and remaining true."

"True?" Diana said softly.

"True to yourself... to the person you are inside. To the real girl within you, who hides herself—for the sake of others, for the sake of all those expectations—beneath the pink ruffles and the perfect manners and the charming smile."

Aunt Josephine reached into the sleeve of her seal coat, and a moment later she pulled a silver charm bracelet from her own wrist. She held it out to Diana, who took it in trembling fingers. Its shining links held tiny bangles of hearts and stars. It was such a sweetly girlish thing that Diana could hardly credit that stoic, stern old Aunt Josephine had worn it.

"You keep this, girl," the old lady said gruffly. "Wear it and remember what I told you today: That you are *more*, no matter what the world tries to tell you. You'll do that, won't you?"

Diana looked up at her great-aunt with shining, grateful eyes. There was such warmth—and such conspiratorial mischief—beaming from the old lady's face that Diana wondered how she'd ever found her intimidating before. "I will, Aunt Josephine. Thank you."

They carried the basket of eggs back to the house together.

THE DANGERS OF IMAGINATION

"I THINK," DIANA SAID THOUGHTFULLY AS SHE AND ANNE WALKED together along the line of the brook, "that my ideal husband would have dark hair, with at least a little curliness to it."

Anne nodded in sober agreement. "I never can take a blond fellow seriously. They always look to me as if they wanted to laugh all the time. I suppose some girls might like a husband who laughs a lot, but I could never lose my heart to anyone who didn't brood at least some of the time."

Each girl held a basket over her arm, in which they were gathering the last round, carmine-red rosehips that had survived the winter. Marilla wanted the hard, shiny berries for her medicinal teas, and Anne and Diana had been only too glad to venture out to collect them, for the long, cold winter had at last given way to spring. The spikes of narcissi were pushing up from damp earth; dew watered the ferns in Violet Vale, renewing them to a vigorous green. All along the Avonlea Road, the new warmth in the air coaxed pearlescent mists from thickets and dells. The dry, brown carpet that had covered the fields since the end of the harvest was rolling back to reveal a new, plush blanket of grass. Choirs of birds filled the sky with constant song, and everywhere drifted the intoxicating perfume of flowers just beginning to bloom.

Perhaps it was the newness of the season, and the promise it made of a precious future, that caused the girls to turn their thoughts so seriously toward the kind of gentlemen they hoped to marry. They had agreed, as they set out together to collect the rosehips, that the morning should be given over to a rumination on each girl's "romantic ideal." Of course, they were only twelve years old, and marriage was a long way off. But on a day that overflowed with hints and glimpses of what was to come, it seemed an entirely prudent, even necessary, topic for discussion.

"No good hero in our favorite books ever laughs too much," Diana said.

"Only with tragic bitterness. That seems like the only kind of laughing a man ought to do." Anne paused a moment, considering what she'd just said. "Well," she amended as she plucked a few more rosehips from the wall of a tangled thicket, "sometimes Matthew laughs a little, when it's only the two of us together, and I don't think it's unseemly. But Matthew is different from a *husband*."

"I think I should like a husband who has a little bit of badness in him," Diana said meditatively.

"Oh, yes. That is a necessity. No one ever has great romantic adventures with a man who is quiet and predictable and does everything the respectable way." Then Anne quoted the poem over which both girls had recently sighed and dreamed:

"He knew himself a villain, but he deemed
  The rest no better than the thing he seemed,
  And scorn'd the best as hypocrites who hid
  Those deeds the bolder spirit plainly did."

"Oh, Conrad!" Diana sighed all over again, feeling the faintness of a minor swoon. "Yes, that's exactly the kind of husband for me."

"Alas, corsairs are in short supply on Prince Edward Island," Anne said, laughing.

"I feel like they ought to be everywhere, and all sorts of other romantic types, too, when you recite poetry like that, Anne. You have such a voice for it."

Anne's cheeks colored as pink as the flowers at her feet. "Do you really think so?"

"Of course," Diana said heartily. "Why, you'll be a great favorite at all the concerts as soon as other people start to realize how well you can perform."

"You are too kind to me, Diana," Anne replied somberly. "I am entirely too skinny to be taken seriously, and my freckles strip away any hope I might have of dignity. Don't try to deny that I'm freckled. I know your denials come from the kindness of your heart, and I love you for it, but it's like denying a hen has feathers."

"If you mention your hair color, I swear I'll scream," Diana warned.

"It is true, though. No elocutionist ever had red hair."

"That's not true, Anne! It simply can't be. Think of all the performers at all the concerts in the world. At least *some* of them must have hair like yours."

"Let us not speak of it anymore today. I want to think only of Conrad. Besides, I still have a hope that someday my hair will darken to auburn, and then I can be taken seriously. I cling to that dream with desperate but hopeful hands, Diana. Well, I suppose we have enough rosehips to satisfy Marilla now. If I stay away too long, she'll get cross and tell me I daydream too much. Oh, look at this sweet path through the wood! Let's take it instead of going all the way back to the foot bridge."

Diana eyed the swath of woodland that separated Green

Gables from Orchard Slope. "I don't know, Anne. I don't think I've ever been on that path before. Where does it lead?"

"It must let out just behind the lower cow pasture, near that big cabbage patch that's gone wild... you know, the one that belongs to the vacant farm."

"That's an awful long way from your house," Diana said anxiously, peering into the veils of dark, cold shadows that hung to either side of Anne's "sweet," fern-lined path. "And isn't the wood here awful thick, too? It's not exactly narrow, as it is down at the foot bridge."

Anne threaded her arm through Diana's. "I'd almost think you were frightened. Of course there's nothing to fear in a forest so close to home, Diana."

"I suppose you're right," Diana said dubiously. But she did not go eagerly along as Anne started toward the forest. Her feet dragged and her heart pounded uncomfortably in her chest.

The wood was thick with old, stately spruces and firs. Their sap was running freely in response to the lengthening days, and the air beneath their boughs was crisp with the familiar scent—one Diana usually loved. But the shadows within the forest were so unlike the friendly sun that shone on the fields beyond that Diana felt nothing but menace among the evergreen trees, and their smell seemed to her like that of freshly turned grave dirt. She shivered, which did not go unnoticed by Anne. Anne's eyes widened as she looked from side to side, trying in vain to peer beyond the margins of the path. All at once the birds stopped singing. That made both girls freeze in their tracks and stare up into the branches that arched blackly overhead.

"What was that?" Anne whispered. "Why have the birds gone silent?"

"A hawk must have flown overhead," Diana said, practical as ever. But somehow she couldn't bring herself to speak louder than a whisper, either.

"Was it truly a hawk? Or was it... something else?"

"Oh, don't, Anne," Diana pleaded. She gazed back the way they had come. The entrance to the wood was still plainly visible, glowing with lemon-bright sunlight. But it seemed a terribly long way off now. "Let's go back. This land belongs to Mr. Bell, anyway; he probably doesn't want us roaming around it."

"Nonsense," Anne said, but her voice was still faint and shaky. "Mr. Bell doesn't mind that we play at Idlewild. He doesn't do anything with his wood, anyway. He won't mind us being here."

Anne went on a few more steps, delving deeper into the eerie silence. Diana had no choice but to go along with her.

"Can't you feel that chill creeping up your spine?" Anne whispered.

"Yes, I can, and I don't like it one bit!"

"Don't be afraid," Anne said, sounding witless with fear herself. "Once I read in a book that spirits of the dead can't hurt you. They can only touch you, but their touch just leaves a cold feeling on your skin. That's all."

Diana, who at that very moment was feeling an icy sensation all over her poor, trembling body, derived no comfort from this information. "Oh, don't talk like that, Anne, please! Let's just get through this dreadful place and out into the sunlight again."

But it was in Anne's nature to talk ever on. Once an idea had seized her imagination, she couldn't keep it to herself. "When I was in the asylum, I knew an Irish girl and she told me that there is a spirit who knows when there is to be a death in the family. The spirit is a lady, all in white with a flowing veil. She walks up and down, up and down, wringing her hands and wailing inconsolably. But the only people who can hear her are the members of the family that's about to be stricken. The girl I knew *swore* it was true. It's not a legend."

Diana swallowed hard and eyed the brook, which had emerged out of the gloom before them. Their path crossed it by means of several flat stones, well placed for stepping over. But Diana gasped when she examined the muddy bank. "Anne, look!"

Small boot-prints—certainly small enough to have been made by the spirit of a lady in a long, white gown—were pressed clearly into the bank, going back and forth as if whoever—or *whatever*—had made them had been pacing in distress.

"It must be the White Lady," Anne said, her voice thick with a thrill that might have been either triumph or terror.

"Let's hurry across! I don't want to stay here any longer."

The girls hopped nimbly across the stepping-stones, spurred on by their unabated chills. When they reached the other side of the brook they clasped hands, each gripping the other as tightly as she could.

"Those dead branches there look just like a skeleton's bones," Diana murmured fearfully.

"On dark nights when there is no moon, perhaps the branches come to life and turn into real skeletons," Anne suggested.

"That's terrible, Anne! How can you say such a thing?"

"We can't prove it *doesn't* happen," Anne said. "So it is probably better to assume it's true, and stay out of the wood on moonless nights."

They shuffled on a few more steps, gazing uneasily from left to right, into the impenetrable shadows of the spruces. Diana's mouth was very dry, but still she felt compelled to speak. "One time I heard the boys at school talking about a specter they'd seen. It was a man who walked up and down a forest path."

"That doesn't sound too overwhelmingly terrifying," Anne said bravely.

"But, Anne, the man *didn't have a head!*"

"Oh!" Anne breathed in stricken admiration. "That is certainly terrifying, then. But where did the boys see it? Not here, I hope."

"They didn't say. They only said 'a forest path.' Somewhere here in Avonlea."

"Then it could indeed be this very path."

"Oh, Anne, I'm awful scared! What if we were to look behind us, and see a headless man coming along the path?"

Both girls froze at that thought and stood in tense, quivering silence for a moment, straining their ears to listen for whatever might be creeping along behind. Heart racing, Diana longed to glance behind her, yet also knew that she simply *could not*. If she were to try, really try, her body would rebel and she would remain facing forward. And yet... anything at all might be slinking along the path in their wake, stretching toward them bony hands toward them, reaching out to brush them with a spectral touch that would leave only an icy chill on the skin...

A twig snapped somewhere in the forest. With twin gasps, Anne and Diana leaped into a run, hurrying along the path as fast as their shivering legs would carry them.

"I once heard a story about a little murdered child," Anne said when they'd slowed to a brisk, urgent walk.

"Don't, Anne!" Diana begged.

"It was desperate for affection, and wanted someone to solve the mystery of its killing, and so whenever people entered the wood where its poor bones lay forgotten, it crept up behind them and laid its tiny, cold fingers on the back of your hand... "

Diana jerked Anne to a halt so quickly that Anne nearly dropped her basket of rosehips. "Look; what's that?" Diana was staring off to the left of the path, toward a little fern-fringed clearing that had formed in a hollow where once, many years before, a grand old spruce had stood. It now lay prone along the forest floor, felled by a storm, with the skeletal tangle of its roots exposed.

"What?" Anne asked, peering into the shadows.

"I saw something move," Diana said, her jaw chattering.

"Maybe it was a bird or a squirrel."

"No," Diana breathed. "No, it was much bigger. And oh, Anne... it was white!"

At that moment, the terrible thing Diana had seen moved

again. As tall as a woman, thin and gaunt, it drifted out into the ferny clearing with a slow, deliberate glide, moving straight toward the girls.

Both of them screamed shrilly, let go of each other's hands, and ran like deer toward Green Gables. They were gasping for breath and sobbing with terror when they burst from the wood, out into the soothing sunlight of the lower cow pasture, and there they locked their arms around one another and wept and gibbered until their fear had abated. Neither of them noticed the sprightly twists and banners of white mist that drifted along the fence line, quite pretty and utterly harmless... and even if they had noticed, it is doubtful whether they would have realized, in their badly shaken state, that the white thing that had pursued them beneath the spruces had been only a stray curl of springtime fog.

SUMMERTIME

As June came to an end, so too did the school year. The children had fidgeted the day away, none of them completing any serious work on their final lessons—not even Anne or Gilbert, who took learning so very seriously. Diana had whiled away the day drawing flowers and fairies with big butterfly wings on her slate, and dreaming of the final bell, when she would step out into the full sun of summer with the entire mid-year vacation ahead of her to savor and enjoy.

But just before he sent Prissy out to ring the bell, Mr. Phillips stepped up to the lectern with a pale, sober, terribly pensive look on his face. Sensing a fateful announcement, the restless class fell quiet.

"The time has come for us to part," Mr. Phillips said. "As the school year closes, so closes a chapter in all our lives, each of us as individuals. I am pleased to say that all of you have succeeded in passing your final examinations, and so will advance when the new school year begins this autumn." There was a happy murmur around the room at that, but Mr. Phillips did not so much as smile, and accordingly the class went silent again. The schoolmaster resumed: "This chapter ends for me, too. The school board has not renewed me, and so I am free to return to my studies at the college, and pursue greater knowledge."

At that revelation, Prissy Andrews sniffled loudly from the back of the classroom. Then she whimpered, a high, keening sound that was so terribly affecting that in short order half the girls in the classroom were wiping their eyes and reaching for their handkerchiefs.

"But we must not allow regrets to hinder us," Mr. Phillips went on bravely, although tears had begun to shine in his eyes. "The future unfolds before us all, with surprising and delightful rewards around every corner, if we are only brave enough to venture out and pursue what life has to offer."

Diana, dabbing at her cheeks (never would she have expected to find Mr. Phillips's departure so moving!) glanced across the room to where Anne sat, upright and alert, beside Minnie Andrews. Anne's lips were pressed into a thin line, and Diana could tell she was struggling to contain her emotions, to resist the urge to weep over the teacher who had often played the role of villain in Anne's personal dramas. But as the schoolmaster went on in a tone of stoic acceptance, speaking of duty to one another and of the obligation to always do one's best, Anne's chin quivered and she swiped quickly at the corner of one eye.

Finally, Mr. Phillips dismissed the school. Prissy was too distraught to be trusted with the bell, so Gilbert was sent out to ring it, which he did with the fullest enthusiasm. Despite their whimpers and sighs, the girls all gathered up their books and slates and pencils, and the children of Avonlea School scampered out to begin their long-awaited summer.

As it was a festival day among the town's small fry, Anne and Diana eschewed their usual private stroll along the Birch Path and the back end of Mr. Bell's property, and opted instead to accompany the other girls along the main road. None of them could decide whether to feel thrilled that vacation time was finally here, or heartbroken over Mr. Phillips's departure. Just when some of them would begin to chatter happily about their plans for the summer, Carrie Sloane would sigh, "The time has come for us to part," and all the girls would lapse into sentimental tears once more, led by Ruby Gillis, who cried the loudest and most determinedly, but always managed to look impossibly pretty while doing it.

As the group of girls reached the Newbridge crossroad, a smart little buggy pulled by a caramel-colored horse slowed and stopped before them. Inside the buggy rode a young couple, sitting very close together. They were both fresh-faced and eager-eyed, even as the man removed his bowler hat in greeting and leaned down with obvious concern to address the flock of teary-eyed little girls.

"Good afternoon, ladies," he said. "Or I hope it is a good afternoon for you, but every one of you is crying. Has something dreadful happened? Do you need help?"

"No." Ruby sniffled up at him. "It's just that our schoolmaster isn't being renewed and we'll never see him again and we only just found out about it, and it's so aw... ful!" She drew out the last word in a long wail, which sent the rest of the girls into fits of noisy crying.

The man and woman in the carriage exchanged a clandestine smile. Then the woman, who looked like the very picture of summertime with her lovely golden hair, blue puff-sleeved dress, and rose-trimmed hat, gave a delightful little laugh and addressed the girls. "So you are the scholars of this town... the girls, anyway. I have some news that may cheer you up. It certainly cheers me, now that I've seen you. I am to be your new Sunday school teacher. And we will have the loveliest time in our classes, too. There, now: Isn't that something to look forward to?"

The girls all gazed up at her in an assessing sort of way. Then as one they broke into sunny smiles and dried the day's tears for good. The woman in the buggy was a very pleasant-seeming lady, with a genuine smile and the warmest twinkle in her eyes... the kind of person any child can't help but want to know better.

"I didn't know we were to get a new Sunday school teacher," Jane Andrews said.

"But you know the old minister resigned in February," Anne said to Jane. Her quick, gray eyes flashed to the man in the buggy, who was returning his hat to his head. "Are you the new minister, then?"

"I am indeed," he replied, with a small laugh like the one his wife had given. He had hair of a deep, mousy-gold color, almost blond—and, as Diana and Anne had previously speculated, his whole person did seem ready-made for laughter. He did not make a very sober impression, which was startling in a minister. But Diana thought him very pleasant and charming all the same. "I am Mr. Allan, and this is my wife." They beamed at one another for a moment, as if having forgotten that the girls existed... that anyone in the world existed, except for one another. "We are newly married. Still on our honeymoon, you might say."

The crowd of Avonlea schoolgirls fluttered and sighed at that unbearably romantic news. And then, having satisfied themselves that all was more or less well with the little girls, the Allans said farewell and drove on toward the manse, which was to be their home while Mr. Allan was in residence.

"She's awfully pretty," Ruby said with an admiring sigh as the couple drove away.

"Did you see her dress?" Josie Pye said. "Those sleeves were splendid!"

"And her hair," Julie Bell added. "Why, I think it's at least as pretty as Ruby's."

"She was dazzling," Anne said. "Like a sapphire set in a golden crown. She must come from some far-off city, the scioness of a noble line, who married a poor minister purely for love, because the least thought of greed has never troubled her worthy brow. I'd bet Avonlea has never seen such a grand lady as that Mrs. Allan."

"Honestly, Anne," Gertie complained, "you'd better stop making up words, because it's just as bad as telling a falsehood. Nobody has ever heard of a 'scioness' before."

"Maybe *you* haven't," Diana said loyally, even though she had never heard the word before, either.

"And anyway," Josie added snappishly, "it's a sin to gamble, so you'd better not let anyone hear you talking about placing bets on anything. Especially not on a minister's wife. That just isn't holy."

Anne was already walking away from the crossroads, leaving the gathering of girls behind her to disperse toward their family farms. Diana ran to catch up with her, and saw that Anne wasn't stalking away in an angry huff. Rather, she wandered with starry, distant gaze, her mind already spinning rainbow fancies around the arrival of Mrs. Allan in Avonlea.

MORE THAN A WEEK LATER, Diana and Anne were playing together in the fields, their day's chores well behind them. A long, drawn-out, violet-soft twilight was lingering over the island, the kind of gentle grading into night that only comes in the summer, with warm breezes whispering in the birches, silver stars gleaming palely in a sky that still holds a cupful of lingering light, and the intermittent music of distant bells on the necks of sleepy, homeward-bound cattle. The girls were sprawling on the flat rocks that surrounded the Dryad's Bubble, listening to the chorus of frogs and crickets and dipping twigs covered in balsam into the water to make rainbows in the night's vestiges of light.

Anne had been enchanted by Mrs. Allan ever since meeting her at the crossroads on the last day of school; the infatuation had only grown after learning what a good teacher Mrs. Allan was during the previous weekend's Sunday school. Marilla had asked the Allans to come to Green Gables for tea, so that she might have a chance to weigh their merits for herself, free from the restricted environment of the church pew. Everyone was dubious of a pastor as young as Mr. Allan—everyone save Anne, who could scarcely contain her excitement.

"They're to come over tomorrow afternoon," she said rapturously as she coated another twig in balsam. "I do hope Mrs. Allan wears another dress with puff sleeves. I suppose if she does, it will most probably be the same blue one we already saw her in, for it wouldn't be seemly for a minister's wife to have a lot of nice clothes. Ministers are supposed to live modestly, after all, as Our Lord did. I wonder if it was hard for Mrs. Allan to give up all her finery when she married her poor, modest husband, or if she did it with a glad heart because she's so good and has such high ideals."

"You don't have any way of knowing whether Mrs. Allan came from a rich family, Anne Shirley," Diana said stoutly. "Not unless you ask her, and it would be a terribly forward thing to ask. You're just making up daydreams about her to satisfy your own imagination."

Anne wrinkled up her nose and gave Diana the strangest look through the veil of twilight. Diana couldn't quite decide whether Anne looked incredulous or hurt. But the expression was gone a moment later, as Anne recited a litany of all the delights she and Marilla were to prepare for the much-anticipated tea. Anne was to make a layer cake, the thought of which was giving her cold terrors, even though Anne had made many cakes before and was by now quite good at it.

"Your cake will be good, all right," Diana said warmly. "We had a piece of one you made for lunch two weeks ago at Idlewild, and it was perfectly elegant."

"Yes, but cakes have a terrible habit of turning out bad just when you especially want them to be good. I suppose I shall just have to trust to Providence and be careful to put in the flour. Oh, look, Diana," Anne said, sitting up abruptly and gazing with wonder down at the rippling water, "what a lovely rainbow! Do you suppose the Dryad will come out after we go away and take it for a scarf?"

Diana stifled a sigh. "You know there is no such thing as a dryad." The incident of the forest shortcut, with its lurking terrors and drifting white things, had left a real impression on Diana. She and Anne had named the place the Haunted Wood, and after that day Diana couldn't look at the dense spruces without a shudder of fear. Nightmares had plagued her for weeks after venturing into the Haunted Wood, and Diana was firmly resolved to keep her head in the practical world instead of following Anne on her wild flights of fancy.

After all, Diana had told herself practically more than once since then, it was best to leave Anne to Anne. She, Diana, would never be like her friend, in form or in personality, no matter how much she might secretly long to be... no matter how she might ache for Anne's popularity, her sharp wit, her rustically charming good looks. Oh, Diana loved Anne as much as ever, to be sure. But she was beginning to understand that there would always exist between them a gulf of difference. Something essential yet difficult to define would separate them for all time, no matter how they cared for one another. Anne was shaped by Providence for a specific world, a particular life, a certain kind of future, while Diana was made for an entirely different life. She did her best not to meditate on whether Anne's or her own predestined world was better, more appealing, more satisfying. She felt instinctively that only unhappiness and dissatisfaction would come from knowing.

Anne looked stricken. "But it's so easy to imagine there is a dryad," she pleaded. "Every night before I go to bed, I look out my window and wonder if the dryad is really sitting here, combing her locks with the spring for a mirror."

Diana gave an uncomfortable little giggle and tossed another balsam-dipped twig into the water so she would not have to look at Anne's beseeching eyes. The truth was, Diana did still *want* to believe in the dryad, deep down in her heart. The dryad, the richness of Idlewild, the fairies that lived in Violet Vale... yes, even the headless man and the white lady in the Haunted Wood. All the delicate, implied magics of childhood still called to her in a voice that was impossible to resist. Yet resist them she must, or risk looking like a fool when the life that was Anne's inheritance by right—a life of passions and prisms, of glories and gold—was barred and denied forever to plain, simple, country-girl Diana.

"Sometimes I look for her footprints in the dew in the morning," Anne murmured. Then she took Diana's hand with a sudden swell of heartbroken longing. "Oh, Diana, don't give up your faith in the dryad!"

"You dear, silly thing," Diana said, rising and pulling Anne to her feet. "I had best get up to bed, and you had better, too. You'll need a good sleep if you're going to make the most important cake of your life in the morning."

The girls embraced and parted ways. As Diana went up through the orchard, she could hear Anne singing softly to herself, though little by little her voice faded as she crossed the foot bridge and vanished into the twilight fields of Green Gables. Diana only looked back once, to the flat stones of the Dryad's Bubble. But the stones were empty. No fairy queen had come out to take up the rainbows that drifted on the waters. The woods and fields were empty as far as Diana could see.

AS ANNE WAS FEARFULLY OCCUPIED with her preparations for tea with the Allans, Diana had no one to play with that Wednesday. Thanks to pure boredom, she completed all her chores at Orchard Slope shortly after breakfast, working with the kind of efficiency and focus that is rare in girls who are tempted by balmy summer days. Her father noticed her "dangling at a loose end," as he liked to say, and took her aside before the lunch hour.

"The Blythes are having a picnic over at their place. Why don't you go?"

For answer, Diana blushed to what she feared was an atrocious shade of scarlet.

The significance of her reaction was not lost on Mr. Barry. He was not a blind man; he'd seen what a handsome lad young Gilbert was now, and though he was reluctant for his daughter to grow up, he was wise enough to understand that the day would eventually come.

"There will be many children there," he said, "*other* than just the Blythes, I mean."

That prospect fortified Diana's nerves. She put on a clean dress and neatened her hair, and allowed her father to drive her down to the Blythes' place, all the while silently admonishing herself to stop feeling so tied up in knots over it—it was just a picnic, after all.

The Blythe farm was small but picturesque. A tall, rather narrow farmhouse of pale, mossy green stood between two neat rows of Lombardy poplars. Beyond the trees lay the potato fields and the orchard, where grew the famed strawberry apples. The picnic was already in progress on the grassy area in front of the Blythes' whitewashed milking barn. Several families had spread blankets and were sharing baskets of goodies, while children ran in the spaces between blankets, throwing balls to one another or playing games of chase.

"I'll come back for you in three hours," Mr. Barry promised as Diana climbed shakily down into the yard.

But she was distracted from her misgivings almost at once by a happy shout from Jane Andrews. Jane and her brother Billy had only recently arrived, too; Diana eagerly joined them on their picnic blanket and was glad to share in the tarts and ham they had packed.

"Isn't this a splendid time?" Jane said.

No one would ever say she was as pretty as Ruby Gillis, for her hair was a plain, dull-brown color and hung rather limply despite her best efforts to curl it. However, with her open, honest ways and naturally kind demeanor, Jane was very pleasant company any day of the week. Diana was glad to be with such a settling and steadfast companion when she felt so positively shaken up.

"It's awfully nice of the Blythes to have everyone over. Is there a special occasion?"

"No," said Jane's older brother, Billy. "Except that Mrs. Blythe likes to put on a big gathering, and I guess the nice weather was excuse enough to do it. She didn't give much warning about it, though."

"We only heard about the picnic this morning," Jane said. "But early everyone from school is here. It's jolly to see everyone again, even though I don't like nearly any of the boys."

"Well, we don't like you, either," Billy teased. Having eaten all the ham and tarts he could comfortably hold, he clambered up from the blanket and wandered away to seek out some fun with the other boys.

"I suppose he's going off to play ball," said Jane. "I don't want to play ball, but we could find some more girls and see what they've got up to. It's sure to be better than what the boys are doing. I saw Carrie Sloane and the Pyes when we first arrived, but I would rather not waste a perfectly nice picnic in the Pyes' company. I know it's dreadful mean of me to say so, but it is true, Diana."

Diana laughed. "I agree, Jane. Gertie and Josie would only spoil a perfectly good summer day. Let's walk around the farm together. I'm sure we'll find out where the rest of the girls are hiding. I suppose they're off in the orchard, even though the strawberry apples won't be ripe yet."

Diana and Jane talked together quite happily as they wandered across the Blythe acres. Jane lacked all the bright imagination and heart-thrilling fancies of Anne Shirley, but she was such an agreeable friend that Diana didn't mind. As they skirted the edge of the hay field and rounded a corner of the orchard, the girls suddenly came face to face with some of their schoolmates... but not the ones they'd been seeking. Some of the older boys were dividing themselves up for a ball game, and there in their midst, tall and confident, brash as the corsair of Diana's fondest dreams, was Gilbert. He gave a little start as Diana and Jane halted some distance away, as if some unseen force had alerted him to the girls' presence. He turned away from the boys' squabbling conversation, caught sight of Diana at once, and offered her a wink and a slow smile. Her knees immediately felt as wobbly as a custard.

"Gilbert Blythe," Jane said appreciatively. "You know, I think he's terribly handsome."

"So do I," Diana admitted.

On the instant, a surge of guilt swept up through her middle and nearly overwhelmed her. It was the kind of secret she should only share with Anne, her one and only, solemnly sworn bosom friend... yet Anne had strictly forbidden her to speak of Gilbert. How *could* Diana tell her dearest friend how she felt about that boy?

"But he's so roguish," Jane went on, as if roguishness were an undesirable quality. "He likes to joke and make mischief too much. I think it will get him in trouble someday. Maybe he'll even grow up to be a criminal."

"Or a pirate," Diana said, heart pounding.

"What?" Jane turned to her with an openly puzzled expression.

"I'm only making fun," Diana said quickly, wishing her face wasn't quite as hot as it was.

"Anyway, there's no point in liking Gilbert because he's dead gone on Anne Shirley. Everybody says so."

Diana's heart sank like a rock in her chest. "Everybody?"

"Of course, no one ever wrote them up in a 'take notice,' because Anne would never stand for it. But it's plain to see. Gilbert's set on winning her heart. I think that's just more proof that he lacks all common sense. Everybody knows Anne hates him. If I were Gilbert, I'd find a girl who actually *liked* me, and set my sights on her. That would be the sensible thing to do."

"That's right," Diana said with more force than was necessary. "Anne *hates* him. And anyway, she doesn't care about boys at all. He ought to be smarter, and stop wasting his time pining after Anne."

"That's what I said," Jane replied comfortably, evidently glad that she and Diana were of the same opinion.

Diana clenched her fists in secret fury and glared at Gilbert as the ball game began to take shape. "It's plain to see that it doesn't matter how many times I tell myself to forget about that infuriating boy, and leave him to Anne," Diana thought. "I will persist in liking him all the same. And it's not fair that he likes Anne, but not me. It's just not fair! Hasn't he known me ever so much longer? And I *am* a fine-looking girl, if I am a little plump... everybody says so. And I'm nice, and good, and have so many qualities. Why won't he just *see* them?"

Diana and Jane quickly abandoned their quest to find more girls, and decided instead to sit under the apple trees and watch the boys play ball. This sudden change in plans, it must be admitted, was most likely due to the presence of Gilbert on the ball field. As the boys ran and threw and rough-housed and shouted, Diana watched the object of her affection with a pensive gaze.

"I must overcome my shyness," Diana thought as the game wore on, "and ask Gilbert straight out if he could ever like me. It's terribly unladylike to do such a thing, and Mother would skin me alive if she found out about it. But I simply must know the truth." Even if the answer was "no," at least she would have an end to all this mooning and wishing and secret longing. Even if he was certain he could never love anyone but Anne, then Diana would know the truth, and could stop wondering, stop tormenting herself with too-heady dreams of "what if."

The ball bounced "out of bounds" and rolled beneath the apple trees. Fred Wright came scrambling after it, ducking to avoid the lowest hanging boughs. The ball rolled to a stop right beside Diana and Jane. Diana picked it up and offered it to Fred with a smile that was far happier-looking than Diana felt just then.

"Thanks," Fred said as he accepted the ball from her hands, with a bow as if the ball were a knight's sword gifted by a queen. "By golly, Diana, isn't it a great day?"

Fred was one of the school boys whom Diana had always liked. In fact, all the girls of Avonlea School thought him perfectly sweet and agreeable, even if no one made him the center of romantic daydreams. Fred was one of Gilbert's closest chums, but somehow when the teasing and tormenting started, he never seemed to be a part of it. He was always ready with a laugh, and had a special knack for making others laugh, too, though never at anyone else's expense. Round and rather red-faced, he made everybody happy just by the grace of his company. When Diana smiled at him again, she didn't feel sad or defeated inside anymore. Just for a moment, as she regally accepted Fred's absurd bow, she felt quite glad to be alive, and content for the world to be ordered exactly as it was.

A moment later, Fred was puffing away, dashing back to the game. Jane rounded on Diana with open mouth and wide, shining eyes. "Diana! Fred Wright *likes* you!"

The emphasis on that certain word left no doubt in Diana's mind as to Jane's precise meaning. She blushed. Diana had never been the object of any boy's fancy before; she didn't know what to do, what to say. She settled on a weak, "Do you think so?"

"I know it," Jane insisted. "I'm awful good at telling when people like other people. They just look at each other a certain way."

"Well, I didn't look at *him* any certain way."

"That's true enough," Jane said thoughtfully. "I guess you don't like him back, though I can't see why. Fred Wright is kind and sensible and real good at making a body laugh. I think that's reason enough to like a boy, and it makes ever so much more sense than liking a rogue like Gilbert."

"*Liking* doesn't happen along such planned-out lines," Diana pointed out with an air of authority. "One's heart reacts however it wants. Besides, you admitted yourself that you like Gilbert, too."

"Yes," Jane said glumly. "But if I could talk myself out of it, I would. It's plain silly, Diana!"

Diana sighed. "Plain silly," she thought, feeling bleak and confused. She watched the ball game resume, frowning as Fred and Gilbert ran together. Fred was perfectly nice; that much was true. And if he did in fact like her, as Jane insisted, then Diana couldn't help but feel flattered.

But oh, if only *Gilbert* would feel the same way!

A SELECT PARTY AND A SINGULAR DISASTER

Toward the end of July, when salt-laden breezes blew in from the Gulf to cool the merciless heat of mid-day, Diana began to feel restless and dull. Summers are fascinating and delightful times, with their long, warm days and their ample opportunities for strolling down green paths or along laughing brooks with no work to be done and only pleasant things to think of. But after weeks of idylls, the days can begin to impart a certain sameness that wears on the nerves. It was in this state that Diana proposed a select party to her parents: Only the girls of her age from Avonlea School. It was Diana's hope that in gathering together they might wring more essence of excitement from summertime before the leaves began to turn and the days to shorten.

Mrs. Barry heartily agreed to the plan. She was glad that Diana had social tendencies. She knew it was not uncommon for girls of that age to cling to one friend only, to the exclusion of all others, and Mrs. Barry was acutely aware of the value of a broad range of friends. She no longer bore any ill will toward Anne Shirley, but as often as Anne and Diana were together—playing by the brook in the middle of the day, roaming the fields at sunset, only parting company when twilight slipped away into full dark—Mrs. Barry worried privately over the health of her daughter's connections. She thought a party for girls was a splendid idea, and volunteered to set out a real "high tea" to make the occasion especially elegant and memorable.

When word spread about Avonlea that Diana Barry was to host a real tea, not a girl in the village could think or talk about anything else for the week before the event. It was to be the affair of the summer, if the fevered talk could be believed. The result of all this was that Diana found herself rather nervous on the morning of the big event. What if her party didn't live up to expectations? Perhaps then the Pyes and the Sloanes would laugh about it behind Diana's back, and she didn't think it possible to survive such depths of utter degradation.

But Diana needn't have worried. Mr. Barry made a big table out of a long plank and a pair of sawhorses, and set it out beneath the apple trees, and Anne helped Diana cover it with a nice, embroidered linen so no one could tell it was only a plank and sawhorses just by looking. The girls gathered bouquets of June lilies and early Queen Anne's lace and the last, faded stalks of May-flowers, and set them out in vases all along the table so that table and orchard alike looked as pretty and fine as the banquet hall at the White Sands hotel.

And then the guests arrived. One by one, carts came up the hill toward Orchard Slope; soon the yard was full of giggling, chattering girls dressed in their party-best. Ruby Gillis had perfectly spotless white gloves, which she had borrowed from her older sister, and which all the guests examined enviously before they made their most civil and dignified compliments to lucky Ruby. Jane Andrews wore a real silk sash of vibrant green, which her mother had allowed her because it had a small stain on it, though it could only be seen if you looked closely. Minnie Andrews and Carrie Sloane had spent considerable time over the preceding week speculating on exactly how special Diana's party was to be. Consequently, they had worked themselves into quite a state of anticipation, so that when they saw each other at last, bedecked in their ruffle-edged dresses and flower-trimmed hats, both girls burst into tears of pure emotion, vented after too long a period of fermentation.

When all her guests had arrived, Diana invited them to the "outdoor parlor," which was what she and Anne had agreed to call the orchard for today only, thanks to how pretty it looked with the table bedizened all in white. Mr. Barry had provided old chairs from the barn (well dusted so as not to soil any girl's best dress), and, murmuring together like a flock of poults, the guests eagerly went to their places.

"This is ever so nice," said Julia Bell, looking at the vases of white flowers and the china place-settings in admiration. (To be sure, the pieces were not Mrs. Barry's best china. In fact, if one looked closely enough, one might note chips on the rims of cups and plates, and mismatched patterns of flowers. But to the girls, the spread could hardly be finer if each piece were gilded and polished.)

"Wait till you see what Mother has made for our tea," Diana said excitedly. "It's all so elegant, you could just *die*."

Mrs. Barry appeared with two steaming tea pots and an indulgent smile. She greeted each girl by name as she poured, and asked after their mothers' health, as if she were playing hostess at the most elite women's group in Avonlea. The girls found it thrilling. Even more delightful were the elegant little egg-salad and cucumber sandwiches that followed, and then darling, tiny scones with clotted cream and strawberry preserves. Last of all came a white cake decorated with walnuts and candied violets. Each girl's slice was of equal size, with an equal number of violet petals on top.

The girls munched and sipped in perfect contentment. The trees overhead, with their glossy leaves and the bright, hard, still-small jewels of apples, cast dapples of sunlight and shade over the linen and over the glowing faces of Diana's guests.

"How perfectly lovely," Ruby said with a sigh as she and the rest of the girls gleaned the last of the cake crumbs from their plates. "I don't think even the queen herself has ever had a tea so nice."

Satisfied that her party was a great success, Diana, in her most grown-up and sophisticated manner, invited the girls to stroll and play among the trees. They dispersed in small groups of three and four, strolling happily around the grounds of Orchard Slope.

Diana and Anne found themselves walking with Jane. Good, steady, reliable Jane; Diana was glad of her company. She felt they were becoming really good chums, and it was nice to know that she had other girls to call true friends, even if she still loved Anne best of all. Anne understood Diana as no one else did—as no one else *could*, and besides, Diana so admired Anne's free spirit, her undaunted sense of imagination and whimsy. But it was comforting to have a friend like Jane, too, who never allowed herself to be carried off by too robust a fancy.

"Oh, Diana," Anne said, "your mother was so kind to give us such a beautiful party. Do you know, at one time I thought your mother entirely too stiff and maybe even a little mean, but now I see that she has a most delightful and luminous spirit. Isn't that a pretty turn of phrase? I read it in a book about a frail young heroine who was a beacon of good morals to all who met her, even though she could hardly get out of bed due to being so ill all the time. Your mother isn't frail, but I do think she's delightful and luminous, now that I've had her violet-and-walnut cake. Do you think she could be a kindred spirit?"

"No," Diana said, laughing, "I don't. She's not like you at all, Anne. She never imagines anything or has any romantic dreams. But she was awful nice to make tea. You know, the older I get, the more I like my mother. Last year was just terrible with her. She and I were at odds all the time. But now I try to be good, because I know all her strict rules are only because she loves me, and the more I try, the easier she is to live with. I think someday when I'm all grown up and have a husband of my own, Mother and I will be real good friends."

"There's someone who will never be a good friend, I fear," Anne said quietly, narrowing her eyes toward a big apple tree with down-curved branches. Josie Pye was seated beneath it, playing a clapping game with Carrie and Minnie. Minnie missed a beat and Josie struck the back of her hand rather harder than was necessary, then threw back her head with nasty laughter. "I've tried and tried to like Josie, and Gertie, too, but I find it impossible. I suppose this is a failing in my own self, because Marilla says that everybody *can* be liked if you look hard enough for reasons to do so. But I've lain awake at nights searching for reasons to like the Pye girls, but none ever come to me. I fear I've lost too much sleep in the trying."

"Everybody can be liked except for Josie and Gertie," Diana said. "I wouldn't have invited Josie at all, but Mother said it would be rude not to, since I invited every other girl in Avonlea who is our age, or close to it. I suppose she's right. But I wish Josie had caught a cold and couldn't come after all. She's always dreadfully mean to me."

"To me as well," Anne said. "Sometimes I think she's far snider to us, Diana, than she is to any other girls. But I suppose that, too, is a failing in me... too much imagination. I'm only seeing faults in Josie because she annoys me so. She is probably just as pig-headed to everyone else."

"Josie is only mean to you two because she envies you," Jane said.

Diana and Anne both turned to their friend in silent startlement.

"It's true," Jane said, smiling ruefully at them. "She's not the only girl who envies the pair of you, but she's the only one who's mean enough to show it."

"Envies?" Diana said incredulously. "But how? Why?"

Jane laughed fondly. "Why, Diana, surely you know that you and Anne are the most popular girls in all Avonlea."

"Surely we are *not*," Anne sputtered. "The very idea, Jane Andrews!"

"It's true. All the girls like you both because you're such good company, and some of the girls like you extra, just because they know how much *other* girls like you." Jane shrugged. "And Diana, you're so good at dressing well and fixing your hair, and you always look so very pretty. And all the boys like you and Anne best of all. It's enough for anybody to be jealous over."

Diana and Anne exchanged a puzzled, rather embarrassed look.

"But I don't want to make anyone jealous," Diana said. "That sounds dreadful... the kind of thing a Pye would do."

"You don't do it on purpose, you goose," Jane said, linking her arm with Diana's. "You don't put on airs, neither one of you. That's why everyone still likes you so much, instead of despising you. If you ever did put on airs, it would be enough to turn all the girls against you."

(Feminine society has ever been disastrously fickle, even among little country girls.)

"I don't believe it," Anne said flatly. "It strains credulity. The only boy who has ever shown me a bit of attention is Gil..." She trailed off, face flaming red, then resumed, "... is one boy in particular, and *he* was only teasing me to be cruel."

"That's what you think," Jane said mysteriously. "But I don't get jealous, because I like everyone just the same, and I know there are enough boys for every one of us to have a beau when we get older. It's not as if there was a shortage of them in Avonlea. I think envy about such things is just plain silly."

Diana, too flustered by the subject to continue with it, brought up another, and the conversation soon tacked in another direction. But she continued to think about what Jane had said. Diana was popular? She had never noticed, but perhaps this very party was proof that what Jane said was true. And... boys liked her? *That* couldn't be true at all. Gilbert only had eyes for Anne; if Diana was the darling of every boy in the school, then Gilbert wouldn't be so oblivious to her very existence!

Once again, an unwelcome wave of envy for Anne, her own dearest and most valued friend, rose up as if to drown Diana in bitter sorrow. She hugged Jane a little closer as they walked, moving subtly away from Anne. It was simply too painful to be close to Anne now, when she recalled all the complexities of their friendship. How could she love a friend so much—to the point that Diana honestly felt she might die of heartache if she were deprived of Anne's friendship—yet also feel so embittered toward her? It wasn't Anne's fault that she was loved by so many... that she was pretty and delicate and enchanting. Anne didn't *try* to be so fascinating. Yet Anne's natural charms hurt Diana secretly, all the same.

"Oh, look over there," Anne said suddenly, drawing Diana's and Jane's attention over to the barn. "What are they doing? Let's go see."

Two of the smaller groups of girls had merged into one ragged circle, and some kind of commotion was going on within it. Diana could see somebody's flowered hat bouncing up and down as if the wearer were hopping in place. Now and then a pair of hands flew up and twirled in the air as the jumper tried to catch her balance. When they reached the circle, Diana saw that a game of dares had sprung up.

Dares were the most popular form of entertainment that year among the Avonlea scholars. Although the boys had begun the tradition, the girls had taken to it with real appetite, for contrary to what most people think, girls enjoy thrills just as much as boys do. Dares were, by that time, so important that to refuse one was to forever smirch one's honor. Consequently, Julia Bell was engaged in hopping on one foot to a count of fifty, without ever putting the other foot down. The girls counted each hop with intense focus, and Julia's face was grim with the same intensity as she busily hopped away. Nothing less than Julia's reputation for bravery and gumption were at stake.

Having completed her task, the panting Julia faced her "darer," Ruby, with a triumphant lift of her chin, then resumed her place in the circle amid a smattering of applause. Diana, Anne, and Jane squeezed into the circle, watching eagerly to see what feats would unfold next.

Carrie Sloane turned to Ruby with an impish twinkle in her eye. "Hopping isn't so hard. I dare you to climb that tree." She pointed to the gnarled old willow that grew near the front of the Barry house.

Ruby's lip quivered. "But I can't! I'm in my nicest dress. What if I tear it? My mother would skin me."

"I dare you," Carrie said levelly.

Ruby sniffled and eyed the willow with obvious misgiving. "There are caterpillars up there," she implored.

Josie Pye had also been drawn to the circle, and now spoke up from her place opposite Diana. "Carrie *dared* you, Ruby. If you won't do it, then you're yellow."

The girls all gasped as one. Ruby couldn't allow such a thing to be said of her... no one could. So she gamely marched to the willow and, without further hesitation, began to climb. To everyone's surprise, delicate Ruby, who was so prone to weeping and hysterics, proved herself quite nimble and strong. She raced up the willow as easily as a monkey would have done, and stuck her head out the top to wave at the girls below. It took her almost no time to descend, without any of the rips in her dress she had feared.

Diana's party guests murmured in admiration as Ruby rejoined their ranks. "So there," Ruby said to Carrie.

The spirit of daring had descended fully on Josie Pye. She narrowed her eyes at Jane. "I dare you to hop all the way around the garden patch on one foot, without stopping."

The girls turned as one to consider the Barry garden patch. It was quite large and muddy in places, but a dare was a dare, and Jane knew the rules as well as anybody. She set off on her left foot, hopping with a steady, plodding rhythm that was characteristic of everything Jane did. She made it to one corner, and then the next, but by the time she was approaching the third she was winded and drooping. She stopped at the third corner and came wearily back to the circle.

"I couldn't do it," she said, downcast. "You win, Josie."

Josie lifted her pointed nose in the air. "I'd think such a thing would be *easy*. Well, I won, fair and square, Jane Andrews. And don't you forget it."

"She's only trying to punish Jane for being our friend," Diana whispered to Anne. "You remember what Jane told us. Oh, she's so rotten! I wish Mother hadn't made me invite her to my party."

Anne scrunched up her nose in the way that meant she was about to do something stubborn and possibly reckless. She stepped forward, into the middle of the circle. "If you think it's so easy, then you won't mind if I dare you to do something harder. Walk along the garden fence. Right along the top of it."

The girls let out a collective, "Ooh!"

Josie eyed the garden fence for a moment, then turned back to Anne with a smile that was far better called a sneer.

"Go on," Anne said. "I *dare* you."

Josie didn't bother with a saucy reply. She went right to the fence and upended a pail that was standing near it, then stepped from the pail up to the top of the board fence. It was narrow and somewhat wobbly in places, and the earth below was wet enough that it would stain Josie's dress if she were to fall into it. The girls held their breath as Josie stuck out her arms to either side, and then, with all the confident grace of a queen in a regal procession, she went one foot in front of the other, straight down the line of the fence. She didn't falter once. Of course, by the time she reached the end and hopped unharmed to the ground, her smug glee was unbearable to Diana.

"I really thought she couldn't do it," Anne muttered in defeat.

"Oh, she'll be just awful now," Diana replied. "She'll never let you forget this, Anne!"

"Don't worry," Anne said. "I have a plan to get Josie for good."

When the guests were finished congratulating Josie on her impressive feat, Anne tossed her braids and said loudly, "I don't think it's such a wonderful thing to walk a little, low board fence. I knew a girl in Marysville who could walk the ridgepole of a roof."

Josie braced her fists on her hips and glared at Anne. "I don't believe it. I don't believe *anybody* could walk a ridgepole. *You* couldn't, anyhow, Anne Shirley."

Anne's temper was roused—so much so that Diana perceived at once that Josie had turned the tables on Anne and gotten the better of her.

"Couldn't I?" Anne cried indignantly.

Josie was quick with her response. "Then I dare you to do it."

A deathly silence fell over the circle of girls. Anne paled; she saw now how Josie had deftly led her into the very trap Anne had intended to spring on her. But there was nothing for it now. The gauntlet had been thrown. Still Anne hesitated.

"I dare you to climb up there and walk the ridgepole of Mr. Barry's kitchen roof," Josie needled.

Anne turned toward the house as if she went into a den of hungry lions. Diana caught her by the hand. "Don't you do it, Anne! You'll fall off and be killed. Never mind Josie Pye. It isn't fair to dare anybody to do something so dangerous."

"I must do it," Anne said rather faintly. "My honor is at stake. I shall walk that ridgepole, Diana, or perish in the attempt." Anne turned to her with sudden intensity, fear and perhaps a little excitement shining from her gray eyes. "If I am killed, you are to have my pearl ring."

With that, Anne disentangled herself from Diana's desperate grip and made her way to an apple-picking ladder, which was resting up against the kitchen roof. Diana whimpered and clung to Jane's arm as Anne climbed the ladder. She pulled herself up onto the roof and crept on hands and feet up its incline, until she was sitting on the ridgepole at its peak. Then she stood, her thin body wavering and tilting alarmingly from side to side as she struggled to find her balance.

Diana was quite breathless with terror. Even steady Jane was shivering as the girls all watched the spectacle on the roof-top.

Anne slowly extended her arms, just as Josie had done on the fence. It seemed to take an eternity for her to quell her precarious wobbling, but once she was more or less still, she slid one foot out along the peak of the roof, paused, and then slid the other. Step by agonizing step, Anne advanced. She seemed to gain more confidence as she went, so that Diana nearly convinced herself that Anne would make it after all. But before she reached the midpoint, disaster struck. Anne wobbled a bit too far; her arms pinwheeled too fast in her sudden panic. She could not right herself, and with a stagger and a lurch she thudded onto the roof, rolled ungracefully down its slope, and dropped with a crash into the Virginia creeper in the flower patch below.

The assembled girls screeched in panic and ran in a herd toward Anne. Diana fought her way through them, desperate to reach her friend's side, fully convinced that Anne was already dead.

The pale form of Anne, sprawled among the tangle of Virginia creeper, did look rather corpse-like, so still and unstirring did she lay. With a wail of grief, Diana threw herself to her knees beside Anne and cradled the red head in her lap. "Anne, are you killed? Oh, Anne, dear Anne, speak just one word to me and tell me if you are killed."

For a moment, Anne remained unresponsive, and Diana was certain her worst fear was true. "Why did I ever feel envy over you, Anne?" Diana wailed on the inside, even as shocked, silent tears spilled over her cheeks. "There's no one I love more than you, no one in all the world. And now I realized it too late! Oh, if I could have you back safe and sound, I would never let envy stand between us again."

But just as Diana was readying herself to throw back her head and shriek with the full force of her anguish, Anne gave a little gasp, a cough, and then carefully pushed herself up until she sat unsteadily among the ruined vines. "No, Diana, I am not killed," Anne said weakly. "But I think I am rendered unconscious."

Carrie Sloane had never heard the word "unconscious" before, and assumed it was something quite fatal. "Where?" she sobbed as she and Ruby clung wailing to one another. "Oh, where, Anne?"

Anne never had the chance to respond. Mrs. Barry was there in a flash, making a way through the crowd of hysterical girls until she towered over Diana and Anne.

"This is the very end," Diana thought, blushing with humiliation and misery as her mother loomed, frowning, overhead.

The event of the summer had turned out to be a disaster after all.

DIANA ON HER OWN

Poor Anne broke her ankle in the fall from the kitchen roof. Diana was grief-stricken, feeling instinctively that it was her fault, for if she hadn't given the party then the disaster of the dares never would have unfolded. Anne was to stay off her foot for seven weeks while it healed—a prospect she found impossible to comprehend, let alone to bear.

Diana made it her mission to visit Anne every day. There was little for Anne to do while lying in bed or propped up on the parlor sofa, except patchwork or embroidery, both of which she despised. Diana hoped her daily presence could at least take her friend's mind off the tedium of needlework and bring a little cheer into her days.

August had already begun to dwindle by the time the Avonlea School board finally settled on a new teacher, a replacement for Mr. Phillips. It had been known for some time that the choice had come down to two lady applicants, but much discussion and debate were given over to making the final selection. There were many in Avonlea who felt that female teachers were no good—either too soft to maintain proper discipline, or not knowledgeable enough to impart anything more than plain common sense to their scholars, and perhaps they couldn't even achieve as much as that. Others, fortunately, held women in higher regard, and their only difficulty was finding some way to eliminate one applicant or the other. Both prospective teachers were well qualified and equally matched.

In the end, though, they settled on Miss Stacy. And even though Diana knew nothing about Miss Stacy, news of the final decision excited her so much that she ran over to Green Gables a full hour before her usual visiting time to tell Anne all about it.

Anne was sitting sideways on the parlor sofa, propped with pillows behind, with her wrapped, splinted ankle stretched along the seat as if on piteous display for God and angels. She was picking disconsolately at a few crooked stitches in her patchwork, but she looked up eagerly when Diana entered.

"Oh, what is it, Diana? I can tell by how rosy your cheeks are that you have exciting news. Is it very thrilling? Please tell me right away, because I am so bored that I think I might actually cry."

"I will tell you, if you'll let me talk," Diana said with a smile and a fond laugh. "What do you think, Anne? They've settled on our teacher for next year. Father just read the letter about it. Her name is Miss Stacy. Isn't that a lovely name? I wonder what she'll be like."

"Now that is exciting news," Anne said. But then her face fell. "Oh, Diana, I've only just realized. I won't be back at school until three weeks into the term. Miss Stacy won't even be new anymore by that time. Everybody will be used to her, and I'll have missed all the excitement of meeting her while she's still fashionable."

"I'm sure she'll be very nice," Diana said. "Or I hope she will be, anyhow. Won't it be dreadful if she turns out to be as stodgy and cross as Mr. Phillips? But I think she'll be nice, and if she is, then she'll feel just as exciting to you no matter when you meet her." Diana pulled a book from her apron pocket and handed it to Anne. "Look here; I've brought you a new book to take your mind off your troubles."

Anne's face lit up when she read the silver-leaf words on the cover. "Charlotte Morgan's newest! Diana, how did you get it?"

"You won't believe it, Anne. My old aunt Josephine sent it to me! It's a good job I went to the post office to get the mail that day, because if Mother had found it first she probably would have thrown it in the stove. But I kept it hidden and read it up in my room, and down by the brook when my chores were done and Mother couldn't see me. It's awfully good. I know you'll like it real well."

"The brook," Anne said wistfully. "And the Dryad's Bubble. Oh, I miss visiting our 'old haunts,' Diana. I can see some of them from my window, like the Haunted Wood and little bits of the Lake of Shining Waters, but it's not the same as being there... walking among our dearest places, and hearing the leaves whisper together, and feeling the sun caress my cheek. This is the very most miserable summer I've ever had."

"It isn't all bad, is it?"

"Well... no. I have had plenty of visitors, and that has given me a nice feeling of being cared for. Even Josie came to see me, just this morning, with a big bouquet of flowers. I think she cut all the flowers from our own garden, because I recognized some of them, but 'it's the thought that counts,' as Mrs. Lynde says. Josie was very apologetic and didn't act smug or nasty once. I think she has come to feel quite badly about the dare, and is ridden with dark regrets. After all, what if I had been killed? I always thought it sounded romantic to be nearly killed, but now that I have lived through it, I can tell you it's a thoroughly disagreeable experience, Diana. But I do think that if Josie dared me again, I might actually try to walk the ridgepole a second time."

"Anne, you never would! I would hope you learned a lesson

from that fall." Diana sounded every bit as sensible as Jane Andrews just then, but she didn't mind a bit.

"Oh, I suppose I wouldn't *really* do it again," Anne admitted. "But it was very courageous, wasn't it?"

Diana had to concede that it was.

ANNE WAS NOT the only girl in Avonlea who learned that summer just how many friends she had. Although Diana visited Green Gables loyally each and every day, she found herself with fare more free time than she'd had since Anne first arrived in Avonlea. For now that Anne couldn't accompany her on their accustomed roamings and ramblings, Diana took to the company of other girls. Jane and Ruby were always game for walks among the wildflowers or shell-collecting expeditions on the red-sand beaches of the Gulf, whenever they could convince someone to drive them out for an afternoon of play. Julia Bell and Minnie Andrews sometimes joined them; once Minnie even invited Diana over to play croquet on the Newbridge Andrews' big, flat lawn.

The girls were good company, but Diana enjoyed her solitary moments just as much, if not better. The fading summer still offered pockets of warmth, and the comforting lassitude one finds beneath murmuring trees or on the sunbaked stones beside gently moving water. There Diana would sprawl on her back, with the tall grasses and wildflowers for a screen, and read her stories until her heart was filled to overflowing.

Treasured, too, were the long walks she took alone. With only herself for company, she could dwell in the unexplored corners of her own mind. She was more thoughtful than she had ever been before, and moved more slowly through the world, noticing more of what she observed, forming her own opinions and ideals. By herself, amid the hum of evening crickets and the sway of ripening oat fields, Diana could be sure that the dreams she dreamed were truly her own, authentic to her own spirit.

The girls were not the only friends whose company Diana enjoyed that summer. One afternoon she followed the Newbridge road away from Orchard Slope, and presently found herself looking out over Barry's Pond... the Lake of Shining Waters, as she couldn't help but think of it now. The lake was very blue—the rich, deep sapphire hue of a perfectly reflected, cloudless August sky. It was a windless day, falling just short of being too warm for comfort, and the lake was undisturbed by the least wave or ripple —except for at its great log-and-stone bridge, where a lone figure leaned on the bridge's railing, casting a baited hook down into the waters below. The splash of his fishing line stirred the water's surface lazily.

Diana stood and looked at the fisherman for a moment, but couldn't tell who it might be from so great a distance. So, idle and curious, she walked on toward the bridge and then proceeded down it. By the time she realized it was Gilbert Blythe, he had taken note of her, and so she couldn't scamper away again. There was nothing for it but to go up to him and say hello.

Gilbert drew in his line when Diana approached, then tipped his hat to her in the most charming way, with a crooked grin. "Good day to you, Miss Barry," he said so loftily that Diana laughed.

"Is the fishing good today?"

"Not at all," Gilbert said. "I haven't had a bite. But that's not the point. I only wanted to get out of the house for a while. The harvest is going to start soon, you see, and there won't be much time for fishing after that. And after the harvest, it's school again. So I must get it in while I still can, even if I don't have anything to show for it."

"I won't take you away from your fun, then," Diana said, and turned to head back toward home.

But Gilbert spoke quickly to stop her. "No; I don't mind some company. Stay and talk a while. It's such a nice day, and I'll never complain about a pretty girl's company."

Diana blushed so hot she knew her face must be as red as an apple. Gilbert was a charmer; no doubt he said such things to all the schoolgirls, when he wasn't dead set on teasing them until they were mindless with fury. Diana knew his compliment meant nothing, but she couldn't help but enjoy it, all the same.

"Have you ever fished before?" Gilbert asked.

"Yes, I've done it a few times with my father."

"Well, cast the line, then. Maybe you'll bring some luck."

"All right," Diana said, "but you must bait the hook. I never could do it; the worms make me feel faint."

Gilbert picked a fat, juicy worm from the can at his feet and threaded it onto the hook. Then he handed the pole to Diana. She flung the line well; worm and float landed with a tidy little splash and drifted on the big pond's slight current.

They leaned together on the bridge's rail, talking of pleasant things while the float remained still in the water below. They spoke of the frolics they'd enjoyed all summer long, the picnics and games and parties. They spoke of the school year to come, the hopes and challenges that lay ahead, and the exciting prospect of a new teacher. The longer they spoke, the less nervous Diana felt, until, after an hour or two, she felt as if she and Gilbert had been the best of chums for years and years... for their whole lives, in fact.

"There's ever so much more to like about him than just the way he looks," Diana realized. "Why, when he's not trying to be a scoundrel for the attention, he's perfectly nice and friendly."

Suddenly the pole in Diana's hand gave a jump. She shrieked in surprise and nearly lost it, but Gilbert reached across to grab it before the fish could pull it from her hands.

"Steady," Gilbert said. He pulled the fish in; it broke the surface with a great commotion and a flash of silver scales in the sun. "You are lucky," Gilbert crowed. He pulled the fish up to the bridge's railing and dropped it in a pail of water. "You ought to come fish with me more often, Diana."

She smiled, but not timidly this time. "I'd like that."

Suddenly the grin slid off Gilbert's face. He busied himself with the fishing line, winding it carefully around the pole and fixing the hook. Diana had the sinking feeling that he was searching for words... and she knew exactly what—*who*—those words would be about.

"Say, Diana," Gilbert finally said, "do you recall when I asked you to talk to Anne Shirley for me?"

"Yes," Diana said cautiously.

"Well... did you ever?"

Diana swallowed hard. They'd spent a lovely afternoon together, and Gilbert hadn't brought up Anne once. And he had to go and spoil everything by getting all sappy about Anne now! "What in Heaven's name can I tell him?" Diana wondered. The last thing she wanted was to let Gilbert down now, after they'd shared such a pleasant day and grown so friendly. But Anne still turned to frost at the mere mention of Gilbert's name. Of course Diana hadn't spoken to Anne on his behalf! To do so would have been to invite the tempest.

Diana decided the best course—the only reasonable one, really—was to tell a falsehood. "Yes," she said rather weakly, for she never liked to be untruthful.

Gilbert's eyes lit up. "You did? What did she say? Has she accepted my apology? Will she be friends with me now?"

"Well," poor Diana stammered, "She's... she's... awful stubborn, you know, Gilbert."

"Oh, I know," he said in a way that suggested he found Anne's stubbornness utterly enchanting.

"I... I think she'll come around eventually," Diana finished lamely. "I must go now. My mother will be expecting me home for supper."

"Wait, Diana." Gilbert reached into the pocket of his vest and pulled out a small envelope. It was sealed, but its edges and corners looked bent and rather abused, as if Gilbert had been carrying it for some time. "I've been thinking I might give this to Anne, but I haven't worked up the nerve to go all the way to Green Gables and face her. Since you've talked to her and you think there's hope, would you be a chum and deliver it for me?"

Diana took the envelope and gazed down at it, her heart sinking as she did. "A. S." was scrawled on the front, right over a little drawing of a carrot.

"Please say you will," Gilbert implored.

Diana looked up at him, helpless to deny his smile and his twinkling, mischievous eyes.

"Oh, all right," she finally said, a bit crossly. "Now I really must go home."

"Good-bye," Gilbert called as Diana stalked off over the bridge. "Come and fish with me again sometime."

When she reached home, Diana ran up to her room and shut the door hard behind her. She stared at the envelope for a long time, biting her lip, wondering what she ought to do. Anne would surely fly in to a rage if Diana delivered the note, or even told her of its existence. "She'd never read it," Diana thought. "She would burn it straight away, without even opening it." Therefore, it couldn't do any harm for Diana to see for herself what the envelope contained. Certainly Anne would never find out.

Despite her excuses, Diana still felt as low as a snake when she slid a finger under the flap and tore the envelope open. Inside was a little post card, decorated on the front with an illustration of blue and pink flowers, embossed, and edged in bright gold. It was one of the prettiest cards Diana had ever seen. It was stamped with these words, also glittering and golden:

May good health
and good cheer
be yours forever.

Diana turned the card over. To her relief, Gilbert had not written out some deathless love poem, but had simply signed his name.

"Oh, I'm a terrible friend, and a truly bad girl, for doing something so mean-spirited and jealous to my bosom friend," Diana mourned.

But what else could she have done? Gilbert and Anne had caught Diana up between them. And now she was stuck as their go-between, a position she did not want, and one that Anne had made quite hopeless and unbearable in any case.

Diana lit her candle and burned the envelope to ash. But the card was too pretty to destroy. She tucked it into her drawer beneath her stockings and shut the drawer firmly. "If only I could shut up my feelings as easily as that," she thought with a distracted sigh.

JOSEPHINE'S LETTER

MISS STACY TURNED OUT TO BE EVERY BIT AS WONDERFUL AS ANNE had hoped and Diana had imagined. She was a soft-spoken, lady-like young woman who nevertheless seemed glad to be teaching in remote Avonlea, not put off by the rustic nature of her surroundings, as some other teachers might have been. She had a great enthusiasm for each and every one of her pupils, and seemed to know just the right way to nurture the best in them, so that each scholar reached instinctively toward his or her fullest potential, like seedlings thriving in the sun. The autumn was full of thrilling adventures that nurtured the mind as much as the spirit: nature walks and studies of birds' nests and earthworms; spelling bees out in the October sunshine along the shore of the brook; recitations in which true feeling were encouraged by Miss Stacy, so that all the plays and poems that were performed left the students prickling with awe and eager to read more for themselves.

Anne was glad to get to know the new schoolmistress when she returned from her convalescence, and of course by that time Diana was already fully devoted to their teacher, leaping out of bed each morning eager to rush to the schoolhouse and learn at the lovely young woman's proverbial knee.

At the end of November, Miss Stacy announced that she intended to hold a Christmas concert, and that she would like every student to perform something, even if they only appeared in a simple tableau. "It's a fine and important skill," Miss Stacy said, "to speak comfortably before a crowd. Concerts can help us become our best, most confident selves."

Diana and Anne shared a look of the purest excitement as they collected their books from their desks.

"Just think, Diana," Anne said, glowing, "we will finally get to perform. Oh, I've waited for this day for so long."

"Diana," Miss Stacy called from the front of the classroom, "will you please remain for a few moments? I would like to speak to you privately before you go home."

"Wait for me outside," Diana whispered to Anne.

She wondered what the trouble could be. She hadn't done as well with her spelling as she would have preferred, but that hardly seemed reason enough to keep her after class. There was no anxiety in the moment, though, for Miss Stacy was a reasonable woman who always spoke to children respectfully, as she spoke to adults. If there was a problem, Diana knew she wouldn't be shamed or humiliated for it, but rather guided and advised in a most sympathetic way.

"What is it, Miss Stacy?" she asked when the school room had cleared.

"It's about the concert. I have noticed, when we've done our group sings, that you have a remarkably fine voice. I would like to ask you to give a special solo performance."

Diana's mouth fell open, before she remembered that it was rude and promptly shut it again. "I... I guess I can do it," she stammered. "But I never sang in front of an audience before."

"I've never sung," Miss Stacy corrected gently, with a smile. "There is a first time for everything, Diana dear. I know it can be intimidating to think of performing before an audience, but you have a rare talent. You know, I think you are a very special and admirable girl, but I get the sense that you don't always shine to your full brightness."

Diana blushed and looked down at the toes of her boots. Hadn't she been thinking that very thing about herself for ever so long now? "It's hard to shine, I suppose," Diana said slowly and rather weakly, "when other girls are so much prettier and gayer and... and more popular."

"That is true." There was no patronizing lilt to Miss Stacy's voice. She took a young girl's troubles as seriously as she would take her own. "I know how that feels, Diana. It is hard to grow up, and difficult to find your place... where you fit comfortably among your friends, your family, the world. But I think you don't give yourself, or your potential, enough credit. You are very popular with the other girls—and with some of the boys, too."

"I'm not as popular as Anne," Diana blurted before she could stop herself.

"But you and Anne are very dear friends, aren't you? Or am I mistaken?"

"No, you're not mistaken. We are the very best of friends. It's only..." Diana shrugged, not knowing how to explain, nor even how to sort out, the jumble of feelings inside her.

"Ah," Miss Stacy said, a sort of understanding sigh. "I see. You love Anne, because she sparkles so brightly herself. But how do you stand out, and truly be Diana—the most whole, most honest version of Diana—when you stand in her shadow?"

"Yes," Diana said, wilting a little, though she didn't know why she felt ashamed, since Miss Stacy was so helpful and caring.

The schoolmistress took Diana's hand briefly, giving her a squeeze to fortify her. "That, too, is one of the hard lessons of growing up: learning how to love our friends without envying them."

"Sometimes I think I do all right at it, but then something will happen to remind me how different Anne and I are, and how I'll never be like her, and how impossible it is to hope for it, and then I'll resent her again." Diana looked up, her cheeks flushed with the sudden force of her feelings. "And I don't *want* to resent her, Miss Stacy! I want to love her just as much as I ever did when we first became friends. But..."

"But it's not always so easy, is it, Diana?"

Miserably, Diana shook her head.

"You are doing a fine job. It's a lesson one learns with time, not all at once. That's the way of most lessons, you know. But I do think singing a solo will help you in this regard. I am sure Anne will wish to give a performance of her own, and she'll do well at it. But you must have your chance to do well, too. You must have an opportunity to stand on your own, and to shine your own light without anything to diminish it."

"I do feel very frightened, just thinking of it."

"Keep thinking about it," Miss Stacy suggested. "With time, the idea will become less frightening. And I look forward to hearing you sing by yourself, Diana. I look forward to it very much."

DIANA DID as Miss Stacy suggested, and thought and thought about the Christmas concert and what it might be like to stand up before a crowd to sing without anyone beside her. She thought about it so much that by the time Christmas vacation came, she was in a cold terror and could scarcely enjoy the weeks away from school.

Perversely, it seemed as if fate wished to prove the good, kind, helpful Miss Stacy as wrong as possible, for the more Diana pondered the solo, the harder her heart grew toward Anne. There was no special reason for it, unless Diana simply envied the ease with which Anne could stand up before the classroom and recite or even spell a word. Performing seemed to give Anne no trouble at all; indeed, it was as natural to her as breathing. But even as Diana felt crumpled and pinched inside with envy, the fact of that envy saddened her as it never had before. For what she had told Miss Stacy was true: she wanted to love Anne, and did her best to feel nothing but warmth toward her. But that warmth seemed harder to maintain every day.

On a mellow evening, when dusk had turned the snow-covered fields to drifts of smoky blue and the spruces of the Haunted Wood were tipped in glittering ice, Diana sat at the tiny table next to her bedroom window, musing bleakly as she gazed out across the dim world. The lamp was burning in Anne's bedroom window, and presently Diana saw the light flash. Five flashes: the signal that meant, "Come over, for I have something important to tell you."

Diana scowled as she considered going. But then she drew down her curtain, carefully and slowly so the motion wouldn't be seen from Green Gables. She lit her own light and took a piece of paper and her ink pen from her writing box. Diana didn't know exactly what she would write, or to whom... she only knew that she must get her feelings out somehow, before they overwhelmed her and spoiled her from the inside out. As she tapped the end of the pen against her lip, the silver charm bracelet jingled softly on her wrist. And then she knew precisely to whom she must write.

Dear Aunt Josephine,

I suppose you will think this is a very foolish letter, but I must write to someone or I think I will actually go mad. I can't talk to Mother because she will think me a very bad girl and will scold me. I can't talk to Father because men don't understand. And I can't talk to Anne for reasons that you shall see.

Aunt Josephine, I like Gilbert Blythe a terrible lot but he doesn't like me one bit, except as a friend. He only likes Anne, even though Anne has refused to speak to him for more than a year because he slighted her once long ago. I feel like the worst kind of friend, because I know Anne would be sore with me if she knew how I feel. She thinks Gilbert Blythe is about as bad as the Devil. I know it is wrong to talk about or write about the Devil, but I don't know how else to be clear in my communication, so you will have to pardon me, please.

I don't know what to do. I'm awful confused. I feel sad nearly all the time about Gilbert, because he is dead gone on Anne, but what if he could like me instead? And I know if Anne finds out, she'll scald me. What should I do about the two of them?

My teacher, Miss Stacy, wants me to sing a solo at the Christmas concert. I am dreadfully afraid of it. I feel that I am a pretty good singer, but the thought of singing by myself in front of a crowd just gives me the chills. Should I sing at the concert, or not?

Do write if you have any advice for

Your great-niece to be pitied,
Diana Barry

The very moment she'd finished the letter, a weight of woe seemed to lift from Diana's shoulders. Often that is the way of things. What we keep bottled up inside only ferments, and builds pressure. But if we can pour out our feelings, we can find some measure of peace again.

A PACKAGE OF GIFTS ARRIVED, sent via the Charlottetown Post, the day before Christmas. Aunt Josephine had been generous, even lavish, with her Christmas giving. There were big, imported oranges and pomegranates for the whole family, and a sack of chestnuts from the tree that grew in her mansion's back yard, which Mrs. Barry immediately poured into a roasting pan and set over the fire. There were sweaters and gloves for Father and Mother, and a porcelain doll with curled hair for Minnie May.

Diana received her present with the smell of the chestnuts drifting smokily around her. It was a long, thin box covered in green velvet and tied shut with a red ribbon. She opened it carefully and found inside a pretty, peachy-soft cameo necklace with an elegant, long-necked lady carved in white. And beneath the necklace was a folded letter.

Diana put on the necklace and then read her letter eagerly. It was written in a thin, cramped, stiffly elegant hand that was so much like Josephine herself that Diana couldn't keep back a smile.

Dear Diana,

Do not think your letter was foolish. Or if it was, I account it no more foolish than any other complaint a girl or woman has ever made on the subject of males. Men—and boys, for that matter—are stubborn, oblivious, eminently frustrating creatures who are better left to their own devices than fretted over by sensible young women like yourself. There exist people who will tell you to disregard the advice of an "old maid," since I have had "no experience" of men. But it is precisely BECAUSE I know the habits of men that I am an old maid!

Your friend Anne is a charming girl, and, I have no doubt, a worthy friend. In fact, I have sent along a present for her, some slippers, which you must give her on my behalf. But if she is in the habit of carrying grudges, then it will be to her sorrow. Fiddlesticks to whatever she may think; I will not hear of any relation of mine holding herself in check for fear of offending a friend, particularly when that friend is behaving like a fool. Diana, my dear, here is one thing proper ladies—those who are not old maids—will never tell you: what you want in this world, you must reach out and TAKE, for no one will hand it to you. Yes, I know it is scandalously forward and entirely unladylike. But if you want something, my dear, you must be willing to seize it, or risk losing it forever.

As for the Christmas concert, you must certainly sing. Wear this necklace when you do, and it will be just like having me there to applaud you.

Yours in shocking crassness,
  Josephine Barry

BY THE TIME Diana sent her first letter to Aunt Josephine, she had already made up her mind to sing at the concert, even though the thought still terrified her. But in the pouring out of her feelings, into a sympathetic old ear, she had found an ounce of courage and run with it. She had chosen "Angels from the Realms of Glory," which seemed fitting for the occasion of Christmas, and had performed it several times now at the concert rehearsals without any tragedy befalling her.

But a rehearsal is a world apart from a concert. On Christmas night, at the Avonlea meeting hall, the school's pupils flocked nervously around Miss Stacy as she directed them to their places. The hall was beginning to fill with the children's families and neighbors, greeting one another merrily, their coats and hats still smelling of horses and winter cold.

The performers were seated in two rows of chairs that spread out from the stage like wings, so that even while they awaited their turn on the stage, each child was still clearly visible to everyone in the audience. Ruby Gillis, who was on the other side of the room from where Anne and Diana sat, was already crumbling under the scrutiny. She dabbed at her red eyes with a handkerchief while Carrie Sloane and Julia Bell tried in vain to comfort her. Gilbert was across the hall, too, lounging unconcernedly in his chair and looking distressingly handsome in wool trousers with suspenders and perfectly shined shoes.

Anne, seated to Diana's left, fidgeted on her hard chair. She was dressed in a lovely new dress of brown gloria with puffed sleeves. It was the perfect shade, mellowing the brassiness of her hair to a nearly auburn hue and keeping a hint of color in her cheeks despite her wide-eyed, pale-skinned worry. Diana had helped her clip a few small, hot-house tea roses into her hair, a becoming shade of ivory-white.

"Oh, I'm terribly afraid," Anne whispered. "What if I forget my lines?"

"Nonsense," Diana said stoutly, though she felt as if her insides had turned to syrup. "You'll do fine, Anne. Really, there's no one better than you at reciting."

As the girls clutched each other's hands and went on whispering encouragement, a shy, hesitant figure approached with shuffling steps. Diana didn't see, for she was focused on whispering in Anne's ear about how dreadful Josie Pye looked in olive-green, but when Anne kicked her ankle she sat up and looked around.

Fred Wright stood before her, shifting his weight uncomfortably from foot to foot, his red face even redder than usual as he smiled timidly at Diana.

"Merry Christmas, Diana," he said.

"Merry Christmas, Fred."

"I got a gift for you." He reached into his pocket and pulled out a tiny box made from folded card. It was small enough to fit in the palm of his hand.

Diana cast a wondering glance at Anne, who nodded in encouragement.

"Th... thank you, Fred. But I'm afraid I didn't get anything for you."

"Oh, that's all right," Fred said gamely. "Go on, open it."

Diana took the box and slid off its lid. Inside was a tiny, pink enamel charm, shaped like a heart. She had never received a gift of that kind from a boy before. Diana was struck quite dumb by the shock.

"I saw that you have a charm bracelet with little silver hearts on it," Fred said quickly, as if he felt he must explain such outrageous behavior. The poor boy's face had turned a truly alarming shade of red. "So I thought you might like one with some color."

"It's perfectly beautiful," Anne said effusively. "Fred, you are so thoughtful and I know Diana is thrilled but she's so overcome with nerves due to her upcoming solo that she can hardly speak anyhow. Here, Diana; let me fasten it on the bracelet for you."

Diana giggled nervously as Anne did just that. The charm fit in well with the tiny silver hearts and stars of Aunt Josephine's bracelet.

"Gosh, Fred," Diana finally managed, "that was awful nice of you. I'm so glad. But..." She glanced across the room at Gilbert, who was deep in conversation with Charlie Sloane. "But..." Anne was a solid force beside her, brimming with energy, and Diana could already hear the rebuke her friend would deliver if she so much as mentioned Gilbert's name. "But the concert is about to start," Diana finally gasped as Mr. Allan took the stage to announce the start of the show.

Fred scampered away to his seat, and with a flurry of applause, the show began.

Diana was the first to be called to the stage, which was an unexpected change from the rehearsed order. But Ruby Gillis was, for the moment, inconsolable with hysteria and could not go on. For one terrible, frozen moment, Diana sat stunned in her chair, not knowing what she should do. It seemed an impossible feat just to rise and walk the few steps to the stage, and then to climb its steps... no, she could never do it!

Anne squeezed her hand. "It's better this way," she whispered quickly. "Then you'll be all done and you won't have to fret about your performance anymore."

"All right," Diana said, as stoically as she could manage. She forced herself to stand and managed to step up onto the stage without stumbling.

Never in her life had Diana felt so conscious of her own

appearance. In a dark blue dress with modest puffs at the sleeves, and with Aunt Josephine's cameo necklace hanging at her throat, she knew she looked as neat and fine as a girl her age could look. But still she felt small and insignificant, and had the uncomfortable certainty that the whole meeting hall was about to burst into laughter—laughing *at her*—although every face was turned to her with smiling, friendly encouragement.

The accompanist struck up the bold, opening chords of the song, and then there was nothing for it but to sing. Diana closed her eyes so she wouldn't have to see the audience. She imagined only two people sat in the chair before her: Miss Stacy and Aunt Josephine. It was easy to feel that Josephine was there, with the cameo lying cool against her skin. "Let your light shine brightly," she imagined Miss Stacy saying. And then, at just the right point in the music, Diana sang out with all the conviction in her spirit:

Angels, from the realms of glory,
  Wing your flight o'er all the earth;
  Ye who sang creation's story,
  Now proclaim Messiah's birth.

Come and worship,
  Come and worship,
  Worship Christ, the newborn king.

She felt like an angel herself as the piano carried her on great, soaring swells of glory. After the first chorus, she forgot all about the stage, the audience, and even the little pink charm dangling at her wrist. She could hear how sweet her voice was... how it blended with the chords of the piano and found each note with delightful ease. She opened her eyes and looked out at the audience as she sang. And there was her mother, smiling with a hand at her throat as if the sound of Diana's voice had moved her that much... and Father, grinning openly with Minnie May on his knee. And there, standing at the back of the hall and beaming as if the accomplishment were her own, was Miss Stacy.

When the song ended, the audience erupted in applause. Diana, with a thrilling new kind of wobbliness overtaking her, managed to give a rather weak curtsey. She had done it! She could scarcely believe it, but she had stood up and performed in front of almost the whole of Avonlea.

"Encore!" someone called. And then another voice echoed back, "Encore!"

Diana hadn't prepared for this. She turned to gape at Anne, helpless and disbelieving. Anne stared back at her with stars gleaming in her eyes. Her hands were clasped before her in a gesture of awed affection.

"What should I do?" Diana mouthed at Anne.

"Sing," Anne replied.

Diana conferred quickly with the pianist, and then gave a brief rendition of "Old Russell's Hen," just long enough to satisfy those who called for her encore. When she was finished, she rushed off the stage and fell back into her seat, glowing with the pride of accomplishment.

Anne wrapped her in a long embrace while the hall was still ringing with applause. "Oh, Diana, weren't you just *wonderful*? I always knew you could sing beautifully, but now everyone else knows it, too, and I'm glad—I'm so glad! I couldn't be happier or prouder if I'd earned all that applause."

"Anne, you're such a dear," Diana said, wondering yet again how she ever could have felt so peevish toward her friend.

To everything there is a season, and Anne's season came in due time. Mr. Allan called her up to the stage several performances later; Anne froze just as Diana had done.

"Go on," Diana urged. "It's not as bad as you think, Anne, honest. And after the first few moments it's even sort of fun."

"I can't, Diana," Anne said breathlessly. "What if I make a fool of myself in front of Gil... in front of everybody?"

"You won't, Anne, I swear it. Don't be afraid; I'll be here watching you. Just pretend like I'm the only one in the audience, and you'll do it fine, just like all the recitations you've done for me at Idlewild."

Trembling, Anne took the stage. But neither Diana nor anyone else, least of all Anne herself, need have feared on her behalf. After one shivery moment, during which she stared out at the audience with a stricken look, Anne seemed to find her composure and her confidence all at once. She drew herself up, in as stately a posture as a girl of almost-thirteen could affect, and took her cue.

Anne gave two monologues: the first one humorous, which was given in a bouncing rhythm and lit by a gleam in Anne's gray eyes which the whole audience found rather contagious. The second monologue was quite a departure. It was tragic and bitter, and Anne's dramatics were so whole-hearted that Diana heard more than a few sniffles from the audience. As Anne wilted into her death scene, her heart-rending groan carried out across a hall gone perfectly silent. Then the thunder of their applause came, and as Anne picked herself up from the stage floor, Diana clapped twice as hard as anyone else. She was glad to find that there was no envy in her now. She felt as proud of Anne's performance as if she had given it herself.

While Anne was still on the stage, Mr. Allan called up the girls who were to join her for their dialogue, "The Fairy Queen." It was sweet and charming, and the girls looked perfectly delightful in their flower crowns and capes made from embroidered table cloths. But after Anne's remarkable monologues, "The Fairy Queen" couldn't help but pale a little by comparison.

When it was over, all the girls on stage clutched each other and gave stifled shrieks of victory. Together they ran off stage and returned to their places. As they went, one of the tea roses worked itself loose from Anne's hair and fell to the ground.

"We'll have the boys' dialogue next," Mr. Allan announced,

"given by Fred Wright, Charlie Sloane, Billy Andrews, and Gilbert Blythe."

The boys sprang up eagerly and made their way to the stage. But Gilbert paused and bent to the floor. He plucked up Anne's rose and, with a small, secret grin, tucked it into the breast pocket of his shirt.

A DEPARTURE IN STYLES

ON A COLD, EARLY TUESDAY MORNING IN APRIL, DIANA WAS dressing for school by lamplight—for the day was so heavily overcast that the sunrise was hardly any brighter than dusk. Mrs. Barry was moving about in the kitchen below, preparing breakfast and starting the stew pot, too, for she would be in town for a Women's Society gala that evening, and it would be up to Diana to set out the family's supper. Diana was just tying her sash and looking forward to a leisurely bowl of porridge when Mrs. Barry's muffled exclamation of "Land's sake!" put Diana on the alert.

"Mother?" she called down the stairs.

"You had better come down here, Diana. It seems you're wanted."

Diana hurried to the kitchen, expecting to find that her mother had spilled something and needed help with it, or worse, that she had burned a finger on the stove. Instead, just as she arrived, there was a timid rap at the kitchen door.

"It's Anne Shirley," Mrs. Barry said. "I looked up and saw her coming through the garden, out there in the rain, looking just like a wraith. She nearly scared the wits out of me."

"Something dreadful must have happened," Diana said,

making for the door. "It's still too early for us to meet for the walk to school."

When Diana swung the door open, she found woe personified waiting on the kitchen stoop. Anne gazed at her silently with quivering lip and teary, tragic eyes. Her black cloth coat was already soaked with rain, and she had wrapped a long plaid scarf all around her head, with its ends knotted hastily beneath her chin, and crammed a straw hat atop the scarf. Its brim dripped rain water in a disconsolate rhythm.

"Anne," Diana exclaimed. "Whatever is the matter?"

"Oh, Diana. 'Pride goes before destruction, and a haughty spirit before a fall.' Mrs. Lynde has said that to me many times, though I never thought before that I was prideful or haughty, but now I see that I was. And oh, how far I have fallen! I fear I shall never recover. And I have only myself to blame for it. That's the worst part, Diana. The very worst part."

Diana and her mother exchanged looks of utter confusion. Then Mrs. Barry said, "You had better come in, girl, whatever is troubling you."

Anne came in and Diana took her hat. There was a moment of expectant silence, as Diana and Mrs. Barry waited to see whether Anne would remove the plaid scarf, too. Finally, with trembling, hesitant hands, she undid the knot and unwound the scarf from around her head.

"Mercy!" Mrs. Barry said when Anne was revealed in full.

Diana couldn't even say that much. She was shocked to pitying silence. Where Anne's long waves of red hair had been, there was... nothing. It had all been cut away, and not as stylishly as one might have hoped. Patches of orange-red curls stood up unevenly on Anne's head. She looked positively dreadful.

"What under the canopy happened to you, Anne?" Mrs. Barry demanded.

Anne seemed to be fighting the urge to cry. She was bravely winning that battle, though not without obvious effort. "Marilla had to cut it all off," she said haltingly. "I... I dyed it, you see. It was terribly wicked of me to do it, and I'm paying for my sin now, so there is no need to remind me of just how bad it was."

"Dyed it?" Diana said. "But why?"

"I wanted to have beautiful raven-black hair like yours," Anne said in a voice that was dangerously close to a wail. "You know how I've always longed for black hair, Diana. I met a peddler and he had some dye, and he promised it would turn it a perfect shade of black, but it only turned green, Diana... *green*! You can't imagine how dreadful I felt. But it was no more than what I deserved, for being so vain about my hair."

"If only Marilla had sent you to me to cut it," Mrs. Barry said. "I don't think Marilla Cuthbert has cut a girl's hair ever in her life!"

"If my hair looks like a patch of weeds now, please tell me right out so I can get used to the idea," Anne said with dignified resignation. "I would rather know the truth."

A patch of weeds was exactly what Anne's hair looked like, but neither Diana nor Mrs. Barry was about to shatter Anne's fragile composure by telling her the awful truth.

"You might even it up a touch, Diana," Mrs. Barry said, going to her sewing basket for her sharpest scissors. "You've trimmed Minnie May's hair before and done a fine job of it. Why don't you take Anne up to your bedroom and the two of you can try some ways of styling it so it doesn't look so—" She stopped herself, pressing her lips tightly together. "Well, I think you can make it look properly rakish and very fashionable if you try. And when you come down I'll have warm scones with honey waiting for you."

"Thank you, Mrs. Barry," Anne said, with an air of bearing an unimaginable sorrow.

The two girls stood before Diana's mirror and took stock of the damage. Anne's eyes were puffy and red, but she refused to let any more tears fall. She sniffled as she stared straight at herself, confronting the atrocity head-on.

"It's not so bad," Diana said cheerfully, snipping here and there to bring the worst of the weed patch under control. "Why, you have all this natural curl, and once you put a little oil in your hair the curls will look real neat and fetching all around your face."

"Do you think so?"

"Just try it and see."

Diana had a small bottle of rose oil; she showed Anne how to twist the curls around her oiled fingers so they lost most of their frizz and lay tame against her forehead and temples.

"Now all you need is a good hair ribbon. You'll have to do a nice, big one. That's the good thing about short hair, Anne; you can put in the biggest, showiest ribbons, and big flowers, too, and no one will think it looks overdone."

"Let them all think whatever they will," Anne said stoically. "I will bear their scorn as my deserved punishment for the sin of vanity."

"Don't be a goose," Diana scoffed as she selected her widest blue satin ribbon. She tied it in a huge bow, just off-center from Anne's curly crown. "There. Now you look real darling, like you did it all on purpose."

"Oh, it will take *years* to grow back," Anne said, giving sudden vent to barely suppressed despair.

"It doesn't matter. And anyway, the most fashionable ladies are wearing their hair short now because it makes it easier to put the stylish hair pieces in. I read all about it in Mother's *Canadian Woman* magazine. They buy the most intricate braids and buns and top-knots, and pin them in on top of short curls just like yours, so it looks like they have masses and masses of hair all piled up to the sky. But at night they can just take their hair off and set it aside, and go right to bed, without fussing with braids and papers and rags. Isn't that clever?"

"It is very clever," Anne conceded. "I think that news would even comfort me, Diana, if I had the money to buy fancy hair pieces. But I spent all my egg money on that accursed dye, and anyway, I don't suppose egg money would be enough to get even one stylish hair braid, would it?"

"No," Diana admitted. "I suppose not. But take heart, Anne. New styles come from somewhere, don't they? Somebody has to be the very first to do something brave and unusual with her dress or her hair, and then everyone else follows along. Maybe you'll set a new trend in Avonlea."

"And soon the Pye girls will be cutting their hair down to the stubble," Anne said with a tremulous smile. She turned away from the mirror and threw her arms around Diana. "Oh, what would I ever do without you? You're the best friend I could ever hope for. I can face the whole school today, looking like I do, because I know you'll be there beside me, and that you at least won't laugh at me, even if all the slings and arrows of scorn are directed my way."

Diana hugged Anne tightly in return. There was a small part of her that rejoiced in Anne's butchered hair, and felt nastily triumphant over it, now Anne's looks had come down rather far... at least where the latest style was concerned. "But that's not the kind of friend I want to be," Diana thought. "A Pye would be glad for other girls' misfortunes. I'm not a Pye."

"No," a small voice seemed to whisper in her head. "You're a Barry... just like Aunt Josephine."

Diana released Anne and busied herself with fixing up her dressing table while Anne talked on about her fear of facing their school mates. Diana wasn't listening to Anne. She was thinking about the letter Aunt Josephine had sent her at Christmastime... the advice the old lady had given her. "What you want in this world, you must reach out and take, for no one will hand it to you."

If ever there was a time when Diana would be able to reach

out and take all that she wanted—not only Gilbert's attention, but greater affection and recognition from her schoolmates, too —then the time was now, when Anne was brought low. Diana had never acted on Aunt Josephine's advice, for rash action was not Diana's way. But she had re-read the letter countless times since Christmas, and thought long and carefully about the advice that letter contained.

"Can I really *take*, without regard for how it might feel to my dearest friend?" Diana asked herself as she and Anne went down-stairs for Mrs. Barry's promised scones. "Can I ever be so mean?"

THE SHOCKING FATE OF THE
LILY MAID

Diana, Anne, Ruby, and Jane hurried down the long, sunbaked hill below Orchard Slope—not the side of the hill that sported the farm's famous apple, pear, and plum trees, but rather the south-facing side, which ran down to the long, blue arm of the Lake of Shining Waters. These fields were planted with Mr. Barry's pumpkins and beans, as the hill provided ideal drainage for those crops. Sweet-smelling shadows of those young, tender vines, climbing so hopefully high up the frames of their wooden trellises, provided the girls with ample cover for their secretive mission.

It was a mission of romance, the seed of which had been germinating within their hearts since the end of the school year. Miss Stacy had assigned to the sixth reader class Tennyson's immortal poem *Lancelot and Elaine*, and not a sixth-reader girl in Avonlea had escaped its enchantment. A full month had passed since the end of the term, yet the glories of Camelot and Avalon had not faded one bit in the girls' collective imagination. In fact, passion for all things Arthurian had flourished, so that even when the girls were fishing or rowing or picking berries among the hedges, they still spoke in hushed, awed tones of Camelot, and played out scenes from Tennyson's poem whenever they found the opportunity. Jane had ordered more stories of Camelot from her mother's book catalogue, spending all the money she'd earned by selling her calves, and Carrie Sloane had hosted a fine birthday party at which the girls took turns reciting lines about the Lily Maid, while Carrie herself lay as if dead on a bier made of sofa cushions. Diana penned her own story about Camelot for the story club she and Anne had formed with their next-best friends. And Anne had declared that her life would be "entirely and undeniably of a better quality" if she had been born in Camelot instead of Canada.

Arthurian enthusiasms had long since reached fever pitch, and every new Camelot game dreamed up by an Avonlea girl was promptly countered by another girl with a game more complex, more dramatic, more thrilling. The stakes rose ever higher. But on that late July day, Diana and her friends had finally hit upon a game that no one in Avonlea would hope to best.

Down through the pumpkins and beans, the girls carried the implements of their glorification. Dina had salvaged from the rag bin her mother's old black shawl, which had been ravaged by moths but still had a pretty, crocheted trim. Jane had supplied an ancient, slightly discolored piano cloth, which was a rather garish shade of yellow but was the most convincing substitute the girls could find for cloth-of-gold. And below them, at the foot of the hill, where a little gravelly spit extended into the water, lay the vehicle of their ascendancy: the tiny flat Mr. Barry used for duck hunting in the fall.

The girls reached the flat, which was pulled up onto the gravel, and clustered together for a moment, giggling and dancing from foot to foot in their excitement.

"Let's begin," Anne said solemnly, and the girls fell reverently silent. "First we must have our Elaine."

"You must be Elaine, Anne," Diana said. "I could never have the courage to float down there."

Diana referred to the long stretch of lake water, with a slow-moving, eastward current, that would carry the flat eventually to the bridge, and then beyond it, where it would fetch up on another gravel strand that waited beyond. The girls had tested the current and the boat's route several times already.

"Nor I," Ruby added. "I don't mind floating down when there's two or three of us and we can sit up. But to lie down and pretend I was dead... I just couldn't! I'd die *really*, of fright."

Anne turned pleadingly to Jane, but Jane shook her head. "Of course it would be romantic, but I know I couldn't keep still. I'd keep sitting up to see where I was, and that would spoil the effect."

"So it must be you, Anne," Diana repeated.

Anne threw up her hands in despair. "But it's too ridiculous to have a redheaded Elaine! I would love to be Elaine, and I'm not afraid to float down, but it's ridiculous just the same. Ruby is so fair and has such lovely, long, golden hair. Just look how short mine still is, and red, too. You know Elaine had 'all her bright hair streaming down.' A red-haired person can't be a lily maid."

"But your complexion is just as fair as Ruby's," Diana said. "And your hair is ever so much darker since you cut it. Why, I'd say it's just about auburn now."

That news cheered Anne considerably. "Do you really think so? I've sometimes thought it was darker, but I never dared to ask anyone for fear she would tell me it wasn't. Do you really think it's auburn now, Diana?"

"Yes, and it's real pretty, too," Diana said earnestly.

"Well, I'll be Elaine, then," said Anne, sufficiently mollified. "Ruby, you will have to be King Arthur, and Jane will be Guinevere, and Diana must be Lancelot. Now, let me see. The barge was 'palled all its length in blackest samite.'"

Diana stepped forward with the old black shawl, and together she and Anne spread it along the bottom of the flat. If you shut your eyes to the moth holes, it looked property funereal. Anne stepped into the boat and lay down along its floor. She closed her eyes and folded her hands delicately over her heart.

Ruby shuffled nervously. "Oh, she does look really dead. It makes me feel frightened, girls. Do you suppose it's wrong to act like this? Mrs. Lynde says that play-acting is abominably wicked."

Anne opened her eyes and said sharply, "Ruby, you shouldn't talk about Mrs. Lynde. It spoils the effect. This is hundreds of years before Mrs. Lynde was born, and it's in Camelot, besides, not Avonlea. Jane," Anne added in exasperation, "you arrange all of this. Elaine can't do the talking when she's supposed to be dead."

Jane placed the piano cloth over Anne's body, tucking it in just below her hands. Diana pulled up an iris from the pond's reedy margin and tucked it into one of Anne's limp hands in place of a snow-white lily. It would have to do.

"She looks perfect," Diana whispered. "Oh, it gives me chills."

"She's all ready," Jane agreed. "Now we must 'kiss her quiet brows' and say our lines."

Diana bent over the flat and kissed Anne's freckled forehead. "Sister, farewell forever," she said, in the most pitiful tones she could manage. Ruby placed her kiss, too. "Farewell, sweet sister."

"Anne, for goodness sake, smile a little," Jane said. "Elaine 'lay as though she smiled.'"

Anne's pale lips curved the slightest bit.

"That's better. Now help me push the flat off, girls."

Diana, Jane, and Ruby leaned into the bow of the boat and pushed with all their strength. The flat gave a loud scrape as it headed away from land. It hung for a moment in the shallows, rotating gently among the reeds and irises before the current took it and tugged it out toward the bridge. Anne did not sit up once.

"That's that," Jane said. "She's on her way now."

"Let's run down to the other headland so we can see her arrive," Diana said. She picked up the cracked old plate that was to serve as Lancelot's shield, to be laid at the tragic maid's feet in her eternal rest.

The girls ran along the lake's shore to the bridge. There they paused to satisfy themselves that Anne was still drifting exactly as she ought to. "Oh, it's better than I'd hoped it would be," Diana said. "She looks awfully romantic, lying so still. It's like we really are in Camelot!"

"Come on, girls," Jane said, and led them on. "We have to be waiting when she arrives."

They hurried up the road and crossed through the woods, turning back toward the pond and the little headland that would receive the lily maid's mournful barge. The girls waited there, puffing to catch their breath and gazing out eagerly at the water. A big willow leaned out over the pond, blocking all view of the bridge, except for the pylons at its northern edge and one end of its railing. But any moment now, the boat would come drifting in through the curtain of willow leaves with Elaine inside it.

"I don't care what Mrs. Lynde says," Ruby confided. "This is the most exciting thing we've ever done, girls. Oh, wait until Carrie and the others hear! They'll just die of envy."

"This is a moment we shall remember all our years," Diana said, trying her best to sound grand and dignified, as Anne always sounded at times like these.

"I do hope word spreads fast," Jane said. "I try to be humble, but this really is the best Camelot game anyone has ever played, and it would be bully to know that everybody else knows we invented it."

"Do you think others will copy us?" Diana asked. "I shouldn't like that. Then it will be a commonplace game. I want it to remain something special, and something only we did."

"We'll be famous," Ruby said giddily. "They'll still be talking about this by the time school starts. Why, maybe Miss Stacy will be so impressed with our dedication to the lessons that she'll let us pick what we're to read next."

"It must be more Camelot stories," Jane said, and Diana and Ruby both agreed.

At that moment, something stirred the curtain of willows. The girls turned toward it expectantly, but whatever had moved there was not the flat they thought to see. It skimmed too low along the water. In fact, it was *sinking* as it came through the green veil of leaves. The girls stared in stunned silence, wondering just what they'd seen slip below the lake's surface. And then, each girl in the same moment realized that it *was* the boat—Anne's boat—and that it had vanished into the lake's depths, taking their friend with it.

Jane gave a long, ragged gasp and covered her mouth with trembling fingers. Diana let Lancelot's shield fall; it shattered on the rocks below. And Ruby, flapping her hands wildly in a display of mindless panic, screamed as loudly and as shrilly as ever a girl had screamed.

"Anne! Oh, Anne," Diana shouted, running down to the water line. "Can you hear me? Where are you, Anne?"

"She's sunk!" Jane cried. "She's sunk and drowned!"

Ruby, having shrieked as piercingly and for as long as she could manage, began to run uselessly from here to there, babbling in terror. "Mrs. Lynde was right! It *was* wicked to play-act! Oh, we're real sinners and we're all going to pay for it now! I tried to warn you girls but you wouldn't listen! Mrs. Lynde told us! She was right, she was right! And now Anne's dead, dead, *dead!*"

Jane, conscious of the fact that someone might hear Ruby's hysterics and then the girls would be in even deeper trouble than they already were, caught Ruby in her arms and clamped her hand over her mouth until Ruby had calmed somewhat. Diana was crouched on the lake's edge, sobbing into the hem of her skirt, with no thought in her mind but one: Anne was gone... forever. What would Diana ever do without her?

When Jane could be sure of Ruby's relative quiet, she released her. "Come on now, girls. Pull yourselves together! If there's any hope for Anne, we must go get help right away. Don't lose your heads. Diana's home is the nearest. We must run back and get her father. He'll know what to do."

Clutching one another's hands with cold, hard, terrified grips, the three girls ran back through the woods, down the road, and over the bridge toward Orchard Slope. If they hadn't been so headlong in their fear—and if their eyes hadn't been half-blinded by tears—they might have noticed a solitary boat rowing easily up the middle of the lake, toward the landing whence the lily maid had embarked on her unfortunate journey. Sitting stiffly in that boat, quite alive but soaked from head to foot, was Anne Shirley, with Gilbert plying the oars.

Diana, Jane, and Ruby scrambled up the pumpkin patch, sobbing and gasping for breath, but found Orchard Slope utterly abandoned. Not even Minnie May was at home; the family, thinking Diana off at Green Gables for the afternoon, had gone into town to shop for needful things.

"What are we to do?" Diana moaned. "Oh, Anne is surely drowned by now, if she wasn't already!"

"We've killed her!" Ruby shrieked. "It's all our fault! They'll hang us for murderers!"

"Is anyone at home at Green Gables?" Jane asked, squinting toward the other farm. It seemed impossibly far away.

"I don't know," Diana said. "Even if there is, won't it be too late? Oh, Jane! Oh, *Anne!*"

"We've got to try," Jane said grimly.

"Murderers!" Ruby screamed again, flapping her hands wildly.

Jane pushed her down on the porch step. "You sit there, and don't move until we come back for you. She's useless when she's in hysterics," she added to Diana. "Now let's run across to Green Gables as fast as we can go. Maybe there's help to be had there."

Diana and Jane left Ruby to cling to the porch post and flew down the hill toward the Haunted Wood. But when they reached Green Gables, with painful stitches in their sides and their breath burning in their throats, they found that house quiet and still, too.

"We must go back ourselves," Jane said. "There is little we can do, but at least... at least we can go back and *hope*, and *pray*."

They returned along the road, running when their legs could manage, and walking quickly when exhaustion overcame them. The whole time, bitter thoughts chased behind Diana, nipping at her heels. How could Diana have ever *considered* being ruthless, as Aunt Josephine had advised her? She loved Anne far too much to ever hurt her. She knew that now... now that it was far too late... now that she had *killed* Anne! "Oh, I would take back every envious moment and every bad thought I ever had about Anne, my own dear bosom friend, if I could just have her back again," Diana prayed fervently. But it was too late. Fate's stamp had fallen, and Diana would be forever marked by regret and woe.

As Diana and Jane rounded the curve in the road, they saw a lone figure coming toward them, walking awkwardly down the center of the lane in the stiff-limbed gait of one who is thoroughly soaked, through and through. In a heartbeat, Diana took in every detail: the long black shawl and piano scarf draped over one shoulder, the familiar blue dress, the mop of red curls—darkened by lake water—and the black velvet bow clinging soddenly to the crown.

"Anne!" Diana shrieked with the force of her relief and gratitude. She and Jane ran to Anne with renewed energy and threw their arms around her, heedless of her wet clothing.

"Oh, Anne," Diana panted, loath to release her friend from her desperate embrace, "how did you escape?"

Anne's teeth chattered, from a chill or excitement or both. "I climbed up one of the bridge piles, and Gilbert Blythe came along in Mr. Andrews's dory, and brought me to land."

Now that the girls knew their friend was not in fact dead, and that they were not murderers, their sense of romance was instantly restored. "Oh, Anne, how splendid of him!" Jane exclaimed. "Why, it's so romantic. Of course you'll speak to him after this."

Anne's chin lifted, though any aim she had for haughtiness was spoiled by her wretched state. "Of course I *won't*. And I don't ever want to hear the word 'romantic' again, Jane Andrews." Seeing the flush on her friends' cheeks, Anne's wrath softened somewhat. "I'm awfully sorry you were so frightened, girls. It is all my fault. I feel sure I was born under an unlucky star."

"But it was lucky that Gilbert came along when he did," Diana insisted. "Anne, how can you deny it now?"

"Deny what?"

Diana exchanged an uneasy look with Jane. She knew it would be easier—better—to remain silent on the subject. But after all she had been through—thinking her friend drowned, and then the bitter repentance of her jealousies, the renouncement of her longing for Gilbert—Diana simply couldn't hold back her words. "How can you deny Gilbert? Oh, Anne, it is so romantic; it's just like a scene from our favorite stories. It's like a scene out of Camelot, in fact."

Anne sniffed dismissively and refused to meet Diana's eye.

"I think Anne and Gilbert are destined," Diana said to Jane. "Speaking of fortunes in the stars."

And even though it tugged ferociously at her heart to say it, Diana knew it was the truth. "I cannot even think about standing between them," she told herself. "I can't get in love's way."

If Diana was ever to have a beau—and she wasn't at all confident that she would—it would have to be someone else. Fate had already chosen Gilbert for Anne.

THE EXPOSITION

The golden September sun had nearly reached its midday peak by the time Mr. Barry's buggy rolled into Charlottetown. Diana and Anne, seated together in the back seat with their overnight bags resting between their feet, had talked ever on, all the thirty miles from Avonlea, which they had left quite early that morning while the sun was still rising. One would have expected the girls to have lost their voices somewhere back before the Charlottetown city limits, but as Mr. Barry turned into the long, curving lane that led back among a thick stand of beech trees still decked in summer green, and Aunt Josephine's big brick mansion came into sight, Anne and Diana found their "second wind." The mansion took its name—Beechwood—from the trees that surrounded it. They made such a thorough screen around the spacious, rolling grounds that Charlottetown was shut from sight.

"What a perfectly elegant place," Anne sighed, gazing around at the plush lawns, neatly trimmed hedges, and bright spots of color where the faces of dahlias and roses peeped over garden borders. "This is exactly the kind of mansion I imagined Lady Cordelia Fitzgerald would inhabit."

"Aunt Josephine has very good taste," Diana agreed. "I've

been to see her in Charlottetown before, but we only came to have visits and luncheons out in the town, and when we stayed the night it was with other relations, not Aunt Josephine. I'd heard before that Beechwood was magnificent, but this is the first I've seen it for myself."

"This is just like a dream," Anne said. "Like a fond fancy coming true at last. I feel as if any moment those front doors will open and Lady Cordelia will be revealed, in a white satin gown with a long, sweeping train, and with her black hair spilling in waves down her back, and amethysts clustered at her throat."

The front doors did swing wide, but it was not Lady Cordelia who greeted them. Aunt Josephine was just as Diana remembered her, small but never frail-looking, her silvery hair swept up in a fashionable yet understated style and her dark eyes sparkling with restrained merriment. She wore a crisp white blouse and a long velvet skirt of a becoming, russet-brown shade, and one of her many pretty cameo necklaces hung below her ruffled collar. She had invited the girls to Beechwood so that she might have their youthful company at the Fall Exhibition in Charlottetown, and neither Diana nor Anne could possibly be any more excited about the adventures that lay ahead of them.

"Diana," Aunt Josephine called gladly from the top of her long and wide brick steps. "How good to see you, my dear. And Anne Shirley. You've come to see me at last, you Anne-girl."

Mr. Barry carried the girls' bags up the steps and kissed his aunt dutifully on the cheek.

"Stay for tea, George," Josephine said.

"I wish I could, Auntie. I must pick up some goods in town and then get back before sunset, if I can. Tomorrow is to be a long day on the farm. We're beginning the apple harvest already, and it will be an especially big one this year."

"Then I shall have to settle for the company of these young snippets," Josephine said with a subtle wink.

Aunt Josephine had a French girl named Marguerite who

helped her around the house... and what a lot of house it was! Marguerite took the girls' bags and carried them off to the spare room where they were to sleep that night. Josephine led the girls into "the green parlor," a distinction which Diana took as a clear indication that Beechwood contained more than one parlor. The mere thought made her feel dizzy.

"Sit anywhere you please," Josephine said, indicating the various carved-legged sofas and mahogany chairs arranged around the large room. "I will go fetch our goodies for tea. I may keep a girl to help me maintain this great old cave, but I do all the cooking and baking, you know. Good food is one of the few sure pleasures in this life. I have always believed that one ought to know how to cook well for oneself, and not rely too much on others."

When Josephine had left, Diana clutched Anne's hand and turned them both around in a slow circle so that they could take in the full splendor of the green parlor. It certainly was green; the floor was covered by a huge, velvet rug, bearing an intricate pattern of pink and ivory flowers against a deep-green background. The walls bore richly shining wainscoting to waist height, but above, where they soared up to the twelve-foot ceilings, they were papered in soft green with a design of garden vines twisting around gold-leafed trellises. A huge window stretched nearly from the floor to the ceiling, paned in leaded diamonds and curtained by silk drapes of a delicate, mossy hue. A huge fireplace stood against one wall, its sides carved in the fashion of two beech trunks with their branches reaching out to form the mantel piece. Between the beech trunks, the fire alcove was lined with tiles of a high-gloss green. Paintings graced the walls—scenes of forests and fields, with men hunting foxes on horseback and waterfalls spilling down into the quiet, green gloom of a woodland dell.

Anne was struck almost dumb with awe. "It's... it's too magnificent for words. And just think, Diana: This is only the parlor!"

"*One* parlor. Isn't it just like a palace? I had no idea Aunt Josephine's house was so grand. I just wish Julia Bell could see this. She puts on such airs about her mother's parlor."

"Velvet carpet," Anne sighed, bending to feel the rug with a trembling hand. "And silk curtains! I've dreamed of such things, Diana. But do you know... I don't believe I feel very comfortable with them after all. There are so many things in this room and all so splendid that there is no scope for imagination. That is one consolation when you are poor: there are so many things you can imagine about."

"Give yourself time," Diana laughed, leading Anne to one of a pair of sofas. "Don't say 'no' to life in a mansion just yet. We've only just arrived!"

"Do you think you could really feel comfortable living in a place like this?" Anne asked, wide-eyed. "After living at dear, sweet old Orchard Slope?"

"Yes, I do," Diana said. "Avonlea is nice, and Orchard Slope is pretty enough, I suppose, but it's nothing like this place. Why, I feel like a queen! That's a feeling I could get used to, Anne. Oh, look at this tea table! The bottom edge is all carved with lion's heads. Isn't that clever?"

Aunt Josephine appeared with a silver tray, which bore a delicate white porcelain teapot with steam ribboning up from its narrow mouth, and several plates full of tempting delicacies— egg salad sandwiches, smoked salmon, real chocolate bonbons, and tiny square cakes dusted with fine sugar. Josephine called them "petits fours"; Diana thought they looked like cakes fit for a fairy's wedding. She set the tray on the lion-carved table and began serving up tea with as much grave deference as if Anne and Diana were honored dignitaries or members of some famous and well-heeled family.

Diana felt satisfaction warm her belly along with the tea as she sipped and conversed with her great-aunt as elegantly as she could manage. "This is indeed the life for me," she thought. "I'm so glad I decided." For you see, after the incident of the lily maid, when Anne had been rescued from drowning by Gilbert Blythe, Diana had made up her mind about her future. She had vowed from that point on to ignore boys altogether—to never think about them, and to avoid speaking to them unless the occasion positively demanded it. She had settled on a life of glorious old-maidhood; her highest ambition was to make herself just like Aunt Josephine, and live out her life doing just what she pleased whenever she liked, without the bother of a husband. And that was before she'd seen Beechwood. Now that she knew exactly how wonderful Aunt Josephine's life was, Diana was certain she had made the right choice.

"I'll never marry," Diana decided, biting into one of the tiny fairy cakes and relishing its sweetness. "After all, Aunt Josephine never married, and look how well she has done for herself. No, never—and won't that just stick it in everybody's eye! Mother's and Gilbert's and Josie Pye's, and... everybody's!"

THE FOLLOWING MORNING, the girls set off with Aunt Josephine for the Exhibition. They rode in her coupe carriage, driven by a real liveried groom, with the window curtains pulled back so the girls could watch Charlottetown go by.

"And so Charlottetown can watch us go by," Diana added. "I wonder if we'll pass anyone from Avonlea. The Exhibition is a big affair, after all. Lots of our school mates have entered for prizes. Wouldn't it be grand if the Pye girls saw us driving in this coupe, Anne? They'd turn green as peas from envy!"

The Exhibition was held on a big ground kept especially for the purpose, as it was one of the most important annual events on Prince Edward Island. There were rows of barns and pens to house livestock, and all manner of halls where the island's best sewing, preserves, baked goods, wood carvings, and more were on display. Aunt Josephine professed a lifelong love of the Exhibition, though, she said, "It never has been so enjoyable as it was when I was a young girl. That's why I wanted you two especially this year. Let's take it all in with wonder and delight, and I think I'll feel just like I'm thirteen again, too."

All day, they walked from one barn or hall to the next. They watched the ponies in competition, with glossy coats and braided manes, being put through their high-stepping paces in a big arena. They wandered starry-eyed through rows of cut flowers, breathing in the perfume as if it were the breath of Heaven itself. They swelled with pride to find Avonlea names among the winners of the sewing and lace-making and baking competitions. Mr. Harmon Andrews won second place for his Gravenstein apples (said Diana, "If Father had entered our apples this year, Orchard Slope would surely have won!") And who should have won the coveted first-prize ribbon in both the butter and cheese contests, but Mrs. Rachel Lynde?

They inspected rows of roosters in identical cages. The birds' feathers glittered with reds and greens and topaz-gold as if their wings and tails were bejeweled. In the next barn over, they found that Mr. Bell had won first prize with one of his big Old Spot hogs.

"Did you ever?" Diana said, aghast. "Mr. Bell is the Sunday school superintendent!"

"I don't see why that should disqualify him from showing his hogs at Exhibition," Anne said.

"I'll never be able to listen to him praying again! As solemn as he is... you know. All I'll think about is his blue-ribbon pig, and how proud he is about it. You know what the Bells are like, Anne."

"I do suppose the sin of pride extends even to prize-winning pigs," Anne answered thoughtfully.

Aunt Josephine threw back her silvery head and laughed. "It

was the best idea I ever had, to bring you girls out for Exhibition!"

They climbed high up into the grandstand to watch the horse races, with Aunt Josephine hooting and cheering beside them. And after the races, a hot-air balloon was brought onto the field. They watched in wonder as the balloon was filled and billowed up against its tie-ropes, straining toward the sky. Then a man climbed into its basket and the crowd said, "Oooh!" with one voice as he rose gracefully into the air.

Late afternoon found them all quite hungry, so they wandered the grounds until they found a pie seller whose wares looked especially tempting. Aunt Josephine pledged to hold their place in the long line, and slipped the girls ten cents each so that they could amuse themselves until their pies were ready. Diana and Anne skipped off, hand in hand, to seek out their next adventure.

They found it in the form of a booth draped with silk cloths of many colors. A man with a pointed little beard stood behind the booth, feeding peanuts to a small, green parrot that perched on his shoulder. Behind man and parrot was a big sign, painted with fancy script: Fortunes Told Here, Ten Cents.

"Oh, look, Diana," Anne said. "Let's have our fortunes told!"

Diana looked doubtfully at the man with the parrot. There was something rather roguish about him. "I don't know. Isn't divination wicked?"

"According to Rachel Lynde," Anne said. "But everything is wicked, according to Mrs. Lynde."

"Well, all right. If you think we ought to."

Diana and Anne approached the fortune booth. "Ah," the man said, taking his parrot down from his shoulder. "Two delightful young ladies come seeking a glimpse of the future. What is your heart's desire? What do you seek to know? No, no—don't tell me. Let my little friend here read the fates for you."

The girls laid their ten cents apiece on the table, and the man set his bird on the rim of a big brass bowl. The bird's bright head dipped into the bowl; it came up holding a tiny scroll of paper, tied with a green thread, in its beak. The man handed the first to Anne. Then the bird extracted another fortune from the depths of the bowl, which was Diana's.

"You read yours first," Anne said excitedly.

"No, you must. I'm too much afraid. What if I don't like mine?"

"Very well; I'll go first." Anne slipped the green thread from her scroll and unrolled the slip of paper. She read it once silently, then, with glowing face, read it aloud for Diana. "'You will marry a dark-complected stranger who is very wealthy, and go across water to live.' Oh, Diana, that sounds so romantic. What does yours say?"

Diana unrolled her scroll, gripped by a sudden shiver of excitement. What would her future hold, after all? Had the little bird predicted a mansion like Beechwood? A life of freedom and luxury, as Aunt Josephine enjoyed?

When she read the words on her paper, Diana felt quite dismayed. "'You will marry one who is known to you, have many children, and stay close to home.'"

Anne set to work at once, speculating wildly about which Avonlea boy was to make Diana his bride. Diana crumpled up the paper and stuffed it into the pocket of her skirt. "Marry!" she thought petulantly. "And stay close to home!"

Just when she had settled on the grandest future she could ever imagine, cruel fate made its contrary plans known.

A DREAM DENIED

NOVEMBER WAS SOFT AND WARM THAT YEAR—AT LEAST, COMPARED to Novembers past. The snows were delayed, leaving fields of stubble and bare furrows to wear jackets of crisp silver. Along the Birch Path, leafless twigs cut enchanting dark patterns against ice-blue skies, and along the edges of the Haunted Wood the last of the autumn's white mushrooms peeked up amid fallen leaves that were edged in pearly margins of frost. Dancing little mists spilled out of woods and hollows in the mornings and lingered almost until the afternoon. And the sky was full of the cries of geese as they winged their way south at the closing of every day.

On one such bright November day, a Saturday, Diana came inside after a long and delightful romp with Anne. They had spent the daylight hours looking for edible mushrooms along the Newbridge Road. They had found none, but the day had been glorious all the same. Now, with the sun sinking lower and tinting the cloudless sky rosy-gold, Diana looked forward to the warmth of the kitchen and a good bowl of Mrs. Barry's venison stew for supper.

Rosy-cheeked and out of breath from her run up from the brook, Diana flung herself eagerly through the kitchen door and tossed her cap, scarf, and coat onto the hooks beside the stove. "Mother," she called merrily, "I'm home!"

The kitchen was empty. "Diana, dear," Mrs. Barry called from the parlor, "why don't you come in here?"

Diana went to the parlor... and froze on its threshold. Miss Stacy was seated comfortably on the sofa, beaming up at Diana in that warm, pleasant way she had. Mr. Barry was there along with Diana's mother. All of them looked perfectly pleasant and not the least bit riled, but still, Diana felt anxious. It usually is not a good sign, whenever a pupil's schoolmistress appears in her home to talk to both her parents.

Diana entered rather cautiously. She sat in a chair beside the fire. "Good afternoon, Miss Stacy," she said carefully.

"Your schoolmistress only just arrived," Mrs. Barry said. "Do tell us what brings you here, Miss Stacy. I hope Diana has not been a disappointment to you."

"No, on the contrary," Miss Stacy said, laughing a little. "Diana is one of my very best students, Mrs. Barry. I want you to know that. I am very pleased with her conduct and her work."

"Well, naturally we are delighted to visit with you any time," Mrs. Barry said smoothly. "But do tell us what has brought you today."

Miss Stacy hesitated only briefly. Her eyes flickered as she took in the sight of upright, prim Mrs. Barry, and Diana's father, who was stroking his mustache and watching her with obvious curiosity. Diana had the impression that Miss Stacy felt rather uncertain of her errand... but a moment later she began to speak, and Diana could think of nothing but Miss Stacy's words.

"I have decided, Mr. and Mrs. Barry, to organize a special class for my advanced students, seventh reader and up. This class would be preparatory in nature—for students who would like to take the entrance exam at Queen's College."

Diana's eyes widened. Her heart thumped so hard in her chest she felt sure her mother must hear it from across the parlor... but she dared not shift in her seat, nor even gasp in surprise. She bit her lip to keep herself still and watched her mother from the corner of her eye.

"Queen's has a very good program for teachers, you know, and teaching can open many doors to good students in a town like Avonlea. I know how difficult it can be to pay for one's child to carry on with education. My own family faced that challenge. By opening up the avenue of teaching, we may provide our better students here in Avonlea with a means to see themselves through several years' more education."

Teaching! Diana had never thought of it before, but now that the opportunity presented itself—indeed, now that it spread before her like a brilliant and beautiful vista—she knew she wanted nothing else for her life. Teaching—working for herself —would provide the surest path to the kind of life she wanted. As a teacher, she could work her way into Charlottetown... or maybe to a bigger city, on the mainland. She might prove herself worthy of a position as a principal, or even a superintendent. There were some women superintendents, Diana knew, though not many, to be sure. "Why, I could live on my own in a city if I were a teacher," Diana thought excitedly. "And the longer I did it, the more money I saved, the more like Aunt Josephine I could be!"

"I see," Mrs. Barry said.

Diana's heart sank. She could tell by the way her mother said those two simple words that she was not favorably disposed to the idea.

"Diana is very bright," Miss Stacy said. "And what's more, she has an excellent way with younger children. I see a dedication and perseverance in Diana that is rare in a child of fourteen. She has all the qualities that make a successful schoolmistress. I do hope you will allow her to join the Queen's class. Anne Shirley will be in it; I know how much Anne and Diana enjoy doing their lessons together."

Mr. and Mrs. Barry shared a long look, during which Diana

had the feeling that whole volumes of conversation were exchanged... but silently, so that neither she nor Miss Stacy could protest.

At last Mr. Barry—Father, who had always been on Diana's side!—cleared his throat in a regretful way. "I'm afraid not, Miss Stacy. You see, we may only be farmers, but still we feel as if our family has a certain... er... reputation to maintain. I hope you will not take offense... you, being a teacher yourself."

Miss Stacy smiled graciously. "I take no offense, Mr. Barry, I assure you. But Diana—"

"Diana must marry," Mrs. Barry said firmly. "That way lies her best hope for the future."

"Of course," Miss Stacy said. "Women who teach are not required to remain unmarried forever. Many work for a year or two, to earn money for more schooling, and then, when they've finished their studies... a B.A., for example... they marry."

"I wonder," Mrs. Barry said, tilting her head with curiosity, "what is the point of attaining a B.A. if one plans to marry? What is the point for a woman, I mean. A wife and mother has no need of advanced schooling. Wouldn't her time and money be put to more sensible uses? Oughtn't she to get started on the business of being a wife and a mother sooner, and leave the B.A.s to the men, who will actually use them?"

"Some would say that knowledge is its own reward," Miss Stacy said, floundering, "and that the pursuit of knowledge is a worthy occupation of one's time, regardless of whether one is a man or a woman."

Mrs. Barry smiled tightly. "I'm afraid my Diana is not destined for a B.A., Miss Stacy. Nor even for Queen's. It is perfectly respectable to marry and keep a home." She added that last with an emphasis that said she considered marriage and house-keeping the *only* respectable occupations for womankind.

Miss Stacy rose and pulled on her gloves. "I understand. Thank you for your hospitality." She turned to Diana with a smile, but Diana could see her own bitter disappointment reflected in Miss Stacy's eyes. "Good evening, Diana. I'll see you on Monday."

Tears filled Diana's eyes as her parents showed Miss Stacy to the door. When they returned to the parlor, Mrs. Barry gazed at the weeping Diana in dumbfounded silence, as if she were truly shocked to her core that Diana could feel such agony over being denied the Queen's class.

"Diana," Mrs. Barry finally managed, her voice faint with surprise.

Diana sprang to her feet. "Oh, how could you, Mother? And you, Father? You of all people!"

"Diana, stop this at once," Mrs. Barry commanded.

"No, I won't stop it! I want to be a teacher... I've never wanted a thing before so badly in all my life. And you ruined my one and only chance!"

"You will *not* be a teacher, Diana Barry. I won't hear such nonsense out of your mouth again. You will marry someday, when the time is right... and marry *well*. We may be farmers, but that doesn't mean you can't marry well."

"Oh, why is it so important to you whether or not I marry?"

"Because marriage is a woman's best hope for happiness, Diana," Mrs. Barry said sternly. "I know you admire Miss Stacy, but imagine what her life must be like. Living in boarding houses, without a home to call her own... being shuffled from one town to the next as the school boards see fit, never able to put down roots... and being dedicated to her work, Diana! That's the worst of it. Teachers, of a necessity, cannot also be wives or mothers. A person cannot divide their minds and hearts in such a way. Every teacher has chosen to devote herself to the school. To a nomad's life, sleeping in damp boarding rooms, and constantly toiling! It's no life for a daughter of mine, Diana, I can tell you that."

"But it's the life I *want*," Diana wailed. "Mother, Father, I want to work. I want to care for myself and go live in a city and make my own way. I don't want to marry well... or marry at all!"

Mrs. Barry's shocked gasp could have sucked the clouds from the sky, had there been any.

"Besides," Diana went on bitterly, "all the boys in Avonlea hate me! So no one will want to marry me anyhow."

That, of course, was not true. It was only Gilbert who wouldn't pay any more mind to Diana than he did to his boy chums. The rest of the boys liked Diana quite well, and in her less bitter moments she was willing to acknowledge that fact (privately, so as not to be accused of being "too big for her britches.") But now, with all the unfairnesses of life throwing their weight upon her, she thought she might as well pull the heaviness of Gilbert down upon her heart, too.

"Stop this crying at once," Mrs. Barry said sharply. "You are carrying on like a fool. No sensible girl *wants* to teach. You heard Miss Stacy; for girls, teaching is a last resort—a way to deal with money troubles. We aren't so poor that we can't provide for you, Diana, and see you into the kind of life you ought to have."

"The kind of life I ought to have?" Diana scoffed. "But what of the kind of life I want? I don't care what you say, Mother! I do want to teach. And it's awful cruel of you to not let me do it."

Mr. Barry stepped between his wife and his daughter, for Mrs. Barry had begun to bristle alarmingly. "Now, now," he said soothingly. "Try and get used to the idea, darling. Your mother and I know what's best for you. Go up to your room and cool off a bit. You'll feel better about things by and by."

Diana did run stormily up to her room and slammed the door behind her with a satisfying thud. She flew to the table by her window and struck a match with trembling fingers... but just before she touched its flame to the lamp wick, she thought better of it. She had wanted to signal for Anne—had wanted to run down to the brook and weep bitterly in her friend's arms, and spill out onto Anne's shoulder how unfair her parents were, how unfair life itself was.

"But Anne will be in the Queen's class," Diana thought, and felt a tightness in her chest. "She won't understand how I feel. She gets to take the extra lessons, and prepare for college, and go on to the exams... and she gets to teach, too."

Diana blew out the match. The smell of sulfur smoke filled her room. She gazed out across the Haunted Wood to Green Gables... to the eastern window, where a golden light was flashing against the royal-blue autumn dusk. Flashing five times, with an exuberant rhythm.

"Anne wants to see me," she realized dully. "And she's so happy; I can tell already. She wants to tell me all about the Queen's class... but how can I stand to listen to her gladness now?"

Diana sighed and sank onto her chair, then dropped her head on her arms and wept afresh. "Oh, Anne. You have everything now. The love of all our friends at school, and Gilbert's affection, and now... now... even this."

Anne even had the bright, happy, self-determined future Diana so longed for.

"How can I love a person so much as I love you, Anne," Diana wondered, "when I also feel so bitter toward you?"

MISS STACY OFFERS ADVICE

THE YEAR TURNED SLOWLY FOR DIANA. IN FEBRUARY SHE TURNED fifteen, and although the celebrations with her friends were gay and delightful, she couldn't help but feel a faint, almost imperceptible dissatisfaction. It didn't feel right, to be fifteen—which was only two years away from being a grown woman—and yet to feel as if one's life had reached a dead end. What real pleasure was there in concerts and games and pretty dresses, if she could never hope to attain the grand, independent life she wanted?

Although her envy of Anne, whose brilliant future seemed all but assured, was still painfully near the surface of Diana's heart, she drew closer to her bosom friend than ever before. Anne never put on airs about being a member of the Queen's class. She seemed to sense Diana's disappointment, and offered only sympathy when it was needed—in the times when Diana cried or railed against her mother for being so unfair—and the simple comfort of good friendship when it was not. The girls were older now. Naturally they played less, laying their flights of fancy and games of the imagination sweetly to rest in the lavender of cherished memory. But they spent as much time in one another's company as they ever had before, talking of subjects both serious and flippant, helping one another through the new, strange, heart-rending thickets of circumstance that seemed to spring up all around them at every turn.

Anne stayed late at school with the other Queen's students, so that Diana had to walk home alone. Sometimes she welcomed the chance to be private and thoughtful, and used her walks down the Birch Path and along the edge of the Haunted Wood to work out the mystery of her own thoughts and feelings. And now, in her fifteenth year, Diana's feelings were a mystery to her as they never had been before. More often, though, Diana missed Anne terribly in the afternoons. What she wouldn't have given to hear Anne's happy chatter all the way home from school, to laugh fondly at her friend's grand declarations and wild ideas, to simply hold her hand and know that no matter how life came to resemble a howling wilderness, she always had a kindred spirit beside her.

Of course, the girls still cherished their time together on mornings and weekends, and made the most of it. Anne told Diana all about the Queen's class, sharing every detail candidly, unless a fleeting expression of pain crossed Diana's features—and then Anne would tactfully change the subject, for the exuberant redhead was learning to read others' reactions and to temper her tongue accordingly. Most of the time, though, Diana liked to hear about the class.

"The geometry is dreadful," Anne moaned. "I fear I am the worst dunce at it. If I don't get into Queen's after all, it will be geometry's fault. No—it will be *my* fault. I heard Miss Stacy correct herself yesterday and own that she had made a mistake, and I thought it was so good and noble of her. I aim to do the same all the time now. So I must bravely admit that if I don't get in... and I think it entirely possible that I won't, Diana... it will be no one's fault but my own. Geometry is my Achilles' heel, though.

I just don't understand it one bit. It feels like wading through a dense jungle of vines and shadows and lurking beasts every time I open my mathematics book.

"Reading is all right, though. Miss Stacy has us finishing the tenth reader, and expects us to get through it before the end of this school year. The tenth! I never thought I would be two readers ahead of our age group, and if I had a say in the matter, I wouldn't be. I love reading, as you well know, but it is so abysmally *hard* when you're reading ahead of your age group. I suppose it's for the best, though. If I'm to teach others someday, I must know how to handle everything up to the twelfth level. But it seems ridiculous to think of myself, at fifteen, ever being a grown-up eighteen-year-old teaching in a school! Can you imagine?"

"No," said Diana, who had been able to think of nothing but teaching for months now. "The classes sound terribly hard, Anne. I guess I'm glad Mother wouldn't let me take them after all. I'm not quick enough to do the tenth reader, and I'm pretty good at geometry, but probably not good enough to satisfy the Queen's class."

Diana stifled a sigh, for she knew what she said wasn't true. She could have handled the work, and would have reveled in the challenge. But it made the disappointment easier to bear, if she pretended otherwise.

"You could have handled it," Anne said. She meant the encouragement in a friendly way, but the confirmation of Diana's inner suspicions only made Diana's stomach sour and her eyes sting with momentary tears, quickly blinked away. "You're ever so bright, Diana. I still think your mother has perpetrated a grave injustice. I would never forgive her, except that *she* forgave *me* for accidentally making you drunk, so I feel as if I ought to remain favorably disposed toward her, just on principle."

"Well, I must forgive her, I guess," Diana said glumly, "for I have to live with her and believe me, it's easier to live with Mother when you aren't at odds with her. She is a positive *dragon* when she wants to be, Anne!"

Anne, for once, said nothing, but squeezed Diana's hand sympathetically.

"Tell me more about the tenth reader," Diana prompted, with more gaiety in her voice than she felt in her heart. "Is the poetry in it very good? Are there any especially romantic lines? I want to know."

And with that, Anne was off again, recounting every detail she could recall of the latest poem the Queen's class had read. Diana stifled her wistful sighs and did her best to listen without nurturing her secret resentment.

IN DUE TIME, the autumn came again, touching the land with the colors of fire and filling the air with the rich smell of dry grass and wood smoke. For most of the Avonlea School pupils, the new school year opened as it did all the years before. But for Miss Stacy's preparatory class, this year was an especially important one. The pressure was on to attain their best marks yet, for when the summer came again, those select students would take their entrance exams at the academy in Charlottetown. That happy and dreaded day was month in the future, but every one of the Queen's students felt the pressure building. Expectations were high—from parents, from Miss Stacy, and from the students themselves. Never before had Avonlea School known such dedication to learning. The focus and determination of the Queen's students seemed to spill over and anoint the rest of Miss Stacy's scholars, so that everyone worked with a zeal that nearly put paid to the usual pranks and tomfooleries that marked the school day.

One student at Avonlea School, though, seemed wearied and

worn. Diana Barry often slouched in her seat, and sighed gustily, and spent more time gazing out the window toward the Lake of Shining Waters than focusing on her lessons. Her marks were beginning to slip—a fact that did not alarm Diana in the least, though it should have.

Miss Stacy, observant and caring as she was, had certainly noticed the change in Diana. That good lady determined to nip Diana's moodiness in the bud, before it could flower into any sort of degeneration. On a crisp Friday afternoon in windy October, she dismissed the class but called Diana back just before the girl could slip out the door.

"Diana," Miss Stacy said, "I would like it very much if you would have lunch with me. Do you think your mother would permit it?"

"I... I suppose so," Diana said uncertainly. She had never been asked to lunch at Miss Stacy's before, and worried that it portended something terrible. But she liked the schoolmistress, and in any case a lunch at Miss Stacy's meant a welcome change from the monotony of her daily routine.

"Good. Why don't you come over tomorrow at noon?" Miss Stacy wrote her address on a little slip of paper and handed it to Diana. "I hope you like fruit cake. My landlady is a sweet old woman who likes baking rather too well. There is more fruit cake than I know what to do with."

Diana smiled. "I do like it, ever so much. I'll see you tomorrow, Miss Stacy."

It happened that Miss Stacy lived very near the Avonlea post office, which was walking distance from Orchard Slope... at least if you enjoyed a good, long walk with plenty of time for quiet musing, as Diana did. The day was fine, too, though a little brisk, and Diana enjoyed the stroll down the red-earth roads with the bright fall leaves skittering past and the birds singing happily in the weak autumn sunshine.

Miss Stacy happened to be the only boarder at her house,

which was a darling little cottage with a white picket fence and gnarled old lilac trees in the front yard. The owner of the house had gone off to Carmody for the day, so Miss Stacy herself answered the door when Diana knocked. The schoolmistress looked smart and professional in a navy-blue dress with modestly puffed-out sleeves. She shook Diana's hand in a way that made Diana feel quite grown-up and serious.

"I'm so glad you could join me," Miss Stacy said, leading Diana into the kitchen.

"Are any other girls coming?"

"No, Diana, it will be just you and I. Does that suit you?"

"Oh… yes, of course. But I thought perhaps you were hosting a tea for several different girls at once. Mrs. Allan, the minister's wife, does that sometimes, you know… to stay in touch with us and to give us a chance to talk to her about things we feel we can't bring up in Sunday school."

"Mrs. Allan is very wise, I think." Miss Stacy and Diana sat at the kitchen table, close beside the warm stove. "And very caring. I have noticed—and I suppose Mrs. Allan has, too—that girls of your age often feel the need to talk about certain subjects, and often those subjects are hard to broach."

Diana sensed that this was the very reason why Miss Stacy had invited her to tea. She sipped thoughtfully from her cup and waited for Miss Stacy to pour a cup of her own, then said carefully, "Is that why you've asked me here, then? So that we can talk about a hard subject?"

"Perhaps." Miss Stacy smiled. "Though I don't know whether the subject is hard or not. I suppose that depends on you… on how you feel. But I have noticed, Diana, that you are losing interest in school. That has me rather worried for you."

Diana blushed and hung her head over her plate of fruit cake. "I'm sorry, Miss Stacy. I don't mean to slip."

"I know you don't, dear. But I am concerned for you. You were one of my very best students, yet now your marks are sliding. I thought... well, I wondered if perhaps you are struggling with things you feel you can't talk about to anyone else. Not to your mother, not to your friends, not even to Mrs. Allan. I wanted to offer myself as a sympathetic ear, in case I can be of any help to you."

Diana looked up, sudden and unexpected tears sparkling in her eyes. "Oh, Miss Stacy. I hardly know where to begin; my feelings are such a tangle, and they seem such a mess to me! And..." she hesitated, took a gulp of her tea to calm herself, and then said, "and I wonder whether I ought to talk about what's troubling me at all. Even if I could sort it out enough to know where to begin. What's the use of talking about one's problems if the problems are unsolvable?"

"Most problems that seem impenetrable are not truly... not when one looks at them the right way."

Still Diana hesitated. She knew she could trust Miss Stacy with any of her secrets—knew it instinctively, for the kindly young schoolmistress had always possessed an undeniable air of honesty. "But how can she help thinking my troubles are silly?" Diana asked herself.

But *would* Miss Stacy think her silly? She had always been so sympathetic before, had taken Diana's concerns to heart and had guided her well through past troubles.

To test the waters, Diana said, "You have made me feel so grown up, just by asking me here to tea. I don't want to feel like a little girl again... not in your eyes."

Miss Stacy's smile had no mockery or amusement in it, only warmth and remembrance. "It wasn't so terribly long ago that I was a girl of fifteen. I recall what that feels like. I recall *all* of being a girl of fifteen, Diana. It is not as easy as older women think. I believe as we grow older, we forget how it felt to be young and vulnerable, and still learning the ways of the world. But I have not grown so old... not yet."

Diana decided she must trust Miss Stacy, or go mad from all

the grief and fear and confusion that plagued her. "You once told me that I would find a way to shine at my brightest, even with... with..." She trailed off, unable to speak on, for she felt so terribly guilty, as if she were committing the sin of a thousand betrayals.

"Even with Anne at your side," Miss Stacy said.

Diana nodded. "But now Anne has gone on to the Queen's class... and oh, Miss Stacy, I wanted to take the classes so badly, and wanted to be a teacher, too. And now Anne is doing it all without me. She's no longer beside me—not very often, anyway —yet I feel farther away from 'shining' than I ever was before. I feel positively dull. And I don't know what to do."

"I see," Miss Stacy said, sipping her tea. "Is that all that troubles you?"

"Well... no."

"Would you like to tell me the rest?"

Diana did tell the rest. For more than an hour, she wrung out all her feelings into her cup of tea, confessing all the anger she felt at her mother—and the guilt over that anger, too, for she knew full well that her mother only wanted what was best for her. "It's only that we have different ideas about what's best for me," Diana said, "and maybe it's wicked of me to say so, but I really think that I know best about me, after all, even if she is my mother." She told about Aunt Josephine and her letter, encouraging Diana to reach out and take what she wanted from the world... and how that advice had haunted her ever since. "I do want to take what should be mine, but the thought of doing it makes me shiver. And I can't take something if taking it might hurt someone I love, can I? Who's more important then—me, or the person I may be hurting?" She even spilled out her conflicted feelings about Gilbert, for she knew by then that there was no danger of Miss Stacy letting the news slip to any malevolent ear. "I feel as if I ought to let all thought of Gilbert go. But then I see him again—just set eyes on him, that's all—and my heart starts to flutter and I just *can't*, Miss Stacy... I truly can't!"

Last of all, she tried her best to unspool the tightly wound, fearfully tangled skein of her love and envy for Anne. "Anne has been nothing but good to me. I can't imagine my life without her. And yet I am consumed with envy whenever I think of her. Imagine, envying a poor orphan! Yet I do, Miss Stacy... I do. She has all the courage I lack, and now that she's in the Queen's class without me, she has the future I lack, too—the future I want. Oh, what am I to do? Anne may not know it, but I've been an awfully bad friend to her, and the knowledge of how ungrateful and mean I am eats at me every day. But I can't seem to stop feeling that way, either."

"Feelings are strange things," Miss Stacy agreed. "They behave without logic. But we all have them, Diana, and even the unwelcome feelings are nothing to be ashamed of."

"I disagree," Diana said calmly. "I feel rotten inside when jealousy overcomes me. Or when I get too angry with my mother. Then I *do* feel shame, and I think perhaps God made us that way, so that we would know when we have let our feelings go to far."

Miss Stacy watched Diana in silence for a moment, then said, "I think you are much brighter and wiser than anyone gives you credit for, Diana dear. Even you don't give yourself enough credit."

Diana didn't know how to respond to Miss Stacy's compliment, so she only bowed her head and picked at the crumbs of her fruit cake with her fork. After a moment, she said, "I do feel a little bit better, just for having told you everything. Not all the way better... but a bit."

"That is usually the way of things. When we can be honest about the way we feel... when we hold nothing back... then we can be sure that others see us most clearly. Even when the picture we must show them is ugly or distorted, at least we know it is a true and honest picture. And it feels good to be sure that our truest self is seen, doesn't it?"

"It does," Diana agreed, brightening a little. Then her face and her spirits fell again. "But Anne is my bosom friend. I should be my truest self with her, shouldn't I?"

"Yes, I suppose so," Miss Stacy said in a practical tone. "Have you been dishonest with Anne? Or kept something back that you ought to have told her about?"

Diana wondered if she had. She couldn't think of anything, other than telling Anne about her feelings for Gilbert, but... but still she felt a strange weight in her heart, as if she had forgotten something important.

When it became plain that Diana had no answer to Miss Stacy's question, the schoolmistress spoke on. "I believe you can still shine brightly, Diana. And I believe your path through life will be just as bright and wonderful as you are, yourself. It may be a different path than what you dream of now, but it will be good and fulfilling and right all the same. You'll know its rightness when you find it; you will recognize its truth for yourself, without your mother or Anne or anyone else pushing or prodding you toward it. You will take your path of your own accord, and do it gladly. You're too smart and good a girl for your life to take any other shape."

Diana did not meet Miss Stacy's eye. She still felt the odd, compelling pressure of something long forgotten—something important—stifling all her gladness.

Again, Miss Stacy seemed to sense that more of her subtle guidance was needed. She thought for a moment, looking earnestly at Diana's troubled face, the downcast eyes and the blushing cheeks. Then, at last, Miss Stacy hit upon advice that felt exactly right, and so she dispensed it. "Diana, dear: Sometimes we must humble ourselves—even when we already feel that the world has humbled us—before we'll find peace."

Diana glanced up, her brow furrowed, her lips pressed together in consternation.

"Peace can only come from inside us," Miss Stacy said, "and sometimes, before we can attain it, we must do the hard thing and make amends with whatever haunts us deep down, inside our very souls."

Diana nodded and offered Miss Stacy a smile, as if she understood the advice perfectly. But to herself, she said, "If only I could know for sure just what haunts my soul. Then perhaps I could finally have a little peace!"

WHEN THE WORLD HAS HUMBLED US

"SPELLING WILL BE OUR LAST LESSON TODAY," MISS STACY announced smoothly from her lectern. "But before you take out your slates, class, I have an important announcement to make."

Although Diana's love for Miss Stacy had only grown in the months since her first tea with the schoolmistress, she struggled to tear her eyes from the window. The first week of June was as bright as a jewel—a sapphire of pure skies, forget-me-nots and bachelor's buttons blooming along the fence lines of the fields, and the deep, inviting, crystal-clear depths of the Lake of Shining Waters, which was even now winking seductively at Diana from beyond the shady spruces. But Miss Stacy had proven herself a friend and confidante many times over since their first memorable get-together. She and Diana had become almost like chums... not quite, for a truly chummy relationship wouldn't be seemly between a teacher and a student, but they had both come to enjoy their chats so well that they shared tea and conversation —Diana earnest if often confused; Miss Stacy confidently guiding—at least once a month as the school year unfolded. Now here they were at the end of the year, with only three more weeks to go before summer vacation started, full already of the promise of warmth and welcome idleness. Fifteen-year-old Diana marshalled all the good sense and self-control she had learned from Miss Stacy, and turned her face away from summer's beckoning. She focused her attention on the schoolmistress... and noticed, with a sudden shiver of foreboding, that there was an unfamiliar reservation in Miss Stacy's manner. In fact, it nearly felt like regret.

"Students," Miss Stacy said quietly when she had all her pupils' attention, "there something I must tell you. I find it rather difficult to say, so I had better just come right out with it. I will not be returning to teach at Avonlea next year."

There was a racket in the schoolroom—groans and wordless exclamations of disbelief from the boys, shocked gasps from the girls, and of course, Ruby Gillis's whimpering. Even at fifteen, Ruby still hadn't lost the habit of hysterics.

Diana felt quite sick to her stomach. She had come to rely on Miss Stacy's good sense and guidance more than she'd realized, until that moment. Now she had no idea how she could expect to get along without her. By habit she glanced across the room to Anne's desk, and there she found Anne's gray eyes, widened and stunned, staring back at her from a pale, sickly face. Diana felt one brief surge of warmth in her chest, for it was good to know that she and Anne still felt as one, even if they were so often separated.

"I know it is upsetting news," Miss Stacy said, "but I want each and every one of you to know how very proud I am to have been your teacher. You have all achieved so much more than even I thought possible. I will always look back with fondness on this school, and the years I spent teaching in Avonlea will surely be some of my gladdest. Now—" she brushed her hands together, as if finishing up some unpleasant business— "let us tackle this spelling, shall we? It's a lovely afternoon, and I know you're all as eager to be out in the sunshine as I am."

But Diana found it all but impossible to concentrate on the

spelling lesson. It wasn't summer's beauty that distracted her now. Rather, a terrible pain had settled deep into her middle. She had never felt anything so sharp, so agonizing before. Never in her young life had Diana known a loss so complete. She had been unprepared for it, and it was all she could do to keep herself from crying at her desk, never mind spelling out the words that Miss Stacy recited from her lesson plan.

When class ended for the regular students and Diana stood to shuffle numbly out of the classroom (leaving the Queen's students behind for their extended lessons), Anne reached up as Diana passed her desk. The slender, white hand slipped into Diana's, cool to the touch from the shock of Miss Stacy's announcement. Diana paused, squeezing Anne's fingers and gazing down at her friend in mute sorrow. Anne looked back at her from a mask of perfect tragedy, but she could find no words to say, either.

Diana might have taken the road home—she often did these days, finding more pleasure than she ever had before in the company of the other girls—but today she felt she had to be alone with her grief. She saw none of the Birch Path's green-robed, light-dazzled beauty, nor did she pay any heed to the tiny purple stars blooming sweetly in Violet Vale. Not even the ghosts of the Haunted Wood could distract her—Diana was pursued by a subtler but far more terrifying phantom now. She paused at the footbridge and leaned on its rail, finally giving vent to the lonesomeness that overwhelmed her, weeping in a storm of sobs.

"Oh, it's not fair, it's not!" she cried, though no one was nearby to hear her except the brook and the trees. "Just now, when I found a grown-up friend—and a friend who's just as good to me as Anne is—now I must lose her!" Who would offer her kind understanding now? Who could she turn to with any trouble no matter how complicated or silly?

Spurred by the unfairness of it all, Diana ran suddenly toward home. She tore up the slope with the air burning in her throat and chest, but no matter how hard or fast she ran, she couldn't leave her sorrow behind. Fresh tears blinded her; she stumbled on a tree root and fell to the ground. But she wasn't hurt—only scraped some, here and there—so she bounced up and hurried on again. "I'll write Miss Stacy a letter," she told herself. "I'll pour out all my truest feelings to her, just as she told me to do, long ago."

The prospect already made Diana feel somewhat better, so the worst of her tears had dried by the time she reached home. She came in through the kitchen door and found Mrs. Barry busy at the stove, with a somewhat harried air hanging about her.

"Diana, dear; you're home at last. Mr. and Mrs. Allan are coming over for supper to discuss getting Minnie May into Sunday school. They will be here soon, in fact." Mrs. Barry looked up from her pot of sugar peas. "Merciful Heaven, Diana; have you been crying? Put a cool cloth on your eyes so they aren't red and puffy by the time the Allans arrive. And change your stockings—you've torn one."

Diana looked down. Her right stocking was indeed ripped just above the edge of her ankle-high boot. She must have torn it when she fell. As she stood there, silently contemplating the stocking with a dull sense of futility, Mrs. Barry snapped, "Be quick, now! I need your help getting supper."

"Miss Stacy wouldn't want me to aggravate Mother by sighing at her," Diana reminded herself. So she stifled her frustration and climbed the stairs to her room.

"Bother everything," Diana grumbled as she changed into a fresh dress and tugged irritably at her hair, which was tangled from her run up the hill. "Bother the whole world!" Now that Miss Stacy was going, nothing felt right to Diana—nothing! The whole world was one topsy-turvy, upside-down place, where she could never feel comfortable or entirely happy again. Despite her best efforts—hers, and the valiant Miss Stacy's—Diana had never quite figured out what mysterious sense of *wrongness* still haunted her... that sense of something long forgotten that had first plagued her at her initial tea with the schoolmistress. "And now I'll never know," Diana told herself sourly. "Without Miss Stacy to help me sort it all out, I'll go on feeling tangled up and lost and dreadfully uncomfortable for the rest of my life!" All those many months ago, Miss Stacy had advised Diana to humble herself in order to find her peace. But Diana had never known precisely how to humble herself, or why. How could she do it effectively if she didn't know *why* she was doing it?

Diana jerked open her stocking drawer so vigorously she nearly pulled it right out of her dresser. She calmed herself with a deep breath, then went searching for her best pair of stockings. She pawed through the drawer with impatient hands, fighting down her frustration, her pain, her rising temper...

... and felt something smooth, flat, and cool beneath her fingertips.

Diana stopped, mid-paw. Suddenly she knew exactly what had haunted her soul since the first tea with Miss Stacy... and since long before that, too. How could she have forgotten? A curious pain, made from equal parts guilt and embarrassment, gnawed at her with teeth as sharp and persistent as a rat's. Reluctantly, Diana took hold of the card and pulled it from the depths of her stocking drawer. It had been years since she'd seen it last, but she remembered the gilt words printed on the front without even having to read them.

May good health
  and good cheer
  be yours forever.

Her cheeks burning with shame, Diana turned the card over to read Gilbert's name. Time had faded his signature, but it was still clear enough. And the lines of his letters may as well have been knife-sharp, given the way they cut into Diana's heart.

"Oh, Anne," Diana whispered. "I have wronged you, though you never knew it. And I must make amends."

SUPPER with the Allans seemed to go on for an eternity. Diana did her best to enjoy it, for the Allans were two of the loveliest souls in all of Avonlea. But all the while, through supper and dessert and pleasant parlor conversation afterward, the card waiting upstairs on her writing table seemed to mock her attempts at good humor. An hour after supper, it was all Diana could do to keep herself from fidgeting like eight-year-old Minnie May. And when at last the Allans took their leave, the sun was already well on its way toward setting.

Diana forced herself to help her mother with the washing up, though her feet danced in place with the urgent need to run up to her room and signal across the wood to Anne. She watched the sunset nervously as she dried the dishes and put them away, and when the kitchen was clean again, she kissed her delighted mother on the cheek and made herself climb the stairs with grown-up dignity. After all, she had a hard conversation ahead with her dearest and oldest friend. She should be thoughtful about it, not headlong.

Diana sat for a minute at her table, staring at the flower-printed card in thoughtful silence, working out what she must say and how she ought to say it. "If only Miss Stacy were here," she told herself. Then she discarded that wish. "Even if she weren't going away at the end of June, Miss Stacy won't be around to help me forever. I must stand on my own sometime, and learn to be a real grown-up lady somehow." This was as good a place to start as any, but oh, she feared the lesson would be hard!

With a long, careful breath to bolster her courage, Diana lit the lamp. Its amber glow suffused her bedroom, and for a minute she sat in its peaceful light, quietly ordering her thoughts. Then she picked up the piece of cardboard that lay beside the lamp and passed it between light and window, in the accustomed signal of days gone by. Five flashes. *Come at once, for I have something important to tell you.*

There was a light glowing in Anne's east-gable bedroom, a small star burning steadily against the pale violet dusk. But perhaps Anne wouldn't answer. "And wouldn't that serve me right?" Diana asked herself. "How many times has Anne signaled for me, only I didn't go, because I was too angry at her, too envious?"

She waited with a lump in her throat. And then, just when she thought Anne had decided to ignore Diana's plea, the light at Green Gables flashed in return—five times.

DIANA WALKED SEDATELY DOWN the orchard hill, through soft veils of early dusk. Crickets and tree frogs sang their evening songs, and above, in the cloudless sky, the first scattering of stars gleamed silver in a velvet-purple night. She moved so calmly, so resolutely, that it almost seemed amusing to her, to remember how, just hours before, she had run up that very path, blinded by tears and not knowing what she ought to do next. "How strange it is," Diana thought, "that I could have changed so much in so short a time." She would have laughed at the thought, had her nerves not been all a-twist with fear over what Anne might say when Diana made her confession.

Anne got to the little bridge over the brook just as Diana did. Her hair had grown out beautifully since the tragedy of the peddler's dye. It flowed down around her shoulders like a cape of the softest silk. Its red color seemed rich and luxurious against the cool tones of dusk, and Anne, dressed in a new white blouse, seemed to glow as she came through the wood.

"You really are lovely; do you know that?" Diana said when

they met. "You look just like a queen, stepping out of a poem. Like Guinevere coming out of Tennyson's pages." And she was pleased to feel, deep in her heart, that she meant every word, and gave the compliment without the least bit of envy. "Miss Stacy was right," Diana thought as Anne clasped her hands in greeting. "I haven't even humbled myself yet, but already I feel freer, better... at peace." The realization gave Diana considerable courage.

"Don't speak to me of Guinevere or Tennyson," Anne said, laughing. "Sometimes at night I wake up from a nightmare, feeling water seeping up through my bed, and I am reminded of the lily maid."

Diana smiled. "You know, the story of our near-fatal re-enactment of *Lancelot and Elaine* never made the rounds at school. We were all so embarrassed and horrified that none of us ever spoke a word about it."

"It's a secret we'll take to our graves with us," Anne said. "You and me, and Jane and Ruby."

"And Gilbert," Diana added.

Anne said nothing. But she didn't rebuke Diana for mentioning his name, either. That, too, gave Diana courage, for now she knew that she could speak of him without inciting Anne's anger. Although when she confessed her secret, Anne's temper might still flare up...

Diana slipped the card from her pocket before her nerves could fail her. "Anne, I have something to tell you, and I'm afraid it's truly dreadful."

Anne's pale brows raised in an expression of desperation. Her voice trembled a little as she said, "Dear me, Diana... after Miss Stacy's announcement today, I'm not sure I can stand—"

"I kept this from you, Anne." Diana thrust the card out, into the space between them, which seemed suddenly to yawn like a vast, black abyss. "It's from long ago, when you fell off the roof and broke your ankle. I don't know why I kept it, except that... well..."

Anne took the card wonderingly. There was just enough light left in the fading sky to read the print on the front. Then, quite slowly and with a hesitant air, she turned it over and read the name scrawled on the back. She said softly, "Gilbert."

"Well," Diana resumed shakily, "I guess I kept it from you partly because you would get so wild if anyone brought him up... but also because... because I like him, Anne. I always have, an awful lot. And I've always felt so... so envious, because he likes you, and not me."

Anne looked up from the card. Something fleeting and indefinable passed across her face, twisting her sensitive features into the briefest frown of pain or anger... or perhaps confusion. But it was gone in a flash, replaced by a grin that shone as bright as mid-day.

"Dear Diana," she laughed. "I was awful to Gilbert, wasn't I? And oh, it was so nice and friendly of him to wish me well while I was stuck in bed with my bad ankle. He is a very nice boy after all, isn't he? I did him wrong all those years. Yes, I think I can be friends with him after all... he did save me from a watery grave, so it's the least I can do. But there's nothing for you to worry about, Diana. Friends is all I ever shall be with Gilbert Blythe. I haven't the slightest interest in him... not in that way. No, it's Conrad the corsair for me—a suitably gloomy, attractively dark and mysterious man. I'll find him someday, I dare say, but not in Avonlea."

"But the card," Diana said. "It was wrong of me to open it, and wrong to keep it."

"You didn't mean any malice by it, Diana. I know that. Don't think of it any longer, dear. It means nothing. You're entirely forgiven... not that you need to ask my forgiveness."

"And the envy, Anne. Oh, how I have envied you! So many times, and not only over Gilbert. Over... over everything! Everything you have, everything you are. It has all but eaten me up inside, and left me feeling miserable and low."

"But it's all forgotten now. We swore a solemn oath of friendship... remember? We may have been just foolish little girls at the time, but I took that oath seriously, Diana. I still do. You are dearer to me than any silly little card, or any boy, or any fleeting envy. Come, dry your tears. It has been a very hard day, hasn't it? I've been crying all afternoon, too."

Laughing with the relief of forgiveness, and feeling more light and peaceful inside than she had for years, Diana threw her arms around Anne. They held each other tightly in the choruses of dusk.

"I can't believe Miss Stacy is going away," Diana said mournfully when at last they broke apart.

"Nor can I. It seems like the most dreadful thing that has ever happened to me, Diana... to *us*. And somehow I must be ready for the entrance exam at the end of June. How can I study and prepare when I feel so broken up over Miss Stacy? Avonlea won't be the same place without her. Oh, that reminds me: I wrote to your aunt Josephine to ask if I might stay at Beechwood for the exam. I think that will do me more good than to get up before the dawn and drive over. Driving such a long way always makes me feel tired. She told me I am welcome to stay at Beechwood while I'm taking the exams."

"I wish I could go with you," Diana said, "to see Aunt Josephine again, if for no other reason. I've kept up a correspondence with her, you know, Anne. She really is amusing. I didn't know such an old lady could be such good fun to write to, but she is. She's not quite a 'kindred spirit,' as you would say," Diana added, thinking of the hard advice Josephine had given in her very first letter, "but I still find her endlessly fascinating. I really do wish I could have a life just like hers, with a mansion in town and no obligations other than my very own affairs."

"I probably should not have any company before the exam," Anne said gently. "But if I could have anyone with me, it would be you."

"I know. I'll go to see Aunt Josephine myself this summer. I've already promised her a visit."

Anne cast a lingering glance over her shoulder, at the light still burning from her bedroom window. Her books were there, no doubt, and two years' worth of notes, painstakingly recorded in preparation for the entrance exam. "I should return home, I suppose," Anne said regretfully. "I have work still to do before I go to sleep... or *try* to sleep, after Miss Stacy's news. Good night, my dearest of Dianas. Don't dwell any longer on the past. It's behind us, and only the future lies ahead now."

When they parted ways, Diana was smiling. For despite the day's high emotions, she found that Miss Stacy was right. Peace did come from an unburdened heart. And although the song of the frogs and the whisper of the brook made her feel a little bit lonely, it was a pleasant kind of lonesomeness... the kind Diana knew she could bear quite comfortably.

Glad of the peace, Diana did not go straight home. She wandered along the line of the brook, following it toward the lake. The evening was plush and gentle. She held out her hands as she walked, allowing the tall grasses to tickle her palms, and cast her thoughts out dreamily before her.

"Hullo," a voice called from the road.

Diana looked up suddenly, glad the twilight concealed her blushing. She hadn't known that she wasn't alone. Her wanderings had carried her almost all the way to the Newbridge road. The road was well lit by the rising half-moon, and there in the middle of it stood a familiar figure. No, not tall Gilbert with his dark, curling hair and roguish smile. This was a stouter figure, with a red, laughing face. It was Fred Wright, with a pail in one hand and a fishing pole slung over his shoulder. Diana felt a tingle at her wrist and recalled the pink heart charm that Fred had given her, long ago at the Christmas concert. She had never taken the charm off her bracelet, though it held no sentimental value. She had simply never thought to do it.

"Fred," Diana said with a self-conscious laugh. "Isn't it late to be out fishing?"

"It is late," he said, grinning bashfully as Diana came up to meet him. "I'm afraid I let time get away from me. I don't mind telling you, Diana... I was so upset over Miss Stacy's leaving us that I had to get out alone with my thoughts. And, well, my thoughts got the better of me, I suppose."

"I felt the same way," Diana confided. Then she hesitated. She did not know Fred Wright at all—not any more than she knew the rest of her school mates. Her friendship with Anne was sacred to her, and even some of the girls from school could be trusted with her secrets—Jane and Ruby, for example. But a boy? If she told a boy too much, he would only make fun of her, or use it against her later, to tease and torment her. That was what boys always did. Even a boy as nice as Fred couldn't be entirely trusted.

Then Diana recalled Miss Stacy's long-ago advice: "When we can be honest about the way we feel... when we hold nothing back... then we can be sure that others see us most clearly." Diana heard the charms on her bracelet tinkle quietly in the evening breeze, and she suddenly felt that she might like it if Fred—nice, friendly Fred, who always seemed like he was about to laugh—saw her most clearly. If nothing else, Diana reasoned, it would be good practice for getting to know Gilbert better... which she was free to do, now that she had aired her feelings to Anne.

So she took the risk. "Fred, I've had an awful day. I cried so much about Miss Stacy that I fell on the way home from school and ripped my stocking. And then I had to... well, I had to tell Anne all about a wrong I did her long ago—confess to an old sin, I guess you could say. I felt dreadful about it, and even though Anne forgave me, I still feel sort of wicked. But you can be sure I'll never do a bad turn to one of my friends again; I've learned my lesson. Oh, but it has been a miserable time. Do you think I'm a fool for crying so much over Miss Stacy? So much that I fell over like a perfect oaf?"

Fred laughed, but there was no nastiness in it. "Not at all! I had a bully cry down by the lake. Boys do cry sometimes, you know... though we pretend like we don't." The grin slid off his face in a sudden show of apprehension. "But you won't tell anybody about that, will you, Diana? Only it's hard to keep face in front of the fellows sometimes, and they'd never let me live it down if they knew."

"I won't tell a soul," Diana promised.

"My mother says boys do cry, even though they tell each other not to, but sometimes I get to believing that none of the other boys ever do it. They always seem so fearless and strong. Most of the time I feel... well..." Fred trailed off, shuffling his feet, his laughing smile entirely gone now. It seemed to Diana that Fred felt he'd confessed too much.

She spoke quickly, to reassure him. "Do you feel as if you're standing in their shadows? Like no one will really see you because of how splendid the rest of them are?"

"Yes," Fred said slowly, his grin returning. "Yes, that's exactly how I feel, but you said it better than I ever could."

"I know just what that feels like," Diana said. And there in the road, with the half-moon shining down on them, Diana spilled out all her feelings to her newfound friend, Fred Wright. Most of her feelings, anyhow. She told him all about Anne—how much she loved her, and how much she also envied her—and told him, too, of her bitter disappointment in the matter of the Queen's class. "I'm glad for Anne, and I know she'll do well at the entrance exam. But there is still a part of me that wishes I could have what she has. I don't feel angry over it anymore, though, and I'm glad about that."

"You know," Fred said solemnly, "that is just the way I feel about Gil. Gilbert Blythe, I mean. Life seems to come so easy for him. He does well in school, the girls are all gone on him... it seems he has everything a fellow could want. But I always try to be a good chum to Gil in spite of my envy, because after all, I like him."

Mrs. Barry's voice came suddenly from Orchard Slope, away up the hill, calling thinly across the night. "Diana! Diana!" There was a note of panic in it.

Diana turned quickly and shouted, "I'm coming, Mother!" Then she spun and impulsively took Fred's hand. "I must go now. But it was so nice to talk to you. Let's be friends, Fred. I think you're a really splendid boy."

Diana ran up the hill toward home, leaving Fred, stunned but not displeased, to stare in amazement after her. When at last he hitched his fishing pole back over his shoulder and sauntered on toward home, he was whistling a jaunty tune, and every bad feeling from that fraught day had been forgotten.

AN ARGUMENT WON

"Where were you?" Mrs. Barry asked sharply when Diana came inside. "It is long past dark, Diana. You had me worried sick."

"I was only down by the road," Diana said, and instantly knew it had been a mistake. Mrs. Barry was familiar with the shared haunts between Orchard Slope and Green Gables. For Diana to have come from the direction of the road meant that she had not been with Anne... at least, not for the whole evening.

"What were you doing on the road in the dark of night?" Mrs. Barry's voice was dangerously low. "Tell me at once, Diana."

"I was only... speaking to a friend, Mother." Diana felt her cheeks color.

Mrs. Barry did not fail to notice. "A *friend*? A boy, don't you mean?"

Diana felt her anger flare up like flames before the bellows. She could have burst out with an accusation, or a tearful storm to leave her mother shaking her head in rueful dismay. She *would* have done just that, on any previous day. But this day's events had changed Diana for the better. Though she was not yet a grown woman, she wasn't a child any longer, either. In one eventful June day, she had faced sudden loss, confession, forgiveness, and the unexpected baring of her soul to a near-stranger. She could never go back and be the Diana she had been before.

It took every ounce of her will, but Diana managed to control herself. She neither sauced her mother, nor behaved icily toward her. She thought of Miss Stacy—always so admirably in control of herself, always genteel and approachable, even when she put her foot down in the classroom. She thought of Aunt Josephine, insistent upon taking what she wanted from life, and making no apologies for it. And most of all, she thought of Anne. Confident, bold, and with an inborn—perhaps overblown—sense of righteousness, Anne Shirley had never failed to stand in opposition to anyone she perceived as unjust. If ever there was a time for Diana to be like dear, oft-envied Anne, this was it.

Diana faced her mother squarely and stood firm. She willed her cheeks not to color and looked Mrs. Barry straight in the eye. "Mother," she said calmly, "I do think it is possible for boys to also be friends. But you have nothing to worry about. Even if I wanted a tryst with Fred Wright, I wouldn't keep it in the middle of the road. You are getting angry about nothing, and your anger is unjust."

Mrs. Barry gasped. "How dare you speak to me in such a way!"

"I haven't spoken to you with any disrespect," Diana said. "And I have no desire to quarrel with you. Arguing never solves anything, does it? I am going up to my room now, Mother. I would be glad to speak to you more when your temper has calmed."

With that, Diana walked steadily past her gaping mother and climbed the stairs to her room. When she reached the landing, and was sure Mrs. Barry couldn't see her face, Diana broke into a triumphant grin. But she didn't clatter up the rest of the stairs with a victorious sprint, even though she sorely wanted to. She made herself move with all the dignity and assurance of Anne, Josephine, and Miss Stacy formed miraculously into one black-haired, dark-eyed, fifteen-year-old girl's body.

DIANA OCCUPIED herself for an hour or two with a novel, reading by the light of her lamp. Now and then she gazed across the darkness to Green Gables, where Anne's light still burned, too. "Anne must cram for her examination, but I get to enjoy myself with Charlotte E. Morgan's latest," Diana thought contentedly. "Perhaps my lot in life isn't so bad, after all."

Orchard Slope was silent, save for the soft chiming of the mantel clock downstairs. It struck midnight. The light in Anne's window went out. Diana assumed the family had gone to bed long before, and, yawning, she thought perhaps it was time for her to sleep, too. She had read more than enough for one night. But as she stood to blow out her lamp, there was a soft tap at her door.

Diana opened it to reveal Mrs. Barry, dressed as Diana was in a nightgown, holding a candle with a timidly flickering flame.

"Mother," Diana said in surprise. "Why are you still up?"

Mrs. Barry pressed her lips together for a moment, then said in a rather contrite voice, "May I come in, Diana?"

Diana stepped back to let her mother inside. Mrs. Barry set the candle aside and sat on Diana's bed. After a moment, Diana joined her, folding up her legs beneath her night dress.

"I... I couldn't sleep," Mrs. Barry began shakily, "because of our quarrel, Diana."

With her newfound patience and wisdom, Diana waited silently for her mother to go on.

"I wronged you, by accusing you. And I apologize."

The words sounded as if Mr. Bell's team of draft horses had dragged them from her mother's throat, but Diana could forgive the reluctance. She knew how rare it was to hear Mrs. Barry apologize for anything.

"Thank you, Mother," she said, rather startled. "But... you know I have always been truthful with you, and have done my best to be good and mind my reputation. Except for my one mistake with Marilla's currant wine... and that wasn't really my fault. Why were you so suspicious of me, Mother? Why did you get so angry over such a little thing? I don't understand."

"Oh..." Mrs. Barry said in a choked voice. "Oh..." And then, to Diana's astonishment, she turned her face away and swiped quickly at her eyes, then clasped her hands in her lap.

Mrs. Barry was *crying*? It seemed impossible. Diana had never known her mother to be emotional at all, unless the emotion was anger. But there the proof was, glittering discreetly on her mother's half-hidden fingertips.

"Oh," Mrs. Barry said again, "it was wrong of me to fly at you that way, Diana, but I... I couldn't help myself. It pains me so to see you—my little girl—growing up. When first I became a mother, and held you in my arms, I felt many things for you... tenderness, joy, even fear for your safety, for you were such a little thing, so helpless and new. And love, Diana... love most of all. But I never imagined I could feel *this*. I don't even know what to call it, this strange, beautiful pain. I am so proud of you, Diana—my little girl, growing up to such an admirable young woman. And yet I am so... so afraid to let you go."

At that, Mrs. Barry pulled a handkerchief from her sleeve and wept freely into it, with several hiccuping sobs. Diana stared at her mother, dumbstruck. Once she'd had an inkling that Mrs. Barry's strictness came from a place of love. But never in her life had she imagined that her mother felt such terrible, tormenting passions over her—plain, ordinary, commonplace Diana. She patted her mother's shoulder awkwardly.

"Someday you will find a young man you like," Mrs. Barry went on wretchedly, "and then I shall have to let you go. And I hate to think of the house without you in it... my life without you in it!" She blew her nose noisily into the kerchief.

Diana, who still clung to her secret ambition of a mansion in Charlottetown and grand independence, said, "It may be a very long time yet before I want any man to court me." To herself, she added, "I may *never* want a man to court me."

But Mrs. Barry, in the calm after her private storm, shook her head. "Your time is coming soon. A mother knows these things— a mother can *see* these things. Even a mother such as I."

Diana smiled fondly. "What do you mean, 'a mother such as I?'"

"I... I haven't always been as good to you as I might," Mrs. Barry said, letting her head hang low. "Your father has always chided me for it, but I always told him, 'Keep to your own business, George, for I was a girl once. You were not. I know more about raising girls than you ever could.' I think now that I was wrong, Diana. I should have listened to your father more, and let you have more enjoyment out of life. I have been so hard on you, because I feared this day... the day when you would grow up. I suppose I thought that if I was strict enough with you, somehow you would always depend on me, and would remain my little girl forever. But tonight I saw the error of my ways. And tonight I also learned..." She dabbed at her eyes again. "... how proud I am of you, Diana. You are such a good girl, confident and sensible and yes, even strong, in a womanly way. I know it's useless to tie you too close with my apron strings."

Diana leaned her head on her mother's shoulder. "Dear Mother. You can't imagine how you've warmed my heart tonight. I feel as if I understand you so much better than I ever did before."

Mrs. Barry kissed the top of Diana's head—something she hadn't done since Diana was a very little girl. It brought a tear of gladness to Diana's eye.

"Let's never let ourselves quarrel again," Diana said. "Let's just be good to each other, and enjoy each other's company, from here on out... and for always."

ANNE EARNS AN ENCORE

Diana held up the white organdy dress and examined it in the lamplight. "Put this on, by all means, Anne."

Anne, dressed only in her shift, peeked out past her blind to the blue twilight beyond. Diana could see a sliver of the early moon's light edge Anne's face with its silvery luster. The soft glow only seemed to heighten the nervous pallor of Anne's face. She had sworn several times that night that she was thrilled to her marrow about the concert—to be held an hour hence at the White Sands Hotel, in aid of the hospital—but Diana knew her friend well enough to read the fear and uncertainty in her tension and quick gestures, too.

"Do you really think the organdy will be best?" Anne asked, coming away from the window and toying anxiously with the white dress's lace-trimmed sleeve. "I don't think it's as pretty as my blue-flowered muslin, and it certainly isn't so fashionable."

Diana rolled her eyes with a fond chuckle. "But it suits you ever so much better. It's so soft and frilly and clinging. The muslin makes you look *too* dressed up. This organdy looks as if it grew on you."

Anne relented and held out her hands for the dress. "I know I shouldn't question your opinion such things; you have the best reputation for dressing in all of Avonlea now. In fact, I wouldn't be surprised if you have the best taste on the whole island."

"You flatter me," Diana said, thoroughly pleased to be flattered.

"I just wish I could get away with your dress tonight," Anne said as she pulled the white organdy on and wriggled into the sleeves. "Or any night. That rosy pink is glorious on you, Diana."

"It does look nice, doesn't it?" Diana said, admiring her color and the cut of her dress in Anne's mirror. "It's almost a shame I won't be performing at the concert tonight."

"They might ask you to perform, when they see how nice you look."

"Nonsense," Diana laughed. "Besides, I don't have anything prepared. I will be quite content to watch you recite tonight." And it was true; Diana looked forward to Anne's moment of glory with all the happy anticipation she would have shown for her own moment on the stage.

Anne stood passively, if anxiously, while Diana fussed with her ruffles and laces and slippers, then braided and pinned up her hair, making her as lovely as if she were to wait on the queen. "This is a very grown-up hairstyle," Diana confessed. "You probably shouldn't really wear it for another year. But this is such a special occasion, I think our vanity will be forgiven."

Diana tied Anne's pearl beads around her neck, then stepped back to admire her. Anne, radiant in the lamp light, was a vision of unique beauty. The pure white of slippers, dress, pearls—even the little rose pinned in her hair—made, together with Anne's alabaster-pale skin, an ethereal, haunting image. The coppery flash of her upswept hair was like an exclamation point at the end of a sentence. She gave an impression of intoxicating contradictions: a bright flame burning at the tip of a candle made of luminous ice. Diana was thoroughly satisfied with her night's work.

"There's something so stylish about you, Anne," Diana said

suddenly, expressing her most spontaneous admiration. "You hold your head with such an air." There was no envy in Diana now. She felt nothing but happiness for Anne, and pleasure at the prospect of watching her take the stage.

With Anne dressed, Diana pulled up the window shade to let in the inspiration of moonlight. But Anne didn't seem to see the moon at all. She wrapped one arm around Diana's shoulders and said quietly, sentimentally, "I'm so glad my window looks east, into the sunrise. It's so splendid to see the morning coming up over those long hills and glowing through those sharp fir tops. Oh, Diana, I love this little room so dearly. I don't know how I'll get along without it when I go to town next month."

"Don't speak of your going away tonight," Diana said. A threat of tears burned in her eyes. The summer was half over, and soon Anne would be off to Queen's Academy, while Diana remained here in Avonlea. "I don't want to think of it. It makes me so miserable, and I want to have a good time this evening. What are you going to recite, Anne? I know you wanted to keep it a secret from our school chums, but will you tell me? Are you nervous?"

"Not a bit," Anne said. Diana saw the lie, but left Anne with her comforting fantasy of perfect bravery. "I've recited so often in public, I don't mind at all now. I've decided to give 'The Maiden's Vow.' It's so pathetic; I feel sure everyone will love it. I would much rather make everyone cry than laugh."

"What will you recite if they encore you?"

"They won't dream of it."

But Diana suspected they would. Anne had become a great favorite at Avonlea concerts; she nearly always earned an encore.

Marilla pronounced a rather grudging approval of Anne's looks, and the girls headed out to the front porch of Green Gables, where Jane and Billy Andrews met them with their buggy. They drove along to the White Sands Hotel beneath a starry sky, with the soft echo of a golden sunset still lingering low in the western sky. Many other parties were on their way to White

Sands, too, for the concert was to be a real affair, not to be missed. The girls called greetings to their friends as they passed, and talked merrily among themselves with the sounds of laughter and distant conversation floating about them in the warm night air.

The White Sands Hotel perched proudly on a hill overlooking the Gulf. It blazed with lamp light, nearly as bright as the full moon that hung above it, high in the velvet sky. As the girls climbed down from the buggy, Diana could hear the pounding of distant surf under the excited murmur of many voices—and could hear Anne's ragged breathing, too.

"Oh, my dress, Diana! I'm afraid it's not nearly nice enough. Look at all the laces and silks and bright colors. Oh, and that woman there! Did you see her diamonds? I must look like a poor little country mouse. Everyone will think me too quaint for words."

"Stop it, you," Diana laughed, pulling Anne toward the hotel. "Trust in the good taste of your old friend Diana. Didn't you say I have the best eye for style on all of P.E.I.?"

"How can I ever measure up to all these grand performers? They've come from all around, Diana! This is no country concert. It's *real*."

"And you belong here, right up on that stage, with the rest of them."

"I don't think I can go on," Anne admitted in a tiny whisper as Diana checked their jackets at the door.

"Of course you can," Diana whispered back. "I'll be here watching you. Just like at our first concert—remember? I'll always be here for you, Anne."

Then Diana thought miserably, "Until Queen's Academy parts us..."

Anne's misery only deepened when she heard that a professional elocutionist would perform that night. The woman was a surprise addition to the concert. She was, in fact, a guest at the hotel, and had nothing to do with Charlottetown or its hospital. But when she heard that the concert was in service to such a worthy cause, she volunteered her services.

"A *professional*," Anne said, sounding very much like she might faint. "I can never do it, Diana."

"You can, and you will," Diana said firmly, dragging the reluctant Anne to her seat at the rear of the stage.

The show began, and Diana, seated down in the audience with Jane Andrews, enjoyed it immensely. Prince Edward Island might be a countryish place, but it had no lack of grand performers. One familiar figure after another came forward to stand in the bright pool of light at the front of the stage. Humorous dialogues were delivered, and thoughtful monologues taken from Shakespeare and other timeless sources. Beautiful poems were recited, with flowing, confident rhythms that surely would have suited the finest concert halls in Toronto or Ottawa. Throughout it all, while Diana smiled and applauded, Anne sat stiffly in her place at the back of the stage, looking quite small and lost among the other performers.

The professional elocutionist took the stage. She was as glorious to behold as she was to hear; her astonishingly expressive voice was in perfect harmony with her enchanting appearance—dark-haired, elegant, with a silver-gray gown made of flowing silk and glinting diamonds in her hair. Her piece transported the audience to a bliss far beyond anything they had imagined possible. Diana felt breathless when her performance ended, so shaken by the beauty of the woman's voice that she could only applaud weakly.

Then, on the heels of that transcendent elocutionist, Anne's name was called.

Anne stood slowly, her eyes fixed somewhere on the back of the hall, and walked as if in a trance to the spotlight. There she stood for a long moment, swaying slightly, so pale that Diana and

Jane squeezed each other's hands in silent fear. The silence seemed to stretch into an eternity.

"Come on, Anne," Diana murmured. "I'm right here... right here."

Anne did not look at Diana, but she did seem to find a sudden rush of courage. She pulled herself up to an elegant posture, as grand as any pose the professional in silver had struck, and lifted her head proudly. She gave the first lines of "The Maiden's Vow" in a strong, clear voice so confident that her show of terror, moments before, seemed a mirage to the rapt audience.

Anne carried the concert hall along with her on waves of hope, love, and crushing despair that broke and crashed with all the drama and inevitable power of the waves on the beach beyond the hotel's shining white walls. Her final word hung suspended in the air, and for a moment the hall was silent. Then uproarious applause erupted all at once—and no one clapped or cheered louder than Diana. Anne, standing in the hot light, blinked and gazed bashfully around, as if only now realizing that she stood on a stage before the adoring eyes of an enthralled audience. Watching her, glowing with pride and love, Diana was glad to call Anne Shirley her dearest friend. Her happiness was pure and clean, without a speck of envy to mar it. And although Diana's cry of "Encore!" was not the first to ring out, she shouted loudest of all.

-THE END-

ABOUT THE AUTHOR

Libbie Hawker grew up reading L. M. Montgomery's books, dreaming of writing her own novels someday. She now writes historical and literary fiction for a living, and Montgomery's distinct influence can be seen in Hawker's work.

Hawker lives on a small island—just like Anne and Diana, albeit on the other side of North America. When she's not writing, she enjoys painting landscapes, homesteading on her one-acre microfarm, and spending time with her husband and two naughty cats.

Would you like to read more Green Gables Variations from Libbie Hawker? Get in touch and let her know! And don't miss her Instagram feed (@libbiehawker) for pictures of kitties and island life.

www.libbiehawker.com
libbiehawker@gmail.com